Two Suns Rising

Can Light Be Destroyed?

Broken Club Publishing LLC

Also from Todd Boddy

Blue Moon Chronicles Novels

The Exit, BMC—Vol I, 2012
Two Suns Rising, BMC—Vol II, 2014
Center of the Sun, BMC —Vol III, 2015

Blue Moon Chronicles Serials

Exit Apocalypse 1-4, 2013
Angel Without a Cause, 2014
Death Flight, 2014

THE EXIT

Blue Moon Chronicles

While two scientists experiment with quantum technology to journey the universe, a demonic insurgency dreams of leaving the earth to establish a new home in a far distant galaxy.

Led by a savvy and ageless CEO and his hybrid daughter, The Sanctuary Corporation acquires the escape technology, plotting to change the course of global and divine history.

To counter them, a weathered angel of light crosses the formal line of authority to recruit an unlikely group who will journey to combat the growing darkness in this new world.

www.ToddBoddy.com

What are people saying about The Exit, Volume I?

"In the spirit of all great science fiction and fantasy, Boddy creates a world in which to explore issues of meaning and human existence, things like truth, commitment, sacrifice, integrity, trust and loyalty."
--K. Crawford

"Illuminates the questions we all ask about good and evil and the relationship struggles of wondering, 'whose side are you on, anyway?'"--S. Mennig

"The Exit makes a great entrance, the story intrigues and entraps." --D. Fischer

"If you enjoy science fiction, frantic and fast-paced, wondering and plot changing novels... you should pick up The Exit. It's very in depth and extremely descriptive."
--J.Ros

"Loved it! This is a unique approach to religious science fiction." --J. Grogan

"If you take my advice and put The Exit on your reading list, you'll understand why it would be an irony to designate this work as 'escape literature'. And, in the final analysis, what makes you think that escape from your Maker is possible?"
--T. Kallenberg

"Is complex and thought-provoking. I thought of C. S. Lewis books, The Screwtape Letters and the Space Trilogy when I was reading The Exit."--S. Pyle

"The Exit is an engaging, moving and surreal fantasy adventure..." --K. Hedges

"It's the Hitchhikers Guide to the apocalypse." –J. Cunyus

THE EXIT
BLUE MOON CHRONICLES
There's no resurrection for Angels.
TODD BODDY

Epigraphs taken from The Exit, Vol I

"I don't share your luxury. I believe in karma. I make karma happen. I rain down karma on my enemies."

"We are the progeny of ancient myths, so we attempt to write our own."

"I see the killing fields of the innocents crying out for justice while we hold our ranks."

"You have ventured into deep waters, leaving your wading pool of shallow pragmatism."

"Divine intervention is not without its own pain."

"When all seems lost, don't confuse this with the end, rather this is the beginning."

"Your redemption is at the gate of your conscience. You have been granted the power of a choice."

"What say you, image bearer? Have you come to save us?"

Two Suns Rising

Blue Moon Chronicles

A SCIENCE FICTION FANTASY

TODD BODDY

Broken Club Publishing LLC
Mckinney Texas

DEDICATION

To Jack Cull, and all his bed time stories

In 1968 while my father served overseas in the Vietnam War, my mother, brother and I moved in with my grandparents, Jack and Shirley Cull of Detroit MI for a year and a half. Every evening Jack would tell a bed time story sure to pump up every young boy's imagination of adventure; stories of working on the Canadian railroad, runaway trains, mountains, and bears. He also related stories about gangsters during prohibition which he had firsthand experience from his barber's chair in downtown Chicago. We gawked, laughed, and begged for more tales each night until we fell asleep. I never realized until years later, the seed he planted.

Two Suns Rising

His is a secret knowledge which is no secret

Chapter 1

Is that post-traumatic enough?

Lucas reread the upcoming ports of call from the edge of his listing crew bunk. The porthole window over his shoulder flashed every few seconds from the night squall line chasing them through the Indian Ocean.

His Swiss bank account bought them undocumented passage on the Liberian registered freighter. The ship's Captain, who Lucas propositioned in a seedy Amsterdam bar joked, "We'll give you and Ms. Lovely the honeymoon suite, a quiet room except when drawing anchor or running at sea. And what did you say the lass's name is? Is she your wife, girl friend, or soliciting company?"

Lucas replied, "I didn't, and no, no, and no. Our relationship is none of your business. Half cash when we get on, half when we get off, and no questions."

The Captain replied, "You don't look like terrorists, never in a million years. You are hiding something more complex. What are you carrying besides clothes? Any weapons?"

"Only a decorative family sword, an heirloom."

Lucas returned to the present as he heard her flip-flops step over the water tight threshold into their room and seal the metal hatch door behind her. Peeking over the ship's schedule, the non-scientist in him noticed Victoria's painted red toenails and white smooth muscular calves disappearing under a towel wrapped tightly around an hour glass figure. Her bare shoulders were covered with beads of water from her wet combed red hair.

Victoria caught the end of his glance as she turned and said, "I can say this for you Lucas, when I fantasized about you at the university, it wasn't in cramped crew quarters of a tossing rust bucket. You caught me off guard. How do you like me now, the throw up queen?"

Lucas chuckled while he circled 'Tokyo' and said, "I warned you about crossing professional boundaries with a colleague. See where it got you."

"I confess, it was the lab coat. I wondered why you always wore it in my presence. I knew you were hiding something."

"Excuse me, but you were the one who kept your lab coat buttoned to the top even on our coffee shop excursions. Awful how you teased me."

"Lucas?"

"Yes."

"What are you doing?"

"I am reviewing places we can get off this ship to meet my parents."

"You were looking at that when I left for the showers. Could you stop and help me? I threw up in there and I feel like my bilge pumps are about to kick in again. This rough sea is making my morning sickness worse."

"Vic Honey, believe it or not, I feel your pain. And you'll be proud, I scrubbed your bucket." Lucas folded the papers under his arm and wobbled his way across the shifting floor carrying the small waste basket until he placed it under her chin, "Reporting for barf duty."

With bloodshot eyes she eked out a smile and asked, "Did you do it with love?"

"Of course," he said as her heaves started.

"Argggh... ohh, why can't we get off this ship? Make the waves stop..."

"Get it all out, you'll feel better."

Coughing and spitting in the bucket she said, "There can't be anything left."

Just as she said this, a large wave slammed sideways into the hull of their vessel, rolling the ship fifty-five degrees and knocking out the lights to their compartment. Victoria, losing her balance and the waste basket, stumbled toward Lucas who blindly opened his arms to catch her in the dark.

In each other's grasp, the incline of the ship and her momentum threw them backwards across the skinny bed and against the wall with a "thunk." Ascertaining what had happened they lay silent listening to the ocean's spray against the porthole window and the slapping of the ship's twin props as they dipped in and out of the ocean swells.

"Darling, do you need your bucket?" Lucas asked.

"I'll let you know. Can you hold me?"

"My pleasure."

With his hands taking notice that her towel had come off in the mêlée, he pulled the bed cover over them and held her tight. As the ship listed hard the other direction he braced his leg against the bunk above to hold them in. Her damp hair on his face and her shifting soft body made all that was wrong with the world flee for the moment. As the ship lurched between swells, Victoria kissed him on the cheek, wrapping her arms and thighs around him.

"I love you Victoria. I'd do anything for you."

"And I love you more than you'll ever know Lucas. Not every man has the stomach for vomit duty."

"I am sorry this all happened on the ship."

"Yeah, and on a night like this. Don't be sorry, my biological clock was ticking."

"We'll get off soon, promise, but tonight will be rough."

As the hull moaned under the strain of the tossing tempest, dresser, cabinet, and refrigerator doors flung open in their room, dumping their contents. The coffee maker slid off the counter. A small card table and chairs rolled across the floor end over end smashing into the TV console, then tumbled back the other direction. Based on what they had witnessed as conscripted scientists for Cuzak, the end of the world was at hand, but who was going to believe them? In an unusual way, the pounding waves and internal chaos of the freighter that night provided enough solace to distance them from their enemies and fall into a deep sleep. And yet in slumber something continued to grow inside Victoria which did not go unnoticed.

With calm seas and dawn light shining through the porthole, Victoria was awakened by another round of nausea. As she came out of her stupor and began to scan the room for the bucket, her eyes halted on a figure standing next to the bed. Stricken by fear she asked herself, *How do they know we're here? Is it the scar tissue hidden in my brain?*

Lifting her view, Victoria recognized the blonde woman Lucas had killed in the lab apartment the day of their escape, a surrogate host of the Vranti collective. The apparition said to her, "You have done well Victoria. They will call you Eve. In time we will return for our child. Keep this as our secret."

"Ahh...!" Victoria screamed as she shuddered in fear. "Lucas, Lucas, wake up!"

Confused and propping himself on his elbows to survey the room's wreckage he said, "Easy, why are you screaming? Did we do all this damage last night?"

"No, I just saw something. Did you see her?"

"Who?"

"The woman who helped kill my mother. She was standing next to us, the bed!"

"Relax Vic," as he caressed the nape of her neck, "that's understandable given the ordeal you've been through. The storm, it could have triggered some post-traumatic emotion."

Victoria rolled over Lucas and out of bed, gathering the blanket around her sobbing, "That thing is still after us. We're never going to live a normal life. You probably won't marry me unless you can invoke a prenuptial with a possession clause."

"Possession clause? Victoria, this is too early..."

Picking up a piece of a broken mirror off the floor she brought it over to Lucas as evidence, "I am not making this up."

Shoving it in front of his face, Lucas saw the normally dormant light from within his eyes had been set off by something evil, and now blazed blue. "Is that post-traumatic enough for you?" she asked. "Why don't you use your super powers and find my pail."

Shem's Log

++

Blue Moon Chronicles Book III, 12.4

Date: At memorial to the vanquished Ouriano,
Binary G-Class star system, Yazad sector
Fifth generation Angelus
Beginning of mass exit to Sanctuary
Subject: Against the night

Because of my friendship with Ouriano, the Magnificon Council has asked me to speak at his memorial. He was unique among the Winds of Light, because he wanted to be human.

In return I asked the Council for something simple; that waters containing Ouriano's memories and prayers be drawn from the Lake of Dreams and presented at his service. Concerned this unusual request might dilute the soothing qualities of the underground lake, I reminded them, "This is the only essence of Ouriano we have left."

They conceded, "It shall be done."

I pray some good will come of this memorial for all is not well on Yare'ach Kachol, our Blue Moon. A new generation of angelus has been released to replace those who have fled their Legions for the Sanctuary's dark light. What shall these new Winds make of their predecessors' desertion?

To become infected is one thing, but to voluntarily leave their millennial position with no explanation? We are all being tested, and the Earth is no better off. The image bearers are being severely tempted as I write. What will become of those who defect when they are cut off?

 Shem, from the Blue Moon, the caverns of Sharu

++

Chapter 2

Can Light be destroyed?

Veezon glided on outstretched wings like a vulture carried by rising drafts. The cool humid air stirred through his war worn gray and white feathers. Beads of iridescent turquoise water condensed and rolled off his wings. Below him he kept careful watch over the tens of thousands of the angelicus ranks funneling toward the Ayin Temple, hewn from the steep hieroglyph covered canyon wall of the Blue Moon. They were dressed in ceremonial white, waists wrapped in golden sashes. Veezon repeated to himself, "She will show... she will show... and she will pay."

Outside the fully recessed amphitheater, miles below the surface of their planet, a growing number of the Winds treaded the misty air. Others hopeful for any remaining space put down on the copper granite landing and continued under the high arch into the immense auditorium. Inside the outward facing Temple, these late arrivals searched for a few empty places on the lofty domed ceiling and walls. When an opening was spotted they flew up and squeezed into the undulating mass.

On the worship platform, centered beneath the high arch dividing the indoor Cathedral from the outdoor landing, was embedded a large Eye some eight wing spans across. The Eye's iris was inlaid with glimmering crystals of gold and indigo, while the center remained a dark hole.

In front of it stood a plain altar—a large slab of gray slate, supported by a base of field stones. On the altar lay an empty light blue worn leather scabbard with its adjoining belt. Next to it rested a large bronze chalice full of a glimmering liquid churning in a whirlpool.

Within and outside of the sacred place of worship could be heard the low buzz of voices as these Winds prayed and conversed their bewilderment. "Could this happen to us?"

"Is evil gaining ground?" "Who sanctioned this?" "Ouriano annihilated? He must have gone down in ignominy."

But all worshipers became silent as the first slow beat vibrated a seismic shock wave emanating from the center of Yare'ach Kachol—the Blue Moon. From the primeval islands--worlds unto themselves like Sharu, Wandu, and Pristia, the Blue planet's mourning caused their ancient hominid peoples to pause. Dropping their spears and plows they looked skyward toward the golden Siyon to remember their fallen friend who stood apart from his kind.

In the seas, the great leviathans, packs of whales, untold schools of fish and serpents alike, floated to the surface from their deep abodes to pay homage. Land mammals, reptiles and fowl temporarily ceased their hunts, escapes, and gatherings. Somehow they knew a tragedy had taken place. Those who could, let out great bellows, cackles, or cries, for one of their keepers was no more. All life on the Blue Moon relented from its normal prey and predator cycles while they became engrossed in the beats. Even the snows on the mountains paused.

By the seventh slow beat, a procession of the twenty-four Magnificon Elders appeared from the back of the Cathedral walking toward the Eye and the altar. They were striking in features, a mix of human, animal and angelic stock, but this day dressed alike; long flowing black robes with white sashes. They were easily spotted moving through the surrounding sea of dazzling white robed Winds of light.

Fifty feet above them, four members of the Royal Cherubim guard with swords drawn, matched their speed to the entourage, eyes shifting from side to side for any potential threats.

"What is this?" many of the host asked themselves, "And swords drawn in a memorial of worship?"

Without a word the packed angelic Winds on the floor parted an opening for these sages of the cosmos and then just as quietly closed behind as they slipped through. Halfway to the altar, a dozen more Cherubim guards arrived, flying in under the great arch. Upon landing they established a perimeter in the center of the platform to each edge of the great Eye. Next, outside of them creating another buffered ring, thousands of Legion Commanders, including the nervous Veezon, glided in to take their stand in a triple deep layer on the edge of the Cathedral floor.

Again many in the sea of white wondered, *Why the high security?*

Unknown to all however, Veezon was attentive to make good on his promise of revenge. It was all he could do to keep his clamoring thoughts to himself, "If this Hybrid were willing to help destroy Ouriano by feinting friendship, why not also attempt to desecrate his memorial? Ru was his fatal flaw, his failed project!"

Despite his anger, all remained solemn while the rhythmic internal beat of the Blue Moon echoed through the faint drone of the hovering Cherubim wings. As Veezon continued his survey along with his officers, the procession arrived two thirds of the way to the front, when the next beat did not sound.

Instead a great rushing wind filled the Cathedral. The gale force breeze swirled through their manes, tunics, and feathers. The droves of Winds treading the air outside the Cathedral were tossed into each other by surprise because of the severity of the drafts.

Yet no one fled. The parading Elders, sensitive to a new presence, immediately prostrated themselves on their knees. Following their cue, the great multitude of the host knelt and covered the top of their heads with edges of their semi-folded wings to mask their hair. The entire interior of the Cathedral from the floor to the ceiling went absolute white with a few shades of gray; that is except for one set of wings.

Veezon noticed, for he alone did not bow his head saying to himself, "There she is, on the top far left corner wall, packed among the legitimate Winds of Light. Her dark wings give her away." He put his hand on the hilt of his sword and grit his teeth; "You will not defile the dead!"

So fuming was his wrath toward her, the knelling and unsuspecting Legion Commanders on each side of him turned to convey their annoyance at his attitude. Veezon quickly reminded himself, *Put your head and hand down!*

Chapter 3

A new day has dawned; your sword without faith is a dead weapon.

When the air calmed another beat from the core of the ancient Blue home of the angels echoed forth, signaling for all to arise. The twenty-four Elders of the Magnificon council resumed their slow procession until reaching the front of the All Seeing Eye. At this point they split to the right and left until their half circles met behind the altar on the far side. Shem continued to the center edge of the altar, facing the indoor audience and pressed his hands against the cool stone table.

The massive Cherubim escorts, who had hovered above them, landed and took their places with the twelve others of their kind outside this inner circle, another line of protection for the twenty-four.

After a brief moment of silence, with his eyes closed he tilted back his head and proclaimed in a loud voice, "What say you, Flames of Fire? Shout to the One who breathes light beneath your wings!"

And shout they did, as a thundering unison of voices with no comparison on the Earth answered back to the mourning guttural beats of the living Blue Moon of Siyon, "To the Heir of the Magnificon! To the One who was, and is, and is yet to come!"

Ru compelled by her love for Ouriano and supposing she had hid from her avowed enemy, was ill prepared for this roar. She clasped her hands over her ears in reaction as the deafening sound waves boomed through the rocks with such force that the Temple shook and the Eye awakened to radiate beams of white and blue light. Even her hybrid bones felt the slam of the bruising concussion.

On the Blue Moon's surface avalanches of snow rolled down mountains, high waves on the seas crashed into shorelines, semi-active volcanoes blew extra steam and hot gases. The creatures on sea and land rocked in motion at the quick burst of change in air pressure caused by these mighty voices.

As the rumble of the Winds' reply faded, Shem lifted his arms and turned his body full circle to take in this momentous but somber occasion. His silvering hair and matching long beard were a sharp contrast to the black robe and his dark brown skin. As he surveyed the audience of sentinels, he thought about the words he had carefully chosen to deliver, *Maybe they are too watered down, maybe these warriors need something more... like the unvarnished truth. But do I know what the end truth will be?*

Shem began a song, by humming.

By the third note he was joined by the throngs who hummed with him, a soft song reserved for grief, rarely used by the Winds,

> *"Hmmm, ah ah ah, hmmm,*
> *Hmmm, ah ah ah, hmmm, ohhh, ohhh, ohhh...,*
>
> *May..., he dance...,*
> *May..., he dance..., like the wind, like the wind...,*
> *May..., he dance, like the wind, rushing wind...,*
>
> *And dance forever more...,*
> *Dance forever more... like the wind...,*
>
> *May..., he fly...,*
> *May..., he fly, like flames of fire through the night...,*
> *May..., he fly, like flames of fire through the night...,*
>
> *And fly forever more ...,*
> *Fly forever more through the night..."*

"This all happened because I couldn't control myself. Why am I like this?" Ru asked herself, still amazed by the colorful rings of smoke flowing from the voices and lips around her. Crying softly she absorbed the worship, as the chorus continued. Their incense like vapors streamed from inside and out of the amphitheater to consolidate as a slow turning pinwheel centered mid-air over the circle of

Elders. Stretching from the floor to the vaulted ceiling, the spinning vapors formed an orange glowing pillar floating just above the Eye and before the altar. The radiance of this cloud lit up Shem's face.

Ru began to dread, *Oh to what can I compare? I should not be here. But if I leave now, I am as good as dead.*

By the time the song ended, the growing pillar had collected all the vapor trails of the slow twirling pinwheel. Shem took a deep breath, unsure of the nature of the concentration of praise and holiness before him. He then began his words with a prayer and bowed head:

"All your creatures gather to worship and submit to you as you have seen fit, to enjoy your presence among us. If what we think be true Lord, then bestow wisdom from the Magnificon to guide us. If we be wrong then may your discipline chastise us, even correct our flight. For you alone are worthy to open that sacred seal of doom and affliction for those who seek to destroy your amnesty and love. But we ask this one thing, be not quick to open that seal, but have mercy on your creation, your image bearers, even the fallen brethren of the mighty Winds here before you."

With these words, Shem raised his head, and spoke, "To those who have ears to hear, let them hear what the Spirit says to his servants, his flames of fire, Amen."

After a unified "Amen," responded to him, Shem began to address the gathering as he walked around the circle of Elders.

"For eons most of you have restrained yourselves from exacting justice on your own, because you knew justice was not yours to dispense. Intervention on behalf of the image bearers is a dangerous business with potential good and grave consequences for all species. Some of you have experienced great joy, and others have suffered confusion, and at times despair, when ordered to intervene. This is true whether you admit it, for not only have we lost ranks in the past due to the infection, but as recent the losses are accelerating. For some reason the infection has picked up strength, as if a new strain.

I suspect we are entering a new era where more will be demanded of all servants of the Wounded Heir and the Angel of Light. A new day has dawned; your sword without faith is a dead weapon. You are not a lost number in a crowd. Our comrade Ouriano learned this. He is our example and this is why we honor him. Let me make it clear, Ouriano did not fall to this infection as rumored. Rather, another form of insidious evil ended him, an evil which dares to strike the Earth, the Blue Moon, and eventually Siyon."

Chapter 4

*Yes, what he was is no more,
and he is better for it.*

"Ouriano made direct contact with this evil that wars against the image bearers and tempts our Legions with the slow decay of pride. But he resisted with his faith, and did not compromise. And for this he is no more."

Shem paused as many of the Winds became restless at his suggestion, wings flexing in response. Some gave bewildered glances, while others nodded in agreement.

Cutting through the protective lines of Legion Commanders and Royal Cherubim, Shem paced across the outer landing, also aiming his address at those hovering over the canyon. "It always has been hard, and will only become more difficult. Times have progressed as they should. Some of those times were known to be sealed for another age. You must be told the truth; this new age is close at hand. And with it a new requirement; to discover the subspace channel of knowing and courage if you are to carry out your mission. Some call it faith!

It is indispensible. There will be more of you who will be called upon to fight in even greater darkness than Ouriano. You will visit worlds where there is no sustenance from the Light as you know it. You may experience the infection, but you must remain loyal even if it means your own demise. For in your demise, the image bearers live." With these words, Shem returned to the altar. Every eye followed him, except for Veezon's.

"On this table rests all we have left of Ouriano, a first generation angelus, an early morning star. Here lies his worn sheath, sword missing. And next to this, a vessel holding his swirling memories gathered from the Lake of Dreams. Observe this marvelous life, and pray it may somehow be united in the Magnificon."

At these words the pillar of cloud in the rock hewn Cathedral began to glow more intense. Bolts of lightning released an overflow of energy, causing some to cower in fear. The Elders in unison then recited in prayer, "Who here is worthy to pour out the waters of this vessel? Who is worthy to receive these sacred prayers, dreams, and memories of Ouriano?"

Ru continued to watch spellbound from the high location, her tears dripping unnoticed on wings far below. Yet, through them, she sensed something good might happen. For she witnessed another deafening response from the sentinels, "There is no one worthy, except the One who reigns from Siyon!"

Through the burning cloud Ru recognized the outline of the Angel of Light, and was touched by the piercing words of her voice. They were the opposite of the shallow and twisted utterances of her father, Cuzak.

"Have I forgotten my humble servants of Light you ask? Does the extinction of one like Ouriano touch my heart? I tell you, his life was poured out so the least among you might stand here and worship. Ouriano was fashioned in the womb of the Magnificon before time, as was each of you. Yes, what he was is no more, and he is better for it."

Her cloud moved and hovered over the altar, while two slender arms extended from the boiling vapors and lifted the chalice of swirling prayers and memories. The glowing pillar then drifted over the center of the glimmering Eye from which her graceful hands raised the bronze chalice pronouncing, "Ouriano, my beloved, you sought the opposite of Lucifer, son of the morning star, and instead became what was intended for all of my sacred Winds. I with the Wounded Heir, therefore declare that your essence will go out to slay our enemies and exact the vengeance of our justice, turning hearts of stone into hearts of flesh. May the redeemed return with you to Siyon, and one day approach the Magnificon gates to receive that which was promised from the beginning.

You will cause the rising and falling of many in a far distant land not of my knowing, a land shrouded in darkness. But you will show it to me when you awaken to the voice who fashioned your light."

Tilting the chalice toward the center of the Eye she said, "Therefore, I now pour you out as a drink offering to the All Seeing Eye, where no shadows can hide the loneliest of good deeds or the dread secrets of evil. No nightfall shall prevail against you. For you will consume it only to spew it in their face."

With the last of the pearl sheen liquid spilling into the center of the Eye, an intense white energy ignited and burst forth. So blinding was the thick pulsar blast that the angelic warriors momentarily hid their sight. Shooting under the arch and up through the great cavern, it left a clamoring wake of collapsing air to rattle the planet.

Those islands near the great crater witnessed the jet of radiation puncture the atmosphere, vaporizing the humid air and searing holes through the clouds along its trajectory. Many entities in orbit of Siyon and residents of its immense floating cities also witnessed the unique energy blast, asking, "What is the source and destination of this great light?"

Veezon temporarily forgot his vengeance, and Ru, her tears as the pillaring tower and the Angel of Light faded away. Amongst their consternation, the worshiping Legions suddenly had more questions than when they arrived, "What does this all mean?" "Fight in the dark?" "Work toward our own demise?" "Become infected? Never!"

Everyone stared at the altar, as did Shem. For the scabbard was now gone, the bronze chalice lay on its side empty, and the All Seeing Eye began to dim.

Shem then raised his arms and said, "Silence... ... That which we beheld, that which we knew from the beginning as Ouriano is no longer here. Behold what mystery has absorbed him. Go now in peace!"

Chapter 5

I hate signs, I hoped we were rid of all that.

"How far are you, we, along now," Lucas asked Victoria, who looked down to rub her belly.

"You should know Lucas, after three months of cramped accommodations on that ship. The first stormy night, the creaking of the bulkheads? Then the last half of our getaway cruise with morning sickness."

"Yes, I guess being on the run brings out the romance in both of us. Do you think you ought to maybe lay off the caffeine since we are going to have a kid?"

"Lucas, you picked Tokyo, a place with a Starbucks on every corner. After what we've been through, this child can't help but to be ADD. Please, let me live a little."

"Don't blame our child for your latté cravings Vic. Those didn't start yesterday. Oh, by the way, can you still do the diva runway walk?"

"If you promise to only propose a toast to me. That kind of got us in trouble last time."

"Not fair Victoria, I am a content man. I'll have you know I am praying for Ru."

"Me too. I can't stop wondering what happened to her and Ouriano. Why would he leave us his sword to help escape without any more communication? Hey, your mom and dad's flight still on time? I'm nervous about meeting them."

"Because we haven't officially tied the knot? Vic, what do you think would happen if we registered for a license and showed up on a data base somewhere? I arranged for this meeting the old fashioned way, paper mail, while we chugged around the world in the hull of that dream liner from hell."

"I know you want us to be careful, I'm just feeling guilty because that's how my mom wanted it to take place; you know, a real engagement, wedding, and then a family. How are you going to explain this to them?"

"'This?' I am going to explain 'this,' is our child. And, I am going to ask my father to perform the wedding ceremony. They'll be ecstatic."

"You really think so? Are you going to explain the whole Juwaan thing, including the Blue Moon scenario?"

"I'll break in ole Henry a little at a time. He can already confirm the few things I told him in the letters, that we were indeed kidnapped, held against our will, and to be on look out for Sanctuary Corporation stock rising in the news."

"I've been praying they won't suffer any retribution from the Vranti because of us, but mostly that they'll like me."

"Victoria, my mom and dad never left me. I left them. I told you the story. Gosh, what a funny twist of fate; I'm going back to where I ran from. And why wouldn't they like you?"

"Cause you are your mama's boy who I am taking away for good, and you are handsome—my nerdy Brad Pitt. Judith might think you could do better."

"Better? I'll have no more talk like that. My mom will love having a red head in the family. I'm the one marrying up."

"I love you Lucas Tanner," Victoria whispered as she kissed his nose and headed for the counter after hearing the loud announcement from the Barista with the Japanese accent, "One venti caramel mocha latté with whip crème and one grande Americano!"

Lucas grinned as she strutted away in her tight blue jeans and high heels with her patented catwalk mocking strut. He savored the moment and thought, *God is good.*

As Vic returned toward their table overlooking the street, Lucas watched a mixed stream of uniformed students, city buses, taxis, and compact cars jousting for position. But Lucas' view was interrupted suddenly by a premonition.

He quickly scanned the café then raised his palm in front of his eyes to check; indeed light was emanating out, a sign something was near. Before anyone could notice he slapped his dark Ray Ban's on to conceal them. "Where is the entity causing me to react like this?"

Victoria tried to hand him his coffee but he wasn't paying attention to her, as he scouted the coffee shop, the patrons, the employees, the street. She sat down concerned and noticed the faint rays through sun glasses. She reached out for his left hand on the table and squeezed, "What did you see?"

"I don't know. I'm still searching, act calm."

"Did you take the battery out of your phone like I mentioned?"

"Yes Vic, over there, the man with the green shopping bag."

"He just smiled at you, and he's missing several front teeth. That's not your person of interest," said Victoria, who then in horror watched him raise his cup in a toast toward them.

Lucas in return raised his Americano acknowledging the gesture. The oriental stranger across the room mirrored the same thing, and added a respectful bow. Before Lucas could say anything, the senior citizen stood, threw his cup in the garbage and entered the men's room.

Lucas moved down the dead end hall toward the bathroom as fast as he could without raising suspicions. Finding the door locked he waited to confront him. But in a few seconds, a bright flash from under the door struck his shoes. Lucas tried the doorknob again, and it opened. Victoria from across the coffee shop, saw Lucas come out of the men's room holding the man's shopping bag, and shrugging his shoulders toward her as if to say, "I don't know where he went." As Lucas returned to his chair,

Victoria asked, "Where did he go? What was the flash at the bottom of the door?"

"I don't know. The door was locked, then after the flash it was open. Gone, water running in the sink like he was washing his hands. Smelled like hand soap and cheap men's cologne."

Victoria felt her stomach again, "This is too weird. Let's see what's in the bag."

Opening the sack and staring inside he began to laugh.

"Let me see," said the unnerved Victoria, where upon she reached in and inventoried the contents one by one; "Clothes for a newborn boy, a little blue and red jumper outfit, matching socks, shoes, and baseball cap. They are so cute."

"How do my eyes look?" Lucas asked as he pulled his sun glasses to the end of his nose.

"They are almost normal again. This some kind of sign Lucas?"

"I'd say so, but... I hate signs. I hoped we were rid of all that. How, who, or what, would be tracking us?"

"Somebody or thing who believes we are going to have a boy. Don't look now, but I bet that's your mom and dad coming toward the door."

"What timing."

Chapter 6

For better or for worse we are standing on the edge of something new.

Lucas stood to greet them and said, "It's been ten years since I've seen them face to face." His parents were searching for addresses to verify the location. "They don't look like tourists, too bold; seasoned missionaries and added gray for both of them."

"Lucas!" his mother said as she came through the door first, enwrapping him with a big hug, "I've missed you so much. Look at you, more handsome every day. Take those glasses off and let me see your face."

Lucas hesitated, "uh, uh," but his mother reached to slip them off. He hoped they were dimmed to normal.

"My, your eyes look as bright as when you were a baby and had the entire world before you. Tell me what happened Lucas. After our experiences in the jungle with everything from parasites, to witch doctors, to Shining Path guerillas, we can handle whatever you want to tell us. Who took you?"

"Easy Judith," his father said, "leave some for me," pushing his wife aside to hug his lost son. Lucas heard his dad sniffle and felt his tears on his cheek as his dad said, "I wasn't sure I'd ever see you again." Taking a step away from each other and locking forearms Henry added, "We thought it strange when the mission office in Lima said we had unmarked envelopes. We saw the news that you and your partner had gone missing after you sold your technology of some kind to a private corporation. The American consulate told us to contact them as soon as we heard anything from you. Your unmarked letter said, "Don't' tell anyone. So we are here officially on vacation."

"You don't know how good it is to see you again. I am sorry," said Lucas.

Victoria inserted herself in the conversation, "Aren't you going to introduce me?"

"Ah, mom, dad, this is ..."

Judith seized the moment and Victoria's left hand, "You must be Victoria, Dr. Pruett. So pretty. He met his match didn't he?" She leaned into Victoria's ear and whispered, "Is it a boy?"

Embarrassed, Victoria asked, "What?" as everyone stared at the baby clothes in her right hand. "Oh, these clothes?" she asked, then slowly released the next sentence word by word as Henry and Judith eagerly nodded their smiling faces up and down with her cadence, "This... is for... our new... that is... Lucas and I... our baby boy."

Henry spoke proudly, "My grandson."

Victoria blinked at Lucas until he rescued her, "Yes, everyone has been guessing it's a boy, but no tests yet. The clothes are samples."

"We love all three of you," chimed in Judith, "and before I forget, I have this for you Lucas," pulling out an envelope from her purse. "We did have one visitor who showed up out in the sticks. I don't know how she reached us on foot. I asked her if she had a vehicle or boat. You need a four wheel drive for the mountain passages, and usually a motor boat to come up the river. She said she didn't need them. Strange, she didn't ask where you were. Only dropped off this envelope to give to you. Said you could use it."

"Who?" Lucas shot back.

His father answered, "Her name was a little difficult to pronounce. Here is her card." Pulling it out of his wallet Henry chopped up her name, "Ruvale Marija Zvonimira, Vice President of Security for the Sanctuary Corporation."

Victoria and Lucas spoke at the same time as they looked at each other, "Ru!"

In a rush, Lucas ripped open the envelope. Inside was a two page letter and a secure bank card.

Ignoring they were partially blocking the door of the coffee shop, Lucas scanned the short note, committing it to memory:

Lucas, Victoria,

I assume you escaped to safety. We found the remains of the Vranti in your lab apartment. Cuzak relished how you defeated them and exacted justice for Ms. Pruett on your own, but upset that Ouriano's sword was not found.

I cannot explain in detail now, but if you don't already know, Ouriano is no more. He is gone. He sacrificed himself for the two of you, and even me. His old friend Veezon has vowed to kill me, blaming me solely for his extinction. Watch out for him. He has gone rogue.

Enclosed are instructions for you to wire currency securely anywhere in the world if you should choose to cash in any shares of your preferred stock in the new Sanctuary Corporation, from a blind trust. Don't use your Swiss account any more, it's traceable. Cuzak made good on his promise to pay you for your work and patents.

Stay off the grid. Too many back office deals could mean the end of any of us. Keep your loyalties with Siyon. There is One there who is faithful and true. At times I don't trust myself.

Maybe in another time or place we can all be friends. For better or for worse we are standing on the edge of something new.

Love to all,

Ru

Lucas put the card in his pocket and handed the note to Victoria, and rested his hand on the back of her neck, "I am sorry Vic." His mom and dad could tell this was bad news. Lucas didn't know what to feel at this point of the reunion; anger, sorrow, joy? Taking a few slow breaths and putting his Ray Ban's on, he said, "Mom, dad, let's find a place with more privacy. We have much to share."

Lucas' mother put her arm around Victoria who was crying as she finished reading the note. Judith said, "I am sorry we brought bad news, did someone you know pass away?"

Chapter 7

I'd call them confused, those doing the best they can with what they have.

"You're making your pop look bad in front of your mother, this penthouse balcony suite... breathtaking. I'm afraid I've taken your mom to the other extreme. Always wished I could afford something like this. That's a pretty penny. You didn't have to do this. Awful expensive."

"Dad, there is nothing financial I can do to make up for my attitude toward you and mom. Please accept this as a small token. Forgive me. We needed to spend some money anyway. It came with a big price. I can't work in my field anymore."

"I am not sure what you are talking about."

Lucas framed his dad in the orange setting sun. His father faced the thick tinted glass, peering over the megatropolis below, baggy khaki pants and ivory print silk shirt. Inwardly Lucas smiled, *Are those shirts mandatory issue for missionaries?*

Mr. Tanner's mind defaulted to what he thought about the most, "Look at this view, the mass of humanity. Many lost souls down there."

"Are you sure they're all lost?"

His father continued to stare, picking up where their conversation left off over a decade ago.

"What would you call them son?"

"I'd call them confused, those doing the best they can with what they have."

His father sensed the renewed tension between them, "And how is that different than what I am saying?"

Lucas answered, "You write others off, when they don't agree with your religion."

"Write off? You mean I act as their eternal judge?"

"No, not exactly, but the negative message is implied."

"Son, I'm not sure what trouble you are in, or what has happened, but you will always be my son. If anything ever separates us, it won't be because I left you. I don't think it is any different with God and his children. The story I preach is: He came back for them."

"I know dad. But how can you be so sure? You've never been there. You haven't seen anything have you?"

"If you are talking heaven, no, I haven't been there. But I have seen the other side." Mr. Tanner turned around to face Lucas. The last of the oriental sun was disappearing behind his father and the groves of steel and glass towers. "Lucas, five months ago we lost your sister. I didn't know how to tell you."

Lucas cried, "No! What happened to Paige? I should have asked why she didn't come. I knew you shouldn't have taken her with you to Peru."

"We moved our school and opened a health station further out to an upper tributary of the Amazon basin. We were working with an indigenous group with whom the mission had a long relationship. Wonderful people, but they had a long standing feud with a neighboring tribe, who thought we brought magic to hurt them.

Their shaman cast a spell against us. I wasn't sure if I believed in any of that hocus pocus until I saw her body riddled with parasites. The locals said this wasn't the first time he had done this to someone. A government medical doctor was dispatched for an autopsy of Paige. She said, 'I've never seen anything like this. It was as if...'"

Lucas interrupted him, completing his sentence, "a swarm of insects had infested her body."

"How did you know this is the other side I am talking about?"

"Victoria and I are all too acquainted. Did you ever hear of its name?"

"Yes, the locals called it 'Branti.'"

"The Vranti? Awful close."

"Let's sit down son. A little much for an old man."

"It has to be the same name of a darkened collective we ran into. A demonic hive if you must. Paige didn't die because of you. She died because of what Victoria and I have been through. It was looking for us."

"Why? Your mom and I are the missionaries."

"Dad, we are both working towards the same end. You have your fight, and I have mine. But I can't let you go back to Peru. Not right now."

"But that's our life. Paige is buried there. We have to return. My support? What will happen?"

"In time we can go to Peru. We need to remain safe as a family, together. That thing, which killed Paige, killed Victoria's mother too. There's more I have to tell. But this time the shoe is on the other foot; I have things to share I don't expect you to believe right away. About the money, fortunately that is not a problem. In fact, I have a more important task for you and mom."

"What?"

"I have a child on the way that will require all the wisdom his grandparents can spare."

Henry scratched his head confused, "Let's back up, you asked if I had 'been there?' Were you inferring you've seen something else?"

"We haven't told anyone. If it hadn't happened to me, I wouldn't have believed it. The technology that Vic and I were working on was a great breakthrough for quantum physics. We found a way to open a controllable worm hole, a door to another universe which intersects ours. But in our case it wasn't just any universe."

"Where did it lead?"

"I followed an angel named Ouriano. He showed me his beautiful home, a blue Earth like planet, except for this continental hole in the crust. It was hollowed out with many caverns but the surface was covered with vibrant life forms, great oceans with many islands. His home was actually a moon orbiting a much larger gas giant planet he referred to as Siyon, where the Wounded Heir of the Magnificon resides.... This must sound absolutely crazy. I met this desert Angel who showed me my life..."

Confused, Henry said, "I was with you Lucas about the darkened collective. That's too much of a coincidence about Paige. But your travel to the kingdom of God, if that's what you are claiming, is a stretch for me to accept."

"I am not finished yet. While I traveled to the Blue Moon, Victoria and our technology were hijacked by the Vranti and their front corporation... How can I say this so you will understand?

Dad, there is no simple explanation here. At the time I didn't believe in God anymore or any personal evil. My reason was guided by blind bias and an over rejection of the beliefs you raised me on. But this experience was real, too real. Unfortunately, Victoria and I were kidnapped and held hostage until we helped this corporation--the Sanctuary Corporation. You may have heard about them in the news?"

"Your stock in this company is how you are paying for this hotel?"

"Yes, we were forced to help them improve the technology for travel to an entirely different realm. They plan on using the technology for, in your words, 'a demonic escape from the Earth, from hell and future judgments of the apocalypse.'"

"Son, if I can believe your outlandish story, then what you are saying is a good thing. Demonic powers fleeing the Earth would be doing the world a favor."

"No! It's not good."

"It's not?" said Henry.

"No, the technology only works with these darkened beings if they are in possession of humans at the time they pass through the artificial opening. They are going to need a lot of jump fodder."

"And the Branti, or Vranti is one of the powers influencing this?"

"I'll explain more later. Wait, I'll show you something I brought with us. The other thing is locked away, too conspicuous to carry."

Chapter 8

You have your own divine journey, as do we.

"Ladies...Vic, Mom, come out and share your secrets. Where are you?" called Lucas who heard the balcony's sliding glass panel open from the other side of the apartment, followed by laughter.

"I spot two handsome guys. Miss us already?" said Judith. A breeze gusted in behind them flaring the curtains as they stepped in from the balcony. "The lightning on this side is spectacular Henry. We saw a couple of strikes hit the Rainbow Bridge crossing Tokyo Bay."

Henry said, "No, we were admiring the passing sunset on the west side. The typhoon we flew around is sending in the first waves of thunderstorms. We'll hear the angels bowling in the heavens tonight. Maybe the building will sway."

Lucas added, "Mom, they construct these towers to withstand earthquakes, don't worry. This is a good evening to stay indoors. Anyone care to join me for a glass of wine? Food is on the way."

Victoria answered, "I'm eating for two, but 'no,' on the wine for me."

"No fruit of the vine for me son, but your mom can be persuaded," said Henry.

Lucas explained, "Glad I picked up a bottle of sparkling ginger ale for our teetotalers. I can't believe we are reunited after all these years. Come on, we have some celebrating and memories to share."

Lucas led them down a hall and through an archway into a large circular room, replete with wet bar, red Plexiglas bar-stools, mixed red and black leather sofas-chairs and a fireplace framed by two steel girders. The walls were covered by a floor to ceiling wrap around video screen, at the moment displaying a loop of a Japanese Shinto garden with Mount Fuji in the background. Centered above the room hung a chandelier composed of hundreds of sparkling tear drop crystals.

Lucas invited his family to recline with him as he slid out a console from his arm rest. Dimming the lights in the room, he opened a retractable panel above the chandelier revealing a clear domed skylight to the dark percolating clouds. Outer storm bands from the typhoon were throwing jagged lightning across the city, illuminating the dome and refracting light through the crystals. While they all gawked, Lucas reached over to the table next to his chair and opened the bottles of merlot and ginger ale.

"Incredible, praise be to God. Let it never be said my son is second class," said Henry.

"That's not all," replied Lucas as he began to push more buttons to retract one at a time the four ceiling panels. In a few moments the only protection between them and a sky interlaced with wild electrical charges was the thin lattice work of supporting metal and glass panes. A few nearby taller towers outlined with neon and LED lights were already attracting strikes.

"You'll close the roof if it gets bad?" asked Victoria.

Excited by the view, Judith said, "'The heavens declare the Glory of God, and the skies show the work of his hands.' Let me be so bold to propose the first toast." Filling everyone's glass, she added, "We never lost our son. You were not ours to lose. You have your own divine journey, as do we. My toast is this, may you complete the journey you have begun with the guidance of His Spirit and your missing angel where ever he now resides. And to you Victoria, may your son surpass your dreams for him." Raising her glass they took a sip in unison.

Henry then moved to the center of the room to make an impromptu speech, "First I'd like to say, if you want me to conduct your wedding, I'd be delighted."

Judith on the other hand interrupted, "Henry...," warning him with a fake smile and sharp voice, as if they had discussed this before.

He paused a moment, to stare at Judith, then resumed, "As I was saying, the Bible says, 'He who discovers a good wife, finds a good thing.' But that's not my toast. Here it is: 'May the two of you be blessed with your firstborn as I have. May this child bring light and freedom to a world oppressed. I am fading, but you are becoming strong. For you Victoria, I give thanks; I can't imagine Lucas with anyone else. Son you've done well.'"

They lifted their glasses together as the sky stirred above them. Lucas rose and said, "Dad, thank you, we'd love for you to perform our wedding vows this week, but we have to postpone any civil registration for security purposes. Mom, God did send an angel to watch over me, an answer to your prayers. I actually met him. I guess Victoria explained to you the disturbing note you handed us at the coffee shop which spoke of his death. We escaped from our captors because of him. His name was Ouriano. He showed me visions, places and things I can barely express. I don't expect you to believe everything. I speak as a scientist, not a loony religious freak."

Lucas' mother said, "You can't make up something like this. Why would you? Victoria explained a lot to me. I didn't know angels could die, but I believe you. She said you were anointed as a Juwaan, a prophet or something. You are anything but a freak." As she spoke a thunder clap rattled the chandelier.

"Here, let me show you something," said Lucas, "a special object not from this world." He lifted a black velvet sack with a gold twine pull sting. Opening the sack he reached in and pulled out the rough hewn mirror. As he did this his pupils illumed. The lap sized mirror's edges were of turquoise crystal and the reflective surface like mercury.

"What in Saint Peter's name is that? And... your eyes, they have light in them," said Henry.

"I wanted to give you proof."

"Like your mom said, we believe you."

Chapter 9

To life, uncertainty, and faith--we are
far better off this way.

"Mom, Dad, I am the one who still doesn't believe everything," said Lucas.

Victoria's eyes kept darting off of him to the bottom of a low thunderhead which had formed over the top of their building. The release of static charges every few seconds lit up the pale green and gray churning cloud.

"Lucas, sorry to interrupt, but why don't you close the atrium panels and let us move to a less exposed room?" appealed Victoria, "This is an unusual storm."

"Please Victoria, let me finish my toast, then we can." She half grimaced acquiescing to him. "And will you hold the mirror while I pour everyone a new toast?" he asked.

Victoria rocked forward out of the thick chair toward the center of the room to help him. She held the mirror in one arm and her wine glass in the other hand while Lucas refilled it with fizzing ginger ale. He explained as he poured, "This mirror was given to me by an ancestral people of this world and reshaped by an angel who cast a new call for my life. It has a special refractive power that cuts through darkness and evil. It is one of the causes of my eyes enlightening at times."

No sooner had he refreshed the glasses of his mother, father, and himself, when the tear drop crystals began to chink together from the down drafts shaking the top of the clear atrium. The flashes of light through the swaying chandelier lit up the room like a disco ball at a teen skating rink. "Hurry Lucas, this is scary," reminded Victoria.

"Raise your glasses high," said Lucas, to which everyone complied.

Victoria however set down the mirror at her feet so she could better raise her toast. She couldn't help but to look through the dangling crystals directly above to see a hollow throat in the center of the brooding cloud.

"Here's to family, my lovely bride, and our new child, praise to the One above who has reunited and blessed us. Everyone take a sip," to which they did.

"Wonderful Lucas, let's move to the next room. That's an awful sky," said Victoria.

"Hold on, part two here. I refilled your glasses for a reason." While he spoke, the gusting typhoon winds and slashing rain grew louder. Straining to speak over the outside elements, Lucas lifted his glass again and said, "To life, uncertainty, and faith--we are far better off this way. In memory of Paige, Ms. Pruett, and not least Ouriano, may their memories and hopes live on through us."

The sound of the atmospheric turbulence became oppressive. As the chandelier swayed, some of the crystals began to snap off and bounce against the marble floor. Victoria arched her neck to see past the chandelier into the stalled thunderhead as a vortex of blazing light energized above.

The mirror she had set down between her feet also began to glow. She tried to warn them of the imminent danger, "Get out of the...," but her muscles froze and the room turned to dead air. Everything stood still before Victoria; no noise of blustering winds, thunder, or familial voices. She saw Lucas, Henry, and Judith had begun to drink from their wine glasses, but were completely rigid.

But ending the short silence were two new sounds. Increasing in intensity, she recognized them; the slower strong pulse of her own heart, and the racing pace of her baby's. Helpless to move she prayed internally, "My God, don't let this happen. I love my baby."

But before she could flee, a beam of white light charged through her from the cloud above. It fired downward through the clear center skylight, through the chandelier, and up from the mirror below. The electromagnetic pulse melted the glass in Victoria's hand, her drink vaporizing, but with no apparent harm to her. In the same way the hanging crystals all fell like hail around her feet, sticking to the floor as a red hot glaze, yet none injured her.

Immobile and temporarily blinded, Victoria felt something kick repeatedly in her womb. Her negative petitions to God continued, "It's too early to feel something like this. What is happening? No don't take this life from me!"

With this plea, she heard a faint but distinguishing reply:

"I take up, and I give life. Protect this little one and set him free.
He is mine, his spirit born of the Lake of Dreams.
Like his father, a sword he will bear.
But unique to him a voice he will hear where no others can hear,
A light he will see where no others can see.
In time, tell him who he is and from whence he was forged.
A great harlot approaches to consume him, yet he will consume.
I will be an enemy to his enemies."

As the present time resumed, and Victoria's family sought to complete the toast, the flash and ensuing concussion knocked them unconscious before they could react. The imminent thunder clap rocked the penthouse suite smashing half the center atrium panes of glass, the shards cascading over them. In a few minutes, the three awoke, startled, brandishing minor cuts and abrasions, but overall unhurt. They ignored themselves as they discovered Victoria's rain soaked body lying crumpled on the floor grasping her stomach. Steam filtered around her as the pouring showers and wind resolidified the molten glass.

Judith stumbled over to her first while Lucas and Henry regained their equilibrium. She noticed a nose bleed from Victoria as she knelt beside her and gingerly cradled her head. Victoria blinked her eyes, opened them and said, "Did you hear the voice?"

"Henry, Lucas, she's talking. Get us some light. Close the roof. Some towels." Then Judith answered her, "No honey, all I saw was a flash. What did it say?"

"The voice said, something like, 'You are going to have a grandson. He will see where no others can see, and he will hear where no others can hear. I will be an enemy to his enemies.'"

Chapter 10

I volunteered for a greater purpose than saving my matrix.

Advanta's wings were bright and sleek, his bronze skin smooth, giving him an edge in speed and agility. His body and mind bore no blemishes, for they had yet to endure significant battles compared to prior generations of Legionnaires. This was all to change.

Previously he had only seen the desecrated Cathedral from a distance as a dark hollowed out spot on the great cavern wall. He was dressed as the other Loyalists on this special day, white with gold sash, sworn to serve the whims of the Angel of Light. But when he observed Veezon, who was far below him, leave his soaring reconnaissance for the memorial, Advanta dove in the opposite direction to the more ancient ruins of the abandoned Diaphthora Temple.

Appearing as a white streak in the distance, Advanta broke off his dive at the last moment, wings counter thrusting-- fanning dust toward the waiting arm-crossed angel. Unimpressed he said, "Save your virgin wings. They will be tested in days to come."

"I am ready."

"No one is born ready for this. Why did you agree to come to this unholy place?"

"My Commander and friend, Veezon said I should become more acquainted with evil to counter it."

"What if he is wrong? What if evil is recruiting you because of your misguided weakness to save the world?"

"What?"

"Maybe you should return to your class mates gathering on the other side of the chasm for Ouriano's funeral."

"And maybe you are no longer the brave one called Fortius. Does your name refer only to younger days?"

"Fortius is a name not of my choosing. In the near future some will say I have wasted my renewed bravery to a lost cause."

"I know somewhat of the Diaphthora's history. It still radiates a dark glow from a terrible time before I came into being. Now that I am standing in this worship tomb, I have seen enough. Let us take our discussion to a more agreeable place," said Advanta.

"The Diaphthora is the perfect place for you, as a new drone of the Heir, to vet your courage."

The younger Wind pondered the hulking frame of this Legion Commander, a co-conspirator of Veezon. He appeared to him frayed, cynical, dark rings under his eyes, caring none to waste energy on his form. The commendations of his extensive service were tattooed on his arms. His previous long satin hair was now unkempt, gray streaked, and thinning.

They sat together on a large boulder fallen eons ago from the ceiling of the mammoth amphitheatre amongst the rubble of broken but once beautiful icons. Advanta spoke, trying to piece together the ancient epoch, "This is the place where Lucifer had proclaimed himself as The Beautiful One, a Co-Regent of the Heir of the Magnificon, isn't it?"

"A brilliant deduction neophyte," said Fortius.

Advanta looked with disgust upon two cesspools, one on either side of them, full of half algae and fungal covered broken statuary of beings like himself. On the walls he observed spill ways where once had been majestic turquoise waterfalls supplied by abundant underground rivers, now reduced to small trickles fed by fog condensation. The thin flow was just enough to sustain a patch work of thorny vines smattered across the high walls and ceiling, covering over many ancient hieroglyphs. Between sections of vines he noticed an immense hieroglyph of two Cherubs. As Advanta observed, he was struck by another detail; borne across the shoulders of the tri-winged Guardians of Holiness, was a colossal serpent. Each end of the snake was wrapped as a tightening noose around their necks.

Advanta repeated to Fortius the history of this once magnificent temple from the story Veezon had told him of Lucifer, "Eons ago, he was brought down in a cataclysmic event when the uninvited Angel of Light interrupted his coronation. In her anger she dragged him to the edge of the Magnificon to display all that his rebellion had cost him. In a rage of spiteful disgust he dared attack the Heir before the time of his wound. Lucifer's being was split in judgment, half cast to Earth and half to distant realm. Is this how you see it?"

"You desire to find out?"

Advanta replied, "Veezon told me, 'To this other realm we must go.'"

"Advanta, they call you?" Fortius broke the young angel's train of thought, "Who gave you such a name? Do not play naive with me. Why do you make it sound so terrible, were you there?"

"No, of course not, but my name is from the same One who gave you your name, Fortius. I must ask, can anything good come from meeting here? Let us join Veezon at the Ayin Cathedral, we all need fresh words."

"Stop it now!" said Fortius, "Veezon wanted you here for a reason. Would you risk being near the all Seeing Eye when you have made a pledge to cross over and desert your Legion? We all are given a name. I'll one day change mine as will you. I will ignore your cowardice, only because Veezon handpicked you."

"I volunteered, for a greater purpose than preserving my newly fashioned matrix."

"Yes you did, neophyte, and did you notice the serpent, the most feared animal by the image bearers? Even if you hate him, Beltshzan did see something in the future you cannot argue against; that one day the image bearers would rise up to overtake us." With these last words, a planet rattling concussion surged through the Blue Moon.

"You know what that is?" said Advanta, "It is our home crying out for one who is no more."

"No," said Fortius, "it is our old home crying out for change. Ouriano wanted a way out. Some think he found it."

"Are you saying he found someone to annihilate him?"

"Isn't that why you volunteered, you want the same—to one day fade away from your eternal servitude."

"No, Veezon told me he needed a group to go with him to the realm of Yazad to start an insurrection against the night. He said the chance of failure was high, but this was not without precedent. He didn't elaborate, but said Ouriano had to die."

"It's a one way trip for sure. Either you convert over to the dark light of the Sanctuary or you will suffer for a very, very, long time."

"The Heir would never leave his morning stars stranded to rot," said the hope filled Advanta, as another beat echoed along the canyon walls. Both turned their heads to see the lightning flare between new brewing thunderheads parallel to their decrepit cliff Cathedral.

"Then where is Ouriano?" Fortius asked as another bellowing vibration resounded, rippling the green filmed cesspools on either side.

"We can still go, we must remember him," pleaded Advanta.

"That would not be wise. We are all going our own way from here, less dangerous. You can hide the infection for a while, manage it. But then it grows on you, becomes you. Did you notice the changes in Veezon?"

"Veezon's infected?" asked Advanta.

"His conscience has been breached. Vengeance is all that is on his mind, despite assuring us he could control the infesting contagion. In following his example, we will have to improve on repressing it."

Chapter 11

And he told us the infection could be mitigated with faith!

Advanta closed his eyes for a second and reopened them, "No, I pledged to help fight against Beltshzan and Yazad as he explained the situation to me. Veezon said the Heir needed someone to infiltrate but not succumb to them. Taking on the infection is crazy. There must be another way."

"It's too late. There is no other way," said Fortius who then gripped Advanta's forearm, "I can't let you go. You know too much from Veezon. You've seen us."

"Us?"

Again, another beat from the bowels of the Blue Moon of Siyon rumbled through the ground, the air, their being.

As Fortius was speaking three other weathered but strong Winds appeared from the back of the Diaphthora--the dark worship cavern, gliding in to surround the young and inexperienced Advanta. Before he could react, one behind him took his sword.

"No, please do not hack off my wings."

Fortius answered, "We are not going to tear, rip, or hack off your wings. You must however take a drink from one of these infected pools, or we will make a visit to the Abyss, and then hack off your wings. Without flight, you would never escape."

"You would maim a brother sentinel?"

Fortius answered, "What? As if this has not been done before? You have much to learn, neophyte. If you plan on surviving an attack by a viper, then you must introduce the poison to your system."

"Never!"

"Lap up a handful. You really won't notice anything. The infection takes time."

"This is how it goes down? I willingly corrupt my matrix?" Advanta looked up but couldn't find Siyon in the sky from his angle, so he prayed, "Oh, great Heir of the Magnificon, save me from myself. What have I committed to? Who are these brothers, these beasts who surround me?"

Advanta then yelled out as loud as he could, but it was drowned out by another radiating beat from the depths on behalf of Ouriano, "I was not born for this!"

"Oh neophyte, I have prayed that very prayer many times. It's always by one's free will. And you already agreed. We know you are true to your word, but this is the only way we insure your silence. Did Veezon leave out this detail?"

Advanta said no more as he hoped one would side with him. *Have they all given up?* he wondered, *Is this what happens from one angelicus generation to another, they lose the ideals of their youth? Grounded, I am no match to them.*

Fortius started to laugh as he plunged his verbal sword, "He didn't tell you? That he has been a carrier for a long time?" The other three roiled in laughter with him, then he added, "And he told us the infection could be mitigated with faith! What do you think of that? Wouldn't you agree he believed his own delusion; the infection can be managed. Here my young one, we will commune together as an act of faith." Fortius ordered, "Azazel, fill the cup!"

One of the sentinels walked over to the cesspool's edge, where half submerged lay a golden chalice. It too was half covered with green scum from the stagnant pond. In righting the vessel, he filled it to the brim and brought it over to their thirsty mutineers.

"Stand up Advanta. It would be sacrilege to sit through this. We will only ask you to do what we have done. All of you take a sip as I pass it." One by one starting with Fortius they lifted the cup to their mouth and drank. To Advanta they did not seem to enjoy it. They consumed the dead broth as a duty, wiping the brown excess from the corners of their mouth with their fingers.

The last to partake before Advanta, the one called Azazel, however was different. Tilting the cup to his mouth, he then cocked his head back and gurgled the liquid before swallowing. To this they all heartily laughed again.

Azazel then handed Advanta the cup. Fortius let loose his grasp. Another tossed Advanta's sword to his feet as they all stood away. Fortius said, "This is your choice."

Advanta now stood free from any physical encumbrances, yet shackled internally, confused by these older generations of Loyalists, Winds who like him had foregone Ouriano's memorial. Deep in his heart he knew he would always be loyal to the One who fashioned him. At this juncture in his life, it was a matter of how?

They all nodded to him that this was the right thing to do. Advanta stared into the cup, a dark repugnant liquid lay at the bottom, green scum clung to the inside walls marking where the others had drank.

The neophyte said, "Before I drink, I do not pretend in the least for this cup to release me from my purpose. Rather may it be for the glory of the Magnificon. With all that is in me I will fight in and against the darkness until the end. If it means my self destruction, then so be it. So say we all!"

And to his surprise, they all looked back at the young courageous one with the same resoluteness, "So say we all!"

Advanta took the cup and pursed his lips over the rim. He felt the rough dirty edges and now inhaled the festering anger, resentment, and pride still brewing in this tea of iniquity. He continued to tilt the cup suspending his conscience, and drank the remainder.

"You were wrong about one thing Fortius," said Advanta as he leaned over and picked up his sword.

"What was that?"

"Maybe you are desensitized by your age, but I already sense a carnal knowledge," Advanta said. He tossed the chalice in the air and hit it with the flat of his sword propelling the smashed vessel out over the dark canyon turning end over end.

They followed it down until the most amazing wonder blazed through the atmosphere; a sight which caused them to question their choices. A thick energy beam of blue-white light pierced up through a spot on the other side of the continental sized cavity. They all realized where this originated. The beam lasted for several seconds, an incredible pulse of energy which blasted through thunderheads, the fog, and the floating drizzle. Tracing the light as it left the atmosphere, they saw a strange orange trail of expanding ringed clouds and heard its reverberating rumble.

As the cup of the infection tumbled lower and lower out of their sight through the cool subterranean air streams, a set of buzzing tri-wings shot like a bullet out of a lower side transit shaft, snatching the vessel in mid air, then circled back to examine the catch. These wings did not glide.

Chapter 12

*Have you the wisdom to dismiss with
all evil for eternity?*

This was not the ending to Ouriano's memorial that anyone had planned. The abruptness shocked the twenty-four Elders, who immediately summoned their return transportation to Siyon. Heading toward the outdoor landing, several of them conjectured, "How could evil raise its head to warrant this type of response from the Angel of Light?"

While the Winds of light, who were packed into the Ayin Temple began to dispatch like morning bees from their hive, Veezon remained. He scouted for her, riling his anger and pride. "How dare she spoil this sacred moment with her presence? She is mocking us, smearing our wings with the refuse from her evil cravings. She is the cause of his fall, and will pay dearly for her treachery. I made a vow. Now where in this Cathedral is she? She is not getting out alive!"

Veezon kept watch for her dark wings and feminine figure. "She has to fly under the arch to get out." He placed his right hand on his sword. The hilt melded with his hand. But this was noticed by one of the Royal Cherubim, the large tri-winged Keepers of the Holiness.

"Sir, I think I have spotted her," said one of Veezon's Legionnaires.

"Think? Give me something definite."

"On the center of the dome above sir, is that definite enough for you?"

"I don't see anything. Wait, the shimmering?"

"Yes Commander."

"She thought she could cloak herself? Remain here and hold my sword until I signal you from the altar."

Veezon had now gained the attention of two Cherubim. They relaxed somewhat when they observed him handing his sword over to a junior of the rank. This would not be unusual if he was going to approach the sacred table before the Eye, for at the altar a few dozen other Winds lingered behind on bended knee.

Veezon kneeled as if to pray, but prayer was far from his heart. In less than a split second he grabbed the empty chalice and hurled it with all his might toward the cloaked entity hanging far above on the ceiling.

The bullet like throw struck its invisible mark, collapsing the bronze cup and deflecting it down toward the floor. His target's cloaked image flickered on and off, the muscles in her left shoulder and wing momentarily stunned. With uncoordinated flapping wings, she fell from the ceiling as a broken glider.

With the Cherubim guards distracted by the falling chalice and black winged sentinel, Veezon motioned to his Legionnaire, who threw his sword above him. Bolting upward, Veezon clasped his celestial weapon on his ascension. But to his despair, a large Cherub intercepted him with two pair of powerful arms clamping over his wings, torso, and arms, grounding him to a halt. Then another joined to disarm him of his flashing blade. What Veezon's body could not do, he announced with a blistering tongue, "This dark half breed Nephilim has defiled all of us. She must pay for her atrocity!"

As he yelled, yet another Cherub seized Ru. They both, bound by the larger Keepers of the Holiness were stood face to face on the floor of the Cathedral.

Shem now moved hurriedly toward them in escort. He could identify Veezon, trying to wrestle free, but the other arrested, faced away from him. "What is the meaning of this Veezon? You would bring violence to this sacred place?"

As he walked between the two, Shem turned to see the reason Veezon was filled with black bile. What Shem saw was a false angel with a soft face, a confused Hybrid now empty of all fight. In her self-loathing she said, "I don't know why I am here. I don't, belong."

Shem, surprised at her presence, asked her, "Were you witness to Ouriano's memorial?"

"Yes, part of me shall mourn the rest of my life. The other half of my heart rejoices that Ouriano is at peace, having completed his purpose."

Shem responded, "Were you not afraid that one or more like Veezon would be searching for you?"

"Ouriano was a father to me. I am without him. What do I care?"

"Was it you who finished him?" Shem inquired, "You know what happened?"

Veezon spoke, "I warned her to stay away from Ouriano. She is a tool of darkness, an illegitimate stillborn with no home. Her kind was never planned for and has no place in this realm or any other. At best her wings should be torn and thrown down to Lamech's island. For her, for her father, and for her father's father, the fires of Gehenna burn continuously. She wants a way out. Can't you see?"

"Veezon, you speak as one who has been shown no mercy. Why this vicious savage language? Have you the wisdom to dismiss with all evil for eternity?"

"No, but I vowed to the Angel of Light that I would use my darkness to help slay her enemies."

"Ru is not the enemy, though she has caused great sorrow. Veezon, your enemy is within you. Call on your inner strength to subdue it, or you will be swept away like the others. Look at yourself. Release him."

The Cherub let go as Veezon pulled up his right sleeve, then his left to reveal the dark surging veins. "What are you gazing at? Do you want to see what the infection does even to the obedient?" he screamed at Shem and the growing circle of post worshipers. In disgust at himself Veezon pulled off all of his clothing, the white robes and golden sash. Everyone gaped at the bruising across his body fed by the varicose veins curling and branching through the warrior's sculpted form.

Bundling the clothes in his hands, he set them ablaze in his anger and threw them in the face of the Cherub who held his weapon. As fast as light he darted and stole his sword from the Cherub, slicing off one of its wings as he passed by.

But Veezon did not flee. He knew that would be an act of futility. For the insidious thing he might become led him to make the attack on one of his own. He stopped and waited for the searing swords of the Holy Guardians to slice through him.

"Suicide by Cherubim," he prayed, but the blows never came. Instead one held his wings prone while the others his arms.

Chapter 13

"Should someone give me briars and thorns in battle, then I would step on them, I would burn them completely."—Isaiah 27:4

Veezon understood the penalty for attacking one of his own, let alone displaying his growing infection. Shem approached him as he finally relaxed against the power of his captors. "Why like this Veezon? You accepted a more noble duty."

"Shem, I know what I have sworn to. I love the Wounded One and would gladly dissipate into nothingness for his sake. But I cannot see where this flight will take me. I am not an image bearer, I am a sentinel."

Shem nodded in agreement, then leaned over and whispered ever so softly in his ear. "You were not asked to be a god. You were asked and accepted to take a new path for your kind. You shall and will be able. The Wounded Heir has deemed it so." Turning away from the bruised soldier of light, he gave the orders, "Hold him for Michael. Regarding the hybrid woman he lusts to kill, bring her with us. Put her on my ship."

"What about her?" Veezon shouted to Shem's back, "Are you going to let her go? Where is justice?"

Veezon's question struck a nerve in Shem as he headed for the outer platform. Raising his hand he stopped the entourage and paused to give answer to Veezon, who with haggard and drooping head, was being led away from him, "Veezon! Know this: justice is a law inscribed into the fabric of creation. Be careful how you hurry justice, lest it come for you. If only evil were like briars and thorns which the Lord would burn up in an instant." Veezon heard him, but he did not look up.

As Shem and Ru continued side by side, passing under the arch toward his descending sleek silver craft which came to a hover no more than a foot above the outdoor landing, he asked her, "Did you intend to kill Ouriano?"

"It happened so fast. It wasn't premeditated. He didn't put up a fight. He didn't even have his sword. I still don't know what exactly happened. Whatever fate you have for me, I will not resist you."

Shem pointed to the huge orange mushroom cloud surrounded by expanding donut rings, glowing with heat lightning and hanging over the center of the black hole of the Blue Moon, "Do you see what I see?"

"Spectacular, beautiful, I have never seen anything like it," said Ru.

"And neither have I. Ru, we are beholding something unique. Justice is at work, but none of us is in control of it."

"What is my justice, my penalty?"

"Like all creatures, it will come. But you have much to accomplish before then. Please get in my ship. It will be safer and shorter for you on your return to Earth."

A panel door slid up on the side of the bi-needle nose cruiser. Ru noticed the two rows of interior passenger seats, four across, facing each other, made of orange cushion vinyl. The floor was covered with a lime green shag carpet. A rainbow of glass fruit and plastic dipped flowers were embedded in the walls above each set of seats. "Time for an upgrade?" she asked.

"I enjoyed some of the 1970's on Earth; maybe they will make a comeback."

They both stepped into the craft, the door resealing seamlessly. Leaving the guards behind, Shem and Ru reclined in their seats as the silver missile launched itself upward through the clouds. Breaking through the canopy of the Blue Moon, Shem marveled at the golden Siyon, "Ru, I'd like to take you there someday."

"I am afraid Heaven and Hell will have to move first to see me on the guest list."

"Much has happened, and you are caught in the center. Honestly Ru, I didn't like you at first. I didn't trust you because of your immaturity, your father, and the legends on Sharu about an evil woman with wings. I didn't see what Ouriano saw in you. He worked with others of your kind in the past to help them change, but unfortunately only to see them die. This time he did something different."

"What are you talking about? I confess, my action—I gave in to the worst angels of my nature."

"Yes and no," said Shem. "You may think you killed him, but Ouriano sacrificed himself on your behalf. He speculated something better would happen to your life and his."

Eagerly Ru asked, "Did it?"

"I am not God. I don't know these things. Every time I put myself in his place, I am wrong. I am inclined to say 'yes,' but divine intervention is not without pain."

"I am feeling the pain, believe me Shem."

"We have almost arrived at your drop off point. Go back, continue your quest. Veezon will eventually overcome his need for vengeance. You have to work with him. He will be cast out of the Blue Moon and Siyon, but not like others with the infection. Keep Lucas and Victoria out of harm's way the best you can. I have been told that the Wounded Heir wants the transport Hubs built."

"I don't understand."

"I wouldn't be surprised if he didn't make the trip himself. He is like that; a strength unseen."

Chapter 14

*"The Earth deprived of her children has cried
even to the gate of heaven."--Enoch 9:2.*

The long sinewy but powerful fingers inspected the damage and began to pull and pry on the metal folds and creases. Next, the four hands of the once holy sentinel smoothed and polished the prized vessel of infection until he could read the words on the bottom of the base.

"It is still here, after all this time," he said. For underneath was inscribed in the language of the Winds, the cryptic words, "The Earth deprived of her children has cried even to the gate of heaven."

This powerful, powerful, Cherub repeated the words again, then pressed the precious cup against his lips and kissed it saying, "The image bearers will reap what they sow, but my Winds will learn to sow anew for themselves."

Pondering how long it had been, he broke out into a wide smile. He then flew as no other entity could, fast and frantic into the heart of the Blue Moon through intricate mazes of tunnels, ventilation shafts, and transit corridors. The deeper Beltshzan traveled into the core of the ancient home of the Winds of light, the more he crossed through channels of steam, gases, volcanic magma, and radioactive decay. No one knew this labyrinth like him, for he had mapped out its design.

In just a few moments he arrived for the summit meeting. Even before he entered, the pulse of his dark energy could be sensed by the three Legion Commanders who heretofore had never met him face to face. They folded back their wings in respect for his power, cunning, and purported beauty as a one of a kind. With them was another from the realm of the Earth, a burly man dressed in a dark blue business suit, white dress shirt with open collar, his face pock marked, the corners of his eyes yellow. In his hand was a lance with straps of leather dangling from the center shaft. As the pulse became stronger a purple fog drifted in across the floor of the inner sanctum catacomb. Cuzak recognized this aromatic presence of Beltshzan and wondered, *In what form will he appear?*

This man bowed with the others toward the large dark red Cherub, twice the size of the Commanders. The pulse now standing in front of them became an aching throb in their chests causing them to tremble and tempting them to flee.

To their relief the overt evil impulse suddenly ceased. Before them now was the appearance of an ordinary man in his early thirties, Caucasian, a short brown beard, a shaved head, an endearing smile. He wore a pair of black loafers, gray dress slacks and a long sleeved pinstripe white shirt. In his hands was the disposed chalice he had rescued from the chasm.

Cuzak tentatively initiated the conversation, "My lord, it is good that we are here with you."

Responding Beltshzan said, "I love these old relics. You never know when they will come in handy--like the lance you hold in your hands, Colonel Cuzak. It rewarded you, did it not? And this cup of the infection, here all the time waiting for those who would drink freely; four more in the Diaphthora before I arrived.

My popularity has suffered among the image bearers, but my talismans bring life to the Winds. You know what they say? 'How ya gonna keep them down on the farm? After they've seen Paris they never want to go back!' But I wonder, is it out of fear that you--Cuzak cower to me or is it disgust for the local entity? Or do you hope in something better for yourself?

Ouriano wanted better, I almost had him converted. For this I commend you Cuzak. By the way, where did he go? And the perpetrator, my granddaughter, she attended the funeral?"

Beltshzan slowly encircled Cuzak while he addressed him. As he did the others noticed something moving inside the back of his shirt. It rose to the top of his collar, coiling around his neck, pausing to rub the top of its viper shaped head against the bottom of his bearded chin.

Cuzak became a mannequin as he feared his schismatic nature, *Though Beltshzan is only half of what he once was, he demands respect and has to be reckoned with.*

The flickering tongued black mambo unwound itself from Beltshzan and transferred over to Cuzak's neck, gliding down inside his shirt.

"You would never lie to me, would you, my son?" asked Beltshzan.

Cuzak felt the snake writhe around his stiff limbs and torso, but dare not move. He knew this question required an answer, "Not to you my Lord."

"I smell the scent of a lie. Tell me how Ouriano pleaded for his life, begged that you not kill him." While he said this, the snake returned up Cuzak's shirt and coiled around his neck gently tightening its grip.

Cuzak answered, "He didn't. He came unarmed."

"The two of you conspired together. For what reason?"

"Only as you taught me to conspire, to fatten for the slaughter. He promised amnesty for Ru in exchange for Yazad's secrets."

"And she killed him, brilliant!" Even though he said this, the snake tightened more so on his neck causing Cuzak's reflexes to take over. The opaque scales came down over his eyes, as he hunched over to unwind the steel serpent with his hands, to no success. While he struggled Cuzak's wings ripped through his jacket and shirt. He could barely speak, he pleaded, "I am not yet immortal, please...Father."

To no avail Cuzak fell to the ground, short on breath and blood flow to his brain. Beltshzan scrutinized the three Legion Commanders carefully for any sign of repugnance to administering such discipline. Resuming the humiliation of his half breed progeny in front of his new recruits he said, "I believe you, son. Today I have become your father. Let me gift you a reminder to never be complacent or double cross me."

As he finished saying this, the viper loosened several of its coils, reared its head, mouth wide open and struck, sinking its fangs deep into Cuzak's chest, locking on--milking its ulcerating poison into his pectoral muscle, while he continued to lecture him. "Until we are united with Yazad, I am not interested in any creative initiatives except those ordered. This bite will not kill you, but it will serve as a permanent reminder until we have established unification. You will be marked with a festering wound which will not heal, a soft spot near your heart. Ah yes, and as for my granddaughter, tell her what she wants to hear. The young deserve false hopes. She knows about the others who tried to turn?"

Chapter 15

One must lust before you have the luxury
to love.

The snake released its fangs from Cuzak, dropped to the floor and slithered over to Beltshzan's benign human form. Climbing up his pant leg it disappeared. Debased, but alive, Cuzak retracted his wings, rolled to his knees and slowly stood regaining the needed pressure to his brain. He unpeeled the wound on his chest and inspected where the poisonous enzyme had eaten through his thick skin and several layers of the striated muscle. What remained was a sunken lesion in the shape of the viper's open mouth, a nagging raw spot.

As Cuzak contemplated one thing, *Is this what merits my loyalty? If I only had another choice. I won't let him touch Ru,* he spoke yet another, "Yes, Ru discovered their bodies in storage. It worked as you said my Lord. She saw through Ouriano for what he was, the Death Angel to your children and children's children. She bemoaned that she had ever befriended the de facto executioner of all of her brothers and sisters."

"Why then did she attend his memorial?"

"She is powerful... like you, my Lord. I cannot bridle her every move. I was unaware until you brought it up. Possibly to defile his memory or as a decoy to our meeting."

Seeing that this did not satisfy Beltshzan he added, "She also loved him like a father, until he broke her trust. He was annihilated before her eyes. She ran the lance through him from behind. He reached out to touch her face."

"This is getting better," said Beltshzan, "I know you would not make this up Nephilim. There is a broken image bearer in her who yearns to be adored. So she loved him like the father she always longed for, which you could never be?"

Beltshzan continued to belittle Cuzak, "Now that is original, and sad. Fatherly love as I have observed is such a primitive filial emotion. But as has been spelled out to me by a reliable source, this love of the Father is as pure as love becomes. For in it there is no lust."

As Beltshzan examined the Commanders faces, they smiled with him, yielding to his presence and will.

Cuzak cupped his hand over his wound and asked, "Why do all of you laugh?"

Beltshzan continued the sarcasm, "Surely you did not ask this question, did you?"

Cuzak rubbed his own neck with his other hand, "What have I not done for you?"

"What have you not done... for me? You have heard the answer quoted many times, no doubt, 'For to which one of the Winds did the most excellent local entity ever say, You are my Son; and today I have become your Father? and again, I shall be to him The Father and he shall be to me the Son?'

Do not forget, before the Heir was rejected by any men, I was rejected by his Father! Yes, forgive me... my son. That slipped your memory?"

Cuzak groveled an apology, "My lord, you were humiliated before all the morning stars. I cannot begin to fathom the experience. The blasphemous thorn's words, then were true, 'To which of the Winds did the local entity ever say, sit at my right hand until I establish your enemies to be a footstool for your feet?'"

"Cuzak, you will be rewarded as those here with you. I laugh because this type of love is a mirage. There is no such thing as a pure love without lust. Without lust none of us would be here; self adulation, pleasure, freedom, domination, creation. These are all lusts. One must lust before you have the luxury to love."

Cuzak, avoiding a flare up of his wrath again, but nevertheless hurting from his humiliation asked, "When will we have this luxury?"

"Soon, very soon," recounted Beltshzan, "the new light of the Sanctuary will restore the mangled beings, minds and appearance of all those who side with me. Those who sip from this cup of liberation will experience relief."

"And those dark Winds who mistakenly abandon allegiance to you for Yazad, who have counted you as irrelevant, soft,..."

Beltshzan cut him off saying, "as powerless, without fangs? To reach this luxury will first require a purging of those who grievously suppose I have defaulted on my revolution. These Commanders will be given new Legions with greater power. Tell me Commanders, what do you lust for? Tell me your names?"

"I am Bengal, from the first generation angelus. I remember the day of your coronation, your beauty. We, or I..."

"Be proud of the word, I," inserted Beltshzan.

"My lord, I am weary of not knowing if I shall be included in the Magnificon when this creation is rolled up like a scroll. With all the attention given to the needs of the image bearers and their transformation, where will I be for eternity?"

"You shall suppress those thoughts no longer."

The next Commander stepped forward, "I am Zomar, from the second generation of angelus. I was under the command of Ouriano at his shedding of your innocents. You can't rephrase it to sound dignified; we slew our own kind. I never said a word until now. I carry a wound which does not heal. I must make amends."

"Talon is my name, for now, a third generation. Why should our kind be deprived of a father, a mother, a partner, the right to bear our own? We are not robots or perpetual drones of chastity. The image bearers have become a sorry lot with little nobility left in them. Their transformation has become like a stillborn birth. Why do we wait on them? They destroy themselves in greater number with each generation. Now, is the chance to claim our destiny!"

Beltshzan, beamed with delight at these new traitors, "You are brave to be here. Disguise your new infection. I need you to remain embedded as long as possible. I will ask each of you to drink from this cup after I depart to allow you the freedom of this choice. Sorry, but I must leave in haste. We will meet again."

Zomar asked, "But where are you going?"

The black snake appeared again from his shirt and circled loosely around Beltshzan's neck before he spoke, "My dear Commander, I have a meeting with the Angel of Light at her request. This is how I was able to access your realm. She has kept me under a no fly zone for some time. She prides herself on staying informed. Never underestimate or trust her. She is cold. She will be arriving at my ship soon. I will make her an offer she can hardly refuse."

Talon spoke again, "I have no need to commune behind your back. I see the weathered face of my more mature comrades. I have no intention of ending up like them. Give it to me now so you can see for yourself where I stand."

"If you insist, my young warrior, I admire those who stand alone."

Bengal stepped forward and looked at the other two angels and said, "We will do this together, and share the secret of our new freedom."

Beltshzan gave an order to Cuzak, "Serve them! This day they will feel a pulse for the first time."

Cuzak took the cup, and stood before them one by one saying, "This is my Lordship's promise to you. You were born for much higher things, together we will taste of new light. Drink you, all of it, seal your destiny."

Chapter 16

The whole universe doesn't rest on
our shoulders does it?

The emergency room Doctor from Tokyo's St. Luke's International Hospital came out to the packed waiting room and stuck his head in the door announcing, "Pruett family?"

Lucas put down his stale coffee. Followed by his father and mother, he weaved through the maze of extended legs, carry bags, and sleeping bodies of other families keeping vigil. They went out into the main hallway and took a quick left into a small private room labeled, "Family Consultation," and were greeted by a Japanese Doctor.

He wore the universal blue-green scrubs, surgical skull cap with mask sideways on his neck, and yellow running shoes. "Hello, I am Dr. Shemoto," he said unemotional, snapping off his rubber gloves, taking a slight bow. As the M.D. stood tall he adjusted his large square glasses and met them with a warm smile.

All three bowed in response. "Yes! Doctor, is she alright? How about the baby? I am, ah, Lucas Tanner, and this is Henry and Judith. We appreciate this, you coming out here."

"This is what I do. Victoria Pruett. She is your, wife?"

Lucas looked at his mother and father, "Almost, why do you need to know?"

Henry spoke up, "Yes, Victoria is our daughter, Lucas is the father. Please, bring us some good news."

"You are here on family vacation, during a typhoon?"

Lucas stumbled again, "Bad timing, we thought it would miss."

"The typhoon has been coming this way for a week. And you did not plan?"

Judith interceded, "Doctor, thank you for your kindness, but how is our daughter?"

"I can say this; they both appear to be stable. Mom-to-be has a few small cuts on her arms and a persistent nose bleed. A staff obstetrician reviewed the 3-D sonogram. Both of their heart beats appear strong and regular. But I have to clarify something with you. The report says she was hit by lightning coming through your hotel room window? Did you see it?"

Lucas answered, "Yes, all three of us, it melted the glass crystals on the floor which fell from the chandelier above her. The concussion knocked us down, but the flash hit her."

The physician responded, "Very odd, she is so lucky. Amazing, this must be one special little boy she is carrying. And you are the father? What were you doing when it hit?"

Judith couldn't contain herself, "I was right."

Dr. Shemoto, apologized, "I am sorry, so you didn't know the sex yet?"

"We had some unofficial opinions that it was a boy," replied Lucas as he hugged his mother. "We're glad you told us."

"It wasn't hard to tell," he smiled, "but I want to observe her through the night before I release her in the morning. Still, I wonder what were you doing when this happened?"

"We were toasting each other to celebrate our passage through a few rough events."

"What sort of events?"

Lucas stood his ground, "Why the inquisition, Dr. Shemoto? That is your real name?"

"Are you a praying man Doctor Tanner?"

"Is that your business?"

"I am a physician, I work to heal people. Please pray Doctor Tanner, everyday, for things that must come to pass. You are a necessary man. Your son will need you. Leave here as soon as you can."

"Pardon me Doctor Shem--oto; is there something you need to tell me?"

As the conversation grew tense, Lucas attempted to stare beyond the man's skin, the structure of his bones, his demeanor, when he heard the words on the loud speaker, "Code Blue, Code Blue…"

Henry blurted, "That means he's got an important emergency to attend to."

The physician pulled out his phone and clicked his newest text, reading it out loud, "'Accident at sea, all ER personnel on standby, first patients in route to St. Luke's.'" Dr. Shemoto pocketed the phone, "Sorry to leave, you can go back one at a time to see her. Now, if you'd like."

Lucas pleaded, "Wait! Why did you call me Doctor?"

The physician hurriedly said, "I am sorry, I must go. We'll meet again. Who would like to see her first?"

"Mom you go ahead. Thanks, Doctor Shem-oto," said Lucas.

"Follow me," said the Doctor," as Judith walked behind his lead.

As the two left the family room, Lucas hugged his father but said, "Now do you believe me?"

"Lucas, I never said I didn't believe your story about being called a Juwaan. It's just that I've never had any real visions to speak of like you. I've never been transported to another world. My faith is plain vanilla, nuts and bolts, here and now.

But another thing, I have seen self-proclaimed prophets in my day drift through churches and show up unannounced at our mission station saying things like, 'God sent us.' 'God spoke to me and here's what you need to do.' 'Everything you've done is wrong.' 'I am here to straighten you out.'"

"You know me dad. That's not my calling card. This is not something I want. I am on the reluctant side."

Henry kept going, "They usually burn out or form a cult, and never become accountable to anybody. God's never talked to me except through the word. In the end that's what I go by. Do I believe the Lord is speaking to you in your visions, travels, in what just happened? Again, 'yes!' But not any more than what can be discovered in the Bible."

"Dad, I didn't know we were choosing sides."

"Your mom and I came to Tokyo didn't we?"

"Look, give me time to come around. I need your help. Wasn't Moses kind of screwed up for a long time? I have money, we need to disappear. I am thinking New Zealand. I have no clue what I am supposed to do yet. Things are not going as I planned."

"Lucas, no one is leaving during this typhoon. As soon as it breaks, I am with you. I want to be around my grandchild. And, relax. No one's call goes exactly as planned. The whole universe doesn't rest on our shoulders, does it?"

As Henry was asking this, Judith walked back in sooner than they had expected with a befuddled look on her face and plunged down into her chair.

Lucas asked, "You're back so soon, how is she?"

"I followed Dr. Shemoto to her glass encased cubicle, past a couple dozen others. Looks like chaos back there. Shemoto pointed to her and kept going down the hall. Victoria was sleeping peacefully with an IV in her arm. Then the charge nurse came in and said, 'It's not visiting hours yet.' So I told her, 'Dr. Shemoto told me I could see her.'

She looked at me funny, checked her computer and went back out in the hall. I heard her consulting with another Doctor in Japanese which sounded pretty heated. Then she came back in the room and said, 'There is no Dr. Shemoto on staff or with privileges at St. Luke's.' I answered, 'But he came and briefed us and said the baby was healthy and told us it was a boy from the sonogram, no mistake.' Well, she started shaking her head no, saying, 'We have not run a sonogram on her, soon, not yet.' That's when she asked me to leave."

Lucas, squeezed both sides of his face, put his head back and bemoaned, "This isn't going away. It's really happening, getting deeper."

His mom added, "So, who was that Doctor who told you to pray?"

Lucas started laughing as Judith and Henry looked at him puzzled, then said, "I know who that was. And what he says has a way of coming true."

Chapter 17

*There are two powers at work seeking to
penetrate you. Who have you allowed?*

Victoria lay sedated on the hospital bed in St. Luke's.
Dissociated from her body, her mind raced with concerns
of how she was going to raise a child under these
conditions. Would her baby be raised on the run, in long
term hiding, under the constant threat that someone or
something might attempt to harm her child at any
moment?

Even with her eyes closed she saw something very real. At
the foot of her bed, centered in a white fluorescent wall-
less room, rested a black leather office chair pointing away
from her. She recognized the chair from the lab where she
worked for Colonel Cuzak Smith. New in this vision
however were the bed mounted medical stirrups holding
her legs, and feet in a birthing position. Horrified, Victoria
struggled to pull her feet out, but they were locked in place.

And worse, she recognized the New Deli English accent
coming from the chair. "My Victoria, you should have
waited. This could have been our child." She identified the
voice as the man who had assaulted her. With the blessing
and presence of Cuzak, he had placed his swarming
essence inside of her to locate Lucas on his trip to the Blue
Moon with Ouriano.

Captive to her inner world, Victoria had nowhere to flee.
He spun around in the seat wearing a white doctor's gown,
stethoscope over his shoulder.

Yes, the same well manicured Indian man from the lab!—
"Why have you followed me? I hate you!"

"Glad to see you too, Victoria. Congratulations on your
significant relationship and this baby boy. Too bad, I
understood we had something between us. Didn't you like
how I tasted, smelled? I can take the truth. Was there

something that bugged you about me? Always a groomsman, never a groom."

Victoria snapped back, "How do you know about my baby, you scum..., you son of a bitch. Leave me alone. Help, someone!"

"Please Victoria. No one can hear you. You are knocked out, I mean knocked up. Ahh, have a sense of humor. You know how this works. I am in you, and you are in me. Wherever you go, whatever you do, we will always share the experience. You are one of the collective."

Victoria responded, "I'd die first. You are not real. I watched you get cut down by Lucas, your blood is the color of a slug's, yellow."

"I give in Victoria. I can see you need more time to think about our relationship. But in the mean time, I want your fetus, your baby boy. Oh, his heart is racing at my presence, a special child."

To Victoria's horror, the man who had once pinned her to a table while filling her lungs with insects until she passed out was putting on surgical gloves. Flies began landing on her face and exposed legs.

"What do you want with my child? What are you going to do?" she screamed at him.

"Babies have a way of growing into hideous monsters Miss Pruett. Some shouldn't be allowed to reach maturity. If we can't have him neither shall you." Snapping the latex of the second glove, he squeezed ointment on his finger tips. Next she felt his hands begin to position themselves between her thighs.

As he huddled between her legs she watched some of the collective swarm ooze out around his eyes, crawling onto his glasses, while his cheeks churned and bubbled.

"He's done this before," she pled, "You can't allow him to penetrate me again. God, no. You can let me die, but save my baby. I know there's One greater inside of me who wants this child to live. Please let him live!"

And then, Victoria heard another voice, one she knew as a child. "My deceased cousin Nicky, she is here."

A frail teenage girl, reddish blonde hair, wearing a tan dress and barefoot, spun the Vranti's chair toward her declaring to the ancient entity with surprising authority, "You have been given no permission to test the anointed in such a manner. To harm this child is to touch the apple of the Heir's eye. Be forewarned you soul invading parasite. You will die in the loneliness of cold deep space where no one will ever remember you."

The Vranti retorted, "Who are you, a runt of an image bearer, and so disgruntled to confront me? You could use a good parasite."

Unintimidated, Nicky replied, "I am a resident of Siyon and a co-heir of the Magnificon."

"What is your kind doing here? All must not be well in the homeland," replied the Vranti.

"I could ask the same of you. Are you preparing to start a war you can never win? Know that if the infection continues to spread and the great Winds fall, we will rally to stop you ourselves. You will be judged. There is no escape."

"Nicky," Victoria called out, stretching her arm toward her, "You came to help. Stop him."

Raising her sight toward Victoria, the innocent girl smiled and said, "He has planted fear in you Victoria. Pay no attention to his tactics. Resist and he will flee like the coward he is."

The Vranti attempted to spin the chair around with the force of his trembling legs, but the sure nimble strength of Nicky held him. In frustration he said, "You have no hint of an altered future. Your charming nest of the redeemed on Siyon has lost its warranty. Fools, all of you, for a new wave of darkness will obliterate your pitiful existence. You would do her unborn son a favor to snuff out his life now, rather than torture him in the pain to come. Better yet, let me infest—connect with the boy. Victoria, join our collective, you are almost one of us."

Nicky intervened again, "You have no deed to Victoria. In time the scars you left in her will be healed. Another of greater beauty has penetrated her. Be gone you son of wormwood."

Nicky then turned the chair toward Victoria. It was empty.

Victoria called out, "Nicky, Nicky, Nicky…"

But a response never came. Instead she was roused by a nurse. "Miss Pruett, Victoria, Victoria, are you all right? Can you hear me?"

Victoria opened her eyes and took in the surroundings of the glass encased ER room as she reoriented herself. The IV drip was in place, the blanket covered her legs. She asked the nurse, "Is the baby safe?"

"Yes, we just completed the sonogram. His heart beat is healthy and strong."

"Thank you Jesus!" exclaimed Victoria. "And did you see like, a twelve year old little girl in here?" The nurse shook her head, "no."

"Please, could you get my husband? You said, 'His?' Like it's a boy?"

"Mr. Tanner? He came by a little while ago to check on you, but yes. He somehow knew the baby's sex before we performed the sonogram."

"It's kind of funny, seems everyone knows about our child."

"I assure you, we do our best at St. Luke's to insure your privacy."

"And I am going to do my best to insure this kid thrives! Oh yeah, he's special," said Victoria.

Chapter 18

But I do not live by fate, and neither does he.

Veezon asked Michael, "Where are you taking me?" Four Royal Cherubim guarded him with swords drawn, as they waited outside the Ayin Temple. The Cherubim took no chances with this seasoned Seraph, clamping his wings, then binding his ankles, wrists and head to a horizontal rod of light behind his back. This solid beam of light was painful to him. Veezon knew what it was; the beam was used to transport the most dangerous. Once one had become infected, this type of Shekinah light was a nuisance, draining rather than restoring, and if tuned too high a dreadful torture.

"I assure you, there will be no outbursts from me again," said the disgraced Veezon, his head hanging down, his once flowing mane, matted tangles.

Michael lectured his prisoner, "You were made for outbursts, but your allegiance is corrupt. I am sending you somewhere you can do no harm until you are dismissed. And believe me when I say, you will be dismissed. If by chance you should meet the end like Ouriano, there'll be no one memorializing you on Yare'ach Kachol. What shame you have brought on your friend, desecrating his service, this holy place. I am at a loss. And on top of this you have hidden your infection from the others. How many more are like you, duplicitous, able to conceal the initial stages and continue to serve? Where do your loyalties lie?" inquired Michael.

Michael took his sword out of its sheath. Its power glowed like steel fresh from a furnace. He held the tip close to Veezon, and used it as an instrument to illuminate the depth and magnitude of the infection inside him. Everywhere he moved the glowing tip, down his legs, along his arms, neck, shoulders, torso, arterial channels of flowing green and blue light were visible. But also, some of these conduits of energy were crisscrossed by blackened vessels. Light as the Winds knew it was no longer flowing in all his veins. Some had become hard and dark, twisting and choking the original vascular design. Michael asked, "Why would anyone want to exist with this bile slowly smothering their true light?"

Astonished, he asked, "This is nothing new, is it?" as he moved the tip of his glowing sword near his chest. Illuminating through his exterior matrix, Michael could see that a third of his heart was dark. "Until you are officially shuffled off to the Earthen realm, you will be held on the island of Wandu. Lamech will be delighted to entertain such an important guest."

"How will I defend myself? They live for the hunt. They are beasts. You do not know the whole story. Ask Shem. I can explain."

"Silence, I forbade you to speak!"

With the power vested in Michael from the Angel of Light, Veezon's lips disappeared and his shape shifting ability was immobilized.

Veezon tried to communicate with him telepathically, to plead his case, "You must know my dilemma!"

Michael slid his sword into its sheath, then turned his back on him as he contemplated the ring shaped orange roll clouds hanging in the middle of the great depression of the Blue Moon. He allowed his inmost thoughts to be shared with Veezon, "How strange your suffering must be. You have to remain silent. You can tell no one without jeopardizing yourself, and your plan. Who have you told?"

"There are two who I trust, Fortius and Advanta."

Michael saw lightning arch between the cloud rings, as he raised his right eyebrow, "Fortius I comprehend, but the neophyte Advanta? The dissimilitude."

"I chose one wise, acquainted with the treachery of Beltshzan, and one naïve who does not yet know enough to fear. But they both share another quality."

"What might that be?"

"They have faith."

"For your sake and the protection of the Magnificon gates, I hope you are right."

"The Wounded Heir has put it all at risk before."

"No!" responded Michael out loud, resuming his vocal communication, "I have beheld him, and you are not the Wounded Heir!"

As he said this, the Cherubim Guard still next to Veezon, raised their wings in alert because of the high speed approaching sentinel, whose own wings were whipping up turquoise vapor trails behind him. To their relief he was intercepted by other Guardians, who guided him in. At the last moment before landing, he reverse thrusted his wings, pushing a swoosh of wind to rush through the group on the landing.

Michael who had yet to move, asked the intruder, "Are you prepared to accept the same fate as this one? What is your name?"

Advanta looked with puzzlement upon the bound, bruised, and bedraggled Veezon, his mouth and lips gone, then over to Michael. Instantly recognizing him, he bowed at his rank and character. "I am Advanta, at your humble service. Veezon is my friend. But I do not live by fate, and neither does he."

"Neophyte, why are you here, approaching us in this manner? Where have you come from?"

"I was asked by Veezon to guard the skies above for any saboteurs of this memorial for his friend Ouriano."

"Then, you did not perform your duty. We discovered a saboteur."

"Never, this can't be."

"Where did Veezon ask you to meet him after the memorial?"

"He said together we would go to the Lake of Dreams. He had something to show me; something that might change me forever."

Turning back to Veezon, Michael asked him, "Is this true Veezon?"

Veezon's eyes blinked, unable to speak, his power draining every moment, he tilted his head, "yes."

"Then I will grant you this, Commander, we will visit the Lake of Dreams briefly where you and Advanta can discuss your little problem. After that your fate is sealed. It will be a cold day in hell before you ever visit Siyon again."

Chapter 19

His is a secret knowledge which is no secret.

Arriving at the Lake of Dreams, Michael ordered the Royal Cherubim to clear the massive domed cavern deep within the Blue Moon. "I want no interruptions." When they had finished searching the area he said, "Unbind Veezon and guard the corridor. No entity comes in or out." With his order they removed the light beam, then the clamps and shackles from Veezon's wings, ankles, and wrists.

Michael escorted Advanta and the weakened Veezon through the fern covered grotto entrance and down the winding path toward the Lake. Michael placed his right hand on Veezon's jaw restoring his mouth and lips, "Before either of you say a word, I want you to know I am with you. But things have changed. It is not so clear who one can trust anymore. When we leave this calm pool of prayers and dreams, our conversation here never happened."

Veezon rubbed his jaw, as if it felt out of place.

Michael continued, "The Angel of Light has spoken. If what she says is true, and I have no reason to doubt her, then you are the first of your kind. May the Spirit of the Wounded One guide you through the darkness you must travel. He works in strange ways which remain unsearchable to me."

"Tell me more about him," inquired Advanta as they reached the Lake's crystalline shore.

"Oh neophyte, where you are going mere explanation and knowledge will never suffice. The Wounded One despises brute power but has the dominion of the Magnificon at his fingertips. He reveals himself to the weak and hides from the prideful. Even the Elders speak of worlds past and worlds to come filled with countless records of his appearing."

"Why have I not met him as of yet?" asked Advanta.

Veezon coughed and said in a gravelly voice, "I have met him face to face. And it is as you say. He carries no sword other than what comes from his mouth, nor displays any power, yet his veiled might is unmistakable. He laid his hand upon me as one of adoption, and showed me his scars. But alas, as you see, I have let him down, allowing revenge to fuel my wrath."

Michael said, "The image bearers we serve proclaim the Heir is closest to the broken, and thus this Lake, filled with their prayers, memories, and tears. His is a secret knowledge which is no secret. I will now leave you alone. But you Veezon, when you are finished will be rebound and transferred to Lamech's island as I promised before your casting down. Do not search for sympathy. This must be."

As Michael walked back toward the entrance, Veezon took Advanta's hand and led him into the shallow mirrored waters along the shore.

Advanta reflected, "You Veezon are the second to take my hand today."

As their matrixes connected with the pearl sheen lake, Veezon admonished, "Please Advanta, quiet your heart and mind. There may be hidden help in these liquid reflections. Kneel with me and place your hand in these waters." Advanta felt the waters creep around his wings as the bottom third of his silky white feathers submerged. Then Veezon, clutching his hand plunged it through the sapphire surface with his.

"I thought maybe this place was of legend," whispered Advanta.

"Please," said Veezon, "I am searching. In a moment you will see, neophyte. The longer you have served the more you have vested. You are so young, so little experience with the image bearers."

Advanta, with wisdom beyond his generation said, "Maybe we have become like them. We have forgotten our purpose."

"There,..." When Veezon said this Advanta's eyes became locked and wide open, staring into the distance as Veezon's vision became his. "What do you see neophyte?"

"I see an image bearer, a man dressed in white, standing alone near the entrance to a small cave on the side of a mountain. I am following him from behind. He is walking toward the front of the cavern and out of the shade where bright rays from a star, no, make it two stars--are blazing down on his face as he scouts the sky and land below." Advanta paused then asked, "Is this a real place? Who is this?"

"Go on," encouraged Veezon.

"He is shading his eyes with his hands, surveying a layered desert plateau below, yellow, brown, blue. There are only sparse dead trees in this area. I also see dry orange river beds winding through the painted desert into the horizon.

The light is more forgiving, less scorching in the distance. Those parts of the river beds, tributaries seem to have water flow. Also, there is a long wall as far as I can see running across the desert, separating it from a more shaded atmosphere. The other side of the wall displays a fertile green rolling land." Advanta asked, "Do you see all of this?"

"Yes, but continue narrating. We must remember everything. Do you see any other life forms?"

"It is hard to make out beyond dead plant species, but yes. Small groups--specks near the wall. Wait, what is that? Coming in high from the shaded side of the wall. I see vapor trails from creatures like our kind. They are diving toward the small specks who are scattering and launching projectiles trailing fire at them. This is confusing. Those Winds, diving from above, are returning greater fire. Leaving patches of burning clouds behind them on the ground, great flames and smoke."

Veezon asked, "The man from the cave, what is he doing? Does he see it?"

"Yes, he appears disturbed by this. I think he might be praying to an entity. Wait, there is something else. A shadowy cloud is moving rapidly through the desert from the region of the wall. It is following the dried river bed in our direction."

"Has the man noticed the cloud?"

"I am not sure, he is not moving. He should flee."

"No, this man won't flee. He is here to meet this evil."

"But he is alone. It is not an even encounter, a slaughter. Can I help him?"

"Watch neophyte! Remain completely still."

Chapter 20

"He sent upon them His burning anger, fury and indignation and trouble, a band of destroying angels." --Psalm 78:49

Assessing the vision from an anonymous point behind the man in white, some twenty humanoid beings came forward into Veezon and Advanta's peripheral view from the rear of the cave. They were larger than the mysterious figure, and took up positions around him. They all were staring below as the ground hugging cloud continued to move like a plague of locusts across the desert floor advancing toward their elevated position.

Frustrated to understand the meaning of the vision, Advanta said, "Those are fallen Winds with him, their wings have been hacked off. Their faces are determined, but their bodies are emaciated. And they also are... praying? What is this Veezon? Is this what is to become of us? Drones?"

Advanta jerked his hand clasped by Veezon out of the Lake of Dreams. Exasperated he said, "I understood the Lake of Dreams contained answers to prayers of the redeemed and from the Earthen realm only. This fight is different than what you explained. Those Winds were maimed. How did the prayers of this man end up in this lake?"

"Can you identify this man neophyte?"

"No, I cannot. This does not make sense."

"In time it will," said Veezon. "What is of importance is we know the subspace channel of knowledge and inner power carried this vision here for us."

"How did you know to look for this?"

"Image bearers talk about hunch, intuition, and their faith. I imagined the Wounded Heir would not send us completely blind. He is also a man, an image bearer. I counted on prayers crossing the space time fabric. Depending on what realm you exist, the plans of what happens somewhere tomorrow may have already been established today. Siyon takes those very seriously."

"Then it is never too late to pray?"

"I have given up before, but now that I grow sickly I am resolved to make it my practice."

"Veezon, if this lake is the place where image bearer's prayers are stored as memories to help us, what pools and cisterns hold our kind's prayers?"

"You have a vivid imagination brave one. I envision a sacred place, hidden somewhere in the stars. In these changes I too am a novice." Veezon uplifted his arms and wings examining where the bruising and dark flow was most apparent, "The infection can be ugly. Though I don't give it credit for everything distasteful about me, it is an insidious slow creep."

"Like you trying to kill the Nephilim Hybrid, in the Ayin Cathedral?" Veezon dropped his head when he said this. Embarrassed Advanta then reflected on his own life, "I think I understand. In some respects I willingly drank from the cup. Something about me craved the carnal knowledge at any price. That's what bothers me the most."

Veezon replied, "I am sorry I did not inform you better. It was the only way. But you have a commission, a charge from the Angel of Light and the Heir, to follow through with this. Doors will open for us if we keep our matrix from disintegrating."

"Yes Veezon, I believe there is a love which saves us, much like the lore of the image bearers. But I wish you had let me make that decision with less encouragement. Do you trust Fortius and his comrades?"

"Who did Fortius bring with him?"

"Three others, two whose names I do not know. One was called Azazel. He was more than eager to drink from the brazen cup."

"Azazel…"

"You know him?"

"Yes, he is the last Legionnaire I would have recruited. There is no faith in him. I transferred him long ago, and since, he has been reassigned four times. He specializes in duties no one talks about."

"I don't understand."

"For one thing, he was with Ouriano when the eradication sentence was given to those abnormally born in the Earthen realm, the ancestors of the Hybrid Ru. For Ouriano, following the termination order was painful enough. But Ouriano told me there was one under him who relished in it. He was told to make death as painless as possible, but instead in the ensuing chaos he took the time to torment the weak, the Nephilim children. Ouriano could never let go of the guilt."

"This was Azazel's doing?"

"Pestilence has been Azazel's specialty. Long before your time, he became the desert consumer of the scapegoat offering in the Earthen realm of the Sinai, during the flight of Moses out of Egypt. Michael thought it suited him well, to be acquainted with the sin of the image bearers, to feel their pain. There is no telling how dark, twisted he would become if he crossed over."

"It is already done," said Advanta.

"God help us all. What is done is done. This is virgin territory. Azazel has special abilities. He could be to our benefit. Meet with Fortius, learn more. They are taking me to a perilous place for the condition I am in. For the most part, the islands are restricted. On Wandu they will ground me until they cast me out."

"How about an escape?"

"I will be cast out regardless. There is protocol. I'd as soon skip the official dismissal than face those under my command. I am both privileged and ashamed. In our case,

I believe the authorities will turn the other way. You also may want to leave sooner than later. We need to prepare. Earth is a good place to hide. It's where we need to be to make the transfer."

"I will do my best, Commander. They will write about our exploits one day."

"Who would that be?"

"Those who want to praise the Heir of the Magnificon. There will be a small section about us."

"A footnote, at most—a Blue Moon Chronicle."

They both turned to see Michael waving at them to return to the entrance and began a slow walk up the hill, continuing to console each other.

When they arrived at the entrance, Michael stepped forward with the Cherubim guard, "You found what you were looking for?"

"That and more," said Veezon, "these waters are deeper than they look. Do you believe in prayer for our kind?"

Michael answered, "I do now."

Chapter 21

If I do what you are suggesting, it would be death to me.

The black leather-clad Goth, revved her engine one last time before parking her red Ducati against the curb on the side entrance of the aging 1950's vintage East Austin Church. The rusty white sign with black letters, "Rev. E.S. Gardner" dangled from an old iron bracket over the cracked concrete sidewalk, squeaking as the wind twisted the short chains securing it. To the right of the door mounted on the old red and black brick wall, a sign read, "Commercial Space for Lease."

What chance will there be in catching him here? She wondered. But pulling on the door, it easily gave way to a clanking set of cow bells and a flood of cool air mixed with rose scented deodorizer. Uneasy she went down the worn but polished tile corridor until she turned into the doorway labeled 'church office.' There, to greet her from behind a laminated counter sat a cheery plump secretary, glasses on the end of her nose, reading a copy of the Christian Century Magazine, "Good afternoon! You must be Pastor Gardner's appointment."

"I didn't make an appointment," said Ru as she started to nervously back away from the secretary.

"Ma'am, I didn't get your name. Are you alright? Can I get you a bottle of water or something?"

"I said, 'I didn't make an appointment.' And I didn't share my name."

The secretary sprang back with a bewildered look, "That's OK, Reverend Gardner sets appointments without telling people all the time. I don't know how he does it. He's old, but he's got this sixth sense about him. You know what I mean?" Mrs. Green stood up to come around the counter.

"I'll come back another time. Ah, thank you," said Ru hesitantly as she backed down the hall and out the old entrance to the street, cowbells clanking behind her as it shut. Walking back to her sport bike she mumbled, "Why did I think I'd find help in this old place?" But before she could mount it, the distinctive loud muffled slaps of a four cycle Harley caught her attention as it pulled in behind her.

Ru watched in disbelief as the tall African American pastor, white goatee, pilot sunglasses, charcoal business suit, with the Brooklyn Tabernacle choir blaring on his radio, turned off the engine, kicked down the stand and held out his hand in greeting. "Reverend E.S. Gardner. We have an appointment. Sorry I'm late. I don't get around like I used to."

Ru stepped back, feeling her eyes begin to dilate, nails unsheathing, wings ready to pop. She thought, *this is not an average image bearer by any means.*

"Why don't we go into my sanctuary? It will be safe there, Miss, Misses...?"

"Ruvale Marija Zvonimira. Single, yes, my friends call me Ru, if I have any friends left, that is. But you already know?"

"Let's take our conversation inside, please come in Ms. Zvonimira." Following Rev. Gardner through the side door, they passed by the secretary, "I think the two of you have met?" he said, "This is Ms. Zvonimira."

"Hello again," said Mrs. Green, wiggling her bright red finger nails at her, "My, you are pretty. I couldn't help but to notice that fine street racer you pulled up on. Does that scare you riding a bike like that through downtown? I've never been on one. I keep asking Pastor Gardner for a ride on his. I came up with a name for his motorcycle. Want to guess?"

Ru, confused at the point of this side conversation said, "No, I wouldn't have the faintest..."

Cutting her off Mrs. Green said, "I nicknamed his bike, 'the beast!' Ha, ha… you don't find that funny? You know the assistant to the anti-…"

Pastor Gardner smiled at the secretary abruptly and said, "Mrs. Green is very friendly. She does research for me. She means no harm, the salt of the Earth. Mrs. Green we will be in the sanctuary. We would like some privacy."

"No one will come through that door pastor."

Ru followed Pastor Gardner around the corner where he pushed open one of the large double oak doors to the rear of the sanctuary. "Please come in." Passing through she noticed the other door had an auction notice pasted on it.

Ru smelled the mildewed air, carpet, wood, paint and the faint moth ball scented paper from the old hymn books and Bibles in the back of the pews. In the front of the high ceiling sanctuary sat a four step elevated oak communion table, with a chalice and loaf of bread. Each was draped by a white linen cloth. "Let's sit in the front row shall we," invited Reverend Gardner, extending his hand toward the pew.

"Now," he said, "how can I help you today? What did you come here to discover?"

"I will tell you, but first Reverend, I know you, don't I? Are you not Shem from the Isle of Sharu? You spoke at Ouriano's memorial?"

"Today I am the pastor of this Church. I am a shepherd. I have been given sheep as a trust."

"But I saw the 'for lease' sign outside, the auction notice on the door we came through. This church is closed, dead? You are an imposter, a friend of Lucas and Victoria?"

"Oh my, I have never been called an imposter," said Pastor Gardner, "The church dead? No, you can't kill the church. No one has that kind of power. Who told you that? How did you find me?"

"I once followed a Dr. Lucas Tanner here. I saw him go inside. What did you tell him?"

"Yes, I recall. A confused young man, he came to pray for a friend. So, what's the trouble?"

"I feel silly. You already know what I am about to say. So, why should I tell you?"

Pastor Gardner asked her, "Why are you here? Is it me you need to talk to? Maybe it is someone else who drew you. Have you never read? 'My sheep hear my voice. I know them, and they follow Me.' I have a feeling you need to talk to someone else."

"I feel like I am carrying the guilt of the world. I drew innocent blood. My selfishness has only caused more mayhem. I am a blight to anyone who comes near me, accursed. Who would I speak to? The Wounded Heir of the Magnificon? If he would even hear me, how would I reach Him?"

The Reverend replied, gently stroking his goatee, "This name you refer to, 'Wounded Heir of the Magnificon,' is new to me, but I like the sound. If we speak of the same One, people reached Him for decades in this place you are sitting. Matter of fact, He never went anywhere. He's got a good set of ears. That part hasn't changed.

You see the cup; you see the bread up on the altar? I can't tell you what to do with your life, but I would let nothing in this or any other world keep me from them."

"Reverend Gardner, excuse me, but if you knew what I'd done. I mean, you do know what I've done. If I do what you are suggesting, it would be death to me."

"Ms. Zvonimira, your eyes are beginning to open. Yes, it would mean 'death to you.' But let me ask you a question; what will it mean if you don't go up to the table?"

Chapter 22

I present a blood poured out to satisfy the blood lust of this darkened world and to that beyond.

Ru considered the vested sacraments as she watched the rays of outdoor sunshine press through the stained glass mural over the choir loft. *Did these refer to a myth, a primordial paradise lost, and--or to a greater coming reality?*

A benevolent Jesus with his hands extended floated under an All Seeing Eye. She thought it odd, off to the right side of this Great Shepherd, was a figure like the Angel of Light who Ru had witnessed at Ouriano's service. In this stained glass version she held a large chalice in her hands and was pouring it out. Opposite her and to the left of Jesus was another figure Ru did not recognize. It was a flying man dressed in red robe, a spear in one hand and a money bag in the other. One cloven foot and the tail of a serpent trailed from under his robe.

She finally broke her silence, "It would mean death or hell if I don't partake. But I deserve as much damnation as can be smothered on me."

Standing he said, "If there is any element of humanity in you, you should try."

Ru hesitated at first and shook her head, 'no,' but when Pastor Gardner offered his hand, she took it following his escort to the elevated table. Like so many communion altars, this one had routed in the front the ancient words, 'This Do in Remembrance of Me.'

As they went behind the communion table, they turned so as to face the empty pews. Pastor Gardner removed the linen coverings. On his right hand stood an old brass chalice, clean but tarnished, half filled with wine. In front of Ru was a small loaf of bread.

"Ms. Zvonimira, are you ready to go through with this, come what may?"

Her chin trembled as she said, "Pastor Gardner I am still in the same sorry state. I don't deserve anything. Let me sit back down."

"On the contrary, what you deserve this moment has already been received by another, so that what you don't merit is freely given."

"That is unjust," said Ru.

Reverend Gardner spoke slow and sure, "Romans 8:38 and 39 says, 'For I am convinced that neither death, nor life, nor angels, nor principalities, nor things present, nor things to come, nor powers, nor height, nor depth, nor any other created thing, will be able to separate us from the love of God, which is in Christ Jesus our Lord.'"

"That sounds like it was meant for me."

"And why shouldn't it?" asked Reverend Gardner. Taking the bread, he divided the loaf in half. Then raising his eyes toward the ceiling he said, "Praise be to your Wounded One, who takes away the sins of the world. His kingdom is everlasting and his redemption falleth nigh."

Then turning to Ru he said, "What sayeth you? Do you with this bread accept his brokenness? That he emptied himself for your sake, though you be feeble in mind, lacking in humility, full of vile intention, bred for the purpose of iniquity, and deficient in divine image?"

In this moment Ru's heart and mind became absorbed by a knowledge from another place; not a projection, not a vision, not a hallucination, but with the true light of true lights, that from beyond the Magnificon gates. "May this be the death of me. Give it to me, but only as one who warrants no mercy."

With this request, Pastor Gardner tore off a thumb size piece of bread and placed it on her split tongue. Forked as it was, he did not hesitate. She chewed the substance, swallowed and waited.

But as she savored the moment a fast moving shadow cast itself across the panes of stained glass along the sanctuary's walls.

"Are you expecting someone?" asked Pastor Gardner.

"No, not unless I was followed, I took precaution."

"We need to finish this," he said in a harsh whisper.

"Yes, that's what I want above all else," said Ru.

While Pastor Gardner lifted up the chalice with both hands to pray, they both witnessed again the swift shadow pass by the windows. Speeding up his words he said, "And likewise with this cup, I present a blood poured out to satisfy the blood lust of this darkened world and to that beyond..."

Before he finished speaking, they heard shouting, and a clamor in the secretary's office, "You can't go in there!" And another voice, "Get out of my way you bumbling church lady,..." followed by an infuriated Mrs. Green bursting through the sanctuary doors as she attempted to block the entrance with her stout body.

"Reverend Gardner, I did my best to stop him and told him you were not to be disturbed..."

"Get out of my way you imbecile and you won't get hurt!" said a large shadow from behind her in the lobby. As the intruder shoved her to the side on the carpet and came down the center aisle, they both recognized him. The unhappy hell's angel, dressed in denim, black leather boots and jacket, donning thin long gray hair, and sword strapped over his shoulder, was not a man.

"Veezon!" Ru and the Pastor said together.

Gardner started his prayer again despite the interruption, "And likewise with this cup, I present a blood poured out to satisfy the blood lust of this darkened world and to that beyond, Lord have mercy upon the one who dare drink from your cup today...."

"What in hell's conscience are the two of you doing!" Veezon boomed, unfurling his wings and flying to the front of the altar. "No, this is unjust!"

Pastor Gardner tried to continue, "... and hold at bay this fallen and confused Wind of light."

But the uninvited guest protested, "You can't let her do this. I swear on the sacred feet of the Angel of Light, she deserves no forgiveness! Either let my sword make swift her sentence, or the scourge devour her like leprosy."

Ru did not look at him but at the cup, for she burned for its absolution. *How fitting*, she thought, *that Ouriano's best friend will be the one to stop me.* But rather than fight him or grope the cup in a frantic manner, Ru quietly walked around the table to meet her accuser.

"Veezon, I hold nothing against you for your loyalty and love for Ouriano. I only wish I had your strength. For your honor I give you the choice of whether my life should continue. If not, then I ask you draw your sword and deliver me to the depths of the pit." Saying this, Ru knelt before him with head bowed and neck stretched out.

Reverend Gardner spoke, "Ru, no, don't do this. You don't have to. This is out of order."

Chapter 23

"Behold, as for the proud one,
His soul is not right within him;
But the righteous will live by his faith."
--Habakkuk 2:4

Veezon pulled out his sword and lightly touched the blade to her bare neck, searing a thin two inch line into her soft skin. He wrestled with her capital punishment, *Is it possible for her to evolve against her own nature? If I don't give her sincerity a chance then my faith will never sustain me. If I kill her, even enslave her, will the justice for Ouriano calm my soul?*

She closed her eyes waiting for it all to end, but when nothing happened she said, "So it is not a rumor. You were cast out."

"Yes."

"Forgive me Wind of light. I killed the only father I had. I have no father on Earth or in heaven. End my misery."

But Veezon relented, "Hybrid, rise and drink the cup which you must drink. If I keep you from this, it would be a greater sacrilege than the slaying of my friend. But promise me, you must turn your loyalty to Siyon. Join our Vigilantes. There are some of us whose infection will be our key into Yazad's hive."

Ru answered him, "Veezon, it is already done."

"Then take the cup of The Image Bearer, and, make sure you drink every last drop. You will need it, Hybrid. You of all creatures need to eat his flesh and drink his blood."

"I will," Ru said as she turned to Reverend Gardner, who handed her the chalice. Grasping it in both hands, she lifted it to her lips and drank the full contents, while her gaze focused on the stained glass All Seeing Eye.

Pastor Gardner set the chalice on the altar, then replaced the linen cloth over it and the bread saying, "Indeed, you have eaten the flesh, and drank the blood of the One who has died myriads upon myriads of deaths, and yet now lives."

"Then I have added to his death and burden," said Ru.

"Yes you have," answered Pastor Gardner. "But some say his yoke is easy and his burden is light."

"Ru," said Veezon, "I have something for you from Ouriano. He told me to give this to you, should anything happen to him." He pulled out of his vest pocket, a folded black piece of cloth.

"What is it?"

"I don't know. Truthfully, I have not cared until now."

Receiving the palm full of black cloth, Ru carefully unfolded it on the altar. It was a pewter cross on a chain, on the front inlaid with beautiful mother of pearl; a crystalline white mixed with streaks of light pinks and shades of topaz. On the back it had an engraving, "Սուրբ Հովհաննէս."

"I can't read this," Ru said, "What does this say?" as she handed it to Reverend Gardner.

He shifted his glasses down his nose to view through the lowest lens of his bi-focals. "If I didn't know better, I would say it appears to be of old Armenian design, but I am afraid I don't read Armenian."

"Let me see," said Veezon. "Hold it for me. Yes, it looks like Syriac but not exactly the same. It might be a common name. I am not good at dead languages."

"Excuse me!" exclaimed a voice from behind all of them pushing Veezon to the side purposefully as she walked up and took it out of Ru's hand. "Mrs. Green, I'm very sorry. Are you OK?" asked Ru.

Mrs. Green said, "Reverend Gardner this is Armenian text type. 'Սուրբ Հռիփսիմէ,' reads as 'Holy Hripsimé.'"

"Who is that?" asked Ru.

Mrs. Green answered, "Hripsimé was an early martyr of the late third century of the common era. She lived during a brutal time of persecution on the Church. She took a vow of celibacy and escaped to Armenia with a female monastic group of virgins after the Roman Emperor, Diocletian sought her for his wife. He had sent artists all over the empire to bring back portraits of the most beautiful women they could find. Once he saw her portrait, he had to have her, but he chose the wrong woman.

In Armenian territory, she was discovered hiding by the pagan King Tiridates the III, who after also being captivated by her beauty wanted her for himself. When she refused him and vigorously fought his advances, escaping from his bedroom, he pursued her, murdering all of her sisterhood, skinning, hacking, and burning them alive. He then turned his wrath on Hripsimé, roasting her too. If he couldn't have her no one could."

Pastor Gardner smiled, "Mrs. Green, thank you. How do you know all of this?"

"Pastor, it is you who encouraged me to study theology. I don't sit around idle while you are out saving souls you know."

"Is there anything else?" asked the Reverend.

"Yes, it is said that Tiridates the III went insane afterward, crawling on the ground and acting like a wild animal. No one knew what to do, so his sister insisted that Saint Gregory the Illuminator be retrieved. He was a famous pastor who Tiridates hated because he was related to a family enemy. For that alone he had him tortured and thrown in a pit for dead. Thirteen years later to their surprise, they found him alive, pulled him out and cleaned him up. He went and prayed that God would show mercy on Tiridates for his murderous ways."

Veezon asked, "Mrs. Green, is that your real name?"

"I am not talking to you," she quipped back at him.

"Thank you Mrs. Green, you've been more than helpful," said the smiling Reverend Gardner.

"Wait, please finish the story," asked Ru.

"Are you sure?" said Mrs. Green, fluttering her hand in front of her face. "I know I get excited and talk too much sometimes."

"Please," said Ru,

Continuing her story Mrs. Green said, "The King was miraculously healed and traded in his idols for the Lord. His entire court converted. Dear St. Gregory, the Illuminator, went back and built a church over his dungeon and started another where the women had been tortured and killed, in part, because he had a vision of their death while he was still in the pit. He had a revelation of one like the Son of God coming down out of the sky and hitting the ground with a Golden Hammer, smashing the local idols.

To this day there is still a monastic order in honor of Saint Hripsimé. About twenty years ago, in the mausoleum tombs beneath the original Saint Hripsimé Church, the beheaded bodies of several women were found. A local church authority believes one of them, is the body of Hripsimé herself."

"Whoa.... the price of being good," said Ru, "there is some connection here I suppose. I need to find out why Ouriano wanted me to have this."

"If you ask for my opinion," said Veezon, "whenever Ouriano did something significant, like leaving you this memento, there was always more layers to his story. You need to trace its origin."

"Brace yourself for what you may discover," encouraged Pastor Gardner, "but I concur with Veezon."

Veezon added impatiently, "We've tarried here long enough. We ought to leave. Too much attention is not good."

"Yes," said Reverend Gardner, "you all must go. Be careful Ms. Zvonimira." To Veezon he said, "You also my fallen friend, know your weaknesses." And to his assistant, "Mrs. Green, my you are full of surprises, thank you."

Lastly he bowed and said, "Godspeed to all of you. You are going to need it." When he raised his head all three were gone.

Chapter 24

*You can acknowledge the truth
without abiding by it.*

Five Years After Ouriano's Memorial

The two continued to monitor the preparations below for the first large scale test. A dozen forest green diesel buses, roofs white with snow, all decaled with the blue and red Democratic People's Republic of Korea flag, descended along the excavated terraces of the old uranium ore quarry. The North Korean military convoy was led and followed by heavily armored personnel carriers.

One of the observers was an athletic young woman dressed in tight black leather pants, steel zippered black leather vest, a matching long duster and snow boots. A Tazer was strapped to her right thigh. "Tell me again why we are running these full scale tests in the middle of this God-forsaken country? You trust this regime?" Ru asked her father, Colonel Cuzak.

As the soft flakes and hard sleet collected momentarily then melted, evaporating off his thick black wool overcoat, Cuzak vented his frustration, "I never told you the first time, so why don't you tell me? You had the stomach to help remove Ouriano, so why are you balking now? Is it because we are so close?... Go ahead I am waiting... And after all, I haven't asked you to harm Doctors Pruett and Tanner, yet, have I? You don't know the pressure I am under. We all have to answer to someone."

Ru put her forefinger across her lips, and then pointed toward the main transfer center some twelve hundred feet below. Its roof supported a large radio telescope dish. "I suppose, in case the tests get ugly, the Sanctuary Corporation, doesn't want any bad press."

"Without saying..." he said.

"Also, there is no red tape, an ample supply of image bearers,.."

Cuzak interrupted, "undocumented humans, supplied by the regime. Good stock for the test. Mostly they are conscientious objectors, generational laborers who don't go for the emperor worship they demand here."

"Yes Father, captive image bearers, who want to escape, anywhere, and also a close supply of—Beltshzan's minions who are stranded and weak. They wish to flee the growing opposition of the Wounded Heir. They are darkened Winds decaying in their own cast down rot. I rather refer to them as 'scavengers of light.'"

The Colonel added, "You have that right my darling to find them disgusting. But sending them into livestock will not cut it. That was tried before as an escape; a waste of good swine."

"What?" Ru asked.

Amused he said, "You should read more theological texts. Whatever happened to a well-rounded liberal arts education?"

"I have to say, you confuse me at times. You act in league with Beltshzan, Yazad, and the Vranti, but you talk of the other side as if you believe their story?"

Cuzak thought for a moment. He kicked around the fluffy snow gathering at his feet, and then stared at the Hub below through the flurries. Finally he turned toward Ru. Her beauty in this stark landscape reminded him of her mother. He said, "You can acknowledge the truth, without abiding by it."

Ru, more confused, replied, "You can acknowledge the truth, but not subscribe to it?"

"Happens all the time Maria. We are helping people to opt out. So your next question is, 'Why are we moving them out of one hell and into another?'"

"And your answer?"

"The important thing is to keep moving, breathing, like these below. For most of them, gulags are all they've known."

"Father, you are impossible. The universe is a big place. Can you run forever?"

"Trust me Maria. The Vranti are rounding up some of your local 'scavengers of light,' as we speak. Be nice; think of them as distant cousins. Why don't we give them the chance they deserve? We've never transferred a group of this size."

"Maybe the minions are your kin, not mine, never."

Cuzak folded his hands together, "We came into this world as we now are. The image bearers have a choice. Watch what they choose."

Protesting she said, "They're not all this barbaric."

Continuing to monitor below, they heard the orders pumped over loud speakers. The thousand men and women were pulled off the buses and marched at gun point into the snowy parking lot to stand at attention. Most were clothed with nothing more than rags to protect them from the brutal North Korean blizzard.

After roll call was taken by the soldiers, Ru became very disturbed by what unfolded. Cuzak held her secure to the ground with his left hand supposing she might dive on them prematurely. The prisoners were ordered to disrobe in the gusting wind and sleet-snow mix. Ru gawked at the frailty of their bodies, "They are so skinny. They've been starved to death."

Cuzak answered, "Lean is a better word, but like you said, 'forsaken by the local entity.'" The discomfort on their frozen soles was apparent, hopping from one foot to the other. Making matters worse, three prisoners were found missing at the roll call. Immediately several soldiers were dispatched to search the buses.

Two hundred yards from the bus, Ru's eyes caught two men and one woman backtracking up the ore mine road.

"Look Father, an attempt to escape since they suspect death to be near; a will to live." When the prisoners were spotted, one of their pursuers methodically climbed to the top of an armored vehicle to take control of a high powered turret, rotating the mount toward the free game and locking on to their heat signature. Ru cringed at the mayhem which took only a few seconds. As least a hundred rounds discharged from the gun's spinning multi-barrels with a short burst squeeze, exploding the targets, leaving a mash of flesh and rags to soak red into the perfect white snow of the road.

An argument ensued among the military officers over who was responsible while the prisoners grew colder in the swirling snow. A North Korean enlisted man, apparently deemed responsible for the bus escape was marched to the other side of the parked buses, asked to strip down of all clothing with a pistol held to the back of his head. Given the choice to die on the spot or enter the transfer Hub with all the prisoners, he got up and gingerly walked barefoot into the formation of the shivering.

A ship horn blasted twice from the roof of the three story Hub station followed by the radio telescope array realigning and a cargo door opening. At this signal half of the one hundred soldiers goose stepped into formation to escort the nearly frost bitten captives into the prototype Hub. Entering by four lines across through two sets of double doors, the limping captives were herded through a black metallic corridor lined with small white lit panels on the floor and ceiling.

While the outside army contingent surrounded the perimeter of the facility, the guards inside shoved the experimental subjects along with the butt of their guns. Forced through a thick open hatch, they spilled onto the dim red lit transfer floor.

The unclothed prisoners welcomed the warmth as the speaker system ordered them to stand equidistant from each other in the large circular room. The oldest of them was forty, as the life of an indentured laborer of North

Korea was not conducive to longevity. The soldiers who surrounded the subjects were themselves at a loss as they waited nervously for their next orders. They wondered, *Might we be microwaved with them? Will we exit before they spray everyone with nerve agents? Will they order us to machine gun them as enemies of our exalted leader?*

As the subjects continued to filter onto the floor, one of them, the stripped ex-soldier made a desperate attempt to approach the nearest officer. Clutching his previous comrade's hand, he begged for mercy to escape the plight which awaited the others. His answer came quickly with clubs to the back of his head and knees, collapsing him in a fetal position on the ceramic floor.

Far above, on the rim of the mine, the father and daughter observed the last of the prisoners entering the Hub. Cuzak scrounged his pockets for a favorite cigar as he spoke to his agitated daughter, "It's remarkable how easy it is to control people in masses, especially when you keep them emaciated. You have to give the image bearers credit for their remarkable lust to wield power over each other. The dark Winds only make them a little more of what they already are. This will be a great day."

Chapter 25

They are as good as dead anyway, please forgive me.

Cuzak ran the Cuban under his nose. He bit off the tips, and spit them out. Within a few deep breaths, a small red ash formed on the end.

Ru asked, "When did you start the habit?"

Pulling it from his lips, savoring the smoke and steam slowly streaming from his mouth and nostrils he said, "It is an old family vice and a gift from our next Hub station host."

"What's in it for these petty dictators, to be early Hub hosts?"

"Notoriety, technology, my dear."

"Perhaps an easy way to dispose of dissidents, and receive stock options from the Sanctuary Corporation?"

"Of course, what do we care?"said Cuzak. While they had been focusing on the mine, dark thunderclouds which clung to the frosty hills behind them gave birth, releasing a low gray cloud bank. Bending and snapping tree limbs as it flooded over the knolls and small valleys, it closed in on their position above the quarry. The cold winds shifted from the disturbance alerting Cuzak who said, "The Vranti's cohorts have arrived."

"Oh joy," said Ru, "Do tell, in what form today?"

"You'll see. Keep watching."

After it passed the tree line, the low gray fog collected in one spot near the edge of the quarry's first tier. From there it poured from one terraced level to the next all the way to the bottom, toward the cadre of soldiers standing guard outside the Hub station. They were amazed as the fog stretched and sifted its way through their legs, around their torsos, and over their shoulders, until a broiling semi-clear gaseous tube had encircled the building.

"Time to join them," said Cuzak, flicking his cigar into the snow, "There's General Sul's motorcade. We'll join in behind him. Get in." Accelerating their vintage Mercedes truck, he called the Vranti from his wrist device, "We are coming in behind you, behave yourself. This must be perfect."

The outdoor soldiers had become preoccupied with poking the unusual ground cloud with their hands, boots, and guns, when a black stretch limousine, an eighty's Lincoln flying two Democratic People's Republic of Korea flags on the hood, pulled in close to the main entrance. It paused then slowly drove around the building. One by one as the guards noticed the General's car, they stood to attention, saluting as he passed by. They all knew the supreme Commander was not to be trifled with. When, the limo stopped, followed by Cuzak's and Ru's truck, two military attachés hastily stepped out of the front of the Lincoln and swung open the last passenger door.

Growing angry at the prospect of yet another meeting with the collective, Ru said, "No, you mean they've infiltrated the head of the North Korean Army?"

Cuzak answered, "Yes, remarkable trait. Listen Ru, I know it is hard, you have no respect for his kind and neither do I. But be careful with him. This Vranti is more powerful than previous forms you have met."

Ru and Cuzak left the cab of their truck. While they approached the limo, the long black leather boots of the General exited first. The rest of him followed, covered in a green wool overcoat with golden buttons and epaulets of his supreme rank.

Walking briskly toward the Vranti's limo, and appearing completely out of place, the General's MP aides ordered Ru to halt. However, when it was apparent that the leather clad vixen had disregarded them, they un-holstered their pistols to kill her. But before they could take aim, she grabbed each of their pistol barrels, forcing their hands backward and breaking their wrists. Ru followed by jerking the screaming men's limp hands down, tearing ligaments and nerves, and causing their faces to ram into her up thrusting knee.

As she stepped over their agonizing bodies in the snow, followed by her father, the guards in the distance all pointed their weapons at Ru. Though she was within striking distance of their Commander, none fired a shot to protect the General because of the open hand he had held in the air.

Unable to hide her anger she said, "So Vranti or General Sul is it? How'd you take control of this man's body? Enter through his mouth, or your favorite access? So this is your big promotion after your last failure? Impressive, but I'm putting you on notice, don't cross us."

The General smiled at her and reached out his hand to embrace hers as a gesture of friendship, asking in his Korean inflection, "We've met before, have we?" Before Ru could react, he backhanded her face, causing her to fall on top of the maimed aides. As Ru crawled to get up, the Vranti took two steps forward and planted his boot in a punt style kick under her chin. The force flipped her violently, landing face down in the snow. Cuzak remained motionless and began chuckling as a cover, hiding his love for his daughter.

"Look at her," said the grinning General. "There is more to her than you concede Cuzak. I doubt her loyalty. She is debating whether to follow or harness her hatred and anger at me." Pointing his finger at her the General said, "Accept defeat and pay homage to my higher life form."

Ru gradually regained her feet and wiped the caked snow from her face. Her dense nails perforated the tips of her fingers like hardened blades. Her eyes' vertical slits opened and closed with her pulse. Her wings posed to burst at the seams except her father put his hand on her shoulder. "Not now Maria."

The Vranti derided her, "I don't know what bloody bastardized half breed experiment you are, but let me give you some quick advice: stay out of our way and listen to your father." Maria continued to look at him with contempt as he turned his attention to Cuzak.

In the mean time the General waved his soldiers to surround them, machine guns pointed toward her. In their native tongue he announced to the hardened killers, "These attachés were not up to the standard I had set up in protecting my life. They did not pass the test, therefore they are expendable. What if this had been more than a drill?" he snarled at all of the young soldiers. "Watch closely as I will hand pick two of you to replace these useless body guards."

By then the two MP attachés, cringing as they held their disfigured wrists, hobbled forward to face the General. "Attention, look at me, put on your hats." he ordered them. Looking over their shoulders to Ru as they fumbled for their head gear, the Vranti said, "Now my little Hybrid, demonstrate your loyalty and show them what the weak and disloyal can expect." Ru's eyes darted toward her father, but he showed no emotion or guidance.

Ru closed her eyes and prayed quietly for a moment, new snowflakes settling on her long eyelashes, "They are as good as dead anyway, please forgive me. I truly don't know what I am doing." When she opened her eyes she positioned the men next to each other, setting their hats at their feet. Leaning over their shoulders she whispered in their ears, "Forgive me, may you wake up in paradise." All the soldiers encircling her could not understand who or what she embodied.

As they speculated about her, Ru spun away from the two attachés and reached behind over her shoulders with each hand grasping a hold under their chins. Quickly shifting her weight forward with bended knee, she leveraged their relatively weak necks against her incredible core power and frame. So fast was the execution, by the time everyone heard the horrible, 'pop,' all the soft spinal tissue in their thoracic vertebra had severed.

Ru then turned around to prop the dead men by their coat collars, as their heads flopped sideways. She darted her eyes back to her father for some kind of sympathy, but none was there; to the young soldiers, but none was there. And last, she looked to the Vranti.

General Sul slowly clapped three times as a sign of his smug satisfaction. When he finished, Ru pushed the bodies forward, toppling them at his feet. She picked up their hats and gently placed them on their heads, then took her place next to Cuzak's side.

Chapter 26

Can technology alter divine providence?

The General unfolded his arms and motioned for the men to lower their guns.

"As you can see behind me, my fodder in the roll cloud is also ready for the first experiment. We've had to energize these infected to an extent to get them in this fluid form."

"Where did you find them? How did you motivate so many?" asked Cuzak.

"Promise of resurrection of course, what's the alternative for them, a lake of fire?"said the General, hands firmly on his hips as he rocked back with confidence.

"Then let's go inside and finish what we came for. This will be our first large scale demo with a direct link to the Sanctuary," said Cuzak.

"Back to your positions," the General commanded the men who had surrounded them, then warned, "and I would not touch the cloud circulating the Hub station. It might hold grave consequences for you."

As they strode over the parking area to the Hub station, they paused at the edge of the dense cloud slowly flowing waist high around the building. The General put his left hand in it, and shoved it to his right, propelling the roiling fog faster.

Wading through the cloud behind the General, Cuzak and Ru heard the faint wailing and echo of words from the infected churning spirits, "Give us the Sanctuary,"... "Give us Yazad,"... "Make it happen,"... "Release us from our fallen state,"... "Complete our hope,"... "Give us new light,"... "Deliver us from the great entity who is prepared to torment us for eternity."

Ru paused in the cloud for a moment even though her father and the Vranti had passed through to the service entrance. They watched with interest as she was mesmerized by all the voices. She had never before heard so many in one place. As she stood still, streams of vapors twisted around her body. An awful dread set in, causing her head to spin, as she heard more voices, "You are not an image bearer. What are you? You... You are what we want to become!"

Horrified, she became immobilized by the desperate beings as more sought to communicate with her. "I am not like you!" she screamed at them. General Sul found this amusing, but when Cuzak realized her predicament, his strong arm reached through the churning mist and dragged her into the doorway.

The General said, "They are so eager. They could sense you, feel you. They want to be healed, live in a fleshly body of their own. They want to become a hybrid like you."

Cuzak cut him off sensing her uneasiness, "Then let's give them what they came for. Lay off of her, she's not your concern."

"Touchy father, we are? And she is yet to meet your father?"

"Enough!" growled Cuzak, "let's remain focused on the task. You can't handle a Juwaan, let alone grapple with me."

With all three inside, they headed for the building's operational entrance elevator, heading down ten floors to the insulated control room which managed both the energy from the supporting twin nuclear reactors and ion antimatter accelerator matrix surrounding the transport room. The accelerators were a unique one of a kind array embedded in the walls, floor and ceiling, surrounding those being transported in a high energy force field. The goal of each transport Hub was to create a collapsing but constant quadrant of time and space, a stable worm hole through which its clients fell through the branes, the structures holding the order and Higgs field of their world.

The high energy quadrants needed for the commercial use of moving a thousand people at a time, required extremely high energy bursts, gained from the afterburner addition of antimatter to excite ions to a super nova and pulsar range. As Cuzak tried to explain this to the five legitimate junior ranking officers present under General Sul, "This is a controlled nuclear implosion, which serves two purposes: inject energy inward into the space time grid rather than outward, and maintain a secure grid around those traveling. Any type of defect in manufacturing, a short, or deceleration of energy at the last moment, could have unforeseen consequences."

Cuzak continued, "Indeed, there are theoretically, an infinite number of positions, dimensions, bubbles, the Hub could land in. Coordinates and pointing this hole all have to be preset, precise. If it works, travel is almost instantaneous, as it is not in linear distance one travels but through the folding of space."

As the General followed Cuzak's tour, he noticed with the others, that the interior of the Hub's control room was engineered with a wrap around screen from the floor to the ceiling, displaying the internal 360 degree view of the transport deck of the Hub. The prisoners could all be seen live, perplexed, standing and waiting for whatever was next. Cuzak explained more, "Because of the force fields generated and flash heat, the control room cannot be adjacent to the transport area. Next, you see, in the center of the control room, our round black granite table supporting five horizontal projection virtual touch computers, and in the center a large 3-D projection of the interior of the Hub, monitoring the vital signs of every person on board: heartbeat, temperature, blood pressure, blood sugar, uric acid output, and more."

But there was something extra Cuzak did not talk about. This virtual monitoring system was equipped with the ability to measure and see symbiotic beings, because of the measurable disruption of Higgs fields, the fluctuations of mass measurements caused by a darkened wind. For milliseconds they could disrupt the atomic weight of specific elements found in the chemistry of humans. Their presence caused a measurable fluctuation, undetectable by almost any other measurement, except the sometimes extreme ill feeling or emotional swing of the host image bearer, that something was wrong. Of course after years of a symbiotic relationship, some image bearers transported would not notice a thing.

In front of the Vranti, his support staff, and members of the North Korean ruling family, Cuzak said, "General Sul, I take it you find the facility first class and state of the art? Please take your seat next to mine as we ready for our initial run."

General Sul accepted the normal chair next to Cuzak, then leaned over to him saying, "I have a question which I've been pondering, regarding this human technology merged with the piggy backing of the infected spirits; What if the house is occupied already? What if the infected--the darkened Winds, cannot find a host, what will happen to them? Left to wander in a foreign universe? Will they be annihilated?"

Cuzak thought for a second, leaned toward General Sul and answered, "We will soon find out won't we," then settled back in his command chair.

Chapter 27

You have been chosen because of your unflinching obedience to your mother land and benevolent leader.

Cuzak and Ru nestled themselves into the shiny white command pods. From the exterior they looked like diagonal cut eggs floating on a magnetic pedestal. Adjusting to the body type, the red gel interior added perfect comfort. Networked in similar seats were the Chief Energy, Chief Symbiotic, Navigation, and Matrix officers. Taking their positions the laser embedded in the left arm rests scanned their mitochondrial DNA, and in recognition extended a custom foot rest. This in turn triggered a green glowing magnetic field supporting a virtual screen which encapsulated the front cavity of their pod.

Once activated it provided a seamless view of the 360 degree panorama inside the transfer floor; zoom in—out on subjects, and effortlessly share the instrumentation of the specialists around them.

As the other staff manned their stations, Cuzak asked for the final ten minute countdown to ensue. "Reactors?" he asked his energy officer.

"Both reactors are now online and peaking at two gigawatt range sir. Anti-matter magnetic baffles also operating at one hundred percent."

"Very good, wait until symbionts have taken up positions before final energy configurations." he responded. To the navigation officer he asked, "How is the communication with the Sanctuary target? Are they ready? We can have no margin of error."

"Yes, Colonel, the quantum teleportation data from our entanglement dialogue is steady. We also have triangulated confirmation from the Europa station signal."

In the privacy of Ru's bubble, as security czar over the process, she scanned the interior transfer deck, where the North Korean guards were nervously bunched near the two exits. She realized most of them had no idea of what the experiment was about, let alone life outside their military cult kingdom. They knew one thing for sure, based on what they had seen at other experimental facilities, whatever was about to take place in this room, wasn't going to pleasant.

Through the universal translator in her egg-like chair she announced, "All security, clear the floor, once the doors are sealed they will not be reopened. Repeat, all security clear the floor." Without hesitation the North Korean military personnel took to the exits, followed by two foot thick ceramic composite doors sliding up into place from the floor. When both of the doors locked into place with a heavy 'clug,' those left inside felt a change in air pressure as their ears popped.

"What are we sending these people into? We are treating them like cattle," Ru regretted. She zoomed in on the weathered face of a woman her age who had lost most of her feminine features due to malnutrition. Her teeth were sparse. Her pelvis and shoulder bones looked like they might pierce her skin. She was holding something in her hands, cherishing it closely, kissing it. Changing views Ru saw that it was a picture of a child, *Soon to be an orphan?* she wondered.

Controlling the computer's kiosk by her vision, she continued to browse through the test subjects. Some had begun to converse with each other. A few were praying and others were scanning the red lit room for evidence of what might happen next or a way out. But to Ru they all looked hopeless.

Up to this point the test subjects had avoided the crows, those black vans swooping in to the labor camp barracks unannounced, scavenging people for military experiments to further poison, biological, munitions, and space research. Those loaded in the vans never came back. Now they figured it was their turn, "What would it be, gas, pressure tests, radiation? The guards certainly left in haste."

Cuzak's voice startled her on a private COM, "Ru, we will be venting in the dark Winds encircling the Hub at minute five. You realize Ru, in this case, these people will be better off."

She attempted to answer through the closed COM in a professional manner but she couldn't conceal the turmoil inside her, "Affirmative, we are ready Colonel. Are you sure your heavy handed methods are the prudent should these spirits misbehave?"

"If called for, you separate them, the Vranti—the General, will take it from there. I expect to have to make an example of one of them. That is how they work," Cuzak answered, then opened the COM back up to all the officers, "Matrix officer--Once everything is set, it will be in your hands to maintain our cargo. Don't let me down."

"Yes sir, I've run the pretests, all circuits are good to go, this is just ten times hotter than anything you've had us run before. We are ready to float the Hub."

"Team, you are about to change history. You will be well rewarded in this life, and should you choose, the alternate life to come."

To the chief Symbiotic officer Cuzak added, "Ready the intake vents for the symbionts on my call. Begin the calming program." Inside the Hub, beautiful mood altering music played in coordination to an astoundingly crisp video feed of some of the most exotic places on the Earth. The prisoners were beside themselves at the scenery, all new to them because of their confined lives in the gulag style encampments, where the only video they were privy to was of their exalted leader. As they watched, the scenery changed to a more instructional video explaining in Hollywood images what was about to take place.

The Hub's transfer room was about to disembark to a new future and freedom. The soothing native female narration started, "You have been chosen because of your unflinching obedience to your mother land and benevolent leader. You will be going to a far distant land to help seed a new world order. Consider this a privilege. Work industriously there, as you did here..."

The General stood and encroached over the canopy of Cuzak's control pod. "Stop this over-sold infomercial! They don't need this. Get on. What is taking so long?"

Inside the Hub, music continued to play with the mingling of narration and pumped in soothing scents of sweet roses, fields of harvest, pine forests, and ocean mists. For many of the conscripts, there was a sigh of relief, oblivious to one slight missing detail.

For in the next launch stage, even one of Cuzak's hearts began to race when he gave the order, through an open COM, "Bring in the passengers, continue countdown." Through his one-way bubble, he could see the General nervously directing his attention around the room, examining the video feeds on the wall monitors, and every worker as if they were suspect.

The Symbiotic officer announced his follow through of the order. "Vents open, bringing in the passengers."

Surrounding the building, the outer sentries observed the fog bank begin to feather off into the vents. Inside, Cuzak left his pod for the central command table to follow the three dimensional imagery of the fallen Winds passing through sixteen ventilation shafts. In the transfer room, two three foot vents silently protruded from the center of the ceiling and floor. While the video and music continued to play the once thick fog divided itself into separate winding streams, clinging to the ceiling and the floor as they selected their unsuspecting hosts.

However all did not remain so peaceful. The beat down North Korean guard, still sprawled on the floor watched the vapors creep almost undetected between the legs of those entranced by the propaganda film. One particular flowing ribbon weaved its way toward him as if it intentionally chose him. He had already resigned himself to death based on the horrors he had witnessed at other facilities. The disposal of human lives was all in the name of science and to the glory of the supreme leader, however, he had never witnessed a method like this.

Chapter 28

"On an appointed day they had been accustomed to meet before daybreak, and to recite a hymn antiphonally to Christ, as to a god."—Pliny to Emperor Trajan 112 C.E.

As the vapor stalked the young man, he sought to scoot away from it on the floor, but his efforts proved futile. He opened his mouth to scream a warning, and as he did the stream entered his mouth as a seamless parasitical worm. For a moment the symbiont paralyzed his lungs. Regaining his feet the possessed man stumbled, flailing his arms for help as he gasped for air and lost control of his bodily functions.

Ru watched helplessly as one by one, people were overtaken by an entity they had no defense against. It was ugly. The first screams erupted as the music and video played on. The fright came from those who were still free for the moment, as they witnessed the mayhem of those around them; convulsions, vomiting, writhing contortions, shoulders disjointed, eyes rolling back in their sockets. Some were speaking languages foreign to them, or using abusive language. Others were acting in intrusive and seductive manners, completely at odds with their normal personalities. Ru asked herself, "Is this what I am related to?"

Cuzak looked up from the 3-D symbiont tracking images to ask the General, "Did you go out of your way to find the worst of the worst?"

Inside her command chair Ru continued to scan for violence, for those entities who at first chance would venture for bloodshed, for they were not without vendetta to each other. She had overlaid each human with a red symbiote view. She noticed that a small percentage of them were not functioning well as hosts. This caused some who had been easily possessed to be harassed again by the darkened spirits desperate to find a receptive body.

Ru tracked the resistance to a small group of humans huddled near the center of the transfer floor, holding hands. A number of orphaned spirits were doing their best to infiltrate them, but something, or someone kept them at bay. She did not know if others noticed but at the cerebral cortex of each image bearer in this group was a unique small blue-white light. "What is that light?"

Ru repositioned her cameras and microphones toward the group. She couldn't believe it, "They are singing, generating their own force field, blocking the symbionts from unification."

Without Ru noticing, the General had moved himself into Cuzak's empty command chair, and was monitoring her private data feed, viewing everything she was focused on from her pod.

"Colonel, we are at ninety-five percent receptivity," announced the Symbiotic officer. "We have extras in the room without a host."

Ru wanted to ask her father for permission, to remove them; a large ex-Cherub, and twenty other darkened seraphs. These blackened Winds were recklessly trying to force themselves into those already taken. She announced, "Some are attempting to breach the one for one ratio."

But her father was now at the table away from private COM channel. Opening her emergency tool application, she found the icon for the tractor beam to focus on their removal. "After all, it is for their protection, but I must be careful. If I accidently lock onto one of the humans, their flesh will be distorted." Waving her hands and fingers before her virtual controls, she began a targeting sequence on those spirits which failed to nest in a body.

The General however, felt he had observed quite enough and pulled himself from the command pod fuming. Surprising Ru as he emerged, he positioned himself across the control table from Cuzak, where he slammed his fist down and demanded, "Why are we not at one-hundred percent fulfillment?"

When Cuzak did not immediately answer, the General announced in a bellicose voice, "Emergency stop to this transfer!"

Cuzak retorted, "But everything is a go, it's not easy to restart."

"I see something I don't like. When we eliminate the problem, we will resume."

"But Yazad is waiting."

"Yes and this first batch will be as pure as the driven snow. Everyone, listen! Open the aft door on the Hub floor. I will be the only one to enter. Then when I exit, you will resume immediately."

One of the North Korean engineers at the table, interjected, "But General, you will be in danger."

Turning against the young engineer, he pulled him from his seat. Grabbing him by the tuft of hair on his forehead he shoved his head backward and pulled down his jaw, finally holding him in a headlock like a wrestler. "You want to talk when not addressed? Leave your mouth open," he ordered. The General then pulled out a pistol sized laser and with precision lacerated the vocal engineer's tongue in four pieces, cauterizing as he cut. As the young man gripped his searing mouth, he spit out the pieces into his hands. The General ordered him, "You will follow me into the Hub."

Turning away from the muted man and toward Cuzak, the Vranti asked, "Does anyone else have an objection to stopping?"

Cuzak, announced, "Emergency stop, decelerate generators to idle at twenty-five percent. Keep the anti-matter isolated. What does our navigation window look like?"

The Chief officers responded, "Yes sir." "Yes sir." "Yes sir." "We have a two hour window, otherwise we'll have to wait forty-eight hours sir."

Except for Ru, who approached General Sul, and saluted with a sarcastic, "Yes sir," at which he turned and left the control room, ordering the agonizing engineer to follow.

Those remaining stayed fixed on their monitors. They watched the General enter into the Hub transfer deck with the engineer in tow. The armed guards cowered behind him in the door way. By now the music and program had ceased.

Forcing his way through the zombie like crowd the Vranti headed for the center of the room. Along the way he threw the young man, still dazed from his oral surgery, on the floor to fend for himself. General Sul, arriving at the resistant group, found them holding hands and free of entities. Breaking into their circle he announced, "Good news, you have earned your freedom,.."

Twice he backhanded a possessed intruder who tried to amble into the small circle he was addressing, "...for we have been testing you to reveal the true believers among you. Your own supreme leader of the Republic is a secret believer. For your courage we are going to return you to your home towns, to your families, new jobs."

The little huddle wasn't sure what to make of this generosity in the midst of this spiritual anarchy, but with no alternative they followed the General off of the Hub floor and into the service hallway.

Now the angry General and his parasitic collective became confused at the number of subjects yet needed to complete the promised one-thousand. Determining there to be nineteen deficient prisoners from this holy huddle, he also added the two he was shorted from the escape attempt.

Therefore he commanded the contingency of soldiers to count off. When the twenty-first had sounded, he commanded them to hand over their weapons and strip of all their clothes before they could protest.

"Now find a place on the transfer floor. Serve your country well. I will see you soon, I promise." As he spoke those final words and finished ushering them in, the thick insulated door slid up and locked into place. Those in the control room winced at the mayhem as the frightened soldiers pounded on the door, pleading to be let out. But slowly they also succumbed to the trailing vapors of no escape; that is, aside from the extra passenger, who himself was an alien among them.

Chapter 29

*Here is what I think; we have a group of
Vigilante Winds-- the lost boys
of the Blue Moon.*

All the monitors in the control room followed the General and his segregated misfits outside. Cuzak said to Ru privately, "He doesn't hate them for being human, for being human he despises them. He hates them because they are Loyalists. They are everything he never can aspire to be, at least in this realm."

Ru asked her father, "So he has replaced those who seemed to be immune with the troops. What is this sick-o-phyte going to do with these poor people?"

"Need you ask?"

"Another thing, the General in his anger has lost count. We have one-thousand and one human passengers; one over target with no symbiote. Do I mention it to him?"

"No, let it go. At this point I want no more absurd confrontations," said Cuzak.

Returning the rejects from the building into the snowy parking lot, the General ordered the shivering prisoners to stand to attention. "So you are of the mindset that the truth has set you free? That your God has delivered you from your fears? Congratulations are in order--you passed your first trial. Now you are free to go except for this final test; to assess your navigation skills. If you climb out of this mine and make it fifty miles to the next city, your criminal records will be expunged. If you remain here, you will be shot. Disperse!"

One of them meekly asked, "General, may we pray and be given clothing before departing?"

The General said, "Of course, take whatever garments lay in the parking lot. By all means, pray if it warms your souls." He then walked away muttering as he signaled the guards to position themselves in a half circle firing squad between them and the Hub station. While the soldiers readied their weapons, the snow and sleet poured harder, whiting out their view to less than twenty yards before them.

As Ru and Cuzak scrutinized this situation, their weather radar tracked a concentrated micro burst directly over the ore pit. From the video feed they saw several bright flashes and heard cannon like thunderclaps echo off the quarry walls. The blizzard conditions and lightning acted like giant strobe lights as the soldiers and subjects felt static charges build around any exposed skin and hair.

Just before reentering the Hub station, General Sul paused and rotated his head one-hundred-eighty degrees to observe the weather phenomena so deep in the Earth. Staring above his soldiers and captives the voices inside him said, "What is that residual glow in the clouds?"....."Someone else is here."... "And they've come to save these mongrels."

"Kill them!" he ordered, going against his word.

However, the young soldiers half circling the hand holding, shivering laborers, lost sight of their targets. The troops panicked in the snow blindness, firing haphazardly and screaming. They sprayed their clips in all directions until every one of them lay still on the frozen ground.

Cuzak leaned over to Ru, and whispered, "It's the spirit of Ouriano come to thwart us."

"No," she discreetly replied, "it's not Ouriano... But I sense the same type of goodness, his justice for the weak."

The General also perceived something. His talons ripped through the fingertips of his fur lined gloves and his eyes glowed red as he ran toward the center of the quieted commotion. When he came across the first soldier's body, he steadied himself, planting his right leather boot on him. Looking up he observed an ascending burst of flashes and dissipating thunder through the billowing snow. "Damn them, every one of them." Calling out to the next of command in the building he said, "Come out here and clean up this mess."

"The storm is clearing," Ru pointed out. "The prisoners, the soldiers, did they shoot each other dead? Did they all die from the gun shots?"

The General continued to survey the damage with hands on hips. The strewn bodies of the bullet ridden soldiers gave off steam from their fresh wounds as they lay on the red blotched snow beside their shell casings. One soldier writhed on the ground gurgling as he breathed, drowning in his own blood from a bullet through his throat. For the Vranti, a few extra soldiers' deaths were nothing more than a hangnail. What troubled him were the nineteen sleeping prisoners lying side by side with no apparent wounds.

"No blood, yet nonetheless dead," the General noted as he rolled several of the pale naked bodies over with his boot. "Colonel Cuzak, Officer Ru, I know you are viewing this. Turn off the outdoor monitoring and come out here. This you must see for yourself. Keep those inside working. We will have our success today."

Arriving at the corpse littered parking lot, the Vranti asked, "Cuzak, you have seen everything. Tell me what or who did this? Not one of these prisoners was killed by a gunshot. This group was unapproachable inside the Hub. Did they suddenly kill themselves? It is as if an ancient mercenary of death visited."

Cuzak said, "This doesn't add up. There are rules, protocols, everything--everyone must abide by. A random lightning strike is doubtful. Something like this can't happen without permission."

The General reminded him, "None of the soldiers died by a lightning strike, they shot each other confused in the chaos. And, where are the burn marks on the test subjects? They appear to have died in peace. Their spirits suddenly left them. Why now? Some of this worthless lot was third generation internment camp slave labor."

Ru spoke up, "Aren't you forgetting, they might be written off in this realm, but still branded by Siyon as Loyalists."

"Aren't you the budding theologue? Hybrid, speak only when you are not fueled by your human ignorance." The General grimaced at her as a fly crawled out of his nose, then continued, "Here is what I think; we have a group of Vigilante Winds, the lost boys of the Blue Moon."

Cuzak questioned his line of thinking, "What are you talking about? Ouriano was the closest thing they had. And if they do, what is one or two? They won't be tolerated by their own Winds of light for long. In a short time, they will join us. I was with Beltshzan to witness the turning of three Legion Commanders. They drank down the infection."

"Don't be so sure Cuzak. What if there are some who have been cast down but want to prove themselves?"

Ru interrupted again to hide what she knew, "To whom would they prove themselves? They have no love which redeems them in this realm, except in the Promised Land we are promoting?" Cuzak nodded in agreement with her.

General Sul laughed, "'A love which redeems them?' Is this what they hope from Yazad? You have taken the archaic language of the Wounded Heir and applied it to Yazad? The only love Beltshzan and Yazad demonstrates lies here on the ground and in that Hub... Power." Treading over another corpse, a few dozen flies from the General's collective inspected the wounds of the dead and returned to his nostrils, where he paused to relish the deceased's aroma.

Ru became nauseous at his morbid pleasure, and asked, "Have you no respect for the dead? Their blood cries out."

"Since when do tramps have the right to judge? I'd say your death count is growing." The Vranti slowly examined her up and down as he said to Cuzak, "I need you to find out who these perpetrators are who interrupted us. Your bastard child here knows more than she leads on; both about the last Juwaan and these Vigilantes. You ought to shorten her leash. She grazes in the wrong fields. Do you know everything about her? She may have her father's eyes, but who can weigh the heart?"

"As I told you before she is not your concern," said Cuzak. "Don't try me on this. Let us leave these corpses to bury their own. We can still make the time window for the first delivery."

Ru wondered, *Cuzak knows more, why is he protecting me? This must somehow be connected to Veezon.*

Chapter 30

"Topheth has long been ready,
Indeed, it has been prepared for the king..."
--Isaiah 30:33a

"All Chief Officers report, countdown thirty seconds," said Cuzak.

Each responded as they hunkered in their control pods along with Cuzak and Ru, "Matrix at full strength, Colonel." "Quantum entanglement data flow is steady, two meter tolerance met." "Symbiotes embedded, quiet as a well fed pack of zombies--sorry sir." "Mix of plasma and anti-matter ready to flow at .00001, sir."

Ru added on her private COM, "It's either fly or fry Colonel."

"I prefer to fly today," said Cuzak.

"Don't we all?" said Ru, as she glanced over at General Sul, who was impatiently rapping his long finger nails on the command table, while scouring the hologram of the transfer floor for any more traitors.

He announced, "What use is a bird which cannot fly? Our fallen brother's ability to sail the universe withered away with the infection, let alone escape the Earth. Leaching off of humans was our last means of survival. They can have this place. Today we reach for the promised light of our salvation." The Matrix officer switched his view to a hologram of the Hub's interlaced magnetic super conducting circuitry, which included mega capacitors to momentarily store the gigawattage. Upon release they would super heat iron atoms to create a quark-gluon plasma. At this point the super charged plasma would be mixed with small amounts of released anti-matter. Dispersed evenly, this flash force field of primordial big-bang energy would then create its own worm hole through time-space, following the entangled guidance system. On a small scale it worked, but on the scale needed to move herds of people and agricultural animals, it had yet to be tested.

As the computers managed the integral timing of all the elements, those inside the Hub reached a point of no return. Now fully embedded, the darkened Winds relinquished control of their hosts and waited in dormant apprehension of their own existence. For the conscripts who had regained self control, it couldn't be much worse than the only life they had known. The North Korean internment camp annual attrition rate for an adult was near twenty percent.

For the last sixty seconds of their Earthly existence, the laborers were as silent as lambs. To the contrary, the last minute substitute soldiers trembled at their unknown destiny; that is, except for one of them who bore a secret wound from the past.

In their last few seconds on Earth, the unknown came alive. The dim red lamps faded until pitch darkness filled the room. All felt the waves of the powerful energy building toward its torrent release and thrust into a new world. Every hair of every follicle was drawn to attention. A stereo hum from the energized magnets and circuits quickly rose from a high pitch turbine whine to a bass deafening pulse, pounding the bones. Some of the image bearing hosts, complete strangers, clung together, groping in the dark, fearful they might die alone. When the noise and vibration had gone beyond bearable, the final burst of primordial energy released into the Hub's superconducting matrix.

This changed everything, as the fabric of space and time released them from their celestial harbor. As gravity lifted, their bodies lightened and floated between the transfer room's floor and ceiling. The darkness and confines of the walls lifted as the light of tangled galaxies, red-green-yellow nebulae, white hot super novae, beaming pulsar blasts, and red giants screamed by them.

Alas, they approached the event horizon of Chronos, the massive black hole two-hundred-thousand light years in diameter. Accelerating their relative position to hyper-light velocity, they bore witness to all who tried to flee this interstellar black vacuum cleaner. Light, radiation, information, stars, glittering gas clouds, all bent backward, funneling into this nether world of no escape. Entering the dark gulf in a compressed and fluid state, the colony of two life forms pushed the envelope of the irrepressible laws of physics.

The Hub plunged like a galactic elevator with its cables severed, plummeting beyond even the edge of the inflating universe to a new space time fabric, even beyond the reach of the local entity, hidden among an infinite multi-verse of possibility, of dimensions, of worlds to be born. For a thousand new sojourners and their symbionts, they were headed for a new home where one could opt out of everything; even escape from their maker, so the designers of this new technology boasted.

Evading the crushing density and the tethering grip of the black hole, the Hub and its cargo shot through, continuing the drop toward a newly fashioned virgin land, where no human eyes had seen and in its new form, no clean Winds of light dare to gather.

For in eternity past and for some unknown reason Siyon and its companion Blue Moon had never charted nor seeded this place. Forsaken and lonely, this region had once flowed as all creation from the singularity residing past the Magnificon gates at the center of the warm glowing Siyon.

From Yazad's experience of creating order from chaos he chose his destiny long ago, staking his ground here, separating from the entity of the Earthen realm. In doing so he forged his plans to establish light of his own making, populate countries with his own seed, and re-establish armies under his control. It would all be his, indebted to no one.

Toward this new world order the image bearing traffic plunged, faster and faster. The stars and heavenly bodies streamed by as stripes, blurs, and then as a faint gray haze. When light was unable to keep up with them, darkness set in, leading their unconscious minds to cross the threshold of nothingness. Soon they were on the other side having gone further than light had ever ventured from their Sun.

Chapter 31

*Well put, the local entity has put eternity in their
hearts, but they cannot fathom
a damn thing.*

The Matrix Officer reported first, "The matrix held intact at the flash point sir. Our magnets suspended the plasma perfectly!"

Next the Symbiotic Chief spoke, "We have left no flesh on the platform. A few high blood pressure readings at the time, that's all."

"I am throttling down the generators to idle. All circuits clear, all superconducting energy displaced with 99.999 efficiency outside the immediate system," relayed the Energy Chief.

"Excellent," said Cuzak as he had one more report before celebrating, "Navigation Officer?"

He did not respond at first then said, "Waiting for confirmation from second entanglement chain embedded in the cargo,... waiting,... waiting,.. verifying tests. Colonel I can report with certainty that the cargo has landed intact."

With this last statement everyone in the room began to applaud, shaking hands congratulating themselves, except for one. Cuzak recessed his pod's green screen and stood, offering his hand to help Ru out of her module, then unexpectedly enfolded her in a hug and kissed her on the cheek. *Wow, his affection is a greater miracle*, she thought, then said, "You did it Father."

"We did it Ru," said Cuzak, pleased that this portion of the plan worked. The General however showed no emotion except more paranoia. Of this, Cuzak was suspicious, but went ahead with his speech, raising his thick hands to commend the staff. "General, Chief Officers, engineers, staff, today we have proven destiny is flexible. All one has to do is change the presuppositions of the immediate universe and you can begin anew. When we finally release the commercial viability of our technology all of you will be richer than you can comprehend. I am sorry for the clandestine nature of our work and the separation from your families. But as you know there is nothing happening anywhere, as important as this."

Before he could continue any further the Vranti interrupted Cuzak. The General removed his army dress hat for a moment as he stroked his oily black hair. "If I may also have your attention, first let me say, I affirm your skills to deliver our cargo despite a few unforeseen problems. The Colonel has spoken correctly about a new Destiny at our fingertips. But before you leap for joy, we have one more jump to make for a very special passenger."

Cuzak, leaned against the control table with one hand and tilted his head, asking, "Excuse me General Sul, but what are you talking about?"

Before he could reply Ru interrupted, "Please, everyone, look at the monitor. Who is that?" Out in the parking lot, a civilian man was examining the fresh dead soldiers and test subjects. He wore a white suit with a red wool stole around his neck. The cameras followed the European with short brown beard and shaved head, as he approached the service entrance, met by two armed guards.

The General quickly gave the order, "Escort him to our control room. Keep your hands off of him." However, the guards, intrigued and ever ready to rough up a would be prisoner, grabbed his upper arms; a fatal mistake, as black power flowed from this unexpected visitor with a pulsating charge, severely disturbing the electrical rhythm of their hearts. Each soldier let go gripping their chest, face turning ashen white, then knees buckling as their hearts convulsed, unable to coordinate positive blood flow. Disregarding his crippled escorts the man stepped over their bodies into the elevator, the camera in the upper corner zooming in on his face.

Cuzak recognized the visitor, while the General said, "An unexpected family reunion, Colonel?"

Ru's eyes darted to the elevator doors then to Cuzak who was rubbing a sore spot on his chest, clearing his throat, and straightening his tie. Cuzak glanced at Ru, "Relax Maria. Let me handle this."

The presence of the Vranti inside the General brought one type of dread, but the presence of Beltshzan delivered quite another. The air in the control room grew humid with unseen bile as the lights above the elevator counted its descent. But for Ru there was also the same ecstatic feeling of empowerment as when she had found the lance which slayed Ouriano.

The doors opened, the relaxed visitor stepped out, pulled off his red scarf, and laid it over the back of a chair. He passed by Cuzak and the General toward Ru. Cuzak thought about blocking his way, but knew that would result in disaster as his chest already hurt. "Cuzak," Beltshzan asked, "Are you not going to introduce me to my own granddaughter?"

The pulse hurt Cuzak's chest, "Yes, my lord... Maria, this is Beltshzan, chief investor in our Sanctuary project, and my father, your grandfather."

Ru's hands instinctually reached out to embrace Beltshzan's. *He looks so average*, she thought, until his hands held hers and she felt his power surge into her body. Flipping her palms, he carefully inspected them. Tracing the lines with his finger nail, he said to her, "These are no ordinary hands. These hands will do my bidding, won't they?"

Ru could not control herself as his power overcame her. There, in front of everyone, her fingers and nails lengthened, her shoulder's widened, her eye's dilated, and the magnificent dark wings ripped through the back of her black leather vest. The wings heaved up and down with every breath. She couldn't help herself as she answered, "Yes my lord."

"Do you like how you feel?" Beltshzan inquired. Ru could not think clearly, but in the emotional high she answered, "Absolutely, my lord."

"Yet, part of you has not been given over to me? Why is that? What keeps you at a distance? Look what I have to offer."

Ru began to fear, *He knows with whom my true heart belongs.*

But Beltshzan said something unexpected to her, "I need this in you. You must persuade others like Ouriano of your love and loyalty, so you can cut their hearts out as well. For this reason you were made. You are everything I hoped for. You are what is right in this world. You are a survivor, a princess, an heir and shall enter into eternal life. You are free to choose your destiny. Ask anything, up to half of my kingdom and I will give it to you."

Was this a horrible trick, she wondered? In spite of being empowered by his presence and the adrenaline surge, she said, "All those who were just transported to live in the Sanctuary, promise me you won't kill them?"

"Ha, ha, ha," Beltshzan laughed aloud as he dropped her hands and turned toward Cuzak and the Vranti, "she has more courage than the both of you combined." By now Cuzak was petrified that yet another of his children would be snuffed out like the others.

"Maria, my offspring, I promise to do what you ask. I will bring no harm to the image bearers who arrive now in that land of Yazad. But as for those riding with them, I cannot give you that promise."

"My lord," the Vranti interjected, "your time frame is getting very narrow if you want to go now."

"Yes, I suppose it is General. My unification is long overdue. Cuzak, what do you think? You are conspicuously quiet. Is this the right time?"

Cuzak answered, "Very soon, my lord, the image bearers of this Earth will be throwing themselves at the new opportunity you give them. They long to invent their own eternal certainty. The supply is plentiful, the choices are few."

"Well put," said Beltshzan, "the local entity has put eternity in their hearts, but they cannot fathom a damn thing. He got one thing right when he labeled them as sheep. Here I am, send me." Laughing at his own sarcasm, his form dissipated into a purple mist.

Cuzak ordered his Chief Officers, "Prepare to launch the Hub in twenty minutes." Then turning to the Vranti he said, "General, gather five live hosts for Beltshzan. I don't care where you get them, but don't touch my staff."

In a few minutes, five stripped soldiers were sealed in the Hub transfer platform. They huddled together, facing outward, leery of what would happen next. The purple smoke encircled them like a slow salivating shark, taxing them of all their fear and emotion before striking them one by one.

Chapter 32

We know you have many questions; after orientation, all of them will be answered.

The conscripted hosts lay on the Hub transfer floor like jumbled pieces of a puzzle; face down, on their backs, some on top of each other. Many were covered in vomit, blood, and or worse. But nonetheless they were alive as testified to by the familiar soothing voice over the intercom and the red service lights, "Congratulations, you have successfully navigated to the Sanctuary, your new home. Please stand so that the disembarking procedures can begin. After you have been cleansed, you will leave through the two exits, where you will receive new clothes and more instructions."

At thirty second intervals the recording repeated until all had stood or been helped up. When the last subjects rose to their feet, receded sprinkler heads protruded from the floor and ceiling, followed by fire hose nozzles from the walls. Without further warning, high pressure water mixed with a sudsing agent sprayed them from all directions, sanitizing them from their own filth. Large grates opened in the floor, quickly sucking down the putrid waters. Finally a clear rinse fell over them followed by high pressure jets of warm air vacuumed out of the ceiling.

As the blow-dried cosmonauts recovered from their hell flight, two hatch doors slid open allowing daylight into the transfer room. No one moved at first as they tried to determine whether they should leave the building. Several times the intercom repeated, "Carefully exit the two ramps on either side to receive your new clothes." On the third time they began to move.

Coming down the exit ramps single file, the new citizens of the Sanctuary paused to marvel at the high stacked yellow and orange cumulus clouds drifting below the aqua green sky.

A white path from each ramp converged around the building to form a wide walkway. As they hesitantly shuffled along this avenue in unclothed bunches, they passed between manicured rows of eucalyptus trees weighed down by glossy red fruit. They gave off the aroma of honeysuckles.

Overtaken by hunger, a group of women left the walkway to sample the fruit. In their hands the fruit resembled red Siamese apples—two grown as one. A teenage girl took a large bite as the others looked on, savoring the sweet cherry-apple flavor. She encouraged her friends to eat with her, but instead, they scowled, pointing to the fruit at her side. "Don't eat it!" they said, throwing theirs on the ground.

Confused but hungry she raised the ripe red fruit for another bite. However, she abruptly stopped when she saw a brown flat worm oozing from her fruit and stretching for her face. Repulsed, the young woman smashed the fruit and worm against a tree trunk. Scampering back to the pavement, the intercom reminded the group, "All guests are required to remain on the walkway, nourishment will be provided shortly." The thousand and one refugees from Earth walked a quarter mile through the trees until the avenue dead-ended at a wide raised platform. The voice told them, "Please board the ferry. In route you will soon receive more instructions. It is important that no one is left behind. We hope you are comfortable on your new planet. We are very privileged that you have volunteered to join us."

Fully loaded the land based barge slowly turned and accelerated, gliding just above the ground, creating very little turbulence or damage to the plants. The wind felt good to the new arrivals, as they skimmed over fields of green clover, sunken rice patties, rows of corn, golden wheat, cabbage and sweet melons. Compared to where they came from, it looked and smelled like a land of plenty. But to the one voluntary traveler among them, it remained highly suspect. For he noticed suspended in the middle of one of the distant fields and hanging on cross timbers, something which looked like a human scarecrow, but with wings.

As they ferried over the tips of the rich agriculture, a male and female Korean hologram divided them between men and women, repeating, "To accommodate you to your new and exciting life please help us prepare you for your orientation by following our directions. No eye has seen nor heart experienced true freedom until now. What do you wish to become? How long do you want to live? In the Sanctuary, all of your needs will be met."

One of the former North Korean soldiers raised his hand and asked, "Where are we? When will we talk to a real person? Where is everyone?"

The male hologram responded with a quaint smile and a preprogrammed response, "Thank you, we know you have many questions, after orientation, all of them will be answered."

A woman asked, "The truck took me from my family. What about my husband and son? Will I see them again?" To which the female projection responded, "Thank you, we know you have many questions, after orientation..." Over and over questions were asked but deferred until disappointed no one asked any more. Slowing, their ferry docked with a regional transit platform.

"Please follow us," said their virtual guides, taking the men one way and women another. The men's line led them to an automated dressing station, where ten at a time stood on prescribed markers. Once situated, metal tri-posts ascended out of the floor around each man, while web sprayers, sewing, and laser riveting mechanisms slid up and down the posts, weaving a glossy red body suit. Once near completion, all in a matter of fifteen seconds, a pattern for the face was cut out leaving intact a tight skull hood. The last item, unknown to the recipient, was an infrared serial number etched across the forehead under the deepest layer of skin.

The women in like manner, received light polished blue body suits. Custom hardened foot soles were sewn into the material as were magnetic released body access panels.

As those who received their new clothes stood to the side and waited for the others, they relaxed somewhat enjoying the surrounding terrain. They found themselves in a green valley of knee high grasses stirring in the wind, surrounded by gentle foothills of terraced agriculture of which they were familiar. But as the surroundings sunk in they realized this was not North Korea, nor South, nor China. Neither was it the planet Earth or even their solar system.

For when the train of clouds drifted away from overhead, beyond the hills, several pointed toward the sky saying, "Look!"

"What?" others asked as they shaded their eyes to see what they were talking about then exclaimed, "Oh, yes, I see it." "Do you see it?"

Amazed they said to each other, "This place has two Suns." "There are two stars in the sky." "Your shadow, it has a double." "Where are we?" "I don't know. Where are we?"

One red clad man answered, "The video said this is the Sanctuary. I am sure they will tell us what we need to know."

Another man asked, "Who are, they?"

When all were dressed, the men and the women looked across the transit platform at each other, a mass of shiny red and blue. A few of them were married, some brother and sister, but most did not know each other very well. In their old home, at least some were allowed to have families. Many wondered, *Will we have family here?*

To the men's side of the platform was a large flexible air tight clear tube, about twelve feet in diameter. The tube came out of a tunnel from a nearby hill and leveled off next to this regional way station. In the other direction the tube was suspended above ground by yellow anti-gravity beam supports as it weaved through the country side.

The first transport sled floated out of the tunnel and through the tube on a bed of air. It came to a halt next to the partitioned red spandexed men. A forward and aft vacuum valve closed on each side of the fifty person sled, sealing the pressurized tube in either direction. With a 'clug' and a 'hiss' the top half of the giant pipe over the awaiting car hinged upward, allowing for passengers to load and unload.

The men's virtual guide gave instructions, "Please process through the grid on the floor and follow the arrows. Remain in line. Move to the furthest seat and place your hands in your lap, where the magnets will safely hold you in place."

Several of the men who had been soldiers in the North Korean Army were not as accommodating to the progression of what they observed. Now free of the General's presence they asked the guide, "Why are the women being separated from us?" "They belong to us, they will be lost. Why are we standing over here?" "No one is stopping us from going to them." "We want answers. We are tired of your same reply."

But the guide gave them no answer except, "All your questions will be satisfied when you arrive at your beautiful new homes."

Most of these disgruntled men moved to the back of the line where they kept looking across the way station at the women in blue who had yet to leave. When about half of the men had been whisked away, some became desperate saying, "We can't leave them." "I am crossing to their side." "Me too, my wife is there." "You are right. We may never see them again."

The women were also asking questions, "Where are they taking the men?" "This is a strange place." "I can feel something is wrong." "We won't see them again." "Look some are running over here to help us." "Won't they get in trouble?" "The instructions said 'stay in the line.'"

And then the blue suited women witnessed the 'why' as five red clad men reached the half way point running toward them. It was as if they had been hit by a microwave or their suits had been wired to inflict the pain of being dipped in boiling oil. "Ahhhh, uggh, eaahh," they screamed, falling to the ground, flailing in terrible pain. Their fingers and toes turned down cramping in reaction to the severity of the burning sensation. Their immediate instinct was to roll back across the deck, but they had no muscle control. The remaining men and women looked on helplessly. No one dare go near them to help for fear of the same; except for one particular man, who no one knew.

Courageous, he asked several men to help tear off his new suit. Clothing removed, he ran toward the fallen and dragged them back one by one, where their burning subsided. Men and women alike feared for his life, "He is a fool." "Why is he helping them?" "They deserve this!"

While this happened the vacuum sleds continued to load the men and jettison away as even the remaining protesters decided it was futile to do anything but to get in. When the men dwindled to the final load, the last automated sled sat idle, waiting for the hero to fill the last seat. He stood alone naked next to the tube and shook his head, 'no.' The holograms stiffened their cheerful attitudes speaking in unison to him, "It is mandatory that you board the car. You must follow protocol!"

But he refused to get in. Those in their seats pleaded with him, "You must come with us." "They will kill you." "Get in."

Eventually the transit system waited no more, with the hatch coming down and sealing, 'thunk, thunk.' In the last few seconds while the tube was re-pressurizing, the men gazed from their sled through the clear transit pipe. In horror they saw what awaited their women. Beings with large brown and white striped wings suddenly swooped low and fast over the platform from nowhere and with no warning. The winged humanoids attacked like a starving flock of sea gulls, many suspended in the air as they waited for the first wave to gather their spoils and move out of the way. Some appeared to have multiple arms, easily snatching the shiny blue screaming females. A few had to make short repeated dives in the frenzy. The women were running wild across the platform to flee, dodging, diving, but it was no contest. Once in their clutches, these frenzied sentinels quickly sailed away for the horizon above the foothills.

Before the lone heroic man could turn to see what was happening behind him, he was lifted into the air by a set of large wings and two sets of claw like hands. The flying predator, sampling to his distaste, released him five stories above the sealed tube. In full view of his terrified and helpless comrades, the naked man landed face first, with a loud "thud," sprawled motionless over their sled, eyes wide open.

They watched him slowly slide over the side of the tube, leaving a smudge of mucus, blood, and hair as he disappeared into the tall grass below. The men in red, now magnetized to their seats, intimidated and powerless to change their outcome, sat silently wondering what new horrors awaited the women and themselves as their sled rocketed forward.

Chapter 33

Do you think you can distinguish heaven from hell?

In a few more seconds all was barren and quiet, until a new vacuum sled of two black spandex clad humanoids emerged out of the tunnel. They were slightly larger than image bearers, one female, and the other male in stature and voice. The more masculine had twin sets of arms, but neither had the expected one to three pair of wings. The anterior portion of their shoulders and lower backs appeared to be able to support such glorious instruments of flight, but none were revealed. As the seals on the hatch opened they both quickly leapt from the sled to the platform then hopped down to the grass below to find the man who had been viciously dropped; a warm welcome indeed from the dual star planet, they called Krator.

As the fallen one lay half unconscious and hidden in the grass he recognized and overheard pieces of their conversation from their second generation angelic dialect, "Is the security momentarily blinded now?" the feminine voice asked.

The larger with much lower pitch and four arms, replied, "Yes, act quickly. We will edit and cut the portion where he was dropped. Blame must fall elsewhere, hopefully on those indomitable Breed Lusters, who could barely contain themselves at the delivery of this first batch of fertile image bearing females. Now that they have some semblance of restoration, they have a profound need to procreate."

"Yes, let one of them explain to Yazad how an image bearer came up missing. If he is the Heir, he must be moved where no one will find him. Our powers are limited. This is so much different than before."

"I think I know what you mean, but how is this different 'than before?'"

Pulling back the high grass she said, "When he showed himself in the past, he brought with him radiance from his home. There it was just below the surface of his flesh. But here he will have no radiance to receive, and no one to pray to. He'll be as forsaken, if not more than we are. Do you agree?"

The deep voice's paranoia came out, "I, I... don't know. Hurry, find him. There is an unidentified cargo set to arrive soon, a rumored delivery of at least three new Legions who have turned to the infection."

She speculated more, "That could be Beltshzan himself transferring over. He'd like to personally greet any new arrivals who betrayed him.... There is nowhere left to hide, he has to be close."

"I am looking... I suppose we were already on the suspect list, having our wings emasculated, a small detail left out of the preview. I was so looking forward to soaring again. If we were loyal and this was our reward, what will Beltshzan do to those he judges to be disloyal?"

"He might say something like, 'Welcome to the Sanctuary, where all your dreams come true, Winds and image bearers alike... but as for you, when I needed you the most, you forsook me. Therefore to the cold wastelands or to the arid deserts of Krator you shall be cast to ebb out a meager life as a drone.'"

The man from Earth heard her as she was standing almost over him, "Here's the human, he's not dead yet; dazed, bloodied, definite broken bones. Do you recognize him?"

Both, of these fallen Winds, restored with Yazad's light, muscular and fit in their sleek black uniforms, but with amputated wings, knelt down next to him, beholding his swollen face, humanity, and vulnerability.

"No, but then again he always was hard to recognize by his outward appearance, a fallen star nonetheless. He has a penchant for hiding among the image bearers, as loathsome as they can sometimes be. Let's take him anyway. If he's someone special, and I doubt it, then we could use him to at least bargain for our wings. The new arrivals should be far enough downstream, we can reverse the vacuum, transfer at the service tunnel, and find a flyer to take him over the wall and the Desert of Sin. We must hurry, his injuries are serious."

"Let's wipe the blood off of his forehead to read his drone number... look at this, 00000000077627. What do you think of this number? Do these remind you of the words long ago delivered by Gabriel to Daniel the prophet by the rivers of Babylon."

The larger responded, "The Seven Weeks of Sevens and the Sixty-two Weeks of Sevens until the anointed is cut off? But these tags are random issue from the Sanctuary Corporation."

While the two sentinels worked to stabilize number 77627, his pain and shock slipped him in and out of consciousness. Picking up pieces of their conversation, he heard the female say, "If it is him, do you think he would help us? Maybe give us limited amnesty or restore our wings?"

"If he survives, it is possible. But he will have no power here--a mere man a long way from his home. This place will not be kind to him."

"Is that not the story of his life?"

The former North Korean winced in severe pain, as they carefully lifted him to the platform and placed him in the sled, "Ohh, ahh."

"Number 77627 is waking," she said, "he is trying to say something." They stood over him in the sled, eager to hear anything.

Mumbling several lines of gibberish, they'd all but given up on comprehending him when he gasped a question with a slight smile on his face, eyes blinking intermittently. "Do you think... you can distinguish... heaven... from hell?" The oriental man from the Earth spoke in the ancient dialect known only to those whose origin was the Blue Moon of Siyon, then sank unconscious again.

The stout half-restored Cherub became convinced of his identity, "Move him now. We have to save him! What mere mortal knows this language?"

Reversing directions, the sled whisked off into the nearby hillside tunnel. As their velocity increased the white rings of lights outlining the tube, flashed by faster and faster. Inside the sled, the seat and backrest lighting cast a pale blue aura over the three travelers who plunged through the underground dark strata.

"What if he dies, what if he should cease to be?" the female sentinel asked. "And what did he mean by, 'Do you think, you can tell heaven from hell?'"

The large one said, "What if he should die?... No one can know such a thing. It would be like asking what if all matter caved in on itself. It has never happened. I have not cried in eons, but for this pure act of courage I will cry. He knows we are deceived; nothing is good or evil, right or wrong anymore. We have chosen our own gods, Yazad-Beltshzan, who does not--cannot love anyone but himself. Our kind has no sense of knowing the truth because we decided, there is none."

The soft voice said, "The rumor about Ouriano, the Death Angel, you've heard? He believed those like us had a chance at redemption."

"If the Wounded One really made it this far, then you can ask him yourself, that is, if he survives."

"I previously had no reason to see him. I am sorry I was enraged with hatred towards him. Things are different now."

Chapter 34

*The Heir has an obligation to help them. But I
have a feeling he's going to be preoccupied.*

Cuzak nestled himself in the plush white leather chair,
high above the Huangpu river, scanning the Shanghai
waterway's front nightline. The Huangpu flowed through
the heart of the business district; a mix of office and condo
skyscrapers, spheres and needles. He could either enjoy
the view or activate the High Definition AMOLED display,
(active, matrix, organic, light emitting, diode), embedded
in the three-story board room windows.

Dressed in symbols of Earthly success, charcoal suit, white
stiff collar wrapped a half size too tight around his pock
marked neck, a shiny red tie tucked beneath the buttoned
jacket, his hair duck tailed, nails manicured, and makeup
softening the dark circles under his eyes--all served to belie
the wounds and creature beneath the drag. It worked for
others but not on him.

He knew too much after the centuries of evading and
plotting for the time at hand. On this night he wondered,
*And my reward for myself and my daughter in all of this
will be?*

The Sanctuary's board room table was equipped to seat
twenty four. Other than his chair and Ru's the remaining
hydraulic seats were recessed under burnished steel floor
plates. Behind them mounted on the wall was the stainless
steel logo of the Sanctuary Corporation; an oval canopy
atop a flaring tree trunk with a lone red, once bitten apple,
mounted against dark mahogany paneling. A single white
beam shone on the emblem, causing the red fruit to
glisten.

For this evening's occasion a thin purple haze of LED's
basked down on the long table for two as Cuzak gently
squeezed his daughter's hand and said, "Ru, as you flew in,

you must have seen the new 797, perched above the penthouse."

Ru answered, "With the spot lights on the logo, nose and tail, how could anyone miss it? You've parked it atop the highest office building in Shanghai, let alone when you crank up those engines."

"Ha, those are the quietest engines in its class. Precisely, we just finished our shakedown tests and want to use the plane to spearhead a world tour promoting the Sanctuary Corporation's transfer technology and the wonderful changes it will bring the oppressed.

On board, I've included suites for the world's religious leaders. And you my darling Maria will have your own accommodations in a luxury apartment at the rear of the superliner."

"What are we calling it, the Ark?"

"Please, I am serious."

"The Traveling Salvation Show?"

Ignoring the joke Cuzak continued, "This plane, with vertical landing and takeoff capability, hydrogen fuel eco-friendly vortex engines, will absolutely bring people out in droves. Our brand will become synonymous with human potential. The Chinese and U.S. Defense departments are next in line for this plane."

"I suppose our twenty percent stake in Boeing helped," added Ru.

"This plane will afford us the ability to hover over a city, an airport… it is the perfect platform for the beginning of our marketing plan to drum up the volunteers we need for the mass exodus. With the keys to this toy, I am giving you the new title of Vice President of Acquisitions and Mergers. You will of course need a little bit of a makeover. I love you but I don't want to see those black wings anywhere, at least not in public. That's where we need the human side, the softened Ru to show up."

"That's not something I always can control," she answered.

"You have to learn!"

"Like you did with Ouriano."

"I will overlook that comment. Dear, the gothic look has to go, at least when you are presiding over a board meeting. Your private excursions, well that is your business. Just don't bring any bad press. I know someone with your energy needs to get out to play now and then. Be discreet, that's all. Anyway, I want to drive up the shares of the Sanctuary stock even higher.

I want the price of our stock inflated to trade and buy out media and technology companies to further control and refine our consumer offers. If you repeat any message long enough, the image bearers will accept it."

"Father, if I might critique you?"

"Listening."

"The religious bent. That's going to make enemies isn't it?"

"What do you mean?"

"The religious acceptance of this new world is going to make or break our efforts. We could have a back lash of suicide bombers, radical millennial types, conservative voices, maybe all joining forces against us as a common enemy. What if the Vatican turns against you?"

"Us, darling, us, together forever, right? The Christians in Western Europe, North America, Catholics, Anglicans, etc, what is left of them, they are like a dripping faucet; no voice, no backbone. They have forgotten who they are. Those in the rest of the world, who are earnest and zealous, unfortunately can be broken by a few well placed crises like SARS, a famine, a revolution.

The fascists within Islam, they may see this as an opportunity to cleanse their lands, drive their unwanted sheep to us. The Hindus, the Buddhists, will simply incorporate our ideas. The Jews, on the other hand--now they concern me. They have interrupted several campaigns in the past. They are small in number, but have leverage over many of their enemies. I will keep my eye on them. If their prophets hold true, the Heir has an obligation to help them. But I have a feeling he's going to be preoccupied."

"What do you mean by preoccupied?" Ru asked, puzzled.

"The Wounded One's weakness is to personally get involved. Put himself, everything he owns, he's gained, at risk."

"You suspect, Yazad, Beltshzan would try to lure him, defenseless once again? That's legend anyway."

"Between you and me, what I am about to tell you in confidence, as father—daughter, this never can get out. Understand?"

"Certainly."

"This is all Beltshzan and Yazad think about. Every second, minute, hour, day, eon, of their contemptible existence, hatred of the Heir is at the core of their being. It is where the power of the darkened light is generated."

"Are you that way Father?"

"Long ago."

"And now?"

"Ru, it's too late for some of us."

Chapter 35

We are selling hope to slugs who believe they can jumpstart their dreary life with a bus ticket.

"No Ru, I am a realist, a survivor, and that's what I wish for you."

For a brief moment Ru felt as if there was a real connection between them, so her heart inquired further, "And the Juwaan, Lucas Tanner?"

Fearing he might appear weak, Cuzak turned his cold dark eyes toward her and said, "Why don't you tell me, about Dr. Tanner." Disappointed, she matched his prying stare reminding herself, *I should never get my hopes up with him. Why can't I have a regular father?*

As he searched for her allegiance, she downplayed her question, "I believe the Angel of Light anointed the wrong person when it came to Lucas. He wants to be left alone. His heart was never in his calling as a Juwaan."

"How do you know so much?" inquired her emotionless father.

Torn between two worlds she said, "There's no fight in him. He's off the map. He's contacted no media, given up his career and has spent little of the blind trust money from his patents."

Cuzak responded, "So Lucas has become a regular paperback writer, but with Ouriano's sword in addition to a pen. What if the Angel of Light's call is no respecter of the recipient? He could be incubating, slowly maturing. That would be an unforgiveable mistake on my part."

"You agreed that if they disappeared for good and didn't interfere, you wouldn't pursue them."

Cuzak veered his sight toward the large windows, and returned to his first line of thought, but not before tossing something unexpected to her, "I know that you love him.

You could have taken Lucas for yourself, killed Victoria, or left her for me. There is no man who could resist you."

For a couple of minutes, Ru and Cuzak sat silent watching the slow flotilla of blue, green, and yellow neon laced tourist ships parade by on the Yangtze tributary below.

Ru mulled his words, *He's right. There was something between us, but I couldn't hurt Victoria, force myself on Lucas, could I? No, that's crazy. Cuzak's planting something in my mind. Not going to let him. 'Greater is he who is in me, than he that is in the world.'*

She broke the silence, "Not everyone has a price. Some people are influenced by something more real, of greater substance. They are willing to die for what they believe."

Cuzak rebutted her, "A few more dying along the way doesn't matter, no one cares. I respect those who are holding out for the, how do they say it, 'Substance of things hoped for? The far distant land? The kingdom?' They of course are the minority of image bearers. Ru, some of the things you are bringing up have me concerned. Are you getting soft?

I expect you to appear, warm and gentle, no Goth, no wings in public. But that doesn't mean behind the scenes you would hesitate to twist a few arms... even necks if necessary. Am I clear?"

"Yes but,..."

"You've known how to inflict fear and pain since you were a teenager. Beltshzan admires your duplicitous qualities. He sees it as a sure way to lure your enemies into complacency. Just keep your good side in check; don't get carried away."

"I don't want to take any more innocent lives."

"Innocent lives? Where do you get innocent from? We are selling hope to slugs who believe they can jumpstart their dreary life with a bus ticket."

"But what is really there waiting for us," asked Ru "if the destination has not developed as planned?"

"The Earth is very ancient. The intricacies are hardly appreciated by the image bearers. They'll be the ruin of this place one day. Replicating this section of the cosmos is truly a God thing." Pausing to clear his throat, "Let me rephrase, a hyper-entity-class building endeavor."

As they talked, Cuzak released her hand to operate the display controls in the table top in front of him. With a few taps of his finger tips, a live high definition feed of Earth from a Chinese satellite filled the board room windows. "Replicating the crust of the planet floating on a molten core with oceans of liquid H_2O, proper land producing plate tectonics, volcanism, heat and cold distributions of weather patterns, has been a nightmare to reproduce."

Switching the view, Cuzak explained more, "This is the binary, or two star system we have named 'Pantos.' Of its twelve planets, the one suited for life is 'Krator.'"

Ru jumped in, "Nice to see actual footage of the secret planet we are launching our test subjects to. I ignored most of my religious instruction at the orphanage, especially Greek, but these names have deeper meaning, don't they? I remember, '*Pantokrator*,' is one of the early Church's titles of the Christ, the Panto-all, and Krator-powerful. The 'Omnipotent One' has a ring to it. How charming that the title has been repurposed."

"Yes, it goes without saying. Yazad began the development process some one hundred thousand Earth years ago; very little time on an evolutionary scale to build from scratch. Of course, once Yazad and Beltshzan have fully united things should improve. They'll be able to do more. That's why some elements of life had to be black marketed from the Blue Moon."

"What?"

"Oh, you have yet to meet Lamech have you? He is a beast of a proto image bearing species, a hunter, warrior, and builder. I am sure it somehow came through him. He took no second to even my species. Everything is for sale by him. He wrote the book on ego. He lives under house arrest on the isolated Island of Wandu. What in the local entity's name he is being preserved for, I don't know. Put that in your places to visit."

"I can hardly wait, especially if you think he is scum."

"That is beside the point. Yazad had a hard time replicating the essence of life itself, particularly at the microbial level."

"But is Krator viable for life?" asked Ru. "That's why we are doing all of this. We sent that first batch of North Koreans there, then other test batches from Cuba, Honduras, and Burma. And now we are selling it as a means to escape the local entity's judgment, restore the infected Winds, breed a better race, and redirect our evolution."

"Well put my dear." Cuzak zoomed in on Krator and its Binary stars, Pantos, on the thirty foot glass. Krator was colored by a purple haze over most of its surface, with a green belt circumnavigating the planet from its north to south pole several hundred miles wide. "Yes, Krator is viable but very crude at the moment. They've had problems with its spin so that most of the agricultural area is limited to the equatorial region where the radiation from Pantos borders with the shade of the back side of the planet."

"Krator is either a hot or cold planet."

"Yes, for now it spins on its east to west axis perpendicular to the binary stars. The fluctuation of Pantos' inter-orbit adds to the width of luminosity for our agricultural and bio-diverse green belt."

"So about seventy-five percent of the planet is uninhabitable for most plants, microbes, livestock, and image bearers? They don't have four seasons."

"You are correct Maria. Plans are underway for subterranean development in the scorched east side and frozen west of the planet to take advantage of milder substrates."

"It's a failed clone of the Earth isn't it? Hardly a Paradise we've sent these first groups to, huh father?"

"Does it matter? For those who want freedom from the local entity, they will receive what they desire. The Pantos planetary system is so distant, light from its two stars will never be viewed from Earth. And besides, the Chronos Black Hole, almost twice the diameter of the Milky Way stands in the way. The technology of Dr. Lucas Tanner and Dr. Victoria Pruett provided the last key to help us travel through the folds of space and time to alter history."

"Is it truly cut off?" said a despairing Ru.

"Yes."

"And that is a good thing?" she asked.

"You've got to serve somebody, darling."

Chapter 36

We orphans have a right to know

"Pam, will you quit being so nervous. You've been producing the 'Around the World' segment for almost fifteen years. You told me if I put this kind of exposé together you would back me. I need a budget for this."

"Like I said, it depends on what you have for me, Rulanda."

"Alright then, sit down. I have proof. I wanted you to be the first outside my videographer to see this." Rulanda operated the curved screen from her controls in the glass surface of the meeting room table. The lights dimmed as the video footage started.

"Tell me what it was like being married to the one entrepreneur the entire media world has come to affectionately refer to as 'The Colonel.'"

A woman's silhouette in a black monk's robe, sat before the popular blonde BBC news anchor, Rulanda Lakee, for the interview. The camera angle from the side had all but the tip of the guest's nose, lips, and chin blocked by the robe's hood. A voice distorter disguised her Armenian accent.

"What is it you are looking for, I understood we were here to talk about my father the late Orthodox Bishop, who suffered under the old Soviet Union's oppression?" said the nun, from the private hotel room in Kiev.

"The CEO of the Sanctuary Corporation," Rulanda showed her a picture on a thin electronic tablet, "you were briefly married to this man?"

"Yes, that's him. He hasn't aged in over three decades. Good for him. We never officially married in the church."

"You had a child together?"

"I would rather not say. Who told you this?"

"So it is true?" said Rulanda, "you know, a nun cannot lie, can she?"

The reluctant interviewee said, "If I told you all the truth about him, you'd call me a liar. He rescued me from a hellish life of prostitution. As I recovered from that, I slowly discovered his true nature, but our short honeymoon period ended when I became pregnant. He is not who he appears to be. I told him I wanted to give the child away fearing it would be like him, but he induced me into an early labor and took my baby from me, leaving me for dead. I never saw him or my baby again, except lately in the media. You must know I am not interested in trying to meet her."

"Hold on. You didn't want the child and he did?"

"Yes, it sounds convoluted, but desperate people do desperate things."

"What do you mean, he left you for dead?"

"The delivery of my child caused much blood loss. He and his doctor left me in a secluded place in the country side, no transportation, no communication, after they took my baby."

"So, you feared having a child that might become like him? Isn't that being overly judgmental on the future of a little innocent baby?"

The hooded woman took a deep breath. Her hands squeezed the cushioned arm rests and then responded, "Ms. Lakee, you don't believe in God do you? In God's judgment of evil? I don't fault you if you don't, but ignoring these realities won't make them go away."

"We are not talking about God here, but your child. But personally, I believe we should not judge others. I am a backslidden Anglican by birth."

The nun continued to speak, rather slow, "Some people have to meet real incarnational evil before they believe in God. I would not pursue this story if I were you. You have no one to protect you. Hah..."

"Why do you laugh?"

"Because your neutrality is a ruse. I will pray for you."

Rulanda shot back, "I am a big girl. I am not asking for your prayers. Whatever happens, happens, right? But let's get back to the subject of the innocent child you abandoned."

"Yes, as you say, 'I abandoned my baby.' Evil can be generational. I was young, and distressed. Socio-paths have family too. I didn't want to be a mother to one. I admit, my attitude was possibly a mistake." Rulanda kept glancing over to Pam to watch her reaction, hoping to set a date for the exposé.

"I promised not to give too much of your identity away, but you said you are of a religious order in the World Wide Armenian Church, with dioceses all over the world. Do you know who or where that child is today? Have you ever met him, or her?"

"Do you really need to know this?" the woman said in a regretful tone.

"Yes, this is why I set up the interview; Colonel Cuzak Runaldi is one of the most influential men in the world and most controversial because of this historic movement to patriate humans to another planet. Yet the public knows little about him. It is as if he surfaced out of nowhere."

"I have never met my daughter."

"So your child was a girl?"

"I am only guessing. I have seen a woman in the media, in the news, who sometimes is with the Colonel. She has some of my features from how I looked years ago, some from her father. But I would have to meet her up close."

"What features would you look for?"

"I can't answer that," the worried nun said, "You won't believe me."

"Please, try. This might have a happy ending."

"Alright, I would check her for wings. Her hands for claws. Her eyes, if they are like a predator."

Pam turned from the screen to give Rulanda a stoic glance she used to kill stories and added, "You're kidding. This is going in the slush pile."

Rulanda responded to the nun in the continuing interview footage, "What are you trying to say?"

"What I am saying Miss Lakee, is, if I ever met her, I could tell if she was our daughter. The Colonel has distinguishing characteristics once you get to know him intimately."

"So you are telling me that he is different than most men you have known and that his only purported daughter, one of his VP's who goes affectionately by Ru, is your common daughter."

The hooded nun hesitated then said, "Yes, it could be as you say. And now I am finished. I have nothing further to tell you. You don't believe me with the few scraps I have given you. Why should I give you more? This isn't what you initially invited me about. You lied to me!"

Blowing past the holy woman's efforts to leave the interview, Rulanda said, "No one is going to believe this revelation. I need something more for our audience."

"You want something to give an audience?" as her words picked up speed in her retaliation, "Tell them this; he is a dangerous man, unlike any other man. I returned home to the church because I felt like I had touched the Devil himself through him. He does not believe in God. Listen carefully to how he says things. He is in all of this for the money and to fool people."

"Do you have a picture of the two of you together?"

"No, he did not permit pictures of us together." Hripsimé hastily got up from her chair, unclipped the microphone and walked out of view of the camera.

Rulanda tried to stop her, "Please, we have a few more questions... I've worked hard to find you."

"Stop--seen enough," said Pam to Rulanda. "If someone finds out, or overhears what you are showing me, we are ruined. This is a personal attack on the Colonel and his daughter. The Sanctuary Corporation could end up being our majority owner soon. We can't air this. And you don't have enough facts. This is slander. Have you even found the two American scientists who you said Cuzak murdered for their technology patents?"

"No, but it's suspicious that his parents disappeared a few months after they went off the grid. His parents were missionaries in Peru, flew to Tokyo, then no one hears from them again. My guess is they are together, one big happy family. Get this, though supposedly dead, on behalf of Dr. Lucas Tanner and Dr. Victoria Pruett, the Sanctuary Corporation still holds a stock trust in their name. Info on it is closed however."

"This is all very enlightening Rulanda. For now, keep up your work-outs, facials, and reading skills. Leave the investigative reporting to others. Enjoy life, OK."

Rulanda protested, "But this woman feared for her life. Couldn't you hear it in her voice?"

"Who cued you in on this hermit Armenian nun? You didn't find her on your own."

"My sources are confidential Pam."

"Tell me..."

"An anonymous tip through a bot-email from an Apple Corporation server. But the lead, bloody panned out."

"Of course, they don't like the possibility of Colonel Cuzak's hostile takeover bid. They want to sink him with tabloid sleaze and let you become the sacrificial lamb."

"Red flags! I'm sorry, this isn't enough. If you can, go and talk to her alleged daughter, maybe see what her reaction is? You'll need to do it in person. Until then, I don't want any piece of this interview being leaked. This isn't your property to shop around."

"Of course, believe me, I tried calling her before. She's never returned my messages. She won't do anything that would hurt their Sanctuary Corporation stock price."

Pam smiled, "Leave her a pleasant message that you've talked to her mother. She'll meet. Now go home and rest. Shut the door please. I am going to do a little work from here."

"Sure thing Pam," said Rulanda as she rose and walked out angry and dejected. She knew she needed more reliable sources and info to prove Cuzak was hiding something. But as soon as she left the room Pam made a video call using the wall screen.

"Pam," the person answered, "what do you need? I told you to only call if this is an emergency." Ru's face, her bobbed hair and black vest filled the screen.

"This qualifies; I have the footage of Rulanda Lakee meeting a woman who claims she is your mother. Rulanda is going to try and schedule a meeting with you. She won't give up on discrediting your father. The woman in the video says some weird things. Sounds like a kook. I told Lakee she needed more credible evidence."

"What weird things?" Ru inquired.

"She alluded to your father being evil and some personal things about you, like claws, wings and such nonsense. She wanted to give you away even before your birth."

Ru did her best to purse her lips and smile, "With the upsurge in our stock values, I've had lots of contacts claiming to be related to me. You did the right thing Pam. I'll handle this from here. Send me a copy of the footage. Thank you for keeping me informed. How's that preferred Sanctuary stock performing for you?"

"Six hundred percent the last year, I'll be able to bloody quit this job and relax instead of escaping through one of your Hub Stations."

"Good choice Pam. I see a promotion coming once the acquisition is made. Keep me posted. Sit on the video. Bye."

After the call ended, Ru entered the restroom on her company plane as the custom 797 streaked toward the next destination. "What are you?" she asked, pressing her forehead and palms against the mirror. "Your mother's alive. We orphans have a right to know."

Chapter 37

I am still defiant, but not against God.

Ru finished her espresso and walked outside into the heart of the city of Vagharshapat, also known to every true Armenian as Etchmiadzin, a mix of new and old. Many of the buildings were destroyed in the great Earthquake of 1988, but some had remained remarkably stable. On this morning she took off on foot, her destination only several blocks away to the Holy Etchmiadzin. In the silhouette of Mount Ararat stood the Cathedral she hoped might provide answers about herself she couldn't get from her father.

Every face she passed on the street, she scrutinized hoping to find the remnants of someone she might be related to: the old woman sweeping in front of a dress shop, young cosmopolitans--heads bent down at their phones while waiting for a bus, children on the way to school. Ru felt good on this morning, dodging cars as she crossed the streets, *Maybe I will recognize someone!* Finally arriving on the campus, she found the admin building and promptly entered the restroom.

She practiced her smile in the mirror then pulled out the cross, given to her by Veezon. "Is this gift a blessing or a burden?" she asked herself. No longer hidden under her vest, she kissed the front and back of the heirloom and then let it dangle over her black leather corset fitting vest. With her long black leather duster coat on to cover most views of the tight hip riding leather pants, her stylish high healed black leather boots were still visible. She knew it was at best border line appropriate attire for visiting the Holy See of the Armenian Church. "Lord please have mercy," she prayed before walking down the hall for her appointment.

Meeting strangers was never a problem, but today she was nervous. The mother of pearl inlaid cross normally rested under her clothing, a private memento, but on this day it seemed right to wear it openly, for it had come home to its place of origin. Ru's tourist pamphlet described the Holy See at the Etchmiadzin as "the place of the Only Begotten Descended, who struck the Earth with a Golden Hammer," headquarters of the World Wide Armenian Church.

Ru knocked on the tall wood door of the communications office, but no one answered. Taped on the door was a small note she couldn't decipher. Just before she found someone to help, she heard hard leather shoes echo off the granite floor, and turned to see coming down the hall to her right a black robed man with a hood, gold rimmed glasses, gray medium beard, a large silver ornate cross jangling on his chest. "Miss Ruvale Marija Zvonimira? Here for the appointment?" he asked smiling.

Fumbling to lift up his robe with one hand, he handed her a stack of administrative papers with the other so he could pull out his key ring from his pants pocket. "Please hold these papers for me so I can unlock the door. Sorry I am late."

"Bishop, Father Svarian?" she asked.

"Bishop is fine, better would be Jerry. You are not of the Holy Armenian Church are you? Croatian?"

"By orphanage. You pronounced my name correctly. I am impressed. It's a long story. Thank you Bishop, Jerry if you insist, for seeing me on such short notice." He appeared to Ru as genuine, around fifty-five, American accent.

"By way of Detroit. We are all over the world now," he said.

"I came by way of vacation in Istanbul, and decided to take a detour to Armenia for personal reasons."

While they exchanged pleasantries in the hallway, several priests walked by taking more than a casual interest in Father Svarian's guest.

"Please follow me into my office, more privacy." Upon entering she noted several ancient wooden shepherding staffs leaning in the corner against his shelves, which held hundreds of tightly packed hardbound books. The paper and bindings gave off a musty smell associated with old libraries. Surveying his office Ru could not help but to notice on the wall in a vertical glass case to the right of his desk an especially dark, twisted, and knotty staff with several carved crosses inlaid with mother of pearl, somewhat like her cross. "Set those papers there, on the one empty spot on the desk. Thank you Ms. Zvonimira. Do you travel everywhere alone?"

Talking to his back while he walked around to the other side of his desk she said, "My friends call me Ru. I couldn't get my girl friends to come with me. We are going to connect in a few days back in Rome. But here I am. You have a remote, but beautiful country."

"Historically, Armenia is a difficult land to tame. Sit down, please. Now on the phone you mentioned your cross and a relative who might be serving in the church? Do you have a name for me? Some information cannot be communicated because of the hostile environments some of our clergy serve in."

"Here, I am not skilled in Armenian," Ru pulled the chain and cross over her head and dangled it above his desk. "The back of this cross has a name. Can you tell me where this came from, who the owner is?"

"May I?" he asked. After taking it from her he slumped back in his chair holding and rubbing the pendant. The only muscles in his face to move were several tense furrows above his brow. To her surprise he kissed the piece, waved it in his hand in the sign of the cross over his forehead and chest. Rolling his chair closer to his desk he leaned forward, "Forgive me," as he shoved half of the bureaucratic reports, budgets, assignments, press releases, and disciplinary notices off of his desk, spilling on the floor, to examine the precious cross even closer.

Father Svarian laid the cross on the surface of his oak desk and positioned a metal spring loaded lamp with magnifying glass in line with his eyes. The fluorescent lamp highlighted the changing shades as he shifted it with his fingers; crystalline white with pinks and blues, also secondary streaks of yellows and purples. The oyster shell lining was held together by ancient but supreme craftsmanship; a frame of heavy silver based pewter with the distinctive flared crowns on the tips of the cross. Flipping it over, he easily read the back; "Սուրբ Հռիփսիմէ," or "Holy Hripsimé." The Armenian language and script had barely changed over the last two thousand years.

Ru's curiosity got the best of her, leaning forward in her chair to ask, "Father, what do you think?"

Reclining from the desk, collapsing the lamp out of the way, he said, "This style of cross at one time was very common in an age when monasticism and celibacy were much more popular. We are a land of old and decaying monasteries. Hundreds of them were destroyed by the Tartars of the thirteenth century, the Ottomans in the genocide of 1915, most of the others decimated by the Soviets, age and earthquakes. But our heritage is also now preserved by our Diaspora located outside our country."

Ru slumped in her chair but wasn't about to give up. She thought, *There has to be a reason Ouriano wanted me to have this cross. The Bishop must know more. Why would he shove half the work off his desk for this?*

"Where did you get this cross?" he asked.

"When I made a profession of faith, a friend in America gave it to me as a gift."

"Hmm, there is more to your story isn't there, much more," said Father Svarian as he read her body language.

Ru fidgeted with how to answer him without letting it get too complicated, "You are a Black Monk yourself. Sworn to celibacy and married to God? Yes?"

He nodded his affirmation under the shadow of his hood saying, "This is true."

Ru said, "In a sense that is why I often dress in black. I didn't realize it until now, Father. You have already enlightened me even if you don't tell me anymore. My black outfit at one time was my defiance against the world, my lostness. I am still defiant but not against God."

Chapter 38

No one comes to Armenia merely to find the craftsman behind an antiquated pendant.

"Against whom or what are you defiant?" the elder Bishop asked.

"Against those unseen forces of the dark realm, the ones people either pretend they can control like a self-appointed shaman or those powers many believe to be fairy tales. I know them too well."

Rubbing again the smooth finish of the inlaid cross with his thumbs, Father Svarian said, "If you follow your path focusing your eyes only in defiance of darkened light, you will fail. Show me your heart child, that I might help you."

"How can I do that? I hardly know you. I didn't think I was asking for much, please just lead me to the owner of this cross. It means so much. So many things I can't tell you."

"Then lead us in a prayer. Your prayer will be the proof of whether I should trust a strange woman in black. No one comes to Armenia merely to find the craftsman behind an antiquated pendant."

"I am not suitable for this Father,"

"Go ahead."

Ru closed her eyes feeling somewhat humiliated, but submitted to his spiritual authority. She gritted her teeth then took a deep breath to relax. Here I go, "Dear Lord, I came looking for answers. I've tasted darkness. Parts of me are still there. I need both your justice and mercy. Forgive me for presuming that you were like me. You are not. You are far superior, more holy, beautiful, and perfect. Surely the plans of evil are always before you, even amusing you. You must laugh. But while you are laughing, I am crying. I... I... want a real father and mother to hold me and tell me who I am. Is that too much to ask?" She exhaled again and peeked up at the Pastor, "That's all I can muster."

Ru lifted her eyes with her head still bowed as Father Svarian stood up and opened the glass case and lifted out the staff she had noticed on the wall. He took it and reached over the desk, gently placing the symbol of his Great Shepherd across the top of her head with one of the shimmering inlaid crosses intentionally touching her hair. "You are in need of a blessing. You cannot accomplish your call alone, for it is not yours to own. His sheep know his voice, and He recognizes them."

He finished with an ancient borrowed benediction:

"Now the God of peace, who brought up from the dead the great Shepherd of the sheep through the blood of the eternal covenant, even Jesus our Lord, equip you in every good thing to do His will, working in us that which is pleasing in His sight, through Jesus Christ, to whom be the glory forever and ever. Amen."

"Amen," followed Ru.

The Father gently smiled at her and returned to his seat holding the ancient staff across his lap. Ru returned with a quick and confused half-second smile, still wondering if she would receive any practical help leading her toward flesh and blood answers.

"This pastoral staff has anointed and ordained many famous priests, rulers, and martyrs in the past. I don't bring it out of moth balls for just anyone."

Ru asked him, "You know something. You must tell me. The crosses match, don't they?"

"Yes they do. In most cases, crosses like this are little more than cheap costume jewelry, but yours is different. There have been some changes in our language but not as much as say, Old to Modern English. The script is reminiscent of fourth century. After the Martyrdom of Hripsimé and the death of over thirty fellow virgins toward the end of the third century, she soon became venerated as a Saint. Many women wanted to be like her, set aside with a vow of chastity for God's work."

"Like in a Convent?"

"Within a hundred years, so many women flocked to this hermitage existence that the head of the church forbid women from such escapism, instead encouraging them to concentrate on raising families."

"Sounds sexist."

"In an ironic way, yes. Some suppose women helped add to their salvation by birthing children; a different time and place."

Ru smiled, "You still don't have women clergy do you?"

"No, but we are experimenting with nuns, deaconesses. But back to your cross, this cross was made by the same person as those in this staff. This much silver with lead is never used in pewter today, mostly cheap tin. Which leads us back to what you want to know, 'Where does the staff come from?"

"They are a match."

"This staff was gifted to my predecessor's predecessor. The office is larger than the man. Back then, under the Soviets our church was at times, in disarray, our places of worship destroyed, desecrated, turned into stables. Anyway he had a beautiful daughter who disappeared. Some say he gave the matching cross to her when he hid the staff."

"What happened to her?"

"He had named her Hripsimé, after the St. Hripsimé Church on this campus. A Russian General wanted her as his wife. When she refused, he sold her to a bar owner somewhere in the former Yugoslavia, who made her earn her keep as a prostitute. Hripsimé's father never heard from her again. He died a few years later in a Soviet Gulag himself because he continued a public protest."

"His daughter, where is she now?"

"She died," he said, causing Ru to bury her face in her hands.

"No! That can't be. I heard rumor, I mean I assumed this cross would lead me to a happy ending."

"She died to the world, Ms. Zvonimira."

Ru lifted her face, wiping a tear, and tilted her head slightly trying to comprehend if there was something else he wanted to say, but he showed no emotion.

Ru probed him to clarify, "What do you mean-- she died to this world, but is still alive? Or she physically died?"

The Pastor tilted his head up and down, "yes," then smiled and said, "Yes, she is one of our deaconesses who would love to become a priest if that change ever comes about."

Ru could not hide the excitement at the prospect of meeting someone who could help her put the pieces of her life together or at least help her understand her father. "Can I see her? I want to return this cross to its rightful owner. I must meet her."

Pastor Svarian pulled his hood backward and revealed his scruffy gray mostly bald head, and began to laugh. "If I send you to Hripsimé, please be respectful of her solitude. She might take the cross without answering any of your questions. There was a reporter from London she met with who wanted to ask questions about her father. It didn't go well from what little she related. I'll call and tell her to expect...?"

"Possibly a distant relative, I am working on a family tree."

"I see. Go then. Let me know what happens. You can find her today waiting for a tourist group at the Khor Virap, the 'deep pit.' She likes to go early and stay late to pray."

Ru changed her mind, "On the other hand I'd rather you didn't tell her I am coming."

"Certainly Ms. Zvonimira, but before you leave, please tell me something. Are the Hub Stations for real? Is there a place we can go to start our life all over if the Earth no longer holds promise for us?"

Ru became flush with embarrassment as she had not acknowledged anything about her job or famous dad. "Oh Father, please don't tell anyone I came to see you or demand exactly why I came to find this woman. I will tell you, talking to Hripsimé is related to the Hub Stations. And off the record, I would advise anyone to remain unless called to go."

Chapter 39

*To discover our ancient roots, we often
presuppose our ancestors found theirs.
What if they didn't?*

Captivated by her surroundings and the rarified air, Ru felt at one with what could be her homeland, in the upper stone courtyard of Khor Virap, little more than an hour's drive from Etchmiadzin to the south. It rested on the edge of the vast green Ararat Plain, where this Armenian pilgrimage center watched guard over the majestic cloud and snow topped Mount Ararat. Shadows cast on the inner courtyard by the thick fortress walls left the five story stone sanctuary to alone absorb the bright late afternoon sun. The seventh century monastery was built on the site of the pit where St. Gregory the Illuminator was held captive for thirteen years at the end of the third century under King Tiridates III. After the cruel King went insane, his sister released Gregory in an act of desperation to come and pray for his healing.

But the land became secondary to the woman Ru identified across the courtyard. "That's her," she almost blurted out. Trying to conceal her attention, she saw nothing distinguishing about the middle-aged tourist guide apart from most women her age, except she wore no makeup, and kept a white head covering. To Ru, her loose long sleeve white blouse and shin length puffy light blue skirt matched with brown laced boots seemed antiquated but not strange to the region. Ru was curious to recognize any shared features. Hripsimé appeared to have lost her once smooth olive skin, to a premature aged tan-leather; a sign of the time she spent in the cold dry winds and harsh summer heat.

"This is wonderful," said Ru, "She is giving her life to greet the Armenian Diaspora, tourists coming home from around the world in hopes to find what I am looking for. Everyone needs to discover their roots, I must know if this is my birth mother." She watched as Hripsimé snapped one last photo of a family, and then waved goodbye escorting the pilgrims toward the exit ramp.

As she began to close the tourist gate, the nun stopped to turn her head and view the straggler still admiring the setting. "Every good thing has an end," she called to Ru, "You should have joined the tour earlier. I am sorry, but we are closing. We will be open tomorrow morning at ten. Can you come back?"

Ru approached, smiling, blatantly staring at her name tag and said, "Sister Hripsimé, I love your name."

"Thank you, but it is common, you know the story."

Ru said awkwardly, "Yes, I do know the story. It is very tragic, how she was killed. But her death set the stage for something very good."

"That is the lesson," said the nun who began to walk Ru out, but noticed that she did not follow her.

"I am interested in another lesson. I'll make a donation, anything, if you will please give me a few minutes of your time right now. I talked with Father Svarian today and he told me you were the person to visit."

"Let me guess, Father Svarian took a staff out of the glass case and prayed for you?"

"Yes, why, did he call you?"

"No, but he is a great PR man. He does that for everyone. He's genuine. I get someone every week who hangs behind and wants to ask questions about the history and the legends. We are an old church, a combination of strange fiction and stranger facts."

"I know I must seem like just another tourist or pilgrim," Ru said, pulling out the cross from her vest. "Please, Father Svarian said you might recognize this."

Ru watched Hripsimé's reaction closely as she held the cross and examined it, lifting it up over the line of shade into the sunbeams. Hripsimé could not hide her bedazzlement by the pendant. As it twirled in the wind and setting sunlight, it glistened and took her to a past painful time in her life. Though her face remained stark, Ru noted the tears welling in her eyes.

"Come with me now," she said to Ru, nervously avoiding direct eye contact, first leading her to the large wooden door-gate she needed to lock, and then to her office, constructed inside one of the outer walls near a small chapel. In her cramped office Ru observed two old metal folding chairs facing her gray metal desk. Behind the desk sat a worn out black vinyl office chair with layers of silver duct tape over the cracks. And on the stone wall behind it hung Hripsimé's framed Deaconess Certificate, a recent color photo of herself dressed as she was today, and a black and white framed picture of a much younger woman. To Ru, the young woman's face in the old picture bore a striking resemblance to her own.

Ru began to sit down but was prevented. "No, no! We will talk standing up because you cannot stay long. Where did you get this cross?" the nun said in a stern manner.

"I can't really tell you. A friend in the U.S., Texas, gave it to me as a gift. I followed the name on the back."

"Who are you? Why are you bringing this to me? Thousands and thousands of these were made after the third century. It means nothing. I have seen many of these. So what? Pilgrims bring them to me all the time."

"My name is Ru, Ruvale Marija Zvonimira," as she searched for a reaction from Hripsimé, but found none. "What would you say if I told you an angel gave this to me?"

The nun extended her hand to shake goodbye and said, "I would say that is nice. I am Sister Hripsimé Madoyan, I believe in angels--so end of conversation. You should go now. I have important things to attend to. Come back tomorrow."

Ru surprised, decided to reveal more, "I met my father when I was twenty-seven. He is, you might say very different. He told me that my mother died in child birth. He left her to die bleeding, never the chance to hold her baby. That is an awful thing to hear about your mother, don't you think?"

Chapter 40

Yet somehow dark places help us see the light.

"That all depends on what type of baby it was," said the nun, her chin trembling. Her immediate response plunged through Ru like an unsuspecting knife to the back.

Ru fought a flood of tears for the second time in one day, "What type of baby was it, you ask? What in the world do you mean?"

Hripsimé stammered through her words, staring at the stone floor as if ashamed, "If the baby was good... and of this world... then it should live. If it was evil, then it would be better off not being born."

"How would anyone know this about their baby? They all come into the world innocent. No one can judge a baby!"

"True for human babies, but not if it is a devil child. They are destined to be evil."

Ru was stunned but escalated her volume with each question like a prosecutor, "Did you try to abort such a child thirty years ago, a baby you carried? A baby you had with a man named Cuzak? Did you?"

With each question, Hripsimé Madoyan sank deeper and deeper into regret about her baby surviving, and Ru could feel it. Cuzak's daughter became so angered, disappointed in the truth, that she didn't notice her own wings had unfurled casting a shadow on her mother, blocking the light from the lamp against the wall.

She heard Hripsimé mumble, 'yes,' then asked, "Did you really not want to give birth to me, but end my existence? Oh, why did I even try and find you?"

Her hands and voice shaking, Hripsimé said, "Cuzak brought a doctor to a remote place where he forced a cesarean section on me and took the baby. I thought I was going to have an abortion. He took my baby and left me to die."

"No, you disgusted him, that's why he left you isn't it? You were abandoning your daughter before she was born!" Ru's anger cut off her seeping tears. "Look at me. Look up at me Sister Hripsimé when I am talking to you. I deserve that!"

Ru's mother refused to look up as she wept, so Ru placed her fingers under her chin, and lifted her head. When she did, Hripsimé's grief turned into horror, knocking Ru's hand away, "You, you are evil! Look at you, I was right. You should not have lived. What do you want from me? Leave me! Indeed, you are unmistakably Cuzak's child." Making the sign of the cross, Hripsimé laid her forehead on her desk and wept aloud.

Catching a glimpse of her own shadow, Ru at once realized how her mother had seen her; the pulsating veins beneath her wings, crackled blue nails grown like short knives, and eyes of a snake. Disgusted she had allowed this unintentional makeover in front of her mother, Ru covered her face with her thick manly hands, concentrating to make it all recede.

Slowly the wings and the nails retreated, the eyes returned to normal, and she lowered her hands. Ru wanted to start over, prove she was not a repulsive creature and said, "I am your child too. I am not evil. I am like everyone else, good and evil. Maybe I should have been aborted, but I am here now, with you. That's all that matters. I've been wearing this cross, it's yours. It reminds me of who I am."

Ru's mother, crying face down on her desk, moaned, "Leave me! You don't want me as your mother. We have nothing in common. The last time I wore that cross, it was taken from me by Cuzak at your birth. He said I was not worthy of it. He ripped it off of my neck. Even so, you are not like everyone else, blackness pulsates in your veins. You are a granddaughter of the great slanderer. In the name of the Father, the Son, and the Holy Ghost I resist and reject everything you stand for. How dare you wear that cross and lecture me! I don't ever want to see it again. It did nothing to protect me."

"Please, Sister Madoyan, look at me. I am back to normal. I didn't will myself into this world. You had a part in conceiving me, so how could you abandon me? Did you ever try to find me? Did you at least pray for me?"

Sobbing less, sitting upright in her chair and wiping her eyes, her mother said, "Why did you come back? You should have never sought me—oh St. Gregory, sweet Jesus, deliver me from this torment."

Ru waited until the peak of her mother's emotions subsided, then stepped around the desk and wrapped her in her arms. She did not fight her embrace, as Ru spoke softly, "But I need your help. Your God needs your help. I don't know what to do. You alone would understand more than anyone in the world."

Sniffling, opening her eyes and wrapping her arms around Ru's waist, Hripsimé said, "I never had another child. I truly deemed what I was doing as right, but then I doubted the rest of my life. I've been paying God back ever since, pretending you never happened. Do you want to know the mother who gave up on you?" Hripsimé examined Ru's face and placed her finger tips on her cheeks. She could not deny the likeness. "You have the image of your mother."

Hripsimé explained more, "I was nineteen. My father was a widower, a Bishop in the Armenian Church, but dominated by the Soviet Occupation. He couldn't protect me. He said my beauty attracted too much attention. A Soviet General wanted me as his mistress. I refused, so he sold me. I was traded as property, passed around from bar owners to brothels.

Cuzak liberated me from a Turkish hotel owner who was using me as his concubine and prostitute for the guests. He was staying at the same hotel in Istanbul. He is ageless it seems. After I cleaned his room, he tipped well and talked to me. I was supposed to bring in extra money from the male guests. But he treated me like a person, not a prostitute. He took me away from it all. When I sensed God had abandoned me, he was there to rescue me."

"So that's how it happened?"

"Yes, we became lovers. He told me he had never married, had no children, no wife. He was rich. Within the year I became pregnant. He had a cabin in the countryside. Sometimes he would go away on business trips for weeks at a time. There was a musty basement in the house he kept locked. I found a key one day and went in. The steps went down several stories. I could sense evil the moment I entered. There was a worship area; half melted candles on an old church communion table, an inverted cross, a pentagram on the wall beneath a tapestry of a multicolored bird like a peacock."

"Yazad," whispered Ru, "what else?"

"I saw dark feathers strewn on the floor, an open coffin with a mummified body with wings, a long spear clasped in its hands. Stacked in the corner were old oil paintings from centuries past. Cuzak was in them. His likeness from different eras of history was in the paintings. I vomited. But then I heard him coming into the house calling for me. I fled up the stairs, but a day later he confronted me. He knew I had found his little secret."

"Did he hurt you?"

"No, on the contrary, he apologized that he had not told me sooner about how he desired to severe old family ties, but couldn't without being killed. 'One day,' he said, 'this will all be over. It will run its course; I must maintain my loyalty until the end.' He refused to give me details in case I was captured."

"Did you believe him?"

"I tried to believe him, but his evil in the basement, his secret past lives, the ties to the Devil and other deities drove me back to the faith of my family. Cuzak had me captive. He permitted me to attend a little chapel service once a week while he waited in the car. That actually empowered me. I told him, 'I don't want the baby. The baby is a mistake. I will not give birth to anything resembling what I saw in the coffin. We both will be better off if I have an abortion and we go our own ways.'"

Hripsimé's explanation grew deeper, "I promised Cuzak that, I wouldn't tell a soul about anything. But no, he wouldn't permit me to leave or take his child's life. I am sorry Ru. I thought I had a devil child in me, so I wrote a long note to the local pastor to explain my plight and ask for help.

When he contacted authorities, all my crazy story did was land me in a mental hospital under anti-psychotic medication until I was near full term. He took you away from me, but I confess, I was afraid to find out about you. And,... here you are standing in front of me, beautiful, and holding the original cross made to commemorate the real Holy Hripsimé. Can you ever forgive me?"

"I don't feel the need to forgive you. I am already blessed to find you alive. But understand, I do forgive you." In saying this Ru and her mother exchanged kisses on the left and right cheek. "I know this is awkward, thank you for telling me what happened. But, how did you come to such a remote place in service to God?"

Hripsimé responded, "Enough about me, I want to know about you. All is fair is it not?"

"Yes, I have much to tell. Where do I start?"

"You can start with what is important. Who do you serve? You sound like you have repudiated your father's ties? Yet, I caught a glimpse of you earlier?"

"Repudiate is a good word. Until recently I didn't believe in anything. It's all very complicated," began Ru.

"Such is the nature of evil; it entangles and gives us excuses. Light is simple, good," said Hripsimé, "yet somehow dark places help us see the light."

Chapter 41

It is a special place, the pit which overlooks the valley of the flood. From there you can see the will of God.

"That is my life story, with a few missing pieces. That's why I am here," ended Ru as they sat sipping coffee in front of the toasty fireplace adjoining her office, late past midnight.

"You really are fighting in the dark. I don't believe I can sleep tonight after digesting so much," said Hripsimé. "What you've told me would be considered the edge of fantasy except I knew your father. Let's go outside for a breath of cool air and see if the angels are playing on Ararat tonight." She grabbed the coffee pot and poured them another cup before she led Ru to the floor above, where they followed a stairway to the roof. "There," Ru's mother pointed, "maybe you have visited? I was hoping you could tell me if you've seen the Ark?"

"On Ararat? No, I've had enough other supernatural things to worry about, but it is most beautiful tonight. I hear the distant thunder on the mountain. Do you hear it?"

"My hearing is not as good as yours, my child."

Ru continued, "The Blue Moon of Siyon has many mountains like this, but they experience no night." A veil encircled the peak which emerged at the center. The smooth ivory cloud bank in the half moon light flashed every few seconds in pink, orange, and yellow from the lightning generated by the static charges as it rubbed against the ice and rock mass in the sky.

Ru asked, "Do you believe the story of Noah, that there was a great flood which destroyed most of the world's image bearers?"

Sipping her coffee first, she answered, "If you vote by whether we humans had it coming to us, yes. If I am to believe your elaborate plot, then it sounds like a deluge will return, but not by water. If the demons are as fearful of the future and the local entity as you say, then they must believe coming judgment is a sure thing. You asked me to help you. I am a woman of prayer. I lead these tourists who come every day looking for mystery, connection. It is not so easy as making a trip to another place.

The real work of faith is to take an inner trip of the soul. Being sick and tired of where you are in life can be the first step in a true pilgrimage. I am not here for the tourists. I am here to pray. If St. Gregory could pray in the dungeon below for thirteen years, relying on scraps thrown down to him to survive, then I can at least enter that dark place of the soul every morning and evening. It helps me to see the light."

"Will you take me there, show me?" asked Ru.

"Child, I am more than happy to take you. It is under this building. But I cannot guarantee you will find what you are looking for or see what I see. It is a special place, the pit which overlooks the valley of the flood. From there you can see the will of God."

"You would suppose from up here you would see more?"

"Be careful little eyes what you see. Come, I will show you the pit, and we will pray."

Ru resisted somewhat, "It's nice here on the roof. Why an old dungeon?"

"You said you wanted help?"

"Take me."

"Then follow," said Hripsimé as she returned down the stairs to the courtyard and next-door to the chapel. "This is the number one spot for tourists, especially for young people. They want the experience of descending through the narrow opening. It is about thirty feet deep. Twenty-five metal steps is all. And it used to be much deeper. It was known as Khor Virap, 'The Pit,' long before this was a holy place. Holy places are made when people touch the face of their suffering."

The steel steps clanked as Ru followed her mother down the steep railed ladder, through the narrow neck into the bottle shaped room. A dozen old framed icon depictions of saints adorned the moldy gray rock walls. Several were inset within a few small alcoves for their devotion.

"I can see you have graffiti artists here too. The air is pretty stank. I can't imagine thirteen years," said Ru.

"Light your candle from mine and place it on the table, before we turn off the service lights," Hripsimé told Ru, "and I know this is not orthodox, but ask Saint Gregory the Illuminator, or the Holy Hripsimé to help you see." They both placed their new stubby white candles on a small table covered with layers of yellowed wax.

"Here we go, lights off." The only other light in the round black stone room came through a small high window, where the sporadic lightning on Ararat sent a small reminder of the outside world. "Imagine if every night the flickering light was all anyone had," said Ru.

"If what you said about your father and the Sanctuary Corporation is true, this will become a reality for many. Yes, you'd better learn to fight in the dark."

"What do we do next?" asked Ru.

"We wait, maybe until dawn. I realize from the predatory eyes you inherited from your father, you can see in the night, but there is another type of vision which must be learned, a gift."

Ru persisted with her mother in silent vigil as the candles slowly burned, the soot thickening and the oxygen depleting. She centered on the flicker of the candles and checked now and then on her mother, whose eyes were almost shut. In the third hour Hripsimé began swaying in front of the candles like she was floating. Ru, concerned she might fall, moved closer to her side, where she also heard her mumbling.

"Hripsimé," Ru gently whispered to her ear, but received no response. Upon closer inspection, her eyes were following something not in the immediate realm. Then without warning she reached out and clutched her daughter's hand, squeezing it much harder than Ru imagined. And as she did, Ru's eyes too began to twitch. The soot covered stones of the confining room faded, giving up their secrets while being replaced with a more certain reality. Together they swayed before the burning candles, their bodies present but their spirits soaring at the beckoning call of another.

Shem's Log

++

Blue Moon Chronicles Book III, 12.5

Date: At the disappearance of the Heir
Binary G-Class star system, Yazad sector
Fifth generation Angelus
Beginning of mass exit to Sanctuary
Subject: Call Through the Dark Cloud of Unknowing

The One beyond the Magnificon Gates once said after descending to the plains of Shinar, "As they have come together with one language, there is now nothing impossible for them."

Indeed it would appear nothing is impossible for the image bearers. Their towers and pyramids reach beyond the heavens to new worlds shrouded in darkness. They have learned to manipulate the fabric of the cosmos this side of the Magnificon. They suppose they will become gods in the land of Two Suns Rising, guarded forever from a love which might redeem them.

And what of my beloved Ouriano and his rag-tag remnant of Vigilantes? Most of them suffer from the infection. I wish I knew of a greater plan, but nothing convincingly coherent has yet been revealed.

And to make matters worse, the Heir himself has gone missing. He has a history of coming and going at his private whims. But what if he needs help? I detest this new place, "The Sanctuary." I'd rather call it "Babylon."

Shem, from the Blue Moon, the caverns of Sharu

++

Chapter 42

But here of all places, in this pit, I am with God.

The power of Hripsimé's prayers pulled Ru with her into a whirlpool of pure black velvet. No reference points, no weight, no created matter, no light on any spectrum registered as Ru's eyes roamed for some hint of even the smallest wavelength of radiation.

"There is nothing to see, to touch," Ru said to herself, "yet there is something in this nothing. What is it? This is no conduit, no worm hole, this is different."

Slipping through the dimensional rift, Ru could clearly hear what her mother was praying, as she communed with the primordial liquid coal enveloping them, "Where can we go to flee from your Spirit? Even if we go down to the depths of the ocean or take up on wings to the far side of the sea, you are there. For even the darkest of nights is as light to you." In the midst of her prayers they sank deeper into the dark as if they had gone overboard mid-Atlantic. But Ru discovered this ocean of her mother's was the source of life itself.

The mother of Cuzak's daughter continued to pray, "Come Holy Trinity, who before time or creation existed. Come Spirit who hovers over the face of the deep bringing order to chaos. Come Holy Father who called all that is, into being and with true light calls us to be transformed into the beloved Kingdom of the risen Only Begotten, who pounded the Earth with his Golden Hammer, smashing the stronghold of his adversaries. Hear our prayers. Let your humble servants be counted worthy to understand these ruminations, which Ru has laid before you. These plans, this counsel was given birth by your enemies in secret to exploit the meek and lowly of the Earth. Let her live to see them smashed to pieces like old pottery. Let the One on your Holy Hill of Zion, who carries the royal scepter of all wisdom, scoff at their machinations. Let not your enemies triumph or desecrate your manifest purpose. Prepare us to guard and defend that which is good and holy against all evil and against worlds with devils filled--Amen."

For the next few moments Ru experienced perfect peace suspended and floating in the dark divine plasma. "I could stay here forever, safe, content. This presence, mother, your prayers, I have never experienced such security, such reality cloaked in darkness."

"You are adrift in the hands of God my daughter, the One who knows all, sees all, is before all. When the mountains fall into the sea and all that you know is rolled up, God will still be here."

Astonished, Ru asked, "But here of all places, in this Pit, you say, 'We are with God?'"

"Our calm assurance before the storm, if what you say is true. Set loose your soul and listen. May God have mercy on us all, lest we be consumed."

Known and searched by the swamp of dark matter, the curtains of the present universe fell before the mother and daughter as they drifted in the current of a new subspace channel provided by the same Wounded One who had caught almost no one's attention on Earth. For part of his strength was to hide his extraordinary inheritance from beyond the Magnificon gates deep in the heart of Siyon, from those who sought to capture that power and wealth for selfish dominance and subjugation.

Through this dark cloud of unknowing Ru and Hripsimé drifted. Amazingly, despite the Heir's lowly configuration from a distant land of Two Suns Rising, the mystical connection was made. From the mother and daughter's view, they exploded from the captive darkness of the musty pit at Khor Virap.

From His view they awakened to the organic and cosmic mind which ordered and sustained everything around them. As Ru flew for the first time without her wings, she asked the One calling "Why have we not met before?"

Yet Ru realized at that moment, "We did meet. We were introduced by the friend I loved--betrayed as I ran a spear though his heart. Then, we were introduced again by Pastor Gardner."

Timeless in pure existence, the dark matter without feeling of acceleration or velocity bore them along in a time-space jet stream from the dungeon of Khor Virap. In an instant they found themselves approaching a green and purple planet, and on its horizon--the tangled pair of stars, Pantos; the same place Cuzak had shown to Ru in Shanghai through a computer generated image.

Descending steeply, they pierced the planet's thin yellow ozone canopy. Nonstop and at high speed, Ru and Hripsimé swooped low, skimming the surface terrain. Their first glimpse of Krator began with a reeling fly-over of a drought ridden lakebed of brown cracked clay, bleached skeletons of farmed fish trapped in evaporated pools, strata of open parched shell fish, and half buried bone riggings of land mammals.

Resting in the hand of the dark matter's carpet ride, they also passed thousands of patches of decayed, burned, and entangled remains of angelicus, hominid, and hybrid species. Hripsimé asked, "What has happened here? Who was fighting who?"

Ru squeezed her mother's hand in reassurance and said, "I can't say for sure, but this planet is devastated."

Rising they flew over rifts and valleys of orange and black granite mountains, streaked by long trenches of jagged bleeding fissures of dark red magma, hissing with steam. The gravitational wrestling match of the twin stars played themselves out through sliding fault lines. Heated by internal churning of the planet, the streams of smoke, dust of pulverized rock, and sulfuric vapors, all rushed upward from deep vents until they belched through the planet's crust.

Next they passed over the narrow green equatorial agricultural zone, where once grew precise fields of legumes, wheat, barley, vegetables of all sorts, orchards of pecans, pistachios, walnuts, and fruits. But the green of the post cataclysmic planet now came from a contest of weeds, fungus, and algae, pocked by black water sink holes.

Across the fields also lay the wreckage of a mass transit tube system, strewn in disrepair like chopped worms. Some of its vine covered sleds contained full loads of harnessed uniformed corpses armed with guns and swords. Moving quickly they passed one city after another, speckled with punctured grain silos, dilapidated multi-story ruins of white stucco apartments, mangled construction cranes, unfinished warehouses and flight decks spattered by damaged alien spacecrafts.

Ru noticed some of the buildings resembled the design of the Hub Stations being contracted on the Earth. They were octagonal with a large radio antenna on the roof--*the receptor sites*. All of them were scorched in the center as if struck by large bolts of lightning.

Not far from each Hub, dotting the landscape in a line from north to south as if they encircled the planet, stood two-thousand foot high double helix structures, supporting a large crystal at their peak. Half of the towers had toppled, their sections having plunged with the crystals into the buildings below.

Onward they flew beyond the green belt, over rolling tan sand dunes interspersed with bleached salt flats dotted by more scars of battle skirmishes. The land was full of exploded craters decorated by legs, wings, skulls, swords, feathers, and disintegrated tram sleds. The debris of war lay silent, paying homage to death.

While the ground still turned beneath them, they rushed over powder red foothills strewn with craggy black and brown boulders leading up to eroded sandstone mountain ranges interspersed with caves and mazes of spindles. In between two ranges as they approached from afar, Hripsimé and Ru observed what seemed to be the giant outline of a human eye. Racing toward the valley, upon closer inspection they saw a land where the sand had been blasted away in a circle several miles wide, exposing the bed rock.

Shades of rainbow colored glass glazed the surface of the raw rock for miles. As they approached the center, their invisible carpet ride decelerated until the they set their feet upon real ground, where an unusual object caught their attention.

Stuck in the rock, in the shiny blackened epicenter of the hardened molten glass was not the evidence of a radical bomb. Instead what they saw wedged into the rock was a hand held sledge for quarrying and breaking stone. The golden head of this large hammer was buried half way into the rock at an angle. A thick iron handle with torn leather grip protruded at a forty-five degree angle. It looked as if it had been melded into the stone for ages.

Hripsimé burst with excitement at this discovery releasing Ru's hand, "The Golden Hammer by which the Only Begotten struck the Earth. This is the Hammer!" But then perplexed she said, "But this is not the Earth. My daughter, do you know where we are?"

Chapter 43

"Is not My word like fire?" declares the Lord, and
like a hammer which shatters a rock."
--Jeremiah 23:29

"Yes, my father-- Cuzak showed me this place, but not like this, only on corporate computer simulation. This doesn't make sense. We've only sent over trial groups and their symbiotes. He made no mention of a Hammer, or a post apocalyptic landscape. What I do know, this place is further from Earth than light has had the time to travel. It was the hope of those suffering from the infection."

"My daughter, some light has no need of travel."

"I am not sure I understand. Maybe the owner of this hammer could explain what we see."

"He is closer than you know," said a familiar baritone voice to Ru, from behind them.

Spinning around, Ru's heart almost burst. For in front of her was the friend she missed so dearly; weathered yet full of wisdom, ancient but somehow displaying a new youthful vitality. She recognized his face and flowing mane, but he was lacking the body builder bulk he once carried, thinner, more like an image bearer.

In joy and disbelief Ru asked, "Is it really you? But your wings are not restored. Are you real?"

"Ru, I wouldn't miss you for the world. 'No wings,' you ask? Please relieve yourself of any guilt or sorrow you may have toward me. I have been changed. My wings are unseen. They are designed to ride the Spirit of the Magnificon."

Hripsimé's eyes doubled in size, saying, "You are the one who insured my daughter received the cross? How did you come by it? Cuzak would not relinquish it so easily?"

Ouriano attempted to relieve their fears, smiling he said, "I come in peace Hripsimé. I knew about Ru because I was asked to follow your early life without making intervention. You've had a hard life Hripsimé, but you added your share of affliction to the opposition."

Hripsimé did not feel her question was answered, "Did Cuzak knowingly give you my cross?"

"The cross Ru wears has a history of its own," he said as Hripsimé was about to interrogate him again. "Yes, Cuzak gave me the cross to pass on to his daughter when the time was right. Sometimes our fathers, even in their weakness want better for their children. I tried to work with him."

Hripsimé blurted, "My God! There is no saving Cuzak."

"I didn't want to disappoint you Ru," said Ouriano.

"But I killed you. I helped my father. I took away your existence. I betrayed you."

"That which was meant for evil by some, became a better kind of good for me. 'The stone the builders rejected has become the chief cornerstone, and it is wonderful in his sight.'"

Ru wanted to wrap her arms and tears around him and moved to embrace him.

Ouriano held his palm toward her and said, "I am sorry, but you cannot touch me as of yet. I am in the midst of transformation."

"Then you are not real," said Ru.

"Please don't say that, Ru. For this age, I am more real than you. The lance once having been dipped into the life essence of the Heir of the Magnificon, would not allow evil to disseminate me. The shell of my person collapsed as you witnessed in your father's lab, but not my essence. As unfathomable as your actions may have appeared, they ensured my redemption. The darkened spear and flagrum you ran through my aging heart of light performed a miracle never experienced by my kind. The original weapon of primordial murder directed at the Heir, the lance soaked in hatred, and preserved as a trophy to kill again, had been infected by his blood. So when you ran it through me, my heart was pierced with the life giving essence from the Magnificon."

Ru shook her head, trying to grasp what Ouriano said, "No, no, here, this vision we are in, it is not real! This hammer, this place,... it is all my imagination. I am going mad," she said in anguish as she pressed the same hands she wished to hold him with against her forehead.

Hripsimé tried to help, "Ru, I will say this: I am here with you. God has not led us astray. But I cannot say the same for him."

"We must all leave this planet. You have work to do. Yours is an adulterous and sinful generation," said Ouriano.

"No, this time you are not leaving without me. I want to go with you," cried Ru. "You are the father I need."

"We will meet again soon. You know this. You have seen it."

Uncovering her eyes she said, "Seen what?"

"The boy," he answered.

Ru paused for a moment, "Daniel, Victoria's and Lucas' son? Are you saying he is more than the sum of his parents?"

"He needs your help to get here," said Ouriano.

Protecting her daughter, Hripsimé asked, "Why have you come into our sacred space with God? Tell me why this Hammer, this forsaken place?"

Ouriano did not answer immediately as he searched the opaque sky for something. Ru and her mother looked up to follow his gaze. Then, through the hazy planet's canopy he found them, proclaiming, "The twin stars, see how the King of Tyre—his shadow swallows them. The darkness will be greater than you can foresee. He failed on Earth. He failed here. But who would have thought it all a test at the expense of every image bearer and Wind alike who trusted him, and even a snare to the Heir himself. You believe your understanding can comprehend this, but don't be deceived. When you suppose you have embraced all of evil's might, you have not."

Ru asked him, "Yazad and Beltshzan are taking the infected spirits and the humans who want to leave the Earth to make a new life in this place. From the devastation I see, I suspect it will fail?"

"No, you must listen!"

Ru was taken aback by Ouriano's corrective, but he explained more, "I apologize but our time is limited. The united force of Beltshzan and Yazad is gathering a storm to obliterate more than this sector. He wants to collapse this far away piece of the universe, causing a domino effect to rupture the Earth, the Blue Moon, and eventually Siyon itself. His intention is to storm the Magnificon Gates and gain control of that which gave birth to creation. In the end he wants to destroy all that was wonderfully fashioned so he may face his Creator alone. But first he intends to critically wound the Heir."

"Night comes upon us," said Hripsimé as she pointed above. The atmosphere cleared bringing into full view the local binary Suns. Beyond them and across the heavens they observed the distant stars, galaxies and nebulae, each bursting with light for a brief moment as they were assaulted by a high energy wave--the edge of an expanding tide of darkness. Ravaged and extinguished one by one, entire quadrants of the heavens disappeared before them.

Next they watched in awe as the planet's two Suns eroded going dim, ripped apart by the super-gravity of the wave. With the luminous edge of the black swath racing closer, the planet's crust began to buckle with a torrent of volcanic eruptions as a last goodbye.

Hripsimé said, "May God save us from this blanket of death which comes for all creation."

"What in hell's name has he done?" Ru said, "He's collapsed the Higgs field and with it the structure of all which exists!" Turning for more explanation from her lost friend, she shouted "Ouriano, where are you?"

With only seconds to survive the mother and daughter clung together, both shouting, "Ouriano... Jesus!" "End this... Wake us!" But like the upheaving land around them, they too were stretched mercilessly toward the ravenous void where no one could hear their screams.

Nevertheless, the musty dungeon of Khor Virap was still standing, though the flames of the candles had long burned themselves out. Early in the morning as the first tourist calls came complaining of the locked entrance to the Monastery, Father Svarian, unable to reach Sister Hripsimé, drove himself from his office at the Etchmiadzin to investigate.

After the black draped pastor begged the crowd in the parking lot to be patient, he headed for the pit. Turning on the service lights, he clamored down the steps and found the two women fast asleep on the cold stone floor. Sprinkling water on their faces until they awakened, he inquired, "What happened here Sister Hripsimé? There is not enough oxygen in here for one, let alone two of you. I forbid you to do this again. You are not Saint Gregory."

Hripsimé slowly sat up on the floor holding her knees and said, "Father Svarian, the end, it's coming. The Golden Hammer, I saw it."

"Yes, I don't doubt you my Sister, but please, we have many on their pilgrimage waiting outside the gates. They need your guidance today, before the end of the world."

Chapter 44

When you've eaten the final fruit off the tree, then there is no going back to Eden.

Nine Years After Ouriano's Memorial

As Victoria went through the delivery of supplies from Cusco, sorting vegetables from the fruit, she called out to Lucas, "Your favorite is on the tele."

"Rulanda Lakee, the British news babe?"

"It's the top of the hour...." said Victoria, "can you believe what she wears? Who is going to take her stories seriously? The camera might as well focus below her neck line and cut off her head. Sorry dear, I wish I was more motivated to dress up for you out here in the rain forest. I did shave my legs for you this morning. You probably didn't even notice."

"Hey, hey, hey... come sit down for a minute," as he waived her to move out of the way of the virtual projection, "Here she goes."

Victoria unfolded the reclining camping chair and placed it next to Lucas, close enough she could lap her left leg over the top of his right. Comfortably situated, she dipped her hand into a hot bag of buttered popcorn.

Lucas looked at her imposition, "What's with the leg wrestling? And new toe nail polish? I'll take the popcorn."

"I have to counter the virtual Rulanda Lakee with real flesh and blood. I hope your mind knows the difference between fantasy and reality."

Lucas took a sip from his tea and asked, "Where were you the last couple of nights? As I recall you were more interested in reading your Bible. Oh, oh, here she is."

"This is Around the World with BBC correspondent Rulanda Lakee. Our lead story once again is related to the Sanctuary Corporation, whose stock continues to sky rocket with most of the initial one hundred transport Hubs set to open within the next year. As you recall, one year ago today, the Sanctuary Corporation completed the largest acquisition in history by purchasing Apple Computers through a stock swap, pointedly for their lock on quantum distance computing technology. This technology allows for precise calculations in quantum or trans-dimensional travel. Apparently one quark of miscalculation and no one knows where you've gone.

This international corporation's market value already surpasses the next ten largest corporations combined despite criticism for not carrying one commercial passenger yet to the confirmed sister universe. They have however reportedly succeeded in all tests and promise to release new confirmation of eye witness testimony from the Sanctuary before initial tickets go on sale.

For now, video and thorough data gathered robotically have satisfied the scientific community. Experts in agriculture, geology, meteorology, astronomy, seismology, astrophysics, oceanography, biology, have all declared the binary star system, Pantos, with its habitable rocky planet Krator, as a prime candidate for supporting large industrial high energy based human cultures.

The notoriety of the Sanctuary Corporation's ability to leap frog nationhood to outright ownership of new habitable planets has countries, hedge funds and individual investors willing to drive the stock's price to astronomical levels never seen before. This has allowed the Sanctuary Corporation to go on a buying spree.

Strapped for cash the BBC is even purported to be in negotiations directly with Sanctuary Corporation's CEO Colonel Cuzak Runaldi in a stock for cash purchase as the UK is rife with budget shortfalls in part to its bloated welfare state. If this purchase is allowed to pass by the busted EU, the Sanctuary Corporation would become the majority owner.

'The Colonel,' as investors like to refer to him for his bold 'take no prisoners captive' attitude in mergers and acquisitions could not be reached at this moment for comment because of his current speech we are about to air.

However no one can forget last year's remark the Colonel made when the buyout of Apple was approved by shareholders and the United Nations' Security Council, despite large investments by questionable partners like North Korea and Turkey. He said quote, 'When you've eaten the final fruit off the tree, then there is no going back to Eden,' unquote. This year the UN gave the Sanctuary Corporation the first seat ever to a non-nation on the Security Council, and also made them a member of the G-8 Council of Financial Ministers, now G-9.

We are going to join a live feed now from where the Colonel is addressing leading scientists, investors, politicians, at the Cosmology Con Expo, at Arizona State University, to relieve concerns about so much power consolidated in one Corporation."

Growing in agitation at the program feed, Lucas inadvertently picked Victoria's leg up off of his and let it drop on the floor, "Ouch!" she complained.

"Sorry Vic, let's see if they take live questions while he is speaking; that two faced pock marked twisted baboon. He'll crap his pants if he knows I'm the one calling in."

"I wouldn't do that Lucas. We'd be hypocrites having sustained our family on the Sanctuary stock. Besides, wouldn't it potentially give away the location of our little sanctuary here? That was brilliant strategy you and dad had, doubling back to Peru, basically bribing the local governor, to stay on the reserve where the land is tied up in heavy litigation."

"It was a political donation, Victoria. Here's Cuzak, let's be quiet."

She pinched his calf with her toes and said, "You're the one making all the noise."

"Shish Victoria, quit rustling the popcorn."

"... and to my esteemed colleagues, including the five Nobel Laureates present. Of course I would not dare claim to be your equal in brain power or creativity in your specialty fields of study. Each of you is a lifetime of vetted scientific experience in mapping and pointing out the undeniable evolution of our species... "

Lucas added, "If they only knew..."

"... but I am your colleague in lending vision and structure that will—or that is providing the gateway to a new kind of thinking that will help you to reach your dreams, a breakthrough in reconstituting what it means to be human, for the betterment of our species. In the first renaissance the restoring of the ideal or myth of the image of God in humanity helped to pull the western world out of the dregs of the dark middle ages; a place where plagues, famines, tribalism, misogamy, feudal systems were rampant and almost destroyed its own species."

Victoria took a handful of popcorn and tossed it through his virtual image emanating from the box on the ceiling, "Please, gaff him," she joked.

"Religion served a noble purpose during this time in diminishing these blows by spreading the good news that we were all created equal in standing before God. For the wrong reason, it served a good purpose in that genetically we are for the most part, very close to each other in genomic imprint.

The great religions of the past were our crude conscience, acting as mediators of important, hard questions like, 'Why is there something rather than nothing?' 'Why is there such pain and suffering if God is basically good?' 'Why the abysmal difference between the have and have-nots of the world with no means to change them?'"

Lucas added his commentary again, "Cuzak sounds like a combination TV preacher and PBS fund raiser."

"Religion, especially those with monotheistic roots helped lead us to the enlightenment and the age of science. We owe them a debt of gratitude, but we cannot stay there. And the leaders of those religions acknowledge such. Speak candidly to them and they will tell you how they have or need to evolve, to experience a new reformation or transformation of their belief system."

For Victoria, thoughts and guilt of how she lost her mother to the oppressive attack of the Vranti kept replaying every time she saw him, "Cuzak's gripping the sides of his blue podium like someone might steal it from him. He sweats a lot, the pig!" She threw more popcorn at his image. "Now he's sipping his sparkling water, and acting all full of himself, like he sincerely cares about these scientists."

Chapter 45

I am that I am

Cuzak continued in his speech, "By the way, we have recruited board members for the Sanctuary Corporation from the major world religions to better listen to their followers' feelings on these subjects.

Nevertheless, it is a concurrent process. Whether people admit it or not, it is beneficial for everyone. From the Renaissance were birthed new burgeoning capital markets, support of the arts and broader economic empowerment. From there we transitioned to the enlightenment and then the modern age with the phrase, 'Cogito Ergo Sum,' 'I think therefore I am!'

A new light began to illume the human mind. Our once sacred institutions of learning, dominated by priests and philosophers found new teachers with greater revelation and supreme truth. The halls of the great European and Ivy League schools slowly adapted to a more reasonable and scientific methodology. Faith as a substance of things we hope for but were indeed unsure of, slowly dissipated. What else could it do? Science has indeed found that which is a more sure reality. Religion should be happy having their hopes realized."

Lucas said to Victoria, "Let me have some popcorn to throw at the talking head."

"Granted, there have been some mistakes and misuse of science, but we don't want to return to a flat Earth. Look at the longevity of humans. There are more people over sixty-five today than have ever lived in the history of the human race. It is very simple, we have and are evolving. For example, in the past ten years we have taken what was junk DNA and fashioned it into new cures in medicine, for cancer, aids, Alzheimer's. Mechanized surgery has turned the corner on health care costs. Families of all make ups can't be stopped from having children.

Yet, some today, like to claim we are in a postmodern age; that we will never get over the tragedy of being human, that no one can give a good answer to the three questions I asked earlier, 'Why is there something rather than nothing?' 'Why is there such pain and suffering if God is so good?' 'Why the abysmal difference between the have and have-nots of the world?' They claim that all our learning has only made us improve at killing and hoarding; that even under the best circumstances, every child will not have a chance of reaching their potential.

Will the poor always be with us? They make some valid points. These are undeniably true and I agree; we are running out of land, we have raped many of our natural resources, humans are a scourge to other species, that fundamentalist religions and technology are a dangerous mix, that weapons grade viruses have been sold on the black market, that a nuclear armed Israel is bad news for its neighbors, that past colonial powers ripped vital resources from the wombs of native people's land!

I agree with these observations." Cuzak paused for a moment surveying the crowd before focusing into the camera, "However, I don't believe the human race has to remain chained to a tree stump, left to drown in a rising swamp of arcane relativistic truths. In the past, when we tried to make, or to force reparations for past offenses against humanity we got nowhere. How do you bring justice to people who don't exist anymore? This may be ideal, but it is not pragmatic. Where does it end? Instead, we must ask, where are we today? Rather than going backwards, is it not easier and potentially more healing to go forward; forgive and move on?" Many scientists acknowledged 'yes,' as he spoke.

"Our science as of today speaks new revelation to us. Where we once wasted brain power on debates over the first cause of the universe; for some to prove God or an intelligent designer exists in the background, we now accept the creation as a closed system. There is no end or beginning. It just is."

"Vic, how can these intellectual elites sit there curtsying their brains in affirmation when he is spouting such nonsense?"

"He's good, wasn't that long ago we would have sucked it all up too."

"True."

"And because we accept it as it is, we are free to explore without the baggage of guilt and shame. We stop looking for a fix to an immoral past. For without guilt and shame driving us toward a pilgrimage to discover a secret deity's will, we also free ourselves from the Freudian analysis of a mythical heavenly benevolent father. In other words we don't expect a thing from our heavenly father, because he no longer exists! Instead we take responsibility for pain and suffering, and we rectify it ourselves."

Victoria blew up, "They are applauding this? He's insane, a megalomaniac!" tossing the empty popcorn bag through the hologram.

Lucas grabbed her left hand, "I thought you were cutting him some slack."

"Lastly, I am a person who likes to get things done. One of my goals is to use the Sanctuary Corporation to help the inequality of those who have not had a fair shake in life. They know, their government knows, their family knows, because of where they were born, or the color of their skin, they will always remain shackled to the same status in life. They are powerless in how others with more power have defined and repressed them. And, I don't have a good answer for them in light of our planet's history.

But I do proclaim this, and I preface it with a question: What if you could opt out of everything? Your caste, your education, your disability, your imprisonment, your religion, your country? What if you could even opt out of God, your entity, your myth? What if you could leave it all behind and start over where everyone will be treated equal?"

Cuzak paused several moments while he received a standing ovation, "Thank you, please be seated my friends and hold your applause. I have nothing novel to say. I am only repeating what you already know to be true.

You see, we have reached a point where a conventional government of the people, by the people and for the people has hit the glass ceiling; they are strapped with too much baggage, including too many promises by politicians and too many ingrained forms of oppression. There is no healing power in trying to fix an old paradigm. Would you try and rebuild a collapsing home over the same sink hole? No, it would be more prudent to start from scratch elsewhere. However, where these old petrified institutions of the past have stagnated, even regressed, the Sanctuary Corporation is prepared to literally move humanity to the stars."

"Vic, I believe I am going to throw this chair."

"Shish honey, here's the finale."

"Where we once said, 'I think, therefore I am,' going forward we will say, 'I am, therefore creation exists!'" The convention center burst into another standing round of prolonged applause.

Cuzak turned up his rhetoric, "… thank you,… thank you for your approval, please if you could refrain for a second. I want you to join me in an exercise."

"Lucas do you know where the sword is?"

"Yes honey, why?"

"Just checking, nearby right?

"Yes, always at hand."

"Too bad it doesn't work on holographs."

Cuzak began, "Since you are all standing, please repeat after me,… I am."

"I am," the crowd responded in unison.

"I am," Cuzak repeated.

"I am," the crowd said more heartedly.

"I am that I am," Cuzak encouraged cupping his hands next to his ears.

"I am, that I am," the crowd said louder.

"Lift your hands over your head like this," said Cuzak. "Proclaim it this time with me, and believe it."

"I am that I am," they said together in full accord, "I am that I am!"

"Yes, let it be as you proclaim!" said Cuzak, "There comes a point where you do not try to fix the past, you move on and begin anew. The Hubs will be open for business, for the sake of all of humanity, for those who claim, 'I am that I am.'

For what tyrants of thought, politics, and religion would dare try to block this fair and deserved rite of passage for who we once referred to as 'Adam's Race?'" With this, the crowd before him roared in adulation, and began chanting, "I am... I am... I am..."

"I suppose I'll join the standing ovation," said Lucas as he stood and clapped. "I'll join in on the applause, that fraud. It takes a lot of guts, smarts to pull off what he has done. I'll hand him that."

"I won't stand even to mock him," said Victoria. "I sense the beginning of the end of our little happy family. And what's this?" as Victoria gazed over at Lucas entering a number into his phone. "Why are you doing this? I know you're not entering the number for a call in to Cuzak are you?"

"Vic, what are the chances I would get through anyway? They can't trace us if I keep it short. The BBC has to be looking for one naysayer, right?"

Victoria said, "Please Lucas, don't let your anger prove something you can't take back. You are not going to change the world. Calm down, maybe pray. And anyway, what are you going to ask if you get through?"

Chapter 46

*"But you have been cast out of your tomb like a
rejected branch, clothed with the slain who are
pierced with a sword, who go down to the stones
of the pit like a trampled corpse." --Isaiah 14:19*

"Damn that Cuzak, because of him we've been living out of
a glorified cave. I'm going out for a few minutes."

"What do you plan on doing? Don't make that call. We
might all regret it. We're OK the way things are." Victoria
wrapped her arms around Lucas, but he unpeeled them.

"Going up to the top of the ridge to make the call. It is a
good time, low rolling clouds and drizzle no one over head
could see if they wanted. You are right, be harder to trace
among all the hikers below on the Inca trail and the cross
traffic relay to Cusco."

As he walked up the steps to the main shaft leaving their
make shift home in the ancient Indian mine, their young
son, Daniel bounced in. "What were you two getting upset
about?"

"Got to go Daniel, be back shortly," said his father as he
disappeared up the stairs.

Victoria called out the voice recognition command to the
holographic television, "sleep" causing the projection to
cease.

"Who, what was it? I know that you and Dad, Gramps and
Grandma are not telling me something about why we are
here."

Victoria cradled her nine year old son against her chest,
rubbing his hair and said, "Time son, give us time. Like
we've said before,.."

Daniel interrupted her with a mocking quote of what she
was about to say, "Like we've said before, 'we are living
here temporarily until we can find a country who will

officially host us. We were working on a top secret experiment and were accused of stealing the technology, so we had to go into hiding and take Grandma and Grandpa with us.'"

"That is completely true Daniel. Don't you believe your mother?" Victoria held both sides of his face, lifting it toward hers. Gazing into his eyes she knew there was something different about her son. He looked appropriate for his nine year old gangly frame, which was always on the run, but Victoria grew suspect. *The eyes look older. They don't match. They are not my eyes or his father's or grandparents. When do we share with him the prophesy of his future?*

"Who are we hiding from?" said Daniel.

"We have been over this Daniel. It is better if you don't know. Please don't worry about this. Each day has ...."

Daniel completed her sentence, "enough worries of its own." Victoria lowered her head with eyes closed for a few seconds as she held him. "Mom?"

"What?"

"Do you believe in the Devil?" When he asked this question Victoria let loose of her son as he went and picked the popcorn bag off the floor, digging into the bottom for the last few popped kernels.

"Why do you ask?" she said.

Between crunches Daniel answered, "Grandpa and Grandma believe in the Devil,... they tell me he is weak... but doesn't give up scaring people... and misleading them. He wants to take them all to hell."

"I think Gramps and Grandma know what they are talking about son. Don't know if I'd state it like that."

"But didn't God make the Devil?" Daniel asked, tossing a last morsel up in the air and catching with his open mouth.

"And?"

"Why did God make something so bad?"

"Little theologian today huh? Daniel, I don't know the answer to that question. Pray, ask God to give you wisdom."

"I did."

"And, what did you learn?"

"God gave me a dream."

"Daniel, are you toying with me? What was the dream?"

"Do you promise you won't get mad at me?"

"What kind of question is that? Of course you can tell me. I have dreams too."

"Did they come true?"

Victoria had a blank look on her face, hesitating on her response, "Some came true, some might come true, I don't know yet. Let's sit down... Tell me what you saw."

"I was lying in bed and I saw the Devil--I guess it was the Devil. He was crying and standing next to a pile of bodies. But they weren't all human. And it smelled like a dead pig."

"Why do you guess it was the Devil?"

"Because he spoke to me."

"What did he look like? Say to you?"

"He looked like a man and had a big stick in his hand. But some of the bodies on the ground had wings. Like people with wings. Pieces of bodies, broken pieces, blood, steam coming off of them. Hundreds, maybe thousands of them. The man who spoke had yellow eyes. He accused me of being a slayer, an angel of death. I yelled back at him no, no!"

"Daniel, dreams are not always what they seem to be."

"Are you mad at me?"

"Absolutely not honey, tell me what else."

Daniel was resolute to get answers, "Mom, am I an angel of death? Did I kill someone?"

"How could you think such an awful thing?"

"The man in the dream said that I betrayed my own kind."

"Daniel, it was only a dream," raising her voice louder, "don't you ever, ever say, or think that again. Do you understand?"

"But I spoke in the dream. I remember the words."

Exasperated, Victoria paused, trying to act calm, but secretly she was frightened and curious, so asked, "What do you remember saying?"

"I was standing in front of him, the man with the yellow eyes, he was very angry, but I was more angry, I was holding a long sword out toward him and said,

'You Beltshzan are cast out of your grave like a disposed branch, and covered with the soiled clothes of those slain, with those cut down by the sword, those who descend to the bedrock of the pit; as a carcass trod under foot.'"

Just then Grandfather Henry came down the front stairs from outside, "Isaiah 14:19, those are the words spoken against Lucifer. I don't remember us memorizing that passage Daniel. Not on my most important list, but glad you are studying on your own."

"Grandpa!" Lucas exclaimed as he ran over and hugged him.

"Hey Daniel, just passed your father, seemed to be in a hurry."

"I'll tell you later," Victoria added, giving her father-in-law that 'don't ask' look. "Yes, that's it. Something you must have read, son. You have a good memory and recited it in your sleep."

Henry, concerned for his grandson asked, "But where did you get the name Beltshzan from Lucas?"

Lucas shrugged his shoulders and lifted his hands, "I don't know, I just said it in the dream, Grandpa."

Henry and Daniel looked at Victoria, as Henry raised his bristly eyebrows, and asked, "Is there something you know which would help my grandson?"

Raising the pitch of her voice Victoria said, "My son, dad-- not in front of him," as she gave him the look again, which did not bypass Daniel.

"Why don't any of you trust me? Believe me?"

"Darling we do believe you. I just don't want you to worry," said Victoria.

Henry added, "Daniel, no matter how terrible the dreams, there is one more powerful and true who is with you always. Remember why you were baptized?"

"I know Grandpa. And he carries a sword too."

"What?" his grandfather said, looking perplexed.

"I read it in the book of Revelation."

Henry's mind instantly pulled down his scripture reference: "From the Apocalypse of John, 19:15, 'And out of his mouth goes forth a sharp sword, that with it he should smite the nations: and he shall rule them with a rod of iron: and he treads the winepress of the fierceness and wrath of Almighty God.'"

"Grandpa, maybe you and Daniel can go exploring for a little while before lunch."

"Let's go Daniel, we'll talk some more. Promise."

As they headed up the stairs Victoria turned around and said, "Resume," and sat down to watch the Colonel Cuzak Runaldi's question and answer session.

Chapter 47

My demise is over rated.

Lucas pulled up to the switch-back overlooking the cloud shrouded peaks and fog covering the rainforest and valley below. Sitting quietly in his black Land Rover he prayed and watched the windshield ionizer cause the precipitation to collect into little pools on the glass and slide off.

"Why Lord do I want to disturb the peace we've had? I suppose I've trained my heart, my soul, my mind for the days ahead. So you have called and pronounced me to be a Juwaan? And I have waited for you, but for what? Now I have a son to take care of. Do you really want me to draw first blood? Then do a miracle and put me through to this passive aggressive tyrant."

With this short prayer mixed with introspection and doubt, Lucas slipped on his communication visor, and summoned the number to reach the live broadcast of his old nemesis. He also took his chewing gum out and covered over the camera lens facing him from the center of the dashboard. Even the notion of talking to Cuzak added a shade of blue to his right hand, something he had kept from Daniel. "Here goes..."

Through the local towers and bundled satellite feed through Cusco, the call went through to the Birmingham UK office. He dare not use direct feed and be located too easily.

"Around the World with Rulanda Lakee. Are you calling to be in queue with a live question for Colonel Cuzak?"

"Ah, you bet, I really got through?"

"Yes! To whom am I speaking?"

"Doctor Lucas Tanner."

"Your name is familiar, the late Lucas Tanner, kidnapped or disappeared?"

"My demise is over rated."

"Hold on! Don't go anywhere."

"Rulanda,"

"What Reina? I trust you to screen the calls, we have about two minutes."

"This is different Rulanda, you are not going to believe this. We have a caller from South America, claiming to be the missing Dr. Lucas Tanner. One of the few mysterious black spots on Colonel Cuzak's resume as you've purported."

"Good God, I presumed he was dead, terrorists or something ten years ago. Put him on privately so I can confirm before the Q and A begins. Oh won't this be juicy if true? Probably a wacko."

"Rulanda here, I am speaking with whom? Let me see your face."

"The camera suits you well Ms. Lakee. As I mentioned to your screener, I am Doctor Lucas Tanner, former researcher at the University of Texas systems, quantum physics."

"Why are you calling, um, ah, Doctor Tanner? The media considers you dead. Show me your face or I won't let your call go through. I won't record it, journalist discretion."

If you are going to war, allow for some control, thought Lucas as he reached over and let his face be broadcast to her and put the gum back in his mouth.

"Pull off the visor," Rulanda demanded "I need to compare your old press photo."

Lucas removed them for a moment, bobbed his head and waved to her, "It's me."

"South America?" she asked,

"Leave it at that, or I'll hang up. Satisfied?" Lucas placed the gum back over the mini-camera lens.

"Yes! I am putting you through first. I can't wait to see the look on the blooming bugger's face. But like I asked, why are you calling?"

"Because I am one of the patent holders on the Hub technology that the Sanctuary Corporation has developed. You know how powerful these people are? We had to go into hiding because we were accused of stealing technology vital to U.S. interests. The reality is that we were kidnapped by Cuzak. They are not who they say they are."

"Ok, I am letting you on. I'll introduce you, but ask a legitimate question." In the background Lucas heard, "three, two, one, you're live Rulanda."

"Colonel Cuzak, Rulanda Lakee on this end, from our London bureau. We'd like to follow up on your brilliant speech with questions from our viewers. As CEO of the world's most valuable company are you game?"

"Absolutely, may I say Rulanda you project most lovely as always. Feel like I could reach out and touch you. You should be given freedom to pursue more of the news pieces you enjoy."

"Thank you Colonel, but right now I am mesmerized by the rock star following you have gained. Are you ready?"

"Yes, who is my first caller?"

"We'll let him introduce himself; he says you will recognize him."

"Interesting, put him through," said Cuzak as he carefully managed his image in the monitor.

"Colonel Smith, I mean Colonel Cuzak, you have served your investors well. You are to be commended for being a man of your word. Thanks to you I have been able to relax."

Cuzak gripped the sides of the podium searching for the voice and said, "Yes, please caller, you sound familiar, identify yourself, our friendship. My age is betraying me, ha. Glad you are happy with the stock's return on investment."

Rulanda on a separate monitor feed to his ear said, "Colonel, we did not mean to catch you off guard this really just came through, I am putting his picture up now."

Chapter 48

Why is there something rather than nothing?

The entire auditorium and worldwide BBC viewers saw the same ten year old photo with the words labeled below it, "live--breaking news! Missing scientist, Lucas Tanner, PhD, calls into Cosmology Conference."

"This must be a hoax," remarked the externally unflappable Cuzak, "but go ahead caller, you worked hard to get through, what is your question?"

Lucas watched the wind blow the leaves in the surrounding trees. Still considering what he would actually ask, he hesitated. Cuzak was about to break the silence as he waited when he spoke, "Colonel, this is Lucas Tanner. We had a short stent together in perfecting your technology, so I wanted to ask what is probably on the mind of many of your stockholders."

"Ha, ha, Dr. Tanner, how are you?" Trying to ingratiate the crowd, Cuzak tacked on "We deliberated that you may have been lost in your own experiments." The immediate crowd laughed with him.

"My question is this: you just mentioned that science has ushered in a new era of revelation, so that what is ultimate knowledge is that which is known through scientific methodology. If that be the case, why do you refer to science as revelation? Is not revelation technically a disclosure of something which cannot be known or found through material observation or metaphysical speculation? Colonel, why is there something rather than nothing—why a universe to begin with?"

Cuzak continued to smile as Lucas seemed to finish his questions. Beads of perspiration became visible on his temples. Rulanda wondered if she should have put Lucas through, after all. As she turned in the newsroom to her aide, clinching her pen, she asked, "What is this bloke talking about, 'something rather than nothing?'"

"Mr. Tanner," Cuzak replied, removing his smile. "I know what your next question is, so go ahead and ask it. Or would you rather I ask it for you since you are a coward, hiding your true image with a mock identity. You are one of the many crazy religious zealots who security had to screen from entering this conference, but still hassle people in the streets, are you not?"

With that statement, Lucas' pride took over, and he pulled the gum off of the camera lens and threw it out the window. Next he looked directly at the lens and took off the visor, his full profile now available for the world to see, including Victoria. The network instantly dropped the live video of Cuzak, and replaced it with the new stream of Lucas, comparing it to the old lab coat picture.

Muting her microphone again, Rulanda screamed in her control room, "Take that you old bugger! You're going to have to be more creative than this. We're not all buying your pile."

Cuzak, except for the heavy sweat acted unruffled and replied, "Dr. Tanner, you are back among the land of the living. I must apologize. You and your partner's credentials and contributions to the Hub technology have taken on a life of their own, but surely you must know this. I believe you might be able to host your own press release. Please tell us where you are? Come to the conference."

Lucas leaned into the camera, filled the stream's entirety with his facial profile and said, "Thank you for acknowledging me Colonel Cuzak and fellow academics. Why don't you first tell me my next question, and then I will answer yours."

"Dr. Tanner, I misjudged who you were. As I said, I apologize. Please, you have all of us on the edge of our seats. Ask!"

Rulanda exclaimed again to her news crew, "There is a God in Westminster Abbey, hush everyone."

"Colonel Cuzak, my question to cap what I asked earlier is this, why are you afraid of God? Are you building, expanding this technology to escape God? Have you no fear to proclaim 'I am that I am?' Better mortals than you and I have died at the hands of humanity for being so bold as to utter such celestial slander."

Many notions traversed Cuzak's mind as he listened for him to finish. He wasn't worried about the endless dialectic of religious and philosophical babble. He reminded himself, *The point is to keep the conversation going—for everyone. The longer Lucas speaks the sooner he and Victoria will be found. But why is he moving his queen so soon?*

"Dr. Tanner, what a delight. So you have found religion in your exile? Are you concerned that God is going to suffer some type of loss because people want to relocate? Surely you don't believe in a God who is so weak do you? We won't protest; he or she can go too if they wish."

Cuzak stepped away from the podium as the auditorium rolled with laughter. He followed up by asking, "By the way, are you going? You wouldn't want to be left behind?" Again the crowd burst out laughing.

Back in the news room Reina reminded Rulanda, "It's a good thing he regained control of the Q and A. If his company buys out the BBC there will be hell to pay for t-boning him like that."

Cuzak saw that he was on the video stream again, and that the live feed of Lucas was gone. Turning his head from side to side, looking many of the convention crowd in the eye, and then the camera, he said, "To address Dr. Tanner's questionable use of the affirmation, 'I am that I am.' Yes, penned by Moses and adopted by the great Rabbi Jesus of Nazareth. You caught me Dr. Tanner. There is, nothing new under the sun.

Doctor Tanner, if you can still hear me, let me give this final answer: We are not apostates against your religion. We have only adopted the ideals and taken them to a new level. Any prophet worth his or her salt would be happy to see the progress of their revelation. As to your other accusation that our science is not technically—revelation, or knowledge which we could not discover on our own, I personally invite you, to come and see."

Chapter 49

I was never able to love. This capacity escaped me. You reserved it for another species.

Having tempted yet another band of unhappy Legion Commanders to sip from his cup, Beltshzan made a quick departure for his main engagement. Like a mad hornet he flew through abandoned tunnels he knew from his over-glorified yesteryears. And when forced, he traveled like a bullet through the high speed intra-planet causeways, illumed with florescent yellow and pink lichens and the ever luminescent turquoise mist.

Entering the bell shaped hollow magma chamber where his dark stalactite ship was moored in the bottom of the mountain, he again began to relax taking the form of a man in a white suit with a red tie. Before he returned to the ship he reached into his pocket and pulled out a lighter and a small gold case. "Ah, home, they say it's where the heart is."

Stabbing the little box into his other hand a single cigarette slid out. Beltshzan promptly lit and inhaled it with a long breath, burning half in a matter of a few seconds. He leaned against the craft with his shoulder as he slowly released the smoke through his nostrils and ears, savoring every plume as he entertained a smug satisfaction that no one had detected him.

"My success is certain to breed her contempt. Waiting, I have spent eternity waiting. Half the time she doesn't even show for our chit-chats. What else has she to do? Give me fair ground and I'll show them how relative they are. All of this is gone too far, too long. What is the point? It lies in the Magnificon. I will have it. It is meant to be. The wretched image bearers, they are but cosmic scum... Where is she? It's always about the entrance. She should ask me about style."

As the last of the tobacco smoke exited his cranial cavities he looked up to see a cloud passing over the cratered summit. This cloud however stopped and began to spin like a white tornado being sucked down through the throat of the old volcano. Beltshzan threw the remainder of the cigarette on the ground and stomped it with the sole of his loafer. "Style," he said as he watched the long whirlwind descend through the shaft, shaking the vegetation viciously, while kicking up sand and debris. As the cork screwing rotation neared him, Beltshzan fell to one knee, knowing in this time and place he was no match. His tie and jacket, shirt, pants, hair, flapped violently in the turbulence while static blue electricity shot out of the cloud, dancing over his ship and him.

When the spinning vortex touched the floor next to the ship, it vanished as the remnant of torn clouds sucked themselves up the shaft in reverse. In their place red velvet flower petals fluttered down over the chamber, punctuating the air with their fragrance. In this sweet aromatic rain, the Angel of Light appeared before her fallen archangel.

She spoke to him as he kept his head bowed, "Raise your scornful gaze if you dare, King of Tyre, deceiver of nations. Any respect you have ever given has only served to feed your corruptness. What will you save by avoiding the eyes of the one who loved you?"

Beltshzan responded in a tiresome tone, "I was never able to love. This capacity escaped me. You reserved it for another species. I was made to create, to bring to order, to sail the Magnificon, to control all that gives shape to time and space. And so shall it be."

"There is still a love which redeems you. But you will never succumb to it, for that would mean the death of what you have made yourself to be. Why do you beckon me? What guile will your twisted tongue tempt me with?"

"To tempt you would be impossible, Heiress of Light, but an exchange to make things fair and decent would be in order." Beltshzan slowly raised his head and lifted his eyes toward her. The petals were still falling around them casting shadows on the walls as they passed through her emanating light. But he could not look directly at her. It was not her light which hurt his eyes so much, he had layers of scales for this. It was something else.

"I was made to stand alone, oh igniter of the stars. And you know this. The Magnificon holds the secret as to my purpose, and the Wounded One blocks my way."

"I have few words for you, son of the morning star, for words are meaningless to you. What is it you petition?"

Beltshzan began to smile as his question slithered to his mouth, "Oh, timeless one, where is the Heir of the Magnificon? Tell me if you know. To what realm has he traveled with empty hand? Is he again cut off from the land of the living?"

The Angel of Light remained perfectly still and spoke sharply, "Your ears have never listened. Does your mind pay no attention that you would tempt the Holy One of the Magnificon? Here I am, privy to your secret meeting, and what will I gain? I gave you everything; beauty, power, ability to fashion, but because you were not an image bearer, you did not see fit to serve. You had to dominate to prove your worth. Who do you plan on taking with you when your head is slain?"

Beltshzan, pulled out another cigarette and lit it, took a long burning puff and resumed his diatribe, "So the Heir is on his own again? And this time he cannot call on any Legions to save him, lest he strike his foot in free fall. Who will hear his cry and save him? Tell me, has he taken it upon himself to enter the Sanctuary of Yazad? Would he be so prideful to dare this rescue? Will he mingle among the image bearers as same flesh? What love will redeem him there, given he barely survived his last spectacle on Earth."

Chapter 50

You always promise what you cannot give.
What you have become is not how
I imagined you.

The blue static electricity continued to send out tentacles from the Angel of Light's body as she spoke, "The Heir walks the stars wherever He pleases. There is mystery of Him hidden in the Magnificon and in the souls of the meek and lowly, as is the reason of His love. You cannot understand because your reason is flawed; reason with no love. It trips your foot and catches your wing."

"And if he should die this time, suffer annihilation in my world, what would become of the Magnificon and your image bearers? Would he risk that or is it simply a meaningless game?"

"Wormwood, you have made your life a very costly reality for others. If the Heir were killed, yes, the Magnificon would be permanently disrupted."

"Such a high price, and for what? Why does the Heir, the Angel of Light, the Holy One of the Magnificon--sorry but your various forms keep me so confused as to your true essence,... why do you not stop the exit before it begins?"

"It is rare that I waste my breath on fools. Let it not be said that Elohim took lead from a wild donkey. Where and when, Fallen One should your infection be obliterated? Was it ten thousand years ago? This instant? A thousand years from now? What is the time frame you request? As there is a middle, there is also a beginning and an end. A hook has been placed through the nose of your arrogance, and on your back the nations will be swept away. You have made careful preparation to sow your tares among the wheat. Will you also dictate to Siyon the timing of the harvest?"

"Angel of Light, it feels so good to be the center of your attention again, but don't you think it is hard for one like me to love when doomed from the beginning?" Waiving his cigarette in a circle like a cheap Vegas act he said, "Hey, why not throw in a little double predestination-damnation? Ha, ha."

Beltshzan raised his voice close to a rage, "Enough of this! You called me out of nothing, who called you? What does it harm you if one of your beloved Winds should arise above the rest? You care for sparrows and fools, but look at us--look at me! You have a secret which I will discover. But if you tell me in what form he might be present in Yazad's Sanctuary, then his life will be spared."

The Angel of Light replied, "You are a murderer and a slanderer to this day. What happened to you? This all came by your choice."

Beltshzan took another long puff, then slowly exhaled the smoke as he sought to dictate terms, "My exchange is this: I will give you the Heir alive, and you will give me the keys to the Magnificon. We can all be happy."

"Never in a thousand of your life times! You always promise what you cannot give. What you have become is not how I imagined you. You will be sifted in the transformation before the closing of the Magnificon gates. You may have the Sanctuary of your choice for a time, times, and half a time. You may even become a shadow of your former self in power and royal array. But is it not written:

'Your splendor has become your ruin. Your vanity consumed you because of your beauty. Your wisdom is a malignant tumor of your vile intelligence. I will gladly cast your matrix to the ground. I will place you on display before the leaders of the Earth, that they might behold the cesspool which birthed the infection.

You have defiled your own home of Yare'ach Kachol and many realms of creation by the sweat of your iniquities; therefore when you can run no more, a fire will crop up in your midst to *devour you, and cause your ashes to rain upon the Earth in the sight of all who behold you!'"*

While yawning and buffing his nails on the lapel of his jacket, Beltshzan retorted, "Angel of Light, how I miss your elegant speech. My ears are awake, I grant that you helped form me, but this is what I will do; I seek not your permission to taste another light. I drink it down and others are getting drunk on it now. Mine is better. Mine will bring healing to my fallen comrades. Mine will bring redemption for my kind!"

In reply the Angel spoke her departing words before ascending, "Yours is poison and results in death. Your house is divided. All that was, and is, and shall be was never yours to own. You are not fit to even bring temptation to the Heir who bears the Wound. Go and do what you must do!"

"Go and do what I must do?" mocked Beltshzan, "Do I need remind you; the very power which wounded the Heir is still very much alive? You are so mistaken if you assume your victory in one world can be applied to another. Another Messiah, another Juwaan waiting to be called out of moth balls? Enjoy, as you watch a people called by your name walk out on everything you stand for." With these last words of ridicule by Beltshzan, the very ground he stood on in the base of the extinct volcano began to quake and shift, venting steam and heat around him and his craft.

Beltshzan beheld the Angel of Light one last time as she ascended in a twirling white cloud in the same way she arrived. "How I hate her," he mumbled, quickly entering his craft. Ripping off his tie he gave orders to leave, "Full immediate thrust out of here!"

Blasting up through the throat of the mountain, his pulsing craft was chased by a sudden surge of red-orange magma and rock as if the Blue Moon itself wanted to expel him.

Chapter 51

There are no coincidences; there are first movers and then there are responders. The responders are the sheep.

Riding the glass elevator to the penthouse suite she shared with her father the week of the Cosmology Con, Ru quietly opened the door and slipped in. *Why sneak in, it's not like he ever sleeps?*

"Ru, come back here to my room."

Ru closed and locked the entrance to the hotel's premium penthouse while she put on a happy face to deflect the vitriol she suspected was about to come her way. Cuzak didn't let her down, chiding on her as she walked into his room, "God forbid your wings come loose and rip through your feminine apparel during a press conference, then what would we do? You have grown soft. I thought you were close with that anchorwoman's producer."

"'God forbid?' Thanks for the encouragement. I've been trying real hard to like who, or what, I was born--made into. Every day I have to deal with the press, 'Hey, what is your father, Colonel Cuzak really like outside the board room? Is he a regular guy? We've heard he is a crusher. When are you going to release real proof about the Sanctuary? Isn't it risky to your investors to build out in such mass?'"

Ru was form fit in a gray one piece short dress with black tight leggings and high heel black boots rising just above her ankles. Her hair was cut short, a classic bob, with her angled shiny dark bangs hanging over her right eye. Her athletic frame and mysterious features made her a magnet for most men. Unfortunate however, since she found most of her suitors annoying at best, unequal to her hybrid genome contributed by her human mother and her half human father, an ancient Nephilim.

Before Cuzak cut loose again she turned away noticing how beautiful the orange sunset was over the Desert Mountains. "You told me Lucas had no intention after their escape of fulfilling his call as a Juwaan! What a jack-ass I am in front of the entire world. And this Rulanda Lakee? Wait until we buy out the BBC. She should have never sucker punched me. She will pay dearly. Does she think there are no repercussions for her actions? And that Lucas Tanner, he should be grateful for the money, the patents. Tell me, is anyone grateful anymore? You didn't look very hard for them did you? Who were you looking for all that time? And don't think I have forgotten, his Eve."

Ru turned toward him. Somehow he didn't look as strong and menacing as he had eleven years ago when he entered--interrupted her life. She answered, "Victoria? His wife? No dad, you handled it well. Every big CEO is a target, not just you. But you are the biggest whale in the sea now. You built up your credibility today. They did you the favor of pulling the naysayers out so you'll know who the enemies of the Hub Stations are. We still haven't seen the backlash of religious fanatics as you projected. You should be thankful no one has harpooned you yet."

"What's that supposed to mean? Thankful? To whom?"

"Sorry, uh, to your father?"

Ignoring her rude comment Cuzak continued, "Does Dr. Tanner really assume that I can't find him if I wanted? I am concerned his fate will be out of my, our hands, and cause him to really disappear off the grid. We were not the only ones who saw him today. It's the little things. Remember what I said about Ouriano's sword disappearing? Too easy I told you. Remember, there..."

Ru joined him in repeating the words, "...there are no coincidences; there are first movers and then there are responders. The responders are the sheep."

But Cuzak added a line, "Don't forget, we hunt sheep. Good, I am glad some things have sunk in." While he spoke she noticed him rubbing the same spot on his chest again and grimacing.

"Father, why are you always rubbing that spot on your chest? Pull up your shirt." When he didn't move she asked, "OK then, have you considered Lucas—Dr. Tanner may want to be found, setting a trap for potential foes who may want him dead. After all, if he is a real Juwaan, then maybe he can't run away from his calling any longer?"

"I've asked you to refrain from so many questions Ru. The problem is, I made the exception of giving them grace. You have never had the joy of meeting Beltshzan, your grandfather, face to face when he is paranoid and inflamed. Thankfully, the time you met him in Korea, he was in a good mood. I believe, even after all we've done, including annihilating Ouriano, he doesn't trust us."

Ru asked, "Maybe he doesn't trust anyone because of his own nature? He hurt you once didn't he? That's why you call him 'My lord.'"

"That is the understatement of the millennium. Stay out of his way." Changing the subject Cuzak asked, "The chain around your neck? What is it?"

"Just a cross, to blend in. Most humans don't even see it."

"I know my crosses; it resembles one your mother once wore, Armenian. Please let me see it. Toss it over here Ru."

Pulling the pewter chain over her head through her hair, she kissed the silver cross, inlaid with colorful mother of pearl, and underhanded it across the bed, where he snagged it by the chain. "Why did you kiss it?" he asked.

"Ritual, that's all."

Cuzak stared at the chain entangled in this thick fingers as he lay propped up against his bed pillows, the cross spinning as it unwound. "The Armenians. I tell you, no humans suffered like they did, an emasculation of an entire people, yet a will to live. Now they are all over Hollywood." When the cross stopped, it faced away from his chest. He tried to turn it around as it dangled, but over and over the keep sake turned away from him. "Did Ouriano give this to you?"

Cuzak tried to lay the cross on his chest, but it acted in repulse to him, comparable to forcing similar charged magnets together. When he dangled it over the wound received on the Blue Moon from Beltshzan, the repulse was more severe, pulling the cross horizontally away from him. Ru watched, puzzled by this. Cuzak then threw it back to her saying, "It wouldn't help me blend in, would it? I am thankful for one thing..."

"What's that?"

"Your mother, or you wouldn't be here. Now, don't wither on me. Our most difficult days are ahead. Please trust me."

Ru questioned why the cross didn't repel from her body as she slipped it back over her head and neck. Moreover she thought, *That old bastard, I don't know whether to feel sorry for him, to love him, or to hate him. I wonder if he suspects I met her. He could have grilled me more about this cross. It doesn't add up.*

Cuzak interrupted her suspicions, "We are at the tipping point. We must complete and open the Hubs. That is our priority. You must stay focused on helping me do this. It has to happen. You've done a splendid job. Don't let anything, or anyone distract you."

Chapter 52

What if for your sake, I simply Am?

Lucas drove by the barren stumps through the drizzle where the rainforest had recently been mowed down in an illegally sponsored clear cutting. As he approached the base of the sharp escarpment of the green and gray mountain ridge which hid his family the last six years in the abandoned mine, he laughed at the warning sign of skull and cross bones planted to ward off wayward explorers. Heavy contributions to local political strong men kept this area free of visitors and hikers. The ridge overhead, the thick trees for several hundred meters buffering their entrance, and the large maze of boulders made a perfect hiding place. "I shouldn't have pulled the trigger," regretted Lucas, "they'll eventually come."

Hopping out of his SUV, Lucas shut the door and gazed at the beauty around him. He mused a prayer of thanks; "This is as close to paradise as it gets, now what? We are going to the Sanctuary, the land of Zion?" Concentrating more on the person of his prayer he asked, "Here I am Lord, not my will but yours be done, for the Juwaan in me, for Victoria, for Daniel, for Henry and Judith. I will go there if you lead me. I am trying, I really am."

Lucas took a deep breath and confessed, "I've broken the long truce and peace you've blessed us with by contacting Cuzak."

He paused for a moment then entreated, "Excuse me, but am I speaking to the wind? It's been so long since I've heard anything from you. I wondered if you've forgotten. You had a purpose in mind, right? After all your word says, 'The Lord delights in the steps of the man who he has confirmed; though he stumbles he will not fall, for you uphold him with your right hand.' I am counting on you to keep your honor."

As Lucas quieted down he tried to listen, just like he did every day, yet he heard only the background noise of the breeze through the top of the swaying trees, and a few nearby birds, but nothing else. But, turning to walk behind the last boulder and up the steps to their secret home's front door, he did hear something.

"The time has come."

Lucas couldn't discern whether the voice was in his head or real. Incrementally spinning around, he tried to locate the origin. "Who said that?"

No response returned, but he noticed a dim light behind the boulder where they collected well water; a small raised pool encircled by medium cut Inca stones, invaded by large tree roots. Cautiously rounding the large rock, Lucas became entranced by a woman sitting on the pool's wall. Dressed in an ivory wrapped gown and head covering, she emitted a warm glistening aura.

When Lucas heard her voice, he recognized it as the one belonging to the Desert Angel he had met almost ten years ago on Sharu. The raspy alto voice demanded more than intrigue. Now, for the first time he could see her. The beauty of her face was mesmerizing; the epitome of every woman, the joy of every man, the security of every child. Her beauty dazzled his mind, not of seduction but of creation and nurture, an assurance that evil will never overcome good.

As she stared through him and spoke he became fearful of her personal intrusion, "I came with as little raiment of power and glory so you could look upon my face. Peace be to you and greetings from the Wounded Heir and the seven spirits before the Magnificon. Do not be afraid, speak."

"Ah, ah, yes, I have to admit to look at you is like peering into the center of the Sun. I have in no way forgotten my painful awakening. You are my Desert Angel. I have seen you as lightning and as one holding my world in your hands. You have a soft voice which disguises your thunder." Falling to his knees, bowing, and slowly lifting his sight to her face, Lucas asked, "Where do you come from?"

"Oh Juwaan, what are you looking for? Why are you concerned with my origins, when you do not know yours? Where do you come from? How far in the past can you imagine? What if for your sake, I simply Am?"

"That would make you... yes, I suppose. What about the meeting Ouriano was preparing me for with the One from Siyon? Was that canceled? What happened to Ouriano?"

The Angel of Light answered, tilting her head slightly, "Am I not with you now? Are you a Juwaan because I called you or because you decided that it befit you? Light cannot be destroyed if its origins are from the Magnificon. The essence of Ouriano continues and will awaken in a distant land of Two Suns Rising."

"Will I know him?"

She answered, "He will be near."

"You are talking about the Sanctuary? Will we, does my family, still have to go?"

"I would not force you, but you will go. For without you, the masses will be led as sheep to a slaughter."

"And Daniel? He's only a child. Is there another way?"

"Always questioning, when the Magnificon is at your finger tips," she said, trying to help him comprehend with something more central to his being.

"I loved Daniel before the creation of the Winds. Of his parent's wisdom and courage, he will surpass. Woe to his enemies, for he will cause the rising and falling of many. You will take him to a land of weeping and gnashing of teeth; a land where you will refuse to be comforted. See, I have not retracted my words I gave to Victoria.

'I take up, and I give life.
Protect this little one and set him free.
He is mine, his spirit born of the Lake of Dreams.
Like his father, a sword he will bear.

A voice he will hear where no others can hear,
A light he will see where no others can see.
In time, tell him who he is and from whence he was forged.
A great harlot approaches to consume him, yet he will consume.
I will be an enemy to his enemies.'

I must go Lucas. You cannot protect Daniel from what he must be or what you must do. Your life is not your own."

Lucas, enraptured by the warmth of her presence, said, "Wait, you can't leave yet."

"I will answer one last question. Do not worry about what you do not know, when you have failed to grasp the fullness of the words the Heir has already given. For those who have ears to hear, they will hear the echo of Siyon in any land."

"Please, I once had a vision of Victoria's death. Will she die in the Sanctuary? Will Daniel ever return? You must tell me."

"You have asked twice, but I will answer once--Yes."

Lucas was ready to plead for more information, when he was interrupted by another more familiar voice from behind, "Dad? What are you doing?"

Reaching quickly to the top of his head, he put on his sunglasses then turned to greet Daniel.

Chapter 53

You and mom keep hiding things from me, why?

Daniel walked hand in hand with his dad half-way up the steps to the secluded home's entrance where his father told him, "Daniel, I need to talk to your mother for a few minutes, do you mind? Where's Grandpa?"

His skinny mop headed son said, squeezing his hand, "He's with Grandma over at the garden. What are you so afraid to tell me Dad?"

"What am I afraid to tell, you? Well, let's see... That you are very special, and that you are going to accomplish much more than your mom or dad. That your birthday party is in a few days?... You aren't buying these excuses are you? I know you want more. Soon, I promise."

Rolling his disappointing eyes, Daniel said, "You and mom keep hiding things from me. Why?"

"I am sorry. Please, a few minutes alone? You know how much I love you."

Daniel let his little dirt and sap stained hand slide out of his father's. As he watched his father climb a few more steps Daniel noticed a blue tint to his dad's right hand. He in turn looked down at his own.

Some of his blue rubbed off. That's weird! he thought, awakening more intrigue. A few seconds later Daniel snuck half way down the inside steps to overhear the heated discussion.

"If Cuzak and Ru wanted something to happen they would have done it by now, Victoria. Please, can you sympathize with me? I pretended this day wouldn't come."

Tears collected in her eyes, "I sat in our living room, and listened to you antagonize Cuzak on the global network.

Admit it. You were baiting him. Are you crazy, putting our lives at stake because of your ego!"

"My ego? You mean my calling. There is a hell of a lot of difference," Lucas responded as he tore off his sun glasses, "please look at me!"

Exacerbated, Victoria dabbed her eyes and saw the brightness coming from his. "I am sorry; I didn't mean to belittle your calling as a Juwaan: the light in your eyes, your blue hand, the sword, the mirror. It's so odd. I've heard you say, 'Cuzak is responsible for your mother's death.' But we've had happiness here. Now I see it all dissolving."

"And if we remain here as a family while the entire world crumbles around us, you suppose we are somehow immune? If we try to save Daniel we'll lose him. This is larger than all of us."

"Lucas, my faith agrees with you, but I locked these feelings in a closet a long time ago. Today Daniel broke the lock. I have to tell you something he said."

"And I need to share something too. Alright, you first," pronounced Lucas.

Victoria pulled herself out of her depressive state, "Daniel admitted to me and Henry while you were out that he's had visions. At least he shared with us a vision. His eyes Lucas, they don't match the rest of him. He's seen things only Ouriano saw."

"Like what?"

As they both leaned on their kitchen island, Daniel crept closer down the steps.

"He quoted a conversation that he had with Beltshzan where he was called the Death Angel. Your dad walked in and heard Daniel quoting some prophetic passage from Isaiah."

"He memorizes verses with mom and dad all the time."

"Not these kind. We are talking gloom and judgment, piles of dead bodies, wings. I wondered about some of his virtual reality games, but we sorted those out, unless he smuggled one in on us. I've never told him about Ouriano, but the vision he shared makes it seem like there is part of Ouriano inside of him, some kind of connection. That's not normal. I am his mother, and I have a feeling there is more he hasn't shared with us."

"Hold it babe, we know what this is about." Lucas turned his head, "Did you hear something? Someone else in the house?"

"No," Victoria said as he leaned around the corner to check on the empty stair well.

"Do you think he heard us? Hey Daniel!" Lucas yelled. But after no answer he continued as his son crept back to within listening distance, "My eyes, my hand. Look at them. I just had an encounter with the Desert Angel from the Blue Moon! God I hope it was her. Only this time she appeared much more human. She said exactly what we didn't want to hear to confirm this vision of Daniel's, as morbid as it sounds."

Victoria questioned him, "The one who energized the mirror and left you temporarily blind in the desert, when you were looking for me?"

"Yes, she quoted the words you have recited over and over about Daniel which you heard the night you were hit by lightning in Tokyo."

"Where did you see her?"

"Just outside by the well," Lucas pointed through the rock.

"That explains your energized eyes and hand."

"She said a string of difficult things which sounded like, 'The time has come--I am still expected to be a Juwaan--That we would encounter the essence of Ouriano, in the land of Two Suns Rising.'"

"Two Suns Rising? Is that the Sanctuary? What else did she say Lucas? Will we come back? What about our son?"

"Concerning Daniel she said, 'Woe to his enemies, for he will cause the rising and falling of many. You will take him to a land of weeping and gnashing of teeth.'"

Victoria paused, put her hands on the kitchen island and bemoaned, "I'd say let's find another place to get away, but where?"

Just then Judith and Henry came rambling down the front steps into the kitchen dining room. Judith said, "Pardon my interruption, but I heard that last sentence. Henry was sharing with me Daniel's vision. I've kept my mouth shut until now. He is a special boy. The fact is there isn't anywhere to get away. The safest place is God's will."

Lucas and Victoria nodded their head in agreement as they grinned somberly. Then Victoria added, "Even if it means going into the darkness."

Henry added, "Yeah, I believe so."

Lucas spoke again, "Something else just occured that I'll have to tell you about, but did you happen to pass Daniel on the way in?"

"Oh, he told me he wasn't wanted inside so he was going to find his little talking sloth friend, Pico." said Henry.

Chapter 54

Find the Sanctuary, find yourself.

The ten members of the Sanctuary Corporation's Unity Team, nicknamed by the press as the "Religious Dream Team," were all huddled around the AMOLED glass U-shaped table in the meeting room of the resplendent Boeing 797. The sixth addition to the Sanctuary's fleet, found itself cruising at sixty-thousand feet over the South Pacific, racing to keep the team's tight schedule of religious solidarity rallies for peoples of all global faiths. Their mandate was "Find the Sanctuary, find yourself."

"In a moment colleagues, the Colonel will be joining us through our live feed. He believes we need some inspiration for our messages," said Ru.

The Colonel, not yet broadcast in front of the team, belly-ached through her close-circuit visor. She saw him fidgeting in one hand with a golf ball which he split in half with his thumb nail, then ground the rest to pulp. "Dammit Ru! What is your group's itinerary this week? I want a surge, a panic rush for these Hub tickets. We handpicked these Cretan-charlatan-shamans to bridge the religious gap for most of the major belief systems where we assumed an endorsement would help. But, I don't see a sufficient increase in the opinion polls, especially with the Evangelical-Pentecostals and Muslims.

I don't want to lump them with the Jews, who I consider to have a low conversion rate, so don't waste time on them. They are too stubborn; last time around they wouldn't even recognize the Messiah. Nobody tells them what to do. But what I envision are guerilla media conferences outside well known and holy places like the Dome of the Rock, the Vatican, Angkor Wat, Machu Picchu, with our plane hovering in the background. These wind bag preachers need to be bold and hit the football, soccer stadiums too. Coach them to leave sound bites to go viral. Team up with rock stars. Do whatever it takes, understand? Some of these religious piss-ants act like they might renege. There will be consequences."

"Colonel, we are hitting Melbourne, Sydney, Jakarta, Kuala Lumpur, Cape Town, and Tehran in the next two days."

"Ru, I'm viewing your God Squad as we speak; cozy, fake smiles, phones, wrist computers, lap tops, overpaid, and lazy. They look more like executives than humble servants. They act like this is a vacation. They obviously don't realize what is at stake. Today I am going to put the fear of God in them, I don't care what religion they are."

"Yes, Father, I will back you up, whatever you say. Do you want a virtual image of yourself in the room?"

"No virtual--live! I'm coming on board. They need a good smack!"

"You didn't tell me, when are you coming?"

"Now!"

Several "thumps" were heard on the roof of the plane. Through the windows several of the leaders saw the shadow of a smaller jet on the wing. Everyone began to look puzzled, first at the ceiling, then Ru. Her choice of power attire for the day: sculpted black business jacket and skirt, dark fishnet stockings with heels, maroon--red lipstick, black pearls, blue nails. Her cross was hidden below the neck line of her white blouse. Also her Tazer was hidden on her upper right thigh, just in case.

Ru addressed them, "Ladies and gentleman, devout leaders, you are about to engage our Founder in person. He makes no apologies for his passion. He is an intense entrepreneur and believes the Sanctuary Corporation supplements your religions with real blood and gut generosity. If you get off this plane only to leave the hordes of the world's hopeless without a chance to win at life, then I doubt any of you are following the true heart of your religion. People will remember you as worse than an infidel."

Cuzak heard every word as he readied himself, complimenting Ru, "Now that's the spirit!"

With his plane locked onto the top of the 797's fuselage, Cuzak stood on the loading circle. At his voice command, "Bring me down," the round white platform descended through an overlapping spiral portal in the conference room's ceiling.

Ru encouraged all the dignitaries, "Please stand and give Colonel Cuzak a well deserved round of applause."

As they clapped, Cuzak descended, his platform sinking seamlessly into the floor at the head of the table. Wearing a dark blue Italian suit, offset by a brilliant light blue tie, he bowed to all with his hands folded together. Without the least bit of a smile, he signaled for them to have a seat and began to ominously pace behind their chairs.

Cuzak recited these leaders' titles out loud as he slowly moved from one to another. "Ah, the Reverend Jane Stalworth, of the World Council of Churches, soon to be labeled as the 'Interplanetary Council of Churches,' representing a declining ecumenical group committed to social justice, identity politics, and apologizing for past colonial and current capital market inequities. How is that progressing for you?"

She smirked back, perplexed, as he continued, "All of you were gifted preferred stock in our Corporation. All of you are multimillionaires by now, if by chance you weren't already. I hope you cash some of your stock in and enjoy yourselves for a change; everything in moderation, even greed."

Moving over, Cuzak placed his hands on the shoulders of the next seated, "The Conservative Rabbi, Isaiah Cohen, psychotherapist and President of the non-profit humanitarian group, 'Mediators for Peace.' Your brother's hedge fund and uncle's law firm profits ungodly amounts behind your secret international negotiations. My kind of preacher!"

Cuzak then stepped behind the third religious leader,

"Here we have none other than gospel preaching, spirit filled evangelical-Pentecostal, wrapped in the American Flag, Hugh McKenzie. Pay attention to this one. Hugh knows how to persuade the ambitious pathetic into believing God's kingdom is focused on them alone, while financing his Gulf Stream gambling trips to Reno and group therapy in Bangkok. Anyone here jealous?

Oh, but next to him is no piker, the Master Shong Lou who in twenty years has branded his own empire of fifteen-hundred international Kalachakra-Buddhist Meditation and Peace centers, while inheriting vast estate holdings of members who decided to enter into voluntary poverty. I am sorry, Master Lou, but your white suit and sunglasses, reminds me of Elvis. By the way, this one owns more white limo's than any man alive." Several chuckled at Cuzak's remark.

"Excuse me Colonel," interrupted the usually quiet man from across the half oval table, dressed in his traditional branded Tibetan yellow and red robes, oversized tinted glasses, bare pale arms.

"Certainly your Holiness," said Cuzak, to the Dalai Lama, tugging the wrinkles out of his suit jacket.

The Dalai continued in his choppy English, "I know you are not finished, Mr. Cuzak, but I need more proof that the Sanctuary is everything your corporation says it is. I am a Buddhist monk. The Earth is the mother to humanity, to all of us no matter what our beliefs. You want us to support leaving the place of our creation and birth, as a way to help the poor. You have given us professional video and news documentaries, but this is not enough proof for me to put my reputation and leadership of souls on the line. Even some scientists are not convinced of the data from Pantos and Krator. The major criticism is valid, given lack of eyewitness accounts."

Cuzak minimally bowed his head toward him, "Thank you for speaking your mind, your Holiness, and noted. You are an honorable man far more than most of us. Are there others here with honor?"

Cardinal Themba Mhaule, of the Pontifical Council on Religious Unity raised his hand. He wore a black cassock, red sash, and clerical collar, with a large gold cross and red silk skull cap. "Colonel Smith, I am not pulling out, for that is not the nature of the Church. The Lord exists outside of time and space, so we have no problem in establishing galactic parishes, but something else has been brought to my attention from several of our previous stops I must inquire about."

Cuzak became cautiously curious, "And what might that be? Get it all out. Another abuse scandal? And you have personal ties?"

Embarrassed by the comment and shaking his head, "No," Cardinal Mhaule clarified, "nothing of the sort Colonel. This did not come from Rome, but from old colleagues who contacted me during our Sanctuary rallies in central Africa. I received alarming information from local priests operating in Benin, Togo, Congo, Nigeria, after this impressive plane you have outfitted with its laser light show and hovering ability, drew great attention."

Cuzak grew impatient, "Please, get to the point."

"The point is this," said the Cardinal, "as you know this area of the world experiences a high number of exorcisms. And in some of these exorcisms the priests have reported something very similar; demons speaking of leaving the Earth for the Sanctuary, for a new god, named Yazad. Do any of you know this name?"

Cuzak smiled robotically, having realized this topic might surface at some point. Wiping the white foam that had accumulated from the corners of his mouth he answered, "Cardinal, people love to start myths. Maybe you believe in demons, but you must realize many dismiss demonic possession as poor psychological care, a schism of the psyche. Would your demons understand quantum tunneling and the manipulation of the Higgs Field involved in the Hub Station technology? Please, Monsignor."

The Cardinal acted intimidated, unsure to the others, "Yes, it sounds outlandish. But I thought you should know. I wanted to dismiss it. They also reported these demented people, strangers to each other, sketching rainbow feathered peacocks."

Quick to maintain control, Cuzak said, "Then dismiss it, and I'll give you and your Pope a new rock on which to build your Church." Ru glanced at each member to see their reaction to his blatant ditching of the question. Most masked their feelings, but Cardinal Mhaule's eyes remained confused.

"Any other substantive questions from the rest of you?" the Colonel asked as he surveyed the room until he caught the Argentinean pastor Dr. Armando Cruz, deep in independent thought staring out a side window of the plane, seemingly disengaged from the others.

What is he up to? Cuzak asked himself as he tried to anticipate who he felt to be the most genuine but also the most unpredictable and least likely to be bullied of the group. With graying temples, immaculate dark brown stripped suit, and shiny copper and black paisley tie, Dr. Cruz held up his old leather bound Bible to make a stand.

Cuzak took the initiative to soften what he might say, "Pastor Cruz, your Solo Jesus movement has impacted millions. Your church is a denomination unto itself. You have spun off some five hundred churches, and your own media empire. You dominate the Latino evangelical mindset, leaving nearby local Catholic parishes lagging in attendance. You sell books by the millions on the motivational market. You are sending Missionaries all over the world. What could be troubling you? "

Chapter 55

How can we fear that which we are by nature
one with? We are not traveling to the stars, so
much as we are the stars.

Dr. Cruz was ready to respond, "I am afraid that I must pull out my support. I have too many questions from my followers raised by Dr. Lucas Tanner who recently called into your international press conference. This former associate of yours, who was reported dead, contacted you live at the Cosmology Conference, raising questions about science and religion. In your speech you claimed to be the author of new revelation, did you not, greater than the Bible?"

"I understand your concern, but that would be a misquote."

As Cuzak moved to explain himself, Dr. Cruz cut him off in a matter-of-fact fashion, "Anyway, my wife has been in prayer with me, and we believe that God wants us to establish dominion here on this planet, not escape. The Earth is the Lord's and the fullness thereof. We don't need the Sanctuary Corporation's money. When God wants a new home for us, He'll make one. Your company's donations are being refunded as we speak."

Again, while Cuzak tried to recover, the eldest statesman in the room, Dr. Mustafa Karim Ali, Secretary General of the Mediterranean Caliphate, was already annoying the Colonel by rapping his thick finger tips on the glass table. Dressed in a sharp kaki business suit, accented by his gray hair, short white beard, he pointed at Cuzak. Speaking very agitated Dr. Ali said, "This is our sentiment too. I have meditated on this very much and have been in counsel with our home office at the Blue Mosque, in Istanbul. Our calling is to establish submission for Allah in the Earth. We feel like it is in our grasp. Within three generations, when all of Western and Eastern Europe, Southeast Asia, and

Africa submit to Sharia law, then we will consider going to your planet.

And as much as I do not always see eye to eye with my Pontifical emissary, I also have received similar communication of exorcisms by Imams casting out Jinns in Egypt, Netherlands, and Iraq. I have pictures and video of the possessed cutting into their arms, others sketching graffiti on walls, depictions of the Cardinal's peacock, the Melek Tous. We know this one is worshipped by the Yazidi as the former Shaytan. You call him Satan." Pulling out a yellow file folder he slammed it on the table, his proof prints sliding out and said, "I for one am not willing to dismiss all of these reports as psychological babble!"

Cuzak wiped the corners of his mouth again. Feeling his shirt collar tighten, he arched his head back, and turned it side to side. Ru heard his reptilian vertebra pop, and felt the tension in the room rise. She became afraid of what her father might do, or worse, ask of her. She also noticed him rubbing the familiar spot on his chest as he moved to the next person.

"Thank you for your insight Dr. Ali," who sat with his hands clasped tightly. "We will miss you, but you must admit you have never liked the Kurds."

"No Colonel, as I see it, you dismiss those who disagree with you."

"Point well taken. Next we have Sheikh Jafar Hammam," said Cuzak to the man seated in the white dishdasha, sporting a black goatee, "an itinerant Islamic preacher for the Planetary Salvation Front. Your home office is in the desert gem, Dubai. You own some of the finest race horses in the world, five star hotels on every continent, and recently a bestselling author. I have read your book, 'The Coming Reformation of Islam,' and so I have to ask you Sheikh Hammam," as Cuzak repositioned behind him, "are you going to pull out with Dr. Ali?"

Nervously shifting his eyes left and then right to try and see Cuzak, Sheikh Hammam said, "Colonel, it is difficult for a Holy man or any Holy woman in this room to comprehend the changes a new world like the Sanctuary brings to one's theology. Although the holy tenets of our book have not changed, the world overnight has expanded beyond our imagination. I have dreamed of seeing two Suns together; one rising and one setting, as mentioned in our sacred Koran."

Ru thought to herself, *If he only knew the true plans of what was intended, he'd never agree to this.*

The Sheikh proceeded, "My message for my brothers and sisters is simple; Allah fills the universe and desires his people to fill every place he has destined to proclaim his truths. He most certainly demands his people establish a Holy Nation, united in faith and peace, even in a new land of Two Suns. I am not preaching a message of escape, but of divine destiny, a tranquil Jihad to occupy the universe."

"Then you disagree with him?"

"Yes, unequivocally," he answered.

Cuzak spun Sheikh Hamman's chair toward him, and shook his hand firmly, smiling, "Yes, this is the attitude I want to hear!" and moved on.

"Who else do we have on our religious team?" asked Cuzak, moving counter clockwise in the room. "Swami Vivekananda III. You have no enemies from what I gather. Live and let live motto all the way to the bank. And you have revived my favorite spiritual discipline, the Kama Sutra. Now you can teach it in a new world. Ha-ha."

"Colonel," he responded in a serious manner, "Nothing in the universe will be withheld from those who go after it with all their heart. How can we fear that which we are by nature one with? We are not traveling to the stars, so much as we are the stars."

Cuzak glanced at Ru quick enough to see her sigh, and then replied, "I couldn't have said it better. Don't you agree Ru?"

Before she could respond he said, "Lastly, my Anglican friend. Dr. Renee Robertson, the Arch Bishop of Canterbury. You've solidified your protestant catholic seat with your nerves of steel and your radical theology. In publishing your new book, 'The Transgendered Jesus, No Marriage in Heaven,' you must have calculated that alienating part of your flock was worth the price."

Dr. Robertson answered, "Yes, but I felt it was the God's honest truth."

Cuzak ran with her words, "That's what we are all after here, isn't it? As you know we cannot win everyone. The Eastern Orthodox Church and Sub Saharan mega-church pastors declined our invitation citing we have linked religion as dependent on science. Like several members here who have decided to break covenant with the Sanctuary Corporation, they will come to their senses later. Besides, I believe many of the members of these groups no longer regard the head of their institution as an authority figure."

Having prodded each member of the religious ensemble, Cuzak returned to his real purpose--motivation. "I want to tell you a story, from years ago about a black Labrador I rescued from being euthanized. I wanted to get an older dog that was mature, already house broken, not overzealous. I had read that older dogs make good pets. They are smart. They know when they have it made. I brought home a two year old male Lab named Fiji. He loved me the first time I laid eyes on him. We became best pals: jog through the neighborhood every evening, special treats, a warm sheltered home.

One day I did not come home at my regular time, and when I walked into the house, it was a disaster. Fiji had gone berserk. Curtains were ripped down. The dog defecated in my bed. It chewed the corner off of a very expensive Persian carpet. But I loved that dog.

When I called the dog's name, 'Fiji,' it finally cowered out of hiding, tail between his legs. I didn't change a thing. We went out for a run. In a few days I had everything repaired, and we were a happy family again. The dog was smart. I taught it more tricks. All was forgiven.

Two months went by without an incident. I came home late again, and it all repeated. Fiji had a deep seated problem. I refused to send it to training school. I desired a dog with a relationship, not military obedience. So having shared this story, what do you believe I did with Fiji or should have done?"

The Dali Lama smiled, and laughed, "There is a reason in some Asian cultures, they eat dogs."

The Rabbi said, "You had him circumcised?"

"You started a monastic movement for dogs," said the Cardinal.

Dr Ali added, "You eliminated the problem. For it did not submit."

"You called the dog whisperer?" asked Rev. Stalworth.

"Ah, you found a new home for Fiji with children," said the Swami.

Disconcerted, Dr. Cruz asked, "Can I excuse myself from this discussion to my quarters, since your beloved pet story no longer pertains to me?" Cuzak raised his right eyebrow and did all he could to contain his wings from rupturing through his blue suit, as his anger began to take hold of him. Ru came to his side to calm her father.

She placed a hand on his shoulder, and whispered to him. "You are about to rip your jacket. Your collar has a ring of sweat, and you have foam on your lips."

Chapter 56

All religions are due for an overhaul, but they need a new context to make it happen.

Cuzak politely answered, "Please Pastor Cruz, or any others who want to vote your conscience. You can leave. I'll be more than happy for my shuttle to arrange a convenient drop off if you gather your things. I'll be departing in about twenty minutes."

The Dali Lama and Dr. Mustafa Karim Ali collected their items and followed Dr. Cruz out of the room toward their quarters, bowing "goodbye." The door to their hall slid sideways then sealed back after they passed.

"How unfortunate," said Cuzak, "they should have recognized the day at hand, nevertheless it will come round to them again. Now let me finish the story of Fiji. How did it end?"

"I hope you did not give up on him," said Swami Vivekananda III as he twirled his long mustache.

"Thank you for asking, Swami. Matter of fact, I tried harder to make my home and schedule perfect for Fiji. But he was a canine who could not be broken. I built a wonderful kennel for him, but he learned to climb out. He dug under the fence and would be lost for days. Finally I paved the entire kennel and put an electric wire on the fence to keep him safe."

Hugh McKenzie added, "You have a soft spot, don't you Colonel, as tough as you come off. You never gave up on Fiji."

"Correct, I never gave up on him. One night I was late and Fiji had to ride out a thunderstorm in his kennel. He panicked and tried to climb out even though he was scared of the hot wire. Unfortunately his collar became caught in the electric wire, where the rain in combination with the current, finally stopped his heart. I found Fiji hanging by his collar on the fence. I cried."

Everyone in the room suddenly shuddered and began searching each other's face for a proper response. Ru looked at her shoes, *What is wrong with Cuzak? This dog torture story is news to me. He's twisted.*

"And the lesson is," The Colonel paused, "if you have to break a dog too many times, that animal will one day kill itself. Don't bother investing your life and emotions into someone who is obstinate and ungrateful. Now, does anyone have a question about what we are doing?"

Cuzak unbuttoned his collar and took off his tie, then said, "No questions?" The volume of his voice increased and the timber more powerful. "You were recruited and paid because of your ability, not potential, to sway opinion for one purpose and one purpose only; to drive people of faith to the Transfer Hubs. You are not being persuasive enough! We don't care about the people who are set in concrete regarding their faith if they don't want to go. Sure we will attract some of those fanatics. Most of them have no life. But that is not enough.

What I don't want is masses of people excited about their decision to begin a new life and then have some two bit preacher-evangelist, suicide bomber, fundamentalist knuckle dragger, self appointed apocalyptic guru, or some pseudo cheesy news reader-reporter, diverting people away. I especially don't want to see the price of our stock drop!"

Colonel Smith lowered his volume as he walked the inside of the table, "The ability for all of us to travel to another universe is just the start. The Hub Stations are only a means to get us beyond the stars. This is about people who have become shackled in history, to be set free from bondage and the old meaningless rules forced on them by unbenevolent overbearing power structures. All religions are due for an overhaul, but they need a new context to make it happen. You are going to have at your means all of your rich history to help people begin anew; to opt out of everything which held them down in the past. And when you do, they will call you 'blessed!'"

With his animated hand gestures and penguin like waddling Cuzak droned on, "We need scientists, but also we need theologians like you to process and incorporate all of these wonderful changes at hand. You will see things your mothers and fathers never dreamed of. Your perspective of the stars will be so different; the first human eyes to chart a virgin universe. All of you know people are scared of death. What if you could promise them that at the very least, 'you will escape the possibility of hell, because it doesn't apply in the Sanctuary?' Behold, you make all things new!"

Ru began to look at her nails, and tried to fake looking interested. The rest were mesmerized by the insinuation of this new world. Cuzak took a deep breath, and reloaded for more verbiage, "And another thing," but was interrupted by blue flashing warning lights mounted on the ceiling. A suave female computer generated voice came over the plane's intercom system, "Warning! Fire detected in residential section A. Warning! Fire detected in residential section A."

A few moments later the computer announced, "Now sealing off section A to contain threat. Now sealing off section A to contain threat."

"What's happening Ru? This is a brand new plane," said Cuzak.

"We rushed the shake down sir," said Ru then gave the computer a command, "Show section A on screen." Behind her and Cuzak, the screen displayed the interior sections of the plane under concern, where a thin white smoke filled the small apartment hall way. Those in the meeting room could see a panicked Dr. Ali, Dr. Cruz and the Dali Lama coming out of their private quarters holding towels over their noses, banging on the meeting room door to open, "Bam, bam, bam."

"Oh my God, "screamed Reverend Stalworth, followed by "You've got to get them out!" from Rev. Robertson.

"Initiating protocol Dog Day One," the intercom blared.

"What is that?" asked a flustered Cuzak.

Ru answered, "The plane is going to depressurize that section while climbing to a higher altitude to starve the fire of oxygen."

"That will kill them," said Cuzak.

"Computer," said Ru, "Open hall way door to allow the trapped to get out."

"We are sorry. Unable to comply."

"That is an over ride directive, code '593-Ice Station Zebra,'" commanded Ru.

"I am sorry. We recognize code '593-Ice Station Zebra,' but for the greater good of the other passengers and the integrity of the plane, we must follow the protocol 'Dog Day One.'"

Desperate Ru demanded, "What type of protocol is that? Computer, where are the oxygen masks?"

It replied in the calm voice, "A short has been detected in the drop down mask mechanism. Sending notification of defect now to manufacturer."

"I am going to knock down that door Father." But Cuzak seized her wrists as her thick nails began to protrude and her iris's split like a predator. "I am not going to let you do this Father," she said loud enough for the others to become alert to the intense conversation. "Those men are the best humanity has to offer. You can't do this."

Cuzak turned his head to the others at the table, grinned and then turned his face back to confront Ru, pinning her against the screen. Speaking softly in her ear he said, "No, not in front of these ministers will you try to confront me. Save it for another time and place. You need to become stronger to take me down. Wise up. You'll die if you go against me today. And then after you, I will kill all of them and start over. These people must fear us." Ru trembled in disgust as tears rolled down her cheeks. Slumping to the floor she covered her face with the fists she made to conceal her nails.

She heard Cuzak say to the remaining dream team, "My daughter is brave. If she could open that door, the plane would decompress this area too, and kill all of us."

Ru curled into a ball under the screen as everyone watched helplessly. While Cuzak pretended to wipe a tear from his eye, the computer's audio and visual tracking showed the victims falling on the floor near each other gasping for oxygen like beached fish. From there, the decompression and injected carbon dioxide, guaranteed them a death sleep.

Cuzak asked the computer, "What are the vital signs of the passengers in the quarantined compartment?"

"Passengers 03, 05, and 08 are critical," said the computer calmly as if giving a sunny weather report, "blood pressure, 40/20, 52/30, and 35/15 respectively. Oxygen levels five percent."

Their chests heaved with lungs starved for oxygen, phlegm and swollen tongues obstructing their airways. The brain stems continued to send signals for their heart muscles to contract, until the cardiac tissues had no stores of energy left to pump. Finally the gurgling gasps ceased and the computer pronounced, "Passenger 03 has expired, no pulse, zero oxygen." A few seconds later, "Passenger 08 has expired, no pulse, zero oxygen." "Passenger 05 has expired, no pulse, zero oxygen."

Pulling her hands away from her eyes, Ru rose to her feet and ordered the viewing screen "off!" then glared at her father, "Are you so cruel that you had to make everyone watch them die?"

Cuzak turned around to the ministers. "I am at a loss for words, would someone please pray. The world has lost some of its finest."

But before anyone could utter a word, the plane's computer announced, "Access to living quarters has been restored, fire abated." To their amazement the door to the apartment hallway slid open, allowing a bank of white smoke to puff into their meeting room. But even more astounding, was the three men striding in behind the smoke. Everyone sat in shock as the three dissenters who they witnessed die minutes earlier, return to their vacant seats around the table.

Reverend Stalworth adjusted her glasses, very disturbed, and voice quaking, "I... You... The three of you... I saw you lying on the floor. There was smoke. Two of you had already put on casual clothes. I mean, you were foaming at the mouth. But here you are moments after being pronounced dead, quite alive, business as usu..." Before she could finish her sentence she passed out in her chair.

At that moment Ru and Cuzak both felt a dreaded dark presence. Ru ran toward the doorway to check for herself on the state of the apartment area. The compartment door slid open, as she approached the hall, and then closed behind her. Turning to her left she attempted to enter Dr. Cruz apartment but suddenly bumped into a man she had met only briefly years ago. He laughed at the prospect of accidentally running into her and acted as if he missed her. Holding her waist and gazing into her eyes, he greeted her, "Ru, I've been waiting so long to see you again. Your father has told me how you continue to grow in your faith, your loyalty to the Company and your family."

Ru could sense a dark pulse of erotic power surge from him into her. She also felt her ancient cross pressing firmly against her sternum as if it were repelled by this man. "Beltshzan?" she inquired.

"What gave me away?"

"I don't know what to say. I can feel you. Your presence is stimulating. I, ah, I, ah. You revived those men?"

Mesmerizing her, Beltshzan said, "I can do many things. And I want you to be with me."

Behind her Ru also heard her father as he entered the hall way. She spun her head to look at him, when he said, "Ru? What did you find?"

"He was here, Beltshzan, just now. Where'd he go? I don't see him." Ru held her father's hands, but he pulled one away to hold over the sensitive scar on his chest.

"My Ru, I am sorry I brought you into this world, that you had to get involved. I am growing weary of his power."

Chapter 57

Never look a gift universe in the mouth.
–C.K. Chesterton

10 years after Ouriano's death

Westminster, London

"Come on Pam, we can't run this bloody story as the lead. Push it down in the teleprompter, and tell the editors to cut the base story in half. This isn't news anymore. This is pure hype for the biggest snake oil rip off in history after the virgin birth."

"Rulanda, I'd kill to have your paycheck, which is not bad for a reader in a tight dress, and FYI the BBC has been commercial for two years. Guess who now owns fifty-one percent?"

"The Sanctuary Corporation... I read, remember? Aren't we glad we're kissin' their arses as news whores?"

"At least their pockets are getting deeper."

"Pam, they're going to own a third of the world markets whether this works or not. This puke your guys have for me to regurgitate is meant to escalate the run on these Hub tickets. The real story here is this whole sham is going to backfire. Look at the thread of the feeds we are featuring today: mega-preachers, self-help gurus, Hollywood, UN, climatologists. Why aren't we featuring the naysayers?"

"The kooks? It's been tested. It works. How can you argue with the Archbishop of Canterbury?"

"Funny, no journalists with independent spines have been asked."

"I tell you what. You're on in fifteen minutes. I'll give you the opening paragraph to put in your spin, after that you read the script and run with the clips as edited. Deal?"

"Thanks, Pam."

"And another thing, he is a powerful man, this Colonel Cuzak Runaldi, and don't underestimate that strange daughter of his. I remember how you caught him off guard by taking the video call from this Dr. Lucas Tanner for his interview at the Cosmological Con. Others may not have noticed, but you made him jump. Lucky for you he knew how to reconstruct your blind side attack into something for his benefit. He's brilliant. Want an unofficial word of advice?"

"Bring it to me Pam."

"People who cross him don't fare so well, and I am not talking about your career only."

"I hear you, but he is hiding something. It's like the children's story of the Emperor with no clothes. How come no reporter has been invited to experience the Hub and return to tell about it?"

"Marketing hype, the more you can't have it the more the masses want it. But many do have legitimate reasons to want this. It's like starting over with your life from scratch. Haven't you ever wondered what that would be like? Hmm? Maybe not, you my friend have the perfect life, don't throw it away."

"Pam, didn't the Sanctuary Corporation sign a release guaranteeing fair and balanced coverage of the news when they bought the BBC?"

"What are you getting at?"

"What if I renewed the special report I was trying to build on Cuzak, the one you pooh-poohed? I am telling you there is an ugly belly to this beast."

"You're out of your league Rulanda; remember when you postulated that Dr. Tanner had been murdered?"

"But he was in hiding for his life."

"Rulanda...," slowly raising the volume of her name.

"Please mum!"

"Rulanda, on two conditions; I'll let you renew your work for a half hour report if you keep it completely hush, hush.

"Oh thank you!"

"And,.."

"You won't be sorry."

"... and I can nix it after previewing. Nothing viral, not a scrap, do you understand? It's got to be you alone."

Rulanda barked back in protest, "That's three stipulations."

"Take it or leave it. Waiver and I'll personally book you a first class ticket to the Sanctuary from one of the three London Hubs."

"You won't regret it."

"I already am. What are your leads?"

"To start with, I have several religious leaders who think this is easy escapism."

Pam countered, "What, a satanic coup?"

"No, on the contrary, I mean there might be some who believe that, but others, more intellectual are arguing that this parallel world is an easy way to get rid of the ninety-nine percent, you know the occupy crowd, the working poor. These leaders oppose it, whether the Sanctuary is real or not on the grounds that this allows capitalist pigs, dictators, fascists, to get rid of their headaches in an easy fashion."

"What do you think, Rulanda, real?"

"I own stock in the Sanctuary Corporation and plan on selling before they implode. Of course I don't believe it's real."

"Are you going religious on me?"

"By birth, Anglican, but I haven't been to church in years. Not since women priests were introduced."

"Any other leads?"

"Do I have to tell you?"

"Yes."

"This Cuzak's daughter, she is a real piece of work, weird. I keep a file on her. I was here in the building when she came through the studio last year assessing everything. I asked her why she never returned my calls. Said she'd get back with me soon. I am still waiting.

She's like his junkyard dog. But he protects her. Remember my investigation you tanked, where her mother supposedly died when she was a baby, but I found out she is very much alive."

"The Armenian nun you interviewed in Kiev—conspiracy stuff?"

"Yes, well, not long after I showed you my video footage, I found out Cuzak's daughter was spotted in the capital of Armenia, likely to pay her a visit."

Pam surprised her, "As much as I hate to admit, you do have several more pieces of your pie. Hmm, what would be the headline? "Spurned lover and mother of Cuzak's daughter claims CEO is of the devil."

"Not the first CEO to be accused of that."

Thanks Ms. Lakee, now do your intro and get back to what you know best... whoring."

"Listen Pam, thanks. One more thing; if we can't run it here, we can sell the story to a competitor."

"No!"

Chapter 58

This is his backyard; nothing bad is going to happen.

"Look at him, Lucas. The rainforest is his playground; no fear of spiders or snakes. He'd just as soon swing on a vine or run barefoot than ride home with us. Call him down and remind him of his curfew – he hears better when dad says it."

"Daniel! Come down here for a second; we need to talk."

"Why does he have to choose the highest trees?"

"Because they're there, why else? He's all boy. Love the perpetual scab on the knee."

Victoria, still not satisfied, poked his shoulder with her left index finger and added, "And your father encourages more risks, taking him exploring deep into those old Inca mine shafts and playing with those antique Conquistador swords."

Lucas caressed her finger and kissed it saying, "Vic, we can't over protect knowing what's at stake."

Daniel bounded down to his parents, immediately appealing for more time, "Let me stay a little longer," Daniel used the puppy-eye look on his best target, "Please, Mom?"

Vic let the sneaky, puppy-eye attack roll over her and stuck to her guns. "Sun sets in two hours. You know the rules."

"Climb with me to the top Dad!" Daniel tried to persuade his other parent. "This Ceiba tree is the oldest out here, it's massive. It'll be fun. Whadda ya think?"

"Daniel, please listen to your mother; you need to be on time tonight. The clock is running while you stand here arguing."

Remembering the occasion, Daniel focused like a laser. "Mom, baked Alaska for my cake? You promised."

"Out here? Absolutely, I'll see what I can do, but no party and no dessert if you're late for dinner, Mr. Tanner. No make-ups for tenth birthdays. Sure you don't want to get in with us?"

"I have a shortcut. Don't worry."

The Land Rover began to inch forward, slowly navigating the water-filled potholes of the old logging road. Lucas looked back in his side mirror as his gangly son with his dark mop of hair, shirtless, shorts, and barefoot, waved goodbye, then darted back for the thicket.

"Honey, when you get to the first switchback, pull over," Victoria said as they went up the hill. "I want to test the broadband reception for my web visor."

Pulling over to a rotted log guarding the edge of the three thousand-foot ravine, they found a clear line of sight to the tower in the valley. Among the peaks' shadows twelve miles to the southwest, Lucas could barely make out Machu Picchu.

"It's getting much worse, Lucas; put yours on too. I want you to see this. Go to preset five."

"This is Around the World with BBC correspondent, Rulanda Lakee. The DOW dropped five percent today on news of more people leaving behind homes, jobs, and family for the Sanctuary Corporation's new transport Hubs. Located in over one hundred cities around the world, they are being touted as the gateways to the new Shangri-La. Many Fortune 500 employers are complaining of lack of job applicants because people are making plans to leave."

"Lucas?"

... ... "...and the stoppage of basic city services like fire and police where civil servants are walking off their jobs, unannounced for good... ... ..."

Lucas cupped his hands around his temples to block the periphery sunlight obscuring the micro-projection being broadcast from his web visor to his retina, "I see it."

"Don't you think it's incredible," said Victoria, "all the masses of people camped around these Hubs? Even in places like Boston, people are panicking, being fooled that they're gonna miss the greatest boat of all time. What's the nearest Hub to us? Lima?"

"They've auctioned off over half a million tickets so far in Lima. In LA, over 700,000; in sub-equatorial Africa, they're trying to double the Hubs. Hold on Vic, listen."

"With the world on the brink of global economic collapse from the dismissal of the Euro currency five years ago, the unification of anti-western Mediterranean rim Caliphate, harsh Asian outbreaks of both H5N1 and military strains of smallpox, and major shifts in weather patterns and crop yields in North America, you can easily see why the world's self-proclaimed ninety-nine percent are throwing in the towel. Rallies are being held in sports stadiums around the world with the fervor of old style evangelistic crusades."

"Watch this clip from well-known televangelist and prosperity minister, Hugh McKenzie of Dallas, Texas," encouraged Rulanda Lakee, with a tint of mockery on her face as the broadcast faded in on a close up of him.

'You've been told all your life you had to suffer to find God's will. I am telling you that this is a lie from the Devil. God has given you the keys to take ownership of the biggest land grab in history. God's not interested in improving this world. Some things need to be thrown away, like old shoes. You ask, what is required to experience a new world and a new life? It is very simple. You have to have faith to leave everything that is broken behind you. No eye has seen nor ear has heard what God has in store for those who love him. There is none who has forsaken mother, brother, father, wife, or child who won't receive, a hundredfold over, mothers, brothers, fathers, wives, children, and with this, eternal life.'"

The news anchor continued, "Here's a clip from another religious dream team member from Jinnah Sports Stadium in Islamabad Pakistan, from Al Jazeera network. The Imam Jafar Hammam speaks highly of the Sanctuary, 'We are the people of the Hajj! Allah commands us to expand our sacred Pilgrimage beyond the monopoly of one country. This has gone on too long. For many of you the sacred trip on Earth will never develop into a reality. But now, you have the opportunity to travel beyond the origins of the Black Rock of the Kaaba, which fell from heaven to our great ancestor Ibrahim. It is your duty to stretch the global ummah of our brothers to include the land of Two Suns Rising. Claim your Hajj for Allah, where no one will subjugate you or your family, or your tribe again. He is the Lord of the Two Easts and the Two Wests...'"

"Take 'em off, Vic. We don't need to see any more of this. We knew this day would come. Watching won't make it go away."

"Lucas, your eyes! It's happening."

He opened the driver's side makeup mirror. "Usually takes more than bad news to get this reaction."

"We should have made Daniel get in."

"Honey, stay calm. This is his backyard. Nothing bad is going to happen. He'll meet us with his Grandma and Grandpa to celebrate his birthday. Good luck to anyone who thinks they can catch that kid in the rainforest."

As they pulled off the main logging road and made their way across several acres of clear-cut fields before diving into the jungle again, they drove through a swarm of black beetles that peppered the driver's side of the vehicle and windshield like small hail.

"Yellow guts on a black paint job. Why do I bother?"

"I don't like this, Lucas."

"Not to worry. If it were them, they would have stayed with us. They're gone. Everything is fine. No more bugs. Let me stop and clean the windshield so I don't hit a tree."

Lucas got out of the vehicle, released the back hatch, and opened the hidden tool compartment under the carpet. Beneath the squeegee and glass cleaner was a bath towel wrapped around a scabbard. He uncovered the hilt and grasped it with his right hand. To his surprise, the handle was warm; after releasing it, his hand retained a slight shade of blue.

Cleaning the bug guts off the windshield, he didn't notice the stirring wake of debris moving rapidly as it followed the vulture-like shadow towards his vehicle. Victoria saw it and froze. There was no time to warn him.

Rocking the SUV in its vacuum and pelting him with dust and gravel, the shadow roared over them into the thick vegetation from where Daniel would be returning. Lucas cleared his eyes and ran to the back of his vehicle for the sword and the small velvet sack underneath.

"Take the Rover to the shelter. Lock it down. Get everyone packed. I'm going to find our son. It's happening."

Chapter 59

There are those who fear what you can become.

Climbing to the top of the towering tree, Daniel curled upside down next to Pico where they watched the late afternoon clouds roll into the valley. "Pico, I don't know any other sloths who speak. Why do you talk to me?"

"Quiet Danielito, learn from me, and remain completely still. Your enemies are looking for you."

"But I have no enemies. My grandfather tells me the one who never sleeps nor slumbers, watches over me, and my grandmother says I can be anything I want."

"True Pequeño, you have the canopy of many prayers, you are the core of the Heir's eye, but there are those who fear what you can become. They fear the warrior in you who might cut them down from within, and for good reason."

"Pico, I don't understand."

"Like the men who illegally hunt in this forest. You have seen them?"

"More and more, and I hide, like you taught me. Those men like to hunt the deer, Mr. Armadillo, the McCaw, the gold, Señor Ant Eater. They harvest the orchids and the trees."

"Danielito, a time is coming when hiding is not enough. These hunters want you. They may be here now. Be silent." The sloth arched his head to see toward the ground. Two forest rangers, dark green ball caps, matching trousers and shirts walked around the trunk of the tree. At the base they noticed the boy's footprints and a four foot sharpened stick with two dead toads on the end. They both looked up.

One of the men motioned to the other to begin climbing. As Daniel remained motionless, he glimpsed one of them through the foliage climbing with ease. The ranger stuck to the trunk, scaling under and around branches like a giant praying mantis. Daniel froze in wonder, *I can't even do that!*

Daniel heard Pico's voice in his head, "Danielito, you have to jump when I tell you. Just do it, you'll be ok." If it were not for the dread he sensed crawling up the tree like a leopard coming to finish its prey, he would not have believed. "On Three... Uno, Dos, Tres!"

He let go and began to free fall some fifteen feet away from the trunk and a hundred and twenty feet above the ground. He passed the ranger going down who put his arm out toward him but missed. Looking up he saw that Pico a second later had let go and was now in a free fall. But Pico didn't remain as Pico. The talking sloth transformed into a young man with wings.

Lucas, fueled by a combination of anger at himself for becoming too hands off as a father and ignoring the inevitable signs of an attack by the Vranti, bolted across the two hundred acre patch of stumps, seedlings and vines, toward the yet to be harvested rainforest. His right arm grew turquoise to the shoulder, fed by the light of Ouriano's double bladed sword.

Lucas' hindsight raced hard as he ran, "Tokyo, New Zealand, Omaha, London, Newark, Buenos Aires, and now here in the state of Cusco Peru; this is the last home place before we enter the Hub station in Lima, but not if Daniel doesn't make it. Daniel's everything. Angel of Light, if he dies, I die."

At the edge of the dark green lush, shadowed by the mountains and pillows of high leafy branches, Lucas paused and listened for the hum of the swarm. "There, in that direction, but no path." He spun the sword like a baton, dismembering the underbrush as he set out for the most direct route; pieces of vine, bark, and leaves sprayed as his sword fanned through the thick growth. "Who was the shadow trailing the pack of bugs? My God, you gave us Daniel, you can't take him away."

Lucas ran to the edge of a rock cliff draped by vines and ferns. There was no hesitating involved. He went head first like he was expecting to fly, arms and legs spread, sword extending out. He calculated during his last step before leaping, he would roll his way down the steep embankment below, ensuring that his own torso stayed clear of the sword. Somersaulting his way through the underbrush for six hundred feet he finally reached the floor of rain forest, and stood up. "The hum's louder. I hear voices, several. This way."

He passed the spot on the road where Daniel had said goodbye just half an hour earlier. A steaming Department of Forestry truck sat idle crashed against a tree with a man hanging out the window. Lucas heard no breathing or pulse. Welts were all over the back of his neck and arm, along with a three foot deep cut through the bottom of the door continuing through the steel side step. He only knew of one weapon that left a mark like that and owned by a human, "Mine."

In desperation Lucas ran toward Daniel's favorite tree where he arrived to see something completely unexpected. Daniel was standing back to back with a young man who appeared to be about sixteen years of age. In their defensive posture, the young man held a sword like Ouriano's. Daniel, holding his own valiance, wiggled his three foot sharpened stick, still with the lanced toads on the end in a circle. Lucas knew immediately, this friend of Daniel's was no ordinary teenager, but a *Legionnaire*. *Could Daniel see him?*

"Daniel, what are you doing? Who is this? I don't know him? Whatever you are, what are you doing with my son?"

Daniel answered first, but the two kept their defensive vigil, their eyes darting at every moving twig, dropping leaf. "Dad, you came back! This..., this is my friend Pico."

"You said Pico was a sloth."

"Sir, I can explain," said the medium blonde headed Seraph. "Your son has a bounty on his head."

"The Vranti?" said Lucas. "How did you know they were coming? Where are they now?"

"That's a long story sir. We should wait until all is clear before I explain."

"You appear to be my son's most imminent danger. How do I know you are not the Vranti?"

"Good question Dr. Tanner. Ah, Ah, Daniel doesn't know any of this."

"Dad, you can trust him. His name is Pico."

"If I can trust you, put down your sword and move away from my son, now!" Lucas raised his own sword with his blue right arm and hand, and began to unfasten the mirror from its pouch. "Come to me Daniel."

"Dad they are still here somewhere. We're in danger."

"Son your greatest danger is next to you. Come to me."

"I don't think so dad, he saved me." Looking over his right shoulder at the angel, Daniel asked, "Pico, what happened to your body, your voice?"

Lucas ordered Daniel again, "Leave him!" at which Daniel gave in and ran from Pico's side next to his father ten yards away. Daniel noticed his father's eyes were lit whitish blue.

"Are you infected?" asked Lucas. "What is your real name?"

The fallen Wind spoke with a look of apprehension, "Juwaan, I am sorry, but my real name is Advanta. I was protecting him."

"Are you a Loyalist or infected," persisted Lucas.

"That's what I need time to explain sir."

"Start!"

"I would but your son is in grave danger. But if you insist to know now, I am a Loyalist of Loyalists, yet darkness creeps within me." Lucas began to aim the mirror at Advanta while he spoke, "What is that Dr Tanner?"

"A gift from the Angel of Light which will sort all this out," Lucas said brusquely. As he stared into the crude mirror, Lucas ignited the energy of the ancient light which began to stir and beam out. Handing his sword to Daniel to hold he aimed the projecting light toward Advanta.

When the light hit him, Advanta felt both pleasure and pain. It reminded him of his predicament, of receiving the infection from the chalice the very day of Ouriano's memorial on the Blue Moon. The light from the mirror revealed the darkened veins in his arms and face, where ever Lucas aimed the beam. Advanta's matrix started to smoke as Daniel's father unrelented.

Advanta winced in pain, "Please sir, I beg you; I am a sworn servant of the Wounded Heir of the Magnificon. If you do not stop I will die."

"Why should I believe you?" said Lucas.

Daniel confused, screamed, "Dad you are hurting him!"

"My loyalty is to Veezon, sworn friend to Ouriano, whose essence was sent to Earth ten years ago."

When he said this, Lucas lowered the mirror, but he had severely weakened Advanta, who was now on his knees, his wings limp.

Lucas rushed towards him, "I am beyond sorry. I am a fool. What can I do?"

"Give me time, I will be alright. You must protect your son," said the weakened Wind. As he said this, Lucas felt wet drops fall on his hand. Examining his hand, he saw the blood.

"Dad, look out," yelled Daniel as his father glanced up a hair too late to see the Vranti infested ranger standing upside down from a large tree limb some thirty feet overhead, who let go, lunging straight down for Lucas.

Before Lucas could raise his sword, he was tackled to the ground, slamming the back of his head so hard, the light went out in his eyes. The crude mirror flew from his hand bouncing into a nearby thick tangle of vines and brush. The possessed forest ranger ran to the spot thrusting his hands in the growth to find it. Daniel in the mean time, picked up his father's sword, and stood petrified at the scene before him. The boy who was his friend and now called himself Advanta knelt, propping himself on his sword while Lucas writhed on the ground struggling to stop everything from spinning.

Chapter 60

You think you can hide from the darkness.
You are wrong.

As Lucas could barely raise his head, the most horrible feeling a father could have--helplessness, roused his anger. *My only son is about to become infested, killed, or maimed by the Vranti and neither I nor this Pico can stop it. Why did I make that call to Cuzak? Victoria was right, it was my ego.... But wait, the Angel of Light made a promise:*

"Like his father, a sword he will bear.
A voice he will hear where no others can hear,
A light he will see where no others can see.
In time, tell him who he is and from whence he was forged.
A great harlot approaches to consume him, yet he will consume.
I will be an enemy to his enemies."

Lucas clinched his eyes and proclaimed from his fetal position on the ground, "My Angel of Light, keep your promises."..."Daniel!"

Crying, the little boy with a man's heart kept guard over his father without Lucas realizing. He heard his dad's words but did not comprehend them in full. He knelt down next to Lucas, confused from the shock. The Vranti moving closer, brooded over Daniel, dripping secretions from its nose on his back. The green clad, swollen faced ranger bragged, "I will rid the Earth of the Vigilante Advanta, and then deal with this Juwaan."

Directing his speech at Daniel, his breaths heaved between every few words, "You little man, are most wanted, most esteemed, most precious, are you not? But then, you have no idea, what I am talking about? You are pathetic; no warrior lives in you or your father. You think you can hide, from the darkness. You are wrong!"

As Daniel knelt next to his injured father the Vranti turned the mirror again on Advanta with no remorse. Kicking his sword out from under him, the mean spirited collective aimed the light meant for good on Advanta like a supernatural microwave. Daniel could smell the burning and hear small crackles. The Vranti added further insult, "You cannot love two masters, for you will love the one and hate the other."

Yet, as the present transpired, Daniel's mind ventured into another time and place. He was in angel's body staring into a reflecting pool inside a domed room. Daniel saw not his own face, but a countenance like Advanta's but older, and with a thick mane of hair. His shoulders were wide, muscular, tattooed with strange markings. In the reflection he recognized them as symbols of rank and accolades. He could not make the image out perfectly, for another angel disturbed the waters with the tip of his sword.

This Wind of light, an alleged friend, spoke to Daniel in the vision, "Ouriano, you must pick up the sword a second time. You were following orders. No one asked your opinion. Maybe it was a test. For this you were made. Now take it!"

Daniel felt the hilt of the sword placed in his hand both in the vision from a far off world and present as he knelt beside his father. The unidentified friend encouraged him more from the vision, "This is a terrible swift sword, and in the precise hands it wields justice. Your hands are the right and true hands. Take it Ouriano."

The vision itself lasted no longer than a split second, awaking Daniel to everything around him. He no longer felt like the powerless little boy. He was still holding the sword handed to him by his father when he rose and faced the Vranti, who paused in his torture of Advanta to turn and gape at the courage of one so young and frail.

"Who are you boy, to do what a man, or a sentinel cannot do?" As Daniel faced him, he noticed insect larva writhing out of the ranger's nose and wiggling just under the skin around his eyes. Despite this the man asserted, "Do not test me, for I have come to take you to the Sanctuary. You have the power of choice; you can go with me, or stay here and die, with these two incompetents. I have a new father picked out for you."

Daniel, to the Vranti's surprise wiped the tears from his eyes with his shoulder and readied the large sword, lifting it to a lopsided angle over his head. Without realizing, the grip slowly conformed to Daniel's hands until it rang with a high pitch as it energized to unite with the life force of the original owner. The sword recognized something in the boy, as did the Vranti, whose instinct re-aimed the mirror at Daniel's soft face, pouring the hot light into his countenance.

Hoping to scorch him, at first it appeared to work, as Daniel struggled to cover his eyes with his forearms to maintain a defense against the searing light. But the longer the wide light beam concentrated on him, the stronger Daniel actually became. In a few moments he no longer needed to block the energized light of this special mirror. He discovered his sight could absorb and even relish in its radiance.

Gaining his own strength, Daniel turned the blade of his sword to reverse the light toward its source. Temporarily blinding the Vranti he charged forward and took a baseball like swing. He missed the collective's body, but struck the mirror, exploding it to bits and powder. The close blow surprised Daniel as well as his adversary, freezing them for a few seconds as they observed the snow of light falling around them from the remains of the mirror.

At that moment, the Vranti saw something perplexing in the boy. It stared into the conscience of good which stared back at him. Within the ranger's possessed body, the collective began trading messages, "This is no ordinary foe,"... "He is both ancient and young,"... "of the likes I have never encountered,"... "no, his father may be a Juwaan,"... "but this little one... is something else,"... "neither must be allowed to survive, to pass to the land of Two Suns." In unison they declared, "Kill them!"

Daniel then replied with foreign words he knew not from where they came, "or you Vranti can perish at the hands of this sword forged beyond the Magnificon gates. It is as you say, 'I have a choice.' And, I choose to slay you."

Lucas slowly staggered to his feet, behind his son, legs yet unsteady and mind unsure of what he was witnessing. For he was staring at the back of his son, who held the sword of Ouriano toward a forest ranger with hands and forearms blue, and glowing ambers littering the forest floor. Beyond them he saw Advanta squatting on the dirt, smoldering and endeavoring to expand his damaged accordion wings.

But something else pulled away Lucas' attention; the noise of shuffling of feet through leaves behind him and the warning of insects swarming his head. He knew what this meant, and instinctually warned, "Son, the other's not dead!" Lucas turned his face in time to see the short log swing down toward his forehead.

Chapter 61

My Jeshurun, my power is made perfect in weakness.

The "clunk" jerked Daniel's attention over his shoulder to see his father waylaid by the twin nemesis behind him. Advanta had earlier flung this ranger through the windshield of his truck, hoping not to kill him, but to paralyze and rid him of the parasites.

While Daniel considered his next tactical move, he had to fight off the urge to stoop in paralyzing grief at his dad's side. As he hesitated, the Vranti in front of him, leapt away, over Advanta's crumpled body, somersaulting across the ground as he snatched the wounded angel's sword.

All of Daniel's senses were now finely attuned. So attuned, that an inner channel opened up to the hidden core of his being, where consciousness, soul and spirit all meet in the center singularity of one's self. And in that place he heard a voice of one normally reserved for those approaching the Magnificon gates. But it did not come from the Magnificon, for it was no longer there. This voice had moved to a far distant galaxy, a place of Two Suns Rising. Now far, far, away, across immeasurable obstacles of mind dwarfing black holes, static of long gone civilizations, time and space, this person was revealing himself to a young boy in the hidden Peruvian rain forest, and none too late.

"Daniel,..." he heard the voice say, and again, "Daniel." Listening, he surveyed the paused scene around him; the swordsman attacking from the front, leaping over Advanta, now frozen in mid-air. The other welt faced ranger, swinging his club from the rear, now gelled motionless for a split second.

The voice was clear, and with the voice he searched outward and within for a face to go with it. What came to him was a countenance totally unknown, the bruised face of an oriental man, not unlike some of the Inca descendents, he had seen nearby, with dark hair, high wide cheek bones. The voice said, "Come over here Daniel, my Jeshurun, my power is made perfect in weakness. I need you. We will meet. The hook is in the snout of my enemies. Do not kill these men. Take not their blood. Your sword will be loosed in another place."

For a millisecond Daniel contemplated these words until the scene resumed to save his father. Stepping to his right, he felt the descending club barely miss his head and left shoulder. Spinning to his right he lowered his long sword to chest high and walloped this assailant from behind with the flat of the blade, causing him to stagger forward into the flashing blade of the other ranger. Advanta's borrowed sword sliced vertically through his green shirt near his heart.

Immediately bugs began to pour out of his chest wound and mouth as he gazed into the eyes of the other possessed ranger who had accidently struck him. Dropping the club, and then falling to his knees, he held his hands over his fatal lesion and appealed to Daniel for mercy. The exiting swarms at once flew into the mouth, ears, and pants of the other ranger to further empower him. His chest expanded ripping open his shirt to reveal the cleavage of his growing pectoral muscles.

Daniel heard the voice again, "Do not kill, provision to escape will come."

Stepping back and straddling his father's body, Daniel looked up at the menace before him. Drops of coagulating blood mixed with unidentifiable chunks oozed from the corners of his mouth. So strong and bulkier had he become, he took the tip of Advanta's sword and flexed the entire blade back and forth in his hands. Daniel marveled, *How can he do that to a human body? What is he?*

"You fool," asserted the Vranti's bellowing base voice.

Daniel in that instant recalled the words his grandfather had told him from the tale of an Amazon missionary decades ago who died unarmed at the hands of those he sought to befriend. So he spoke to the man, the thing, across from him, "My grandfather once told me, he is no fool who gives what he cannot keep, to gain what he cannot lose."

"Your grandfather is a *fool* as well, for it was I who vanquished his daughter. He has done his own damage, and for that I will add more pain to your end."

Daniel then did something, which made no sense to the Vranti. He had not seen this reaction in ages; an unlikely courage, a sign of ultimate strength and possibly a sign from the Wounded Heir himself. Daniel laid down his sword, tossing it to the ground.

The Vranti began to grin, raising his sword, but then diverse voices within its collective began to argue. He looked confused at Daniel. Inside the ranger's body a conversation was taking place, "We are foolish,"... "No strike him down,"... "Flee at once,"... "No, take him alive,"... "Kill his father and finish the Vigilante,"... "Do not hesitate,"... "Yazad wants him alive!"

Daniel at this point, refocused on his father's injuries and squatted down to hug his neck, where he found him still breathing. Noticing the ranger's feet approaching him from the side, he determined he would not look up... that is until gusty downdrafts began to shake the surrounding trees and the huge Ceiba limbs above him. Even the preoccupied Vranti hesitated on slaying Daniel, instead nervously gazing around to confirm his suspicions of sabotage.

As Daniel waited on his knees for the inevitable, he saw new legs and feet like Advanta's appear around him. Bewildered, he stood to witness the three strangers, one of whom had told him to "pick up the sword" and addressed him as "Ouriano" only moments ago. But now he appeared in a much more wretched state, like the other two.

The first spoke boldly, "You ought to return the neophyte's sword immediately. And if you should try to escape, we will make sure you and your bug friends will be whipped into a paste and fed to a school of piranha."

With double the insects inside him, the forest ranger's thoracic vertebra crackled as his head ratcheted in a full circle, sizing up the three ancient Winds who surrounded him, two he recognized; Veezon and Azazel. Unintimidated he replied, "What is your name, one who speaks so bravely, that I may warn my trembling enclave?"

"I don't fear you. You are less than a maggot brained ring worm with wings. I am called Fortius."

"So proud we are? So who calls on your name? Is there a love which redeems you? What have we here, the Flying Vigilantes? Your light is dim. You are sick. Like so many image bearers, you also pretend you can choose your destiny. Have you looked in a mirror lately? You are not yourselves anymore. Don't make me laugh! Ha, ha, ha, it hurts."

Chapter 62

What are you progressive Vigilantes going to do,
take over this dilapidated Earthen realm?

Azazel, another of the Vigilantes, with wild bushy hair and a beard to match shouted, "Shut up you unholy carcass of condemnation. Do you know who I am? For I will not hesitate for one moment to suck down your larval essence into my bowels, if only for the joy of excreting you into a form more suited for your family portrait!"

The Vranti leaned on Advanta's sword like a walking cane against his hip, and replied half laughing then became stern, "You wouldn't believe how I have taken others up on that offer. Azazel is it? You are renowned as an example of all that is unjust in the universe. Consuming scapegoats no more are we? You should be careful what you ask for."

"And you should never speak unless spoken to," said Azazel as Veezon cautioned him back with the dilation of his eyes.

Turning to Veezon, whom he recognized and shaking his head, the Vranti continued his poetic lashing, "And you lost your nerve. You organized this group because of sorrow over Ouriano. Kicked out of Yare'ach Kachol for your human like vengeance against Cuzak's daughter-- word gets around you know. I am amazed; you tried to kill the celestial slut, in front of the Magnificon Council. Was that courage?... No, that was the infection enraging you. Come with me and I can help you control it, soothe it."

Daniel tried to follow all of this angelic banter, but was unsure of who was a friend or foe. These powerful sentinels before him were strange, but in a way, not so strange. He incidentally caught pieces of their alien dialect and read their body language.

Veezon answered in an almost agreeable manner, "Yes, I warned Ouriano of Ru, that his prime breeding Hybrid project, would be his end. And further, I made a vow to her that if she should do anything to entrap and hurt Ouriano, who was closer than a brother, I would personally hunt her down, hack off her wings and make her a specimen of the Blue Moon."

"You know, I have confirmed, indeed it was her who annihilated him, no doubt," said the Vranti, "a second rate Lilith with no loyalty except to her pleasure. In time I have a ruse for her. She has done my kind no favors. All is fair in war. But you and your friends must know I have no bounty on any of you. I've waived my personal grudges. Tell me Veezon, have you and your comrades, made yourself known to me to save this boy? Or is it to make an equitable trade, for the Hybrid? Has the infection helped you to see how things really are?"

"What do you mean?" asked Fortius.

"Tell me more," added Azazel, "I am listening."

"What are you progressive Vigilantes going to do, take over this dilapidated Earthen realm? This has been tried for millennia, a waste of time. Your infection will not be healed in this place, ever. Where is your heaven? Join us, and if not, you can have this spent Earth if you wish. We are tossing it like an old rag. You have Beltshzan's word. I speak for him in these matters. Only let me take the boy, and I'll..."

Veezon stepped forward within sword's length of the Vranti and replied, "All of us here mean you no harm, except maybe Azazel, but there is no one's company he enjoys." Veezon paused, smiled at Azazel, then said, "We have no discrepancy with you or your kind. Now that we have tasted freedom, the price of infection is all the more worthwhile. You must now realize that you have awakened my insatiable thirst to bring this Ru back to a secret place on the Blue Moon, for justice."

"We have an understanding?" the gruesome parasitic filled ranger asked, as flies crawled in and out of his nose, a repulsive sight to Daniel.

"Yes, we do," said Veezon smiling, "but first I must ask, how were you going to dispose of Cuzak's daughter? Is Cuzak not watching out for both of them? He himself is powerful. It's as if he has been given sovereign shelter from reprisal until his task is completed."

"Exactly Veezon, and may I say you were—are, a Legion Commander among Commanders. As instrumental as Cuzak has been in furthering the human's technology, no one is indispensible. He and his protégé daughter will be disposed of together once they come to the Sanctuary."

"Am I missing something?" asked Veezon.

The Vranti explained still taking large gasps of air, "Yazad has no use for them, once the quotas come in. There is of course more; they are suspect of a secret loyalty to the Wounded Heir. They suppressed the truth about this boy, and his father's whereabouts. Can you believe these two little mortals have been in possession of Ouriano's sword? How it has grown on the Juwaan and his son. Perhaps they should taste the cruelty of Ouriano's sword."

At this point in the conversation a shadow flew over all of them several times, breaking beams of the setting sun. Vultures like the Andean Condor were not uncommon, but this shadow had much larger wings. No one ventured to see what it was, except for the Vranti and Daniel. The others kept their undistracted eyes, fixed on the ranger, as if they may have expected this.

Daniel and the Vranti caught sight of the owner of this shadow, an approaching black leather clad bird of prey. Riding the wind at ease on her sleek wings, she weaved under and around the rain forest's tree boughs and dangling vines. Landing next to Lucas, Daniel picked his sword off the ground and raised it to protect his father, but was met with her soft words.

"I come in peace, Daniel. I mean you no harm. I am Ru, a friend of your father and mother." Assessing the small boy she said, "Little one, now that I've laid eyes on you, it is true--you carry the sword well. You make your father proud, a real warrior's son, forged from the Earth and Siyon." Refocusing her attention to the grave injuries of Lucas she said, "He's hurt. He has to survive."

Ru fell to her knees and bent over Lucas while both Daniel and the Vranti continued to marvel at her. Having just explained the details about her death sentence, the Vranti collective disbelieved their fate was being squeezed by these unconventional Loyalists, "No, this cannot be a snare of these plebs' invention,"... "this is beyond their feral minds."

Ru could barely contain her emotion as she placed both hands on Lucas cheeks, caressing his temples and examining the ballooning welt on his forehead. Absence had made her heart grow fonder. She did her best to speak to his unconscious mind with reassurance through the power of her telepathic touch, "Lucas, I have never stopped loving you. I could never come between you and Victoria. Your son is beautiful. He will be in good hands. I am sorry; this is how it must be. It is the only way he will be safe. Trust me. It is His will."

Chapter 63

Love is a light you can never diminish.

Daniel shifted his eyes and head several times at this woman-creature, her wings tightly retracted to her shoulders. He said sheepishly, "I know you? Where are you from?"

"No, we have never met. Of that I am sure, but I knew your mother and father in another time and place," Ru responded, keeping her eyes attentive to Lucas. Gently touching his father's bruised forehead, she reached over to Daniel and said, "Give me your hand," whereupon Daniel slipped his powder blue right hand off the hilt of the sword and placed it in hers, kneeling down with her next to his father.

"Pray with me," she said. He innately knew he should trust her, but he didn't know why.

To her surprise Daniel began to lead the prayer. To those standing round, they felt an intimidating presence almost forgotten. The feeling was repulsive to the Vranti, but to the others it was a pain mixed with joy, rekindling a lost hope that might one day return. All those standing knelt in this sacred presence, except the disfigured forest ranger, who continued to ooze and drip his hatred, standing in defiance.

Daniel's brow furrowed and his chin trembled. "God, this is my dad, the only one I have," he cried, "he's the best dad in the world. Who will climb trees with me? What's mom going to do without him?" Pausing to sob for a minute, Ru squeezed his hand in assurance and comfort. The words he spoke next, gained more attention from the Vigilante Winds around him.

"Jesus, if Grandpa were here, he'd say, 'by his stripes we are healed,' and he'd quote his favorite old song to you:

'The Prince of Darkness grim,
We tremble not for him;
His rage we can endure,
For lo, his doom is sure;
One little word shall fell him'"

As Daniel quoted these old stanzas mentored into him from his grandfather Henry, the half darkened Winds, Fortius and Veezon, helped recite more words of this hymn with him. From Daniel's point of view, they were immense in size, built like his toy superheroes but with patches of knotty dark varicose veins barely under the surface of their skin, and voices so powerful, they vibrated the ground. Yet in this case, Daniel's strength became theirs, and theirs became his:

"'That word above all Earthly powers,
No thanks to them, abideth;
The Spirit and the gifts are ours,
Thru him who with us sideth.

Let goods and kindred go,
This mortal life also;
The body they may kill;
God's truth abideth still;
His kingdom is forever.'"

With wisdom from another place, Daniel finished his prayer, "Please Lord, fell the devils around me with one little word, and let the rest remain. I cannot tell them apart. Help my friend Pico, he needs to fly again. Protect me from what I don't understand. Fix my dad's head. Heal him. Amen."

Next, Ru reached for her own neck and pulled up the chain from under her vest which held the Armenian cross from her mother. Grasping the sacred trinket in her right hand, she continued to also hold Daniel's hand on his father's chest as she now prayed, "To the Wounded One who is merciful to me, and birthed me into being by my young mother, to the One who forgives all of our youthful indiscretions and willing sins, who guides the Winds of light and silently herds his darkened enemies into their own snares, please hear our prayers. We are not worthy of one breath more in any of your worlds, and we wonder at why you have yet to cut us off."

Ru continued, "Guide us in our faith, and keep us from falling any further toward the abyss of no return. Do not let the darkness overtake us. I plead, for the sake of Ouriano who gave himself away, that you heal this beloved Juwaan, Daniel's father. Surely in all your wisdom, you don't have to let Lucas' life end this way?"

Releasing Daniel's hand, she touched her cross on Lucas' forehead and said, "So say we all," to which the others of the lost clan of angels repeated, "So say we all."

In response to the growing anxiety of the Vranti, repulsed by their tidy prayers and his predicament, the Winds all placed the tips of their swords on his torso to keep him from fleeing. Still amazed they all watched as Ru place her lips on Lucas' lips, and her hands on each ear. She breathed into him, and exhaled for him several times, releasing her own anti-inflammatory agent into his blood stream. But more than that, it may have been the power of the prayers and her love for him that began to enact healing.

"Look, his swelling is going down," said Daniel, "His eyes are flickering."

Ru replied, "Yes, Daniel, I believe he will be healed. He should be able to stand in a few minutes. But by then we will have to leave."

"Leave?" Daniel asked.

The Vranti, growing in indignation, snarled out at Ru, "I sensed you as less than a half breed vermin the cold day we met. You snapped the necks of a few useless soldiers. Why are you so interested in saving him? You are losing a battle that will rot you from the inside."

Ru stood and faced him, "No, General Sul, there is something here you cannot fathom; a few image bearers with faith can do far more than any Legion, good or bad.

That is a reality you cannot change. Love is a light you can never diminish."

Oozing and chewing unidentified debris in its mouth then swallowing, the Vranti again issued more threats, "Spare me the devotions." Hoping he might persuade the weakened state of Veezon, he focused on him and said, "Here is something you will never change; your life is a wasteland. Everyone needs a home, but you will never know one. Mark my words. She annihilated your friend, and will betray you and this boy in the same manner. I've seen evil up close, and she is its grand-daughter. Why do you think she wants the boy? She wants to ingratiate herself with Beltshzan--Yazad."

Azazel cut him off, "You've said your peace, times up *worm boy*. We don't deal with maggot heads. You have an appointment with the abyss. Remember what that is like? Oh yes, you were right about my eating habits."

Ru asked Daniel a question, "Daniel, this is hard to understand. Please don't strike this man down, but I want you to hold your sword up to his mouth." Still somewhat confused, he complied and held Ouriano's sword higher than the others to the lips of the man hosting the infestation. The sword's initial faint ring resonated louder and louder, as the double edge blade became a shimmering blue-silver, aglow with a special light of its own."

The sword in its energized state, became such an irritant to the Vranti, the forester's body began to shake as masses of insects in various stages of development readied to leave. As some began to swarm and secrete themselves, many parasitic larvae rose to the surface of the man's skin, drilling holes, squeezing out his face and forearms through expanded sweat pores.

And with this exorcism Azazel made good on his earlier threat, as he began to hover in the air above the Vranti infested man, dislocating his own jaw in a grotesque manner. Opening his mouth very wide like a whale straining krill, he vacuumed up every fly, gnat, insect, larvae, which left the sickened body below. When he had finished, with his belly bloated and shifting, Azazel shot up into the sky to negotiate an exchange for his valuable but ignoble cargo.

Chapter 64

Trust doesn't cover taking someone's son without asking.

With Victoria and his parents by his side, Lucas shook his head to adjust his eyes and shoved away their bottle of water inquiring, "Where's Daniel? Did you find him? I tried to fight them. I was blindsided. My head is throbbing. Where is he?"

"He's not here," Victoria apologized, "We've looked, but we found...."

"What do you mean? That's impossible. Not in the cards. Not supposed to happen. Help me up, this is an emergency. Why aren't you looking for him? Why are you all standing here? This is my son!"

Lucas' mother, Judith blurted out, "It's in the note. Read it, and be reminded, he's my grandson too. A little thanks might be in order. Victoria wanted us to stay locked in the compound, but I told her we'd best find you."

"What note?"

"In your shirt pocket," his father, Henry snarked.

"Who left it?"quipped Lucas.

"You best read it yourself," sighed Victoria. "This all started with your calling in stunt."

"Where did this come from?" As Lucas unfolded the white paper note he exclaimed, "This isn't Daniel's writing." The recovering man in the blood and mucous stained green uniform moaned on the ground a few feet from him. "Help him, somebody. See if he still has the parasites."

"Did he do this?" said Victoria. "It was the Vranti after all wasn't it?"

"Yes, but let me read this," Lucas said hastily as he focused on the note, speed reading it once, shouting "No...!" then combing through it word for word the second time hoping it would read differently.

"Dear Lucas," he could hear her voice distinctly as he read the note:

"I pray you are recovering from the terrible knot on your forehead. We treated you and had to leave. I know how much you love your son. He is adorable, so much like you, brave, instinctual, a warrior, and like his mother, kind, deliberate, loyal.

But, I had to take him with me once I met him. It is for his protection. Daniel is like no other. Somehow the spirit of Ouriano lives inside him, so that Daniel poses a great threat to Beltshzan. I won't allow Daniel to fall into the enemy's hands. I know this sounds complicated, but I am not the enemy. I am not sure that Cuzak is even the enemy, but I am not sharing any of this with him. The Hubs must open. This is bigger than all of us. You should not have called into the conference, but I know you had your reasons.

Please understand, no one will suspect that Daniel is with me. I can protect him before he must answer his call. Ouriano was feared above all of the Winds, so just the rumor that Daniel reflects something of Ouriano makes him wanted. You must leave this place at once. Don't worry. I'll find you. Let me arrange which Hub you take.

May the one who is enthroned above the Winds of light, shine forth for eternity--

Ru

P.S. Daniel has Ouriano's sword with him.

When Lucas finished reading, he crumpled the note in his fading blue right fist and pumped it to the sky, "Why, why are you doing this?" he cried. Victoria wrapped her arms around his waist and tried to settle his emotions, but instead sobbed with him.

Henry came alongside and put his arms around both of them for comfort. Judith followed suit. Henry said, "They've got at least an hour head start on us. This woman who left the note had help and they didn't arrive by any vehicles that I can tell, there's enough foot prints around for ten people and some are mighty big. No sign of extra vehicles except the wrecked forestry truck. We might be able to call for help, cut them off if you want."

"Dad, there is no finding them. They didn't leave by a car or truck."

Henry spoke, "In that case, I believe Daniel is going to survive this. We know that he belongs to someone else first. They just poked God in his all seeing eye. They'll have more than they can handle. My grandson is strong in mind, body and spirit. Now, you've mentioned this Ru woman before. Do you trust her?"

Victoria dabbed her tears, "Trust doesn't cover taking someone's son without asking, but I know what she said about Daniel is true. Ru's never lied to us, she saved my life. She was kind to my mother. Lucas you haven't talked in a long time about your experiences with her."

"I think she means well, but she's too close to evil. And as an understatement, you don't kidnap someone's son. We knew he was special, but he's not ready for anything like this. God, come on. Please, where are they taking him? Give us a sign."

As Lucas lifted his eyes, he saw a sloth hanging upside down from the lowest tree limb, "When I got here, there was an infected Wind brandishing a sword to defend Daniel. Daniel said this was Pico, but he went by another name, Advanta or something. In the tussle I lost the mirror and the Vranti used it on him after I had mistakenly fried him with it. I believe I may have made a mistake. That's the last I remember."

"I thought Pico was his imaginary sloth friend?" asked Judith.

On a hunch, addressing the brown and white sloth hanging above, Lucas shouted, "Hey up there, are you Advanta? What happened to my son, Daniel? Talk to us if you can," to which the sloth remained still except to rotate his round head slowly toward them.

"He doesn't know what you are saying," chimed Victoria, who demanded of the sloth, "If you know what is good for you tell us where Daniel is. I have a mother's wrath and some Holy water reserved for you," she said pointing her pistol at him.

"Why do the both of you want to hurt me? Danielito is safe for now," replied the sloth. "He will live another day to help crush our enemies. You cannot keep him from his destiny. I do not know where they went. Only the woman, the Hybrid knows."

Judith responded horrified, "Tell me that the sloth didn't talk. Hold me Henry. And where did Victoria get the gun?"

The sloth spoke again, "El Niño Pequeño is a powerful force for good. He prays very loud, and he has ears to hear. You should be proud of him. You will meet him in days to come. You should leave this place immediately. It is no longer safe for you Juwaan."

Lucas answered, "Before we leave, for the honor of Ouriano, show your true self again." With this request, Pico dropped from the branch above and on the way down transposed himself into the young infected angel. They were aghast at the lesion filled former Wind of light, hunched over in pain.

Chapter 65

Ah, so you serve the man who fell from the sky.

On the surface, Advanta's skin was smooth but had become like that of an aged image bearer, thinning and translucent enough to see the dark twisted veins inside of him. His wings were singed in places. Patches of what were silky aerodynamic feathers, now resembled parched gray leather hide supported by a boney frame.

"I am sorry I appear this way. My wounds have weakened me."

Lucas interrogated him, "What were you doing with my son? He spoke of you often as Pico, his sloth friend."

"Ru, the Hybrid sent me. She's trying to protect your family. She knew the Vranti would come looking for you and your son."

"Did she force Daniel to go with her?"

"No, she told him she was an old friend of yours. He asked her about a vision he had of an oriental man telling him to come to the land of Two Suns Rising. The man in the vision called Daniel by name and also gave him another name, 'Jeshurun.'"

"What does that mean?" Victoria worried.

Judith spoke, "Jeshurun, means, 'the beloved or righteous one.' That sounds like my Daniel."

Advanta continued, "Ru told him, 'I can help you get there.'"

Victoria spoke up, "You are coming with us. You are not fit to fly, and you are the only connection to my son. If you are so good, why did they leave you behind? We can see all the footsteps. Who was here?"

"As I tried to explain to the Juwaan before he turned the reflective light of Siyon on me, I am for lack of a better word, a Vigilante. My goal is to reach the Sanctuary like you, undetected and fight. They left me because I can barely fly at the moment, and transporting Daniel to a safe place was a priority. What is left of me is at your service."

"How many are like you?" asked Henry.

"Five so far, but one of them, Veezon, was a close friend of Ouriano. I am sure there must be others. It is better if our confederation remains hidden."

"Five?" questioned Henry. "That's what you are sure of? And how many defections have there been over the millennium who share Beltshzan's sentiments?"

"I don't know. My generation was created to replace the many previous defections."

Lucas hurried them, "I for one am not ready to be replaced yet. Let's get back to the compound and pack. We'll leave in the morning and figure out where Daniel is along the way. You are coming with us, Pico."

"Yes, but while I am healing I feel more comfortable as a sloth. Do you mind?"

"Of course, you'll be less conspicuous."

On the short return trip Pico the sloth sat wedged between Judith and Henry in the back seat of the SUV, where Henry inquired, "Can I ask you something, Pico?"

"Si, I will try to answer."

"Who do you serve?"

"I serve the One whose nombre you call on; El Hombre que cayó del cielo."

Henry was startled by his answer, "Ah, so you serve 'the man who fell from the sky.' Interesting, that would be the Devil?"

"No, no, Señor Henry, the Devil was never fully a man."

Somewhat flustered Henry asked more, "But how can you serve God, as infected and condemned as Lucas has described your plight?"

"Señor, I can't answer you sufficiently. For the few of us, we do it the same way you do, by faith."

Henry became somewhat perturbed, "But salvation is only for humans. You have no second chance."

"I am not doing this for a second chance. I am doing this for the sake of the Keeper of the Magnificon Gates, and my infected hombres. Did not the Wounded Heir do the same for your kind?"

Henry, somewhat confused, said, "No, I mean yes! But that's different. Your kind was never made to rule but,..."

"Como no? But what?... 'to serve your kind forever?' Si, of this I am well aware Señor Henry. And when our servicios to your kind is over, what then?"

"I don't know," said Henry.

"We came into this world as we now are and remain. You were born into existence for what you will become. Is it wrong for me to hope that mi hombres can change too?"

Henry quoted the Bible, "God is the same yesterday, today, and forever. He doesn't change his mind like man."

Pico reflected for a moment, his round claw touching his lips then spoke, "Si, I agree, the Lord is the same, but maybe God hasn't told us everything there is to know; only what we need to know for now. Have you not heard from Isaiah the prophet?

'From this time on I will tell you of new things,
of things hidden, unknown to you.

They are created now, and not from of old; before today you have not heard of them.'"

"Please dad, can we focus on finding Daniel and cut the Bible quiz?" demanded Lucas as he rubbed his forehead and took over the questioning. "Pico, where would Ru take Daniel?"

"La mujer was careful not to tell us, in case we were subjected to interrogation."

"Does she still have access to the Blue Moon?"

"I suppose she does. It would be difficult for the Vigilantes to gain access, but not impossible. I wouldn't think she would risk going. The time is too close to the exit. Cuzak needs her. And, the Vranti revealed to us that Yazad plans on exterminating the Señorita and her Padre once their relocation program is under way. Señorita Ru must be very careful."

"All the more reason I don't understand why she took Daniel," bemoaned Lucas.

Victoria, listened intently to the conversation, but her mothering instinct told her the worst of their day was yet to come. The sun became a giant red disc, setting behind the Andes as they made the final switchback, headed down the hill, and turned off through the clear cut area toward their compound. Nearing the boundary where the trees and incline began again, everything they saw reminded them of Daniel until another warning sign went off.

"Your eyes and your hand, Lucas, they are still... " said Victoria. Lucas quickly turned off the Range Rover's headlights and inched up the drive close enough so that his enhanced sight could scout out the rocks, brush and trees hiding their home's entrance. "There could be another ambush," he whispered.

Chapter 66

"Your wisdom and knowledge mislead you,
When you say to yourself,
I am, and there is none besides me."
--Isaiah 47:10

Pico asked Lucas, "Did they send más bug hombres to find Danielito?"

"That's a good question. Change of plans, we've got to leave as soon as possible."

"We've already packed the essentials in the other SUV," said Victoria, "but leaving so soon without my son? What if he's hiding in the forest all alone? I'll remain till morning, see if he comes back, then join you."

Lucas put the vehicle in drive and slowly crept up to their parking area behind two boulders, "Honey, you said Ru's never lied to us. I can't leave you here alone through the night." Shifting to park, he added, "Let Pico and I go in and check the compound."

Henry said, "I'll stay out here with the gals."

Lucas held Pico's claw, who scampered just behind him, and entered the rock doorway and down the stone steps. At the base of the stairs they turned on the lights. From the main kitchen-living room, they searched for evidence of an invader, but found none. "Looks clear Pico," said Lucas.

In a few minutes they emerged to find everyone else searching with flashlights, "Nothing inside" said Lucas.

"But why is your hand still blue darling," asked Victoria, "I feel something in the air."

"Señor Lucas, *aquí*," said Pico, "shine your lights on the pond."

Walking around the two parked vehicles, they aimed their flashlights at the holding pond where Pico was pointing, who said, "The very bad bug hombre did come by here." Floating on their source of drinking water was a thick layer of white and yellow writhing insect larvae.

Victoria said, "I am never drinking that water again."

"Turn off your flashlights," insisted Lucas. Turning them off they saw what Lucas had spotted, the outline a logging truck coming down the mountain, across the field running parallel to their compound. They all heard the truck gearing down, the staccato reverberation as its high compression cylinders helped it decelerate. Behind it trailed a bouncing, noisy, half full log carrier. Next the tractor trailer turned toward their compound and accelerated through the clear cut field, adding gear after gear.

"Pico, get back in the vehicle," ordered Lucas. Respecting him the sloth hooked the top of the mirror and swung up to the open passenger window and dropped into the seat, "Shot-Gun!" he said, "Ah, you no like Señor Vranti, the bug hombre."

"That's an understatement," added Lucas.

"Why are you getting in the car!" screamed Victoria, "The truck is coming up the drive!"

"Victoria, settle down. Go with mom and dad. Lock the compound down, and finish packing. Give us half an hour. Pico and I are going to lead it away from here. After that I'll meet you at the Cusco safe house."

"But Lucas," protested Victoria.

"There is no time to discuss it," Lucas said as he jumped in the Range Rover. "Do it! Please, Dad, Mom, make her. It's going to be OK." And before Victoria could reply, Lucas dropped the transmission into reverse, spewing gravel, and whipping the front end around toward the drive. Without braking, he jammed the transmission forward with his blue hand, all four wheels accelerating down the hill toward the approaching demonic diesel.

"Pico, are you healed enough to help us?" asked Lucas, "Now would be a good time."

In an instant the sloth transformed, into the neophyte, Advanta, "Open the sun roof," he said. Standing through the opening, Advanta unfurled his wings, half feathered and half leather patches, his hair tussled by the wind. The driver of the truck saw the expanded wings in his headlights and still did not relent, as the vehicles rumbled toward a lopsided collision. Within twenty-five yards of the head on truck joust, Lucas veered his vehicle off the road, bouncing through the shallow drainage ditch, while jerking his SUV left and right to avoid the field stumps.

Unfortunately, he saw one stump where his only recourse was to straddle it; a mistake, flipping his Rover onto its side, rolling him twice, before coming to rest on a log suspending its front wheels in the air. His side and front air bag had exploded, deafening and stunning him for a few seconds. He sat still, momentarily recovering from his third blow, his head aching, smothered by the bags. Then in frustration he ripped the empty bladders out with his blue hands stuffing them out the missing side window.

With only one headlight functioning, Lucas attempted to adjust his left mirror, but it broke off, dangling by its thin control cables. His rearview mirror and camera were likewise malfunctioning. Advanta was gone, but his sword still lay tucked between the seats. He slammed the vehicle in reverse and began to roll off the log, but a large root jammed itself under the left front wheel weld, holding the Range Rover stuck, as the four wheels spun.

Grabbing the sword and shoving against his car door to get out, Lucas hyper-extended the hinges which snapped, allowing the door to fall to the ground. Lucas crawled out to locate the wild truck in pursuit and Advanta. The semi was turning around through the shallow ditch, while the laden trailer leaped off its wheels from side to side with every stump it hit. He heard it gearing up again along with the pounding of its trailer. The headlights bobbed toward him over the rough terrain. Its logs jostled within the creaking steel cradle, one managing to fly loose behind the truck.

Meanwhile, Advanta's weakened wings flew him into the cab of the truck through the open passenger window, hoping to disperse the insects from the unlucky driver.

Lucas found the problem and hacked at the large root with Advanta's sword, splitting it, then jumped into the SUV to out run the oncoming lights of the semi. "Lord help me lead it away from the compound," he prayed.

To Advanta's surprise, a woman about nineteen years old, was at the wheel. *"I must be careful, I cannot take this innocent life,"* he said. But as the strength of the collective inside the driver became evident to Advanta, he realized his current weakened state was no match for what controlled her.

Determined, he addressed her in the native darkened speak of the infected. The driver instantly recognized the patches of eczema-like damaged hide with molting feathers as one who had turned his back on Siyon.

Chapter 67

"From the far east I summon a bird of prey;
from a distant land, a man to fulfill my
purpose." --Isaiah 46:11

"This territory is mine, what are you doing?" Advanta screeched at her.

As the cab bounded over the rough terrain, pulled and tugged by its loose trailer, the driver turned her stiff robot like head and neck toward him, "This one must die. You, we do not know. Rid yourself. You are weak, half darkened, and a neophyte."

Advanta countered, "Cuzak, son of Beltshzan, sent me to drive the Juwaan insane, not kill him."

"That is impossible. You are no match. We were sent to exterminate this one and his son. They stand in the way. He has decimated my kind before."

"Where is his son now?" said Advanta as their racketing semi truck neared Lucas, head lights growing more intense on the banged up black vehicle.

"Why do you wish to distract me? Are you not preparing for the exit? Is this not why you succumbed?"

"Listen to me you foolish bug eyed banshee! This Juwaan's son, Daniel, has escaped, and your cohort was taken by the known Vigilante Azazel to be traded into the abyss. If you don't stop I will force you from this body." With no abatement the young woman gave off a laughing hiss, shoved the truck into a higher gear, accelerating through the ditch onto the dirt road, the trailer weaving wildly, closing the gap on Lucas' damaged vehicle.

Praying for what to do, Advanta flew back out of the cab, covering the front of the semi's windshield with his emaciated body and flimsy wings just as the truck was about to strike Lucas from behind. But then he received a better idea.

Back near the tree line on the edge of the compound, Victoria, Henry, and Judith watched the bouncing headlights, and listened to the banging trailer, screeching wheels and revving engines. They each prayed for Lucas and Advanta, for divine intervention to stop whatever, whoever this enemy was, and by all means to be with young Daniel.

"You two get our stuff together; meet me here at the car. I have to take care of something," said Henry.

Advanta hated the idea of invading the already cramped woman's body. However, his matrix did crave for the raw energy a live body of flesh could provide, for the infection no longer allowed him to be nourished off of the pure light of Siyon. Relaxing his bodily matrix, Advanta slipped into a vaporous cloud through the cab window and entered the body of the young woman, already host to something more insidious.

Inside Advanta could feel the roiling multitudes of this Vranti, and hear their internal chatter, "We did not invite this one to enter."... "Does he want to join us, and be a part of our collective?"... "No, this one may be a traitor."... "Look at him, he cannot hide his disease."

Swimming his way through the multiple entities swarming in her flesh and soul, Advanta felt disgust with himself. *How have I deteriorated to this level?*

Veezon, Fortius, and Azazel had warned him it might come to this. Tracing her neural pathways and synapses, Advanta looked for vestiges of any true light in her. The Vranti made it difficult to see anything redeeming in her mind. The woman's hands bled from the tight grip on the steering wheel, while anger and adrenalin fueled the collective entity's control over her.

Advanta noticed a light toward her cerebral cortex as he pressed his way through the others and their incessant mutterings. He saw she had ceded all control of herself to this pariah, but there remained in her, an eternal gateway, a trapped consciousness, a place at the center of her heart and mind where one's spirit can meet the inner sky. Yet for the moment this innermost connection of space and time between Siyon and this woman was blocked by an enemy she probably didn't even believe in.

As Advanta tried to dismantle her from the inside, Lucas tail gate was smashed from behind by the rusty oil pipe bumper of the truck, boosting his vehicle forward, whiplashing his neck, while relentlessly bearing down. With only a right beam head light functioning, bent forty-five degrees off center, Lucas attempted to lead the truck away from the compound in the dark as he reached the T in the road. Taking a hard right he headed up the hill for the switchbacks. To his amazement the truck was gaining on him. "Advanta, where are you? Hello..."

"Bamb," the semi rear-ended him again. Lucas glanced down to see all the engine warning lights on. He was losing power, and so was Advanta, who decided the best he could do was to try and blind or asphyxiate the woman until she passed out.

The darkened sentinels inside the driver said to the extra parasite, "You will not stop us, for we are many." "Vomit him out at once."... "He is not with us! He is a Loyalist in disguise."... "You are a Vigilante, and a poor one at that. Your secret will be known."

But to this admonition Advanta countered with his own pronouncement, "I have shared in your cup of wickedness, but I have discovered another cup, dipped in a far sea which drowns the sorrows of the infection and sprinkles the nations. I will share with you a hidden word which does not die."

The collective implored him, "What is this secret word?"... "I demand on Beltshzan's grave that you tell me."

"If you have ears to hear then listen," said Advanta, "'From the far east I summon a bird of prey; from a distant land, a man to fulfill my purpose.'"

"What kind of foolery is this word? He will never come to the Sanctuary," said the entities. "He doesn't even come to Earth anymore."

"He has come already to the land of Two Suns," said Advanta, "He knows no fear."

In the short distraction from the inner visitor, the collective paused to doubt themselves as the logging truck raced for the first switchback overlooking the dark rift valley, a drop of three thousand feet to the ravine along the Inca trail, full of mountain jungle and large boulders. Aiming to ram the rear of Lucas' Rover, she steered a straight line as long as possible, planning to pull away at the last second. But it was too late.

The possessed driver mashed hard on the air brakes, locking up the wheels, causing the worn tractor trailer to jack knife to the right. The rear of the trailer slid past the cab, pounding Lucas' SUV, as he attempted to swerve sharply to the right to escape the kamikaze truck. However, the rear dual trailer tires hit him head on, catapulting the exploding mangled fireball off the precipice, into the night.

Moreover, the momentum of the rig dragged its own rear axles helplessly backwards toward the cliff where they dropped first. Next, weight and leverage hoisted the cab up into the air, flipping the tractor-trailer in a back somersault. The tumbling truck chased downward end over end after Lucas' fireball in front of it. The cracking of large limbs and twisting of the body and frame of the SUV echoed through the canyon first as it crashed and burned like a meteorite through the tree canopy, and then to the jungle floor thicket. A few seconds later the awful metallic moans of stressed steel smashing and bouncing on the jagged edges of rock formations, resounded for miles. Its descent carved a further path of vegetative destruction as it slid down the escarpment, followed by a rain of burning diesel fuel from the ripped saddle tanks.

Chapter 68

I am tired of no one telling me the truth about who I am.

Gliding onto the tarmac of the Jorge Chavez--Lima International Airport, under the cloak of a moonless night, Ru landed with her young shirtless, shoeless quarry in her arms. Dismissing her Vigilante escorts after they cleared the plane, Ru and Daniel boarded a cylindrical magnetic elevator beneath the six story tail of the Boeing 797 luxury liner, equipped for vertical takeoff and landing. By owning a majority stake in Virgin Airways, the Sanctuary Corporation insured that a dozen of these planes were outfitted with private rear fuselage offices for their special board officers.

As Daniel turned his eyes to the bottom of the plane, a whirlpool opening recessed above them, then corkscrewed closed after they passed inside. The twelve hundred square foot, two story apartment-office, was furnished with much technological advancement."

The first thing Ru showed him was the well stocked refrigerator. "Are you hungry Daniel? If you don't want to make something yourself, here is the menu from the plane's galley. Push the item and without question it will show up on the turn-style counter over there when it's ready."

"This is all real cool," said Daniel, momentarily side tracked from the heartache of being separated from his parents. As he put on a pair of computer visors and scrolled through the recent menu items, he quickly found the laser light decoration controls and began changing the apartment's décor. From 'Urban Andean,' to 'Turkish Delight,' to 'Uptown Shanghai,' to one labeled 'Ouriano's Lair,' his retinal reflex made this selection, causing the flat square dividers and ceiling to meld into arched walls and a multi pastel illumed dome ceiling, known only to one who had visited the private living quarters of a Blue Moon Legionnaire. In the center of the virtual apartment appeared an elongated bed with a small reflecting pool in the floor behind it. Daniel took off the visor and walked over to the bed. He reached down to feel the silky smooth white coverings, spreading out his arms and hands. To Ru it appeared as if Daniel was more than familiar with these surroundings. "This is mine, isn't it?" he said, pausing to look back at her.

"This is not real Daniel," said Ru.

"But it is real somewhere, isn't it?" he reminded her.

Ru had not anticipated this, but desired to discover where this was going. Clutching the cross around her neck, Ru prayed, "Is my old friend toying with me? Is Ouriano in Daniel somewhere? Does he have any idea who he is?"

Next he took a few steps over to the small reflecting pool and stared into it. To his amazement Daniel could see a reflection other than his own. Cautious, he asked, "Who is this apparition?" For in virtual waters he saw the image of a weathered first generation Wind of light, a muscled physique whose prime was of another age, like the abs which now had slumped into a paunch. It was immensely real to him; so much that he reached up to feel the engrained furrows on his own forehead and lines in his leathery cheeks. Along the neck and right shoulder he saw the long scar in the pool, but also could trace the healed scar tissue on his own neck and shoulder.

Daniel continued to stare into the waters as Ru stood silent in horror, afraid that her departed, but murdered friend would rise up somehow to confront her through the boy. She said under her breath, "This should not be happening. It is only technology imprinted from my memories, programmed for interior design, nothing more." As Daniel made a happy-sad connection with the image, she added, *"But it's true."*

Tear drops rolled off the face of Daniel and the image of the old warrior, striking the pool at the same time, their ripples crossing. But in a few moments the rings in the water became as one, through which the weathered reflection gently smiled at the young boy. Returning the gesture, Daniel and the image pulled away from the reflection pool. This was all the emotion that Daniel, the newly called Jeshurun could handle.

Daniel wiped his eyes, reached for Ru's hand and said, "I am beginning to understand, but are you going to let me talk to my parents?"

Failing to conceal her own wet eyes, Ru answered, "Daniel, like I promised, I am never ever going to hurt you. Look, here is your sword."

Holding it in both of his hands, Daniel for the first time marveled at its beauty; double edged, a shining blade inlaid with strange hieroglyphics. As he held it over his head, once again it began to hum ever so faint, a light blue energy flowing through to the hilt and up into his hands, forearms, and shoulders. The energy made the long battle sword feel light. "This belongs to my father," said Daniel, "I saw his hand turn blue from holding it, like mine."

"The sword was in his possession, but it has always belonged to you."

Still unsure whether to trust her, Daniel began to move in rhythmic exercises with his sword, spinning, twirling the blade as if the two were one, and buying time as he deliberated on his surroundings and feelings. Though he was lanky, thin arms and legs, Daniel's coordination amazed even Ru, *"He is truly a wunderkind."*

As he continued his mock combative moves, Daniel tested her with a question. "My grandfather would quote to me during hard times, 'And they overcame him by the blood of the lamb and the word of their testimony, and they loved not their lives unto death.' I have wondered who or what these words are talking about?"

Gripping the cross on her neck she reflected on the name engraved on the backside of it, *'Holy Hripsimé.'* "Help me," Ru prayed in silence, *"for not only does he have the coordination of Ouriano, but the early Death Angel instincts."*

"Why are you asking me this?" she countered, "You already know."

"You won't answer?"

Daniel became more aggressive in his exercises as if a new instinct guided him. Then, in the blink of an eye he leapt into the air, spinning, scissoring his legs over his head, the remainder of his body and sword whipping after them. Landing with perfect balance in front of her, Ru had no time to react. She could see and hear the sword coming for her, but it was too fast to defend. The tip of the blurring blade stopped at the top of her neck line. Breathing a sigh of relief, she pushed the tip to the side, while more tears streamed from her eyes.

Daniel held his position to evoke an answer, "Why am I asking you this? I can't believe you don't know. I am asking because behind your tears, you look like someone who is from the darkness. You know much more of me than I do of you. Why do you wear that cross you are holding in your hand?"

"A gift from the past, that's where I want to take you. It will explain so much. You can trust me Daniel."

Daniel, still unsure, slowly dropped his sword, "I am tired of no one telling me the truth about who I am. I feel so weird inside. Help me."

"I will... We will help each other."

"It's hot in here. I am getting light headed," said Daniel, swiping the sweat from his forehead.

"It has been a very long day for you and your family. Come let me show you your room so you can get some sleep." As Ru led him through an automatic door to a small room with a bed, a dim spotlight focused on his place of rest. Daniel still only in shorts, barefoot, lay down on his back, covering his eyes with his fading blue forearms, where he began to doze off from the stress of the day.

Ru lingered over him. Overcome by a deep love for the boy and a link to her old friend, she sighed in her soul, "How often has Victoria looked down on her sleeping son like this and loved him? But not tonight, I am so sorry I had to do this Victoria."

As the light in the small room dimmed, Ru couldn't help herself but to kiss him on his shoulder. And that is when she noticed it for the first time. Marring the perfect skin of the boy was a scar on the center of his sternum. She swore, a few minutes earlier that it was not present.

Chapter 69

You think evil goes away just like that?
Think again.

"What's that noise like thunder from the ridge where the road turns? Can't be good." Victoria panicked, asking Judith, "And where's Henry? Forget anymore packing. We just need to take off and see what happened to Lucas."

"I thought you wanted to stay behind," said Judith.

"No, Lucas was right, we need to leave now. Henry, Henry, Dad! Let's go. I have a bad feeling about this. Where is he?"

"He probably went back into the compound to gather a few more things."

Victoria raised her line of sight toward the canopy of trees above them, "Hey, do you hear what I hear?"

Judith pointed her flash light up into the trees, "Yes, a humming. It wasn't there a few minutes ago. Look at all the insects attracted to my flashlight all of a sudden. Oh Jesus help us," fretted Judith, crossing her heart. "I have to go in and get Henry.

"No you are not," whispered Victoria emphatically, "Mom, turn out your light and get in the car. Do it now." They both darted for the driver and passenger front doors. No sooner had they locked themselves in, when a sound like hail, began to pelt the Range Rover in the dark, pinging the roof and hood, pounding thuds on the windows, and increasing in frequency.

"What are we going to do?" screamed Judith.

"We can't sit still Mom," said Victoria spinning the wheels in reverse then snapping forward into four wheel drive, the vehicle straddling small boulders while bounding up the compound steps. Victoria pulled as close as she could to the front door, where she turned on the head lights and honked the horn for Henry to come out. But the door never opened.

Frantic, Judith tried unsuccessfully to open her passenger door. "Unlock the door for me Victoria. I am not leaving Henry here to die like our daughter Paige!"

Energizing the front and rear windows, hundreds of green sparks spewed from the aggressive contact with the electrical insect repellers. "Mom, you are crazy, maybe dad is locked in, secure. I know these bugs. They are going to try and get in this car. I am sealing all the vents."

"Oh my gosh the car is moving on its own," screamed Judith as they spun sideways and slid backwards down the ten steps, the vehicle shifting by the force of thousands of insects attached to its sides and chassis.

Victoria tried to aim the SUV toward the front entrance, then floored the gas pedal. The RPM's soared as the engine raced and the wheels spun. "We are off the ground, we can't get traction."

"Unlock the door darling. I mean it," said Judith. "I know what I am doing. Then see if the car can get away. I'll die here with Henry if I have to."

"I can't," Victoria said as the SUV swayed back and forth like a flight simulator in a storm.

"Do it for Daniel, my grandson," Judith said, "if you want to see him again. He needs his mother."

Reluctantly, Victoria's finger tips unlocked her door whereupon Judith slung it open, but only to have it slam shut against her, knocking her backwards into her seat even quicker. She heard her husband's muffled voice, "Don't come out!"

Through her side window she saw an outline of man with a wide head in a white jump suit, "Henry has his old Bee Suit on." No sooner had she said this, when they heard a low pressure jet sound from Henry's make shift propane blow torch. He normally used it to start family bon fires. They watched in confusion as a bright blue-yellow flame baked the hood of the SUV, followed by a cloud of smoke. They heard again the muffled jet of pressurized gas igniting as Henry roasted all four sides of the car to burn off the parasites. Those surviving flew away as windblown ambers.

"I forgot he had that suit from back when we served in the Amazon basin. The mosquitoes were sometimes terrible, the bullet ants, the bees, where they had clear cut some of the forest. He used that suit when he had to control them," said Judith. When the insects had disappeared she opened her door to Henry standing with the propane nozzle on low flame in one hand and an insecticide sprayer in the other.

"Henry, what in heaven's name are you doing?"

"What does it look like dear, roasting weenies? Don't get out, I am getting in," he said, opening the back passenger door, dropping the sprayer and propane tanks off of his shoulders, head gear still on, "Let's get the tarnation out of here."

The smoldering Range Rover with scorched paint job took off down the drive for the main road.

"Dad, you saved our lives."

"When I saw all those larvae in our little pond, I knew something was up. I went in the storage building after I heard something in the trees. Now, where do you think Lucas is?"

Victoria answered, "We heard what sounded like thunder up on the ridge, possibly a crash. If we don't find Lucas we are to keep going to Cusco, to the safe house, and wait." In five minutes they arrived at the scene of the wreckage. The overhead beams, fog, and head lights illuminated the evidence, which led to a thin smoke rising beyond the cliff.

Scattered on the brown dirt and gravel lay pieces of Lucas' SUV; a crumpled passenger door, a deformed steel grate bumper, a collapsed hood, a front winch and loose cable. From the tractor trailer, a bent wheel, a leaking diesel saddle tank, and burst tire lent testimony to the hard impact.

Victoria scrambled for an explanation, "You can see where the truck slid sideways, digging the trench in the road and broke through the guard rail. Oh my God! It must have hit Lucas and taken him down too!"

Henry jumped out of the car, pulled off his bee hood and ran to the edge, staring down, anticipating some sign of survival. "Somewhere my boy is down there Lord. Help him," he prayed. A fire raged thousands of feet below, partly covered by its own smoke. Miles away he saw a helicopter, maybe a drone, flying down the valley toward the fire to investigate. Depressed he slowly walked back to the SUV and got in, "I don't know anyone who could survive that. I saw a plane or something headed toward the fire below coming up through the valley. I am sure it will fly our way if we wait. Lord Almighty, this can't be happening."

"Then we need to go dad. I will cry when we reach the safe house. We don't need to wait for more unfriendlies to show. Cuzak is a powerful man. We need to keep all of our options in play."

Judith, covered her face in her hands sobbing, as Victoria turned and headed down the mountainous logging road. Judith said, "I feel like I have lost two sons today, Daniel and Lucas." Henry leaned forward, reached around the front seat and held her shoulders.

"I know, darling."

Into her tear filled hands she spoke again, "And I know if the Lord desires, he can raise them up. He raised His Son, why not two more. Is that so hard?" Judith prayed.

Victoria reached out and grasped her hand, "Come on everyone hold it together. This has to be part of the plan... And no Judith, I believe two more, even a million more to raise up is not so hard." After a few seconds, she released Judith's hand as disappointment and anger raced to replace her faith. Victoria squeezed the steering wheel as if to break it off. She pounded the wheel and column with her fist and shouted, "Is it, God?" Then pounded it once more and yelled louder, "Make another son for all of us, go ahead! Isn't that what you are good at?"

Henry tried to calm her, "Victoria, be careful what you say."

Chapter 70

Heroes? We are disfigured.
We are an embarrassment,
a wound that won't heal.

The Vigilantes hovered above the vertical ascending Virgin Airways 797 with Ru and Daniel safely secured inside. At a mile high, the hydra-vortex engines rotated forward to propel the super luxury liner to its cruising altitude of sixty-thousand feet, toward an undisclosed destination.

From the vantage point high above Lima, Veezon and his companions sensed an evil concentrate of long infected Winds leaching into the city of eight million souls. As Lima was host to one of the new Hub transfer stations, long suffering sinister entities deliberately filtered down to the coastal city, for the image bearers were not the only ones preparing to leave.

These tattered raw hide wretches carried their despair to trade for a chance to begin anew; a place where their independence from the local entity would know no limits. Every day the oppression of this city and ninety-nine others around the world grew in labor like contractions. Something had to give.

Veezon called to his comrades to encourage them, "This is our crucible. Consider yourselves fortunate and give thanks. We are a forsaken lot, but not forgotten. We have nowhere to rest our wings, for our destiny is before us. There is no time to waste. We must retrieve Advanta."

Fortius agreed, "Well said my friend. There is a spirit who gives lift to our frayed wings, but Advanta does not have the strength to weather a frontal assault alone." Tightly packing themselves into a stream lined diamond formation for the return trip to the Tanner family compound, they blasted through the sound barrier approaching mach five, rattling the windows across the city.

Veezon continued through telepathy, "The Vranti scum will send another. Our neophyte is wise for a fifth generation, but he won't crawl out of that jungle alive unless we retrieve him. Ru has good reason to hide Daniel, but the boy needs his father alive. Lucas is after all a Juwaan."

Azazel added, "Then this Lucas Tanner, PhD, he needs to be pushed. He should be more on the attack. Too much a pacifist if you ask me."

Veezon retorted, "You were not consulted for a reason Azazel. He must enter the Sanctuary quietly, like us."

"Yes," Fortius added, "But he has a point; if we are to recruit more infected Winds, they'll need a leader they can support. Not just a boy with potential and a reluctant man."

"What did you exchange for the Vranti you swallowed?" Veezon asked Azazel.

"I traded for a favor."

"Are you saying you didn't hand him over to those who would take him to the Abyss? That was my order."

"Order? No, the way things have gone lately, I sent him somewhere he might be tamed. We need someone like him on our side."

Veezon said, "His kind cannot be tamed. He is a cold blooded murderer. Where did you send him?"

"I requested the transport forward him to Wandu, to Lamech. I left instructions for my old friend to hold him. We need information."

"For what gain?"

"A transport of our own to the Blue Moon, with Ambassador status."

"Representing who?

"The Vigilantes, of course."

"No one knows of us Azazel, no one cares."

"Of this Veezon you are wrong," said Azazel, "we have become heroes on Yare'ach Kachol."

"Heroes? We are disfigured, an embarrassment, a wound that won't heal," said Veezon, the former Legion Commander.

"Veezon, you have more pride than all of us combined. I have a place we can go," said Azazel.

"Where?"

"Didn't I just say, 'To see Lamech'?"

Their diamond formation reverse-thrusted through the sound barrier with wings tucked, leaving a white ring vapor cloud between two mountain peaks. Passing Machu Picchu in their descent toward the hidden Tanner Family compound, Veezon said, "Hold that thought, ahead, the truck chasing the Range Rover toward the cliff, not good."

Fortius said, "Another one of the collective. Do they have a factory for these things?"

"It's Advanta, he's in the truck," said Azazel.

Veezon commanded, "Azazel, take the truck, we're going for the car."

The Vigilantes could not respond with nearly the speed they once had as infection free Winds, whipping in and out of dimensions at will. Now, they had to stoop to most of the same laws of physics which bound humans. Like high speed jet fighters they split formation, improvising their next plans of action as they observed the logging truck slide sideways toward the front end of the dented Range Rover. They calculated by instinct that they would arrive a split second after impact.

An incredibly loud "Ka-chunk!" blasted out as the vehicles collided. The thirty thousand pound double rear axle of the semi slammed the front of Lucas six-thousand pound car like a giant mallet to a pecan shell.

"Keep the steering wheel from jamming through his neck!" Veezon directed Fortius. The force of the truck pushed the engine block of the SUV backward four feet. Fortius redirected the steering column at an angle out the broken door. Veezon punctured through the sunroof and grabbed Lucas by the shoulders, pulling him out before the Rover became a fire ball hurling over the cliff.

In the mean time Azazel swept into the cab of the truck calling out, "Advanta!"

Shocked at his presence, the truck driver stared at him with a wide grin as Azazel found her arms locked around the steering wheel while the cab swung to follow the inertia leading log trailer over the edge of the cliff. When the cab lifted off the ground to flip over backwards, the wounded Advanta left the woman to perish on her own as he was pulled to safety by Azazel.

Floating in the air while holding Advanta, he watched the truck trailer, and heavy lumber, descend end over end backwards down the steep cliff. Lifting his gaze he saw coming to him in the night, Veezon cradling Lucas' unconscious and limp body across his arms.

Veezon asked as they hovered in the air, "Can either of you heal anymore?"

Azazel and Fortius answered one after another. "You must be in denial, look at the shape I am in," "No, not at all. I barely have energy left to sustain my form."

"Then we need to get them to a place which can help. Look in the distance, coming up the hill. A smoking vehicle, it looks seared," said Veezon.

"We don't have the strength to make a confrontation after these flights," lamented Fortius, "we need rest too. The vehicle is stopping. Who is this getting out—white suit and head dress?" They all watched as Henry took off the bee keeper's hood and walked to the edge of the cliff. "Poor man, is that Lucas' father examining the wreckage? The Juwaan should be well enough for us to leave him with them. Check his eyes."

Veezon took his right hand and lifted his eye lids; there was still a dim light coming from them.

Azazel responded, "We need to save Advanta, our kind. No one is watching out for us."

Veezon looked with compassion on the decrepit Advanta, "Neophyte, can you maintain your matrix a short time more? What in the world were you doing cohabiting inside the woman's body?"

"He cannot answer you," said Azazel, "all his strength, energy are gone. He looks horrible. And we are not far behind." As the three Vigilantes examined him, the once fair and handsome Advanta had become a shrunken entity, half his original size, leathery in appearance. The spindle bones of his featherless wings were poking through the stretched dry eczema patched hide, the once muscular athletic arms, now gaunt. Advanta curled up into a fetal ball to conserve his essence.

Azazel added, "He is going to disintegrate if we don't do something."

"We won't let that happen. Make good on your favor. We'll leave this Juwaan with his family. Someone on the Blue Moon will help Advanta. No one comes more innocent."

Chapter 71

Identify Yourself

About a mile down the dirt road from the point of the accident, Victoria slowed the SUV to a stop at the fork in the road. One went south toward Cusco and the safe house, a four hour high altitude driving adventure, the other toward remote area of the wreck. Resting her head on the steering wheel, she made a private apology, "I didn't mean it that way Lord."

"What did you say Vic, you need me to drive? To the right is the way down to the wreckage. Let's pray about it, then make our decision," said Henry.

Victoria shot back, "Let's not do the share the prayer thing right now. I've been praying a long time. And we can't use any electronic device. It gives away our location, OK? So if we want to find Lucas either we jump over the edge of the ravine or we drive two hours down ragged logging roads, and then hike another hour to reach the bottom of the crash site. I don't expect you to understand, but I'm for sticking to the plan and going to our rendezvous point."

Judith added, "She's right. The wreckage is in a remote area. There is a train which runs in the valley towards the base of Machu Picchu from Puno. Maybe Lucas will jump on that train for help. Henry, you shouldn't drive at night on these roads, and you know it."

"Let's take a vote," said Henry. "All in favor, of going down to look for my son..."

But before anyone could argue further, a knuckle wrap on the driver window in the middle of nowhere caused everyone to jump, "Ahh...!"

Victoria stomped on the accelerator pedal out of fright, spinning the stranger and tripping him to fall in the road. Judith was just able to make the man's two blue radiating eyes, "It might be Lucas, his eyes. Stop, back up." Opening her door, the passenger light displayed the singed and smudged face of her son, who was dragging a sword in the dirt behind him. "Lucas!"

"Mom?"

"Hurry Lucas, Get in. We thought you were dead."

"Do you know where a fella can get a lift?" mumbled Lucas, as Henry and Victoria jumped out of the SUV to help him. "Your car smells burnt," said Lucas, reclining his head back, rubbing his temples and closing his eyes. "Have you seen Pico, the sloth--Advanta? He was trying so hard to help me, but he was already weak. This is his sword."

"No, but Daniel will be broken hearted if something happened to him. How'd you end up on this part of the road without your car?"

Gently dabbing his forehead scabs, Lucas said, "I'm not sure. I was heading fast to the edge of the overlook and veered right, believing I could out maneuver the truck, then,... here I am stumbling on the road."

"We heard a horrendous crash. Your SUV and the truck chasing you went over the cliff. We were trying to decide whether to search for you in the ravine or continue. We just knew you went to the bottom," said Victoria, shifting the SUV into drive and taking the fork to the left. "It was another of the Vranti, they were in the tree's waiting for us. Instead, your father had a surprise waiting for them. He toasted the paint job of course, but we're alive."

Forty-five minutes later, the snow capped Andes and star lit clouds were below window level. Everyone but the driver had fallen asleep, aided by the high altitude of the sixteen thousand foot pass where they approached the main road to Cusco, the ancient capital of the Inca Empire. Cusco itself lay at twelve-thousand feet, a tourist Hub and small cosmopolitan launch point for seekers of mystery and intrigue, serviced by plane, train, and slow buses.

The pass, even in the summer maintained its cut snow banks on each side of the highway. Tonight the road was empty. The southern hemisphere's bright Milky Way allowed Victoria to relax and absorb the beauty of the shadowy sleeping giants, blanketed by their glistening snow and ice sheets. In many of the steep hair pin curves, memorials of crosses mixed with religious statues, stapled pictures and flowers adorned the last places they were known to be alive before going over the edge.

At least with Lucas in the car she realized, all was not as lost as it could have been, "Thank you God that they are alive. But tell me, where do you have my Daniel tonight? This was supposed to be his tenth birthday today. I didn't even get to wish him happy birthday or attempt the baked Alaska. Where is Ru hiding him? You know everything, so tell me. If we make it to Cusco we can disappear into the city and regroup, have our family again. Lord, I want my family together, is that too much? I am not sure if I care what your plans are. Forgive me."

As she finished, Victoria crested over a mountain pass, the yellow lights of Cusco miles away sparkled over the top of her dash board. Her entire world was tranquil for the moment, when a blue light for an incoming call signaled on the visor, setting off her defense; *This is mom and dad's vehicle. Nobody has this number but Lucas and I. Do I take the call and give away our location? Maybe it is about Daniel.*

Victoria slipped on the visor, the Sanctuary Corporation's Eden Tree insignia came into view. "Identify yourself," she said.

The icon faded and Ru's face appeared, "Victoria, thank you for answering."

"How is Daniel?" Victoria demanded. "Why did you take him?"

"By now you know, Vic. Your location was given away by Lucas. They wasted no time in finding you. For some reason they are scared of Daniel's more than Lucas' potential. They will never suspect the boy is with me. As we speak, he is en-route to somewhere very safe."

"Let me see him," Victoria demanded in a soft voice as not to wake the others, while descending a new set of sharp curves cut into the mountains.

"I can do that." The video showed Ru's hand motioning a panel door to open, and then her view leaning over Daniel's body where he lay fast asleep curled around a pillow. "That's all I can afford to show you."

"Tell him I love him."

"Of course, I can't talk long. I need to tell you to skip the safe house you have in Cusco as a precaution."

"What? How did you know?"

"I have a message from Shem."

"God, I haven't heard from him in ages. You sure? Shem the leader on Sharu, the Elder from Siyon? That Shem?"

"That is the one. Go to Cusco, but go to 110 Portal de Panes, off of Plaza De Armas."

"That is the club and bar district. Are you sure? The safe house is on the outskirts."

"Vic, I don't know all the reasons. Yes it is off the main square in Cusco. Shem has contacted me and asked that you go there. He is the one who told me to take Daniel to protect him. Do you remember the address?"

"Yes, 110 Portal Panes."

"Go straight there. You will get help."

"No tricks?"

Ru pulled out her cross and put it in front of the lens. "Do I look like I would dupe you? Now, I am going to hang up, and you are going to throw your communication visor out the window." The Sanctuary corporate insignia flashed just before the visor's projection fuzzed out.

Victoria rolled down her window, the cold high altitude air slapping her in the face, and threw her visor out the window. The glasses bounced on the pavement and slid under the guard rail tumbling over the sheer cliff.

Chapter 72

*Why don't you put on a iron shirt
and chase da Devil outta Earth?*

The cool air roused her passengers. "Everybody out," commanded Victoria, "on foot from here. Let's abandon our SUV in this church parking lot. We're about five blocks from our destination."

As they got out into the crisp evening air, Judith ordered Henry, "Lose the bee suit. I am not going into any restaurant with you in that thing."

"Of course, am I that big of a putz to keep this on?" Henry said, peeling off the garments and stuffing them in a nearby trash can. Like always underneath he had his panama shirt with slacks. "They didn't build this city for full size American cars did they?" he said.

"No dad," said Victoria, "almost all the narrow streets predate cars, especially those with blow torched paint."

"It wasn't my best detail job, but it worked."

Lucas added, "Dad that was ingenious. I wish I would have been there, roasting those sons a.... "

"Hush. Chilly in this altitude. Here's everyone's coat we packed," said Judith.

"Mom I need a favor of you. You have the only full length coat among us, and I am not abandoning this sword. It will be like when you would sneak popcorn in the movies for us."

"Hiding a sword is like sneaking popcorn? At this venture, I am not going to ask why son. Hand it over. No one suspects a little old lady."

"Come on guy's, this way," said Victoria. She led them across the city square, then through an alley with old white stucco and cinder block construction on one side of the street and a retaining wall of precise Inca stones on the other.

"Victoria," Lucas asked as they walked hand in hand, "Ru actually spoke to you?"

"Yes, like I told you. I believe she was in an airplane. She showed me a live feed of Daniel sleeping."

"Where would she try to hide him?"

"If I knew, I'd be on my way. Hey, up ahead, there's our address. Am I reading the sign correctly?"

"Can't say I've ever been in the 'Club Afro-Andean,'" said Henry. The neon pink and blue sign hung over the door with the street number 110. "And aren't we lucky. Sign says it's ladies night."

Lucas added, "You gals are free cover and drinks half price."

The front of the club was painted with three diagonal thick green, yellow, and red stripes. Two young Latin-Andean men in similar colored long soccer shirts and baggy jeans controlled the front door, their hair braided in dread locks. A mix of young adult tourists and locals were lined up at the entrance to get in: a cross-pollination of tight skirts and high heels, hiker grunge casual topped with Inca knit ski beanies with tasseled ear flaps. Among them, many internationals set to explore the Inca mysteries. But all of them came in stark contrast to the indigenous Indian women in the street, enterprising to take photos for tips in their colorful, skirts, blouses, intricate serapes, and top hats.

As they stood in line Henry remembered a conversation he and Lucas had years ago when he was home on break from undergrad studies. "Lucas, when you were in college you resented me for trying to change indigenous people when you found out I was going to be a missionary. Do you still feel that way?"

Checking the deflated swelling on his forehead, Lucas replied, "Ah, dad, given the circumstances why are you asking me that now?"

Henry raised his voice as the loud rhythmic sounds of the reggae band started inside. "I mulled over what you said for years, 'what right do you have to come and push your way of life, your religion on others?' Truth is everyone I ever came across has been oppressed or is oppressing someone. Even the Incas consolidated power from many tribes. More than once I had to help villages where the Shining Path communists had murdered the local shaman and priest."

Trying to speak over the band, Lucas answered, "And your point?"

Henry moved close to his ear, "We are moving toward a common oppression of all humanity. That's what this is all about."

"Yes, I am afraid so," yelled Lucas who was cut off by Victoria pulling both their shirt collars toward her, "Hey gentlemen, we are next to go in. Keep an eye open for whoever we are supposed to meet."

Entering as the band played, the four crossed between a brightly lit small elevated stage and the soft blue lit dance floor. Both were outlined with turquoise blue LED lights. The rest of the club was dark except for the highlighted artwork of band posters pasted over old murals of Inca ruins. A host led them to an empty booth where Judith examined a wall poster over their table. It read, "Afro Andean Reggae," above the artwork of Bob Marley standing atop of Machu Picchu singing before an Inca King.

Judith was mesmerized by the young people, the aromas, and the energy. She leaned over to Lucas and shouted in his ear, "Your father would never take me to places like this. I always wanted to learn to dance."

Lucas laughed with her as the song ended, while the electric guitarist with spiked hair continued to pluck his reggae beat. The lead singer was a tall dark Caribbean mix, middle age, red slacks, green soccer shirt, yellow sports jacket, big smile of pearl whites, pilot-sun glasses, goatee, and long dreadlocks capped with a local Inca woman's brown top hat. Between songs he began to address his audience through his English-Jamaican accent, "Tonight, you have come to da highest pa-ti in da world...."

Many in the stuffed club howled with enthusiasm, "...so happy to be here and hopefully add to your repertoire of Andean-Afro-Reggae; where da people come from all ova da world to find Jah." A few less responded to him with claps and shouts. The singer motioned to the guitar to pause so no music would mask his words.

"You ah already so close to Him," the singer added, lifting his top hat forward to block the flood lights to better make out the crowd. "Dat is why so many of you traveled to da mountains, to be closer to Jah and each other on dis long, long journey. My prayer to you, dat you find your way, eternally. You ah all aliens, pilgrims on dis Earth. How many of you have your Hub tickets already? Can I see da hands?" A few beer bottles raised into the air accompanied by a couple of whistles and yells. In a more serious tone he asked, "You tink if you find a new home in anuda world, every little ting gonna be alright?"

A few people clapped, but overall the club grew more unresponsive as his banter was perceived as actual communication, "Ya man, dat is good, but why not start your life ova on dis planet? Repair da injustice here, no? Oh why don't you put on a iron shirt and chase the Devil outta Earth?" Given these odd questions and suggestions by the band leader, the crowd on the dance floor, at the bar, tables and booths went mute, unsure and uncomfortable in how to react.

Sensing the patrons awkwardness, he let them off the hook, "Ha ha! Don't you worry bout a ting, I know you want de next song. Dis one is off our new release, titled, 'Dat Man Who Came to Town.' My name is Shem and dis is my band, Island Picchu. Enjoy!... One, two, three..."

The club relaxed in celebration, *sermon avoided.* "Crank it... Rasta man... Wuhu!" some yelled. Shem twirled his hat through his finger tips, until it came to rest over his dreads.

When the electric guitarist jump started the pulse of the band, Shem yanked the microphone from its stand, caressed it, and rolled his shoulders back and forth with the music. The steel pan drum and bass joined in on his cue as the questionable Rastafarian readied to mix his words into the rhythmic syncopation.

When Lucas turned toward Victoria, she was already glaring at him with raised eyebrows.

Chapter 73

Dat man he came to town,
He tried to tear dis mountain down...

The Reggae Rastafarian from another dimension fused his
words together in his song for this night alone:

"No mo rain, no mo rain, no mo rain...
No mo rain, no mo rain, no mo rain...

Dat man he came to town,
Dat man he came to town,
He tried to tear dis mountain down...

He come in and cut down da tree,
Make room to grow more coffee,
He say dey no room for someone like me,
So Blind you cannot see...

Dat Man he came to town,
Oh, oh, Jah will cut him down,
Who try to steal HaShem's crown...

Buildings, temples and stones dey raise,
Mountain Cathedrals, Worshipping Sun ablaze,
We stack one more block for our future days...

From Ancient of days, da son of man will come,
Dat man who came to town,
Oh, oh, his stone will cut him down...

So blind you cannot see...

Cry forest, cry river, cry all da dead,
Cry jungle, cry lakes, cry all who suffer bled,
No coca leaves left for healing, only red...

Dat no man, who came to town,
He tried to cut dis mountain down,
He always wears a smiling frown,
Oh, his stone will cut him down,
He will not steal HaShem's crown,
Can you hear da kingdom sound...

So blind you cannot see...

Cry forest, cry river, cry all da dead,
Cry jungle, cry lakes, cry all who suffer bled,
No coca leaves left for healing, only red...

But Jah will send his kingdom down,
Lift up your voice when all falls to da ground...

He say der be room for someone like me...

Hey dat no man who came to town,
Rejected stone will cut him down,
He will not steal HaShem's crown...

So blind you cannot see...

Let him reign, Let him reign, Let him reign...
Let him reign, Let him reign, Let him reign...
Let him reign, Let him reign, Let him reign..."

The music slowed down while the soloist's voice faded to the applause of the crowd, "Thank you Cuzzcoooooh!... We will take a break, and be right back. We love you..."

Stepping off the stage and edging his way through the crowd who stayed on the floor as the Bob Marley tune Three Little Birds kicked in, Shem headed directly to Lucas' table. Lucas told Henry and Judith, "We've met this singer before, and he's not from this world. Listen to what he has to say. He is old school like you."

Shem slid into the booth on Victoria and Judith's side, broke into a big smile and removed his sun glasses. "Oh, Juwaan. It has been so long. Time feels slow, but it is sure to arrive. You have a last bit of preparation before your trip to the Sanctuary." Judith and Henry scoured the man up close—his long dreadlocks, the goatee.

Victoria replied, "Is this a game? Our son Daniel is gone. We haven't heard from you in ten years. Now you are coming to claim your Juwaan, my husband? And appearing as a reggae singer?"

"Mrs. Tanner I presume," said Shem, "and Lucas' parents, Judith and Henry. Very nice to meet you. Yes, Daniel should be shielded for now. He is in good hands. We are entering into very tough times, like no other in the past. I wish there were somewhere to run away, but these things must come. No one on the Earth escapes this turn of events. No living thing, Daniel included. All of you will be going to Krator."

Henry spoke up, "My grandson should be safe? Why wasn't something done about this in the past, allowing evil to linger only to strike again? I believe in the Church. If this is such a real threat, why haven't I seen God mobilize the Church better?"

Shem scratched his goatee, "I have asked the same question Henry, and have never received a satisfactory answer. I am afraid all who live on Siyon and the Blue Moon will be affected by this too. The mystery Church you ask? Yes, a good question. It seems to have outwardly faded in this last age. But maybe all the better if it is called to fight in the dark. After all Henry, are they not referred to as, 'exiles scattered throughout the provinces of the world'?"

Henry responded, "You are referring to Saint Peter aren't you? We have to keep faith in our living hope, shielded until that day appears. In our case we have to live out our salvation."

Lucas spoke, "You ideologues can split hairs later. The Hubs are about to open. What is the plan? Has Cuzak and the Sanctuary Corporation really perfected this technology to cross through the multiverse?"

Shem nodded, "Da man, have been testing it for over five years."

Chapter 74

I have a third way; always have.

As the music played in the background, "...every little thing, gonna be alright..." a plump waitress tucked into a tight tuxedo body suit with dark hose and a bow tie, butted into the conversation offering two drinks on her tray, "Te gusta? Would you like?"

Shem waved off the waitress, "Please come back." But she would not relent, "Tonight we have Inca Gold margaritas half-price for the ladies!"

Victoria acted perturbed, "No, we don't want anything now."

The waitress insisted, "Top shelf, everybody is having one. Please try," while placing the frozen drinks on white napkins in front of Victoria and Judith. The waitress then leaned over to Shem and whispered into his ear, "How am I doing sir?"

Shem sat up straight in the booth, caught off guard, "Mrs. Green, I can't believe I didn't recognize you. Where did you get the big hair and outfit? What in the Blue Moon are you doing here?"

"Sir you know how dangerous things are getting. I couldn't remain home. I have done so much research on this place. I thought you might need me. Things have become so unpredictable and all."

Shem turned to the others at the table, "I am sorry, this is my assistant, Mrs. Green. I didn't recognize her at first. Tell me Mrs. Green, what is the best way out of this place?"

"Sir, it depends on where you are going."

Shem answered her, "We need to split up. I need to take Lucas to Wandu. The others need a place to stay near Lima and acquire Hub tickets."

"In that case sir, may I suggest that you leave immediately. There is a sump pump room underneath the kitchen in the back. It leads to an ancient pre-Inca tunnel which meanders through a maze under this city. Supposedly it is connected to the Island of Wandu on the Blue Moon. It was sealed after the infection. Here is a map and trans-corridor mechanism. Prior to the infection this passage was often used as a short cut by Legions."

"Why can't I get a transport?"

"Sir your transport was recently borrowed by your Vigilante friends. I approved an exchange for an emergency they had."

"Why, Mrs. Green did you do that?"

"It was to save the life of a young infected Wind named Advanta. Awful sir." Shem tugged the dread locks near his side burns in angst.

"Are you mad at me sir?"

"No, Mrs. Green. Let's not dally around then. Get Victoria, Judith, and Henry to a safe place on a boat or something off the coast of Lima. Things are going to get ugly."

"Yes sir. I will protect them until the last moment."

Shem looked at Lucas across the table, "Lucas, say goodbye to your family. Next time you see them we will unite on Krator."

"Wait, wait a second. That's it? This whole thing, this war, this fight against evil has been so unorganized from the beginning. Who's in charge? I am not leaving my family to travel to Lima with this cocktail waitress and get in one of those Hub Stations!"

Shem countered, "We are organized, but not the way you would like. You really believe a mechanized army of humans and all their techno-wonders is going to win this? There is a plan, but it's not mine or yours. So let's go. You will see your son and someone else you care about if you follow me out of this place. Do your part Lucas and no one else's. You are in a war, but it is not yours to control. Have faith. When all seems lost, this is not the end, only the beginning."

"Sir," interrupted Mrs. Green, "Sir..." Shem quit his speech to look up.

"What now Mrs. Green?"

"They are calling you on stage for one more song."

"But we have to go Mrs. Green."

"Sir, you should sing one more, you know, maintain your cover, and besides your sales are doing well this month."

"I'll do it on one condition."

Mrs. Green asked, "What condition... please don't ask me to..."

"...sing? Yes, we'll do our version of 'Red Red Wine,'" said Shem. "Pardon us for a few minutes, say your 'goodbyes,' then we'll leave."

Pushing their way through inebriated hordes, Shem and Mrs. Green took center stage. As the music started they danced as mirror images of each other to the delight of the crowd, then began their duet, "Red, Red ...."

Henry asked, "Son, can you trust them?"

"Mom, Dad, Victoria, I don't know what else to do, I wish there was a third way out." As he said this a new waiter stopped in front of their booth holding a tray of drinks.

Before turning to him, Lucas felt a rush of adrenaline, heightened more when he heard the waiter's words; "I couldn't help but to notice how you need a drink, and I overheard what you said, 'I wish there was a third way.' Can I say, whatever you were talking about, it sounds rather interesting."

Taking an extra large shot glass off of his tray he proceeded to put it in front of Lucas, saying, "This round is on the house."

Yet before the glass hit the table Lucas snatched his wrist to shove the drink away, "No thanks, we were just leaving."

The waiter in his early thirties, Caucasian, short brown beard, shaved head, tattoo of a snake wrapped around his neck replied, "Oh, I insist."

Overpowering Lucas despite his sudden bright blue hand and iridescent eyes, he forced the glass on the table. Victoria, Henry, and Judith looked on, paralyzed by the stranger's bad aura.

The overbearing waiter said, "Drink up, I have a third way; always have. I'll even guarantee your son's life. Just give me Ouriano's sword. You know what I'm talking about."

Lucas, unsure what to do and sensing this being's oppressiveness, let go of his arm. He turned to his family who were too numb to give advice, but his mother still had the wherewithal to slide Advanta's sword under the table to him. Reaching for the shot glass with his left hand, he picked it up and held it to his lips.

"I knew you were a reasonable man," the waiter said, eager for him to finish his drink.

Tilting his head back Lucas downed the triple shot while taking a firm hold of Advanta's sword. Slamming the thick glass on the table he began to grin at the embodiment of evil and extended it to a hearty laugh. When he stopped, Lucas said, "You know, you've made one big mistake in coming here."

The waiter responded, "We mustn't give up should we? Tell me."

Before Lucas spoke his eyes burned brighter than they ever had before, gaining even the attention of those on the stage, causing the music to stop. Then he said, "Beltshzan, you're not going to win any converts tonight."

Shem's Log

++

Blue Moon Chronicles Book III, 12.6

Date: At the edge of losing it all
Binary G-Class star system, Yazad sector
Fifth generation Angelus
Beginning of mass exit to Sanctuary
Subject: They know we are coming

Is this all a trap? They know we are coming. The numbers we are sending seem so insignificant. For the first time, the residents of Siyon have been put on alert for possible intruders. Siyon is a place of peace, but I sense even the Angel of Light is troubled.

Worse, I have determined the Heir is indeed, gone. It has been reported to me there are only a lowly few who have heard from him directly. They say he may have taken a new form and has called them by a vision to come to the land of Two Suns Rising.

Questionable information from the captured Vranti claims the Heir's only support so far comes from drones disloyal to Yazad, who labor non-stop in preparation for the coming Exodus of Earth. Surprisingly these decrepit dark sentinels may have sided with the Wounded One.

I considered asking the council about going myself, but I know what their answer will be, They'll say, "We need you here." Therefore, I have determined to go without their permission.

If my faith does not move me to do something now, it never will.

Shem, from the Blue Moon, the caverns of Sharu

++

The End

**Find out more on the following pages about the
Blue Moon Chronicles.**

Blue Moon Chronicles

Keep up with the continuing saga of the **Blue Moon Chronicles** and your favorite Characters. You can do this two ways:

In the **full Length Novels,** now released:

"The Exit," Vol I of the Blue Moon Chronicles, 2012

"This time you won't be left behind."

"Two Suns Rising" Vol II of the Blue Moon Chronicles, 2014

"Can Light be destroyed"

Cover art by Sue Northcutt-Kelly

Blue Moon Serials

Also in **the Blue Moon Chronicles Serials**

Cover art by Sue Northcutt-Kelly

Blue Moon Serials

ANGEL WITHOUT A CAUSE

Ru shares her plight as an orphan and search for true identity through the help of an ancient angel, a sworn enemy of her family line.

2014, Cover Art by Ammi Howard

Preview:

ANGEL WITHOUT A CAUSE

They say everyone hopes for a love to redeem them, someone who will come along and blindly give their whole heart to your worthless scrapbook of existence. I believed this fairytale when I boarded in the Coventry School for Girls—call it what it was, an orphanage for little XX chromosomes estranged by the Bosnian war, dead beat parents, or unwanted pregnancies.

If you were one of the lucky ones and adopted early then maybe a magical little fairy sprinkled your pitiful life. A lot of potential parents inquired about me, "oohed" and "aahed" over me, handpicked me, but when they left, I was still an orphan, alone again.

My imagination roamed through the sunny hills and forests outside my class room. At night I prayed, clinging to my pillow, assured someone out there was praying for someone like me; that we would meet, fall in love, escape the past and live happily ever after. I told the story in my scrapbook and covered it with pink lace and bows.

But here is what no one told me; "Don't over estimate yourself." And, I forgot to ask, "Does anyone really want to see my frilly bound hopes and dreams?"

Most of us don't even begin to scratch the surface of our worthiness to be loved. If we did then we might discover things we'd be better off not knowing. That's what happened to me. After the accident I discovered a whole new world my mandatory religion classes only touched the surface of; one where I certainly no longer fit in.

My classes basically outlined life like this; let's see, there is good and there is evil, there is heaven and hell, people who spend their lives laboring to be a saint, and others who dive into the dregs of life--the bottom feeders. I

Preview Continued

wasn't comfortable with either of those choices. I was caught in between, confused with no one I trusted to guide me.

Until my graduation I was a perpetual teenage orphan, one of those girls people feel sorry for. Our nicknames from the staff nuns were, "Angels Without a Cause." This may come across as a bad attitude from a perpetual loser, but little did they know how much this label applied to me.

My given name is Ruvale Maria Zvonimira. That's hard for most people to pronounce. What few close friends I have, call me Ru.

Blue Moon Serials

DEATH FLIGHT

Ouriano, a first generation angel, anguishes over fulfilling orders to exterminate the Nephilim and is witness to the beginning of the great infection.

2014, Cover Art by Michelle Bauman

Index of Names

Abyss: holding place for violently infected dark Winds, also called Abyss of Gameroon

Advanta: is a fifth generation angel from the Blue Moon, who occasionally takes the form as Pico the sloth.

Angel of Light: also known as the Desert Angel, divine like being who directs light from the Magnificon, governs Winds of light

Angel of Death: derogatory term for Ouriano because of his past

Archangel: angels who oversee Legion Commanders

Ayin Temple: rock hewn Cathedral for worship by the Legions of the Blue Moon

Anquanga: name given to Victoria by people of Sharu

Azazel: is a first generation angel who has a blemished past, a comrade of Fortius

Beltshzan: Earthly leader of the infected

Bengal: Legion Commander who sides with Beltshzan

Blitz: Ms. Pruett's little dog

Blue Moon: also known as Yare'ach Kachol, the ancient home of the Winds of light/Angels, a turquoise blue planet in orbit around the gas giant Siyon

Colonel Smith: leader of the Sanctuary Corporation, last of surviving original Nephilim, half fallen angel--half human, father of Ru, alias Cuzak

Cuzak: leader of the Sanctuary Corporation, last of surviving original Nephilim, half angel half man, father of Ru, alias Colonel Smith

Daniel: Child of Lucas and Victoria, foretold by the Angel of Light as one to help bring deliverance in a land of Two Suns Rising, rumored to have the spirit of Ouriano.

Darkened Winds: infected angelic beings, demons

Desert Angel: name given by Lucas to the Angel of Light

Desert of the Dark Winds: previous center of culture and worship for people of Sharu, now cursed and deserted wasteland on island of Sharu.

Diaphthora Temple: remnant place of worship on Blue Moon where Lucifer attempted to coronate himself as co-heir of the Magnificon

Drone: angel of light or fallen who has had wings removed

Father Svarian: an Armenian Priest

Fortius: A Legion commander from the Blue moon, friend of Veezon

Gamaliel: head of the Magnificon council

Gameroon: name of the abyss, holding place for violently infected dark Winds

General Sul: is high ranking North Korean Army General who is possessed by the Vranti

Great Cavern: also great canyon, chasm, continental sized hole in the Blue Moon as seen from space

Henry Tanner: Lucas' father

Image Bearers: term used by angelic beings to describe humans

Judith Tanner: Lucas' mother

Juwaan: person called by the Angel of Light for a new prophetic purpose

Krator: main habitable planet of the Sanctuary in orbit of twin stars Pantos

Lake of Dreams: place on Blue Moon reserved for reflection by Winds of light, composed of prayers and memories of humans

Lamech: an early proto type image bearer/human with such extreme intellect and warrior qualities he was removed from the Earth and exiled to the Island of Wandu on the Blue Moon, where he governs his own city-state.

Legion: Military regiment of Winds of light

Legionnaires: angelic members of a Legion

Leviathan: a great sea creature in the depths of Blue Moon's ocean

Local Entity: diminutive name for God of immediate universe, by darkened Winds

Lucas Tanner: PhD, human, scientist specializing in quantum physics, also Mr. Luke, Dr. Tanner

Lucifer: first of the first generation of Angelus, and originator of the infection

Magnificon: that which existed before the creation of the universe and to which all shall return

Magnificon Council: council of twenty four Elders comprised of different races, species from different epochs, also known as the Council of Elders

Marge: first name of Ms. Pruett, Victoria's mother

Michael: an archangel

Mrs. Green: is the assistant to Shem

Ms. Pruett: Victoria's mother, calls herself Marge

Neanderthals: name given by Lucas to the ancient people of Sharu

Nephilim: an ancient race of beings who were thought to be the offspring of darkened Winds and humans

Nicky: cousin of Victoria, died as young teenager

Ouriano: a first generation Angelus, given special operation assignments, previous Legion Commander

Paige Tanner: Lucas' younger sister

Pam: producer of "Around the World" BBC news show

Pantos: the twin stars of the Sanctuary's planet Krator

Peleg: a tribesman leader of the people of the island of Sharu on the Blue Moon, mate is Wayla

Reina: assistant to News anchor Rulanda Lakee

Royal Cherubim: or Cherubim Guards, powerful tri-winged creatures who guard the most sacred on Siyon

Ru: most recent daughter of Cuzak/Colonel Smith, her mother was human, genetically refined by her father

Rulanda Lakee: reporter for BBC

Ruvale Marija Zvonimira: long name of Ru, most recent daughter of Cuzak/Colonel Smith, her mother was human, father Nephilim, genetically enhanced by her father.

Sanctuary: a fabled parallel universe under the supervision of another entity

Seraph: type of angel filling the ranks of the Legions

Sharu: an island on the surface of the Blue Moon, home of Neanderthals

Shem: recorder of the Blue Moon Chronicles, Elder of the Magnificon council, governor of island of Sharu

Siyon: golden gas giant multi-dimensional planet, the Magnificon is at the center

Talon: Legion Commander who sides with Beltshzan

Trans Corridor Café: also called The Well, tavern for Winds of light and visitors to the Blue Moon

Veezon: a Legion Commander of the Winds of light, former student of Ouriano

Vic: short for Victoria

Victoria Pruett: PhD, human, scientist specializing in quantum physics, also Vic, Dr. Pruett

Vranti: or The Vranti, a demonic collective of darkened/infected Winds, who once helped organize the cosmos

Wandu: island on the Blue Moon governed my Lamech

Wayla: female leader of the people of Sharu, mate of Peleg

Winds of light: angels, flames of fire, sentinels, serve Angel of Light, home is the Blue Moon

Wounded Heir: also Wounded One, Heir of the Magnificon, the One, co-regent with Angel of Light

Yare'ach Kachol: Winds or Angelic name for Blue Moon of Siyon, home of the Angels

Yazad: the entity over The Sanctuary, favorable to The Vranti and said to offer new light to darkened powers

Zomar: Legion Commander who sides with Beltshzan

Acknowledgments

Special thanks goes out to my editors, Judy, Shari, Bill, Loretta, Hank and Sue, who read over and over generating reams of feedback; for their courage to confront and pray for me. I especially appreciate their hard work to slog through early rough manuscripts. And of course, I give thanks to the One whose secret knowledge is no secret.

About The Author

"If you play golf, you are my friend," is an invitation to building bridges with people about something you love.

Todd is a graduate of the University of Texas at Austin and Dallas Seminary. He is an ordained minister in the Christian Church, Disciples of Christ.

He offices and writes on his North Texas "ranchette" with his wife Loretta, two dogs, varieties of native plants and animals, including their children and grandchildren, who come and go.

Todd is known to frequent many coffee shops and golf courses in the Princeton and McKinney Texas area.

Passionate Author, Texas Golfer

Contact

For information regarding speaking engagements, interviews or
press information, address:

Todd Boddy
Broken Club Publishing LLC
3001 S. Hardin Blvd. #110-351
McKinney Texas 75070

Email: BCP@ToddBoddy.net
Voice mail @(214) 310-1834
@Twitter: Todd_Boddy

WWW.TODDBODDY.COM
WWW.BLUEMOONCHRONICLES.COM
www.facebook.com/bluemoonchronicles

www.ingramcontent.com/pod-product-compliance
Lightning Source LLC
Chambersburg PA
CBHW031425240626

47154CB00001B/201